No Secrets
No Lies A NOVEL

by
TAMARA TILLEY

No Secrets No Lies

By Tamara Tilley

Library of Congress Cataloging-in-Publication Data is on file at the Library of Congress, Washington, DC.

ISBN 13: 978-0-578-71891-0

Cover design: Design 7 Studio
Cover images: Shutterstock
Photo credit: Rachel Sydlosky

ARCHER
PRESS

Dedicated to my husband, Walter.
He is so patient with me and forgiving of all the hours I spend pouring over my manuscripts. I could not do this without his sacrifices.

ACKNOWLEDGEMENTS

I am so thankful for the readers who have taken the time to contact me and bolster me with their words of encouragement. Though writing is a solo art, it's fueled by the appreciation of those who take the journey with me.

I am also thankful for family and friends who support my writing with words of affirmation and a listening ear. Though a lot of strategizing takes place inside my head, it energizes me to process out loud to an audience who is genuinely interested.

And then there is my editing crew. I absolutely could not do this without them. I love telling stories that shine with the redemptive power of Jesus, but the polish is applied by friends who are willing to pour over my words until they gleam. Thank you-Mom, Michele, Charlene, and Jessie.

And what is a book without an amazing cover. Thank you, Scott, for always capturing my vision and making it even better than I could have imagined.

And to my Savior, Jesus Christ - Thank You for allowing me this avenue to point others to You. I pray for those who are searching for a true relationship, that they realize there is nothing so terrible, so dark, or so unforgivable, in light of Your grace. Grace you extend to all. They have only to ask and believe.

Chapter One

Hunter Jennings sat in his luxury tour bus, his phone pressed to his ear. "Come on, Rob, can't I just send an autographed CD with the tickets and backstage passes and call it good?"

"No!" His manager was emphatic. "I landed you a top sponsorship; now you have to come through with your end of the bargain."

"*My* end of the bargain? I never agreed to this promotion. It was all your idea."

"And a personal appearance is what clinched the deal. So buck up. It will only take an hour of your time, two at the most."

"Two!" Hunter shot up from his custom cowhide couch, ready to chuck his phone down the hall. "You said I would be in and out. Come on, Rob, I hate this, and you know it. For cryin' out loud, it's awkward."

"Hey, if making millions of dollars and having women throw themselves at you is awkward, then sign me up," Rob chuckled.

"That's easy for you to say. You're just the manager who comes up with these stupid promotions and divvies out the cash. You don't have to deal with psychotic or truly desperate women."

"Hang on now, I take exception to that. Getting Desperado—one of the largest manufacturers of boots, saddles, and gear—to sponsor your tour was a stroke of genius. You said so yourself."

"Yeah, well, that was before I found out I had to hock their goods at every major city along the tour. You've turned me into a glorified delivery boy."

"You can whine all you want, Hunter, but you're doing it. The promotion clearly states the winner will be presented with a saddle, tickets, and backstage passes by none other than yours truly. So get on board. The car will be by to pick you up in an hour. Be ready. And make sure you check the crappy attitude at the door."

When the phone went dead, Hunter tossed it on the couch, plopped down beside it, and swore under his breath. Raking his fingers through his hair, he massaged his scalp and leaned back against the overstuffed pillows.

"I need a new manager."

Chapter Two

Charlie had just finished lunch and was putting her dishes in the sink when there was a knock at the door. Startled, she dropped the plate and juggled to right the glass. Luckily, nothing broke. "Come on, get your act together," she scolded.

It had been six months since moving to Connor, Tennessee, but the paranoia she carried around like baggage was never far away.

Looking through the peephole on the front door, she took a step back, shocked by who she saw.

It can't be.

Taking a breath, she looked again.

Sure enough, country music star, Hunter Jennings, was standing on her front stoop.

Walking away from the door, she stood in the middle of the living room completely mystified.

What in the world?

Then she remembered.

Hunter Jennings was in town for a concert. The feed store had been promoting it for months. A flyer was even stuffed inside her bag when she bought Goliath's hoof dressing. It advertised not only the concert, but a giveaway that included concert tickets and a gorgeous Desperado saddle.

But what does that have to do with me? I never put my name on anything.

Her mind whirled with possible explanations, but there

were none.

Another heavy knock on the door reminded her she needed to do something and had better do it quick. So, with a cleansing breath, she reached for the deadbolts and slowly disengaged all three of them.

———————— ● ●————————

Hunter's agitation was growing by the second. He saw someone approach the peephole, but that same someone refused to open the door. He was about to knock for the third time when he heard the click of a lock being released, then another, and still yet another. Finally, the door eased open.

He was not at all prepared for who stood on the other side. A beautiful brunette, wearing faded jeans, worn boots, and a simple plaid shirt. Except on her, it looked anything but simple. Everything about her was amazing, except for her eyes. Though they were rich brown, captivating, and mysterious, they communicated one thing: Back off.

But I can change that. He gave her another glance. *So maybe this gig isn't that bad after all.*

He took a step forward, removed his hat, and flashed the seductive smile he had perfected over the years. "Good afternoon, ma'am. I'm looking for Charlie Foster. Is he home?"

"Is this about the contest at the feed store?"

"Well, let's see," he glanced at the man with the store logo on his shirt. "We have a store owner with a saddle in his arms, a couple of photographers, and I'm standing here with a pair of concert tickets and backstage passes in my hand." He put his hat back on and chuckled. "I don't think I'm selling Girl Scout cookies." He smiled again, but it was obvious she didn't appreciate his humor. Her already frigid look cooled a few more degrees.

"There must be a mistake. I didn't enter the contest. I'm sorry." She took a step back and started to ease the door shut.

"Wait a minute! You're Charlie Foster?"

She stopped, clearly annoyed. "Kind of looks that way."

Okay . . . good looking or not, he didn't appreciate the woman's barbed attitude. Not in the mood for games, he shook his head. *Just give her the saddle and get out of here.* "Well, this card has your name and address on it which means you're the winner of the Desperado contest. Congratulations," he said, minus any enthusiasm.

"Then someone must've entered me in the contest without my permission because I didn't fill out that card. I decline."

She tried to close the door again, but he stuck his custom alligator boot between the door and the jamb.

"What does it matter who filled out the card?" he snapped. "You won. Your name was drawn. Just take the saddle, pose for a few pictures, and we can all call it a day."

"But I don't want the saddle or the tickets. Give them to someone who does." She looked down at his boot, then square in the eye. "Excuse me."

But Hunter didn't budge. "Listen, lady, I don't know what your beef is, but I'm not going door to door like a freakin' salesman to find a winner. You're it. Now, let's just get this over with."

When one of the photographers snapped a picture, she threw the door open and catapulted out onto the porch. "Hey, you have no right taking my picture without my permission! Delete it. Right now!"

"But when you filled out the entry form," the feed store owner spoke up, "it stated that pictures would be taken for promotional reasons. Charlie, what's wrong?" he took a step closer to the woman and whispered. "Why are you making such a big deal out of this? If you don't want the saddle, you can sell it later. It's worth over five grand. But, please don't ruin this for the store. We need the publicity."

Hunter looked at the owner, then back to the belligerent woman. That's when he noticed her pale complexion, and the way her clenched fists shook at her side. "Umm . . . lady, are you okay?" His irritation quickly turned to concern. Something wasn't right. He watched as the woman reached for her forehead, her fingers shaking, her eyelashes fluttering. "Ma'am?" He reached out to her.

"I . . . I'm fine. I just need to sit down for a second. If you'll excuse me."

Hunter watched as she backed away from the door and took a seat on the arm of her couch. Resting her hands on her knees, she lowered her head.

"Wait here a minute," he said to the small entourage flanking him, then stepped over the threshold and approached the woman with caution. "Are you all right, Miss Foster? Is there someone I can call?"

"I'll . . . I'll be okay. I just need that picture erased."

That's what this is all about? A stupid picture? What a whack job. He had heard of people who didn't like to be photographed, but hyperventilating seemed a bit extreme.

After a few seconds, she was breathing normal again, and color slowly returned to her face. When it appeared that she wasn't going to pass out, he decided it was time for him to leave before things got any worse.

"I'm sorry for upsetting you, Miss Foster. I'll talk to the store owner and have him pick another winner." He tipped his hat, turned and headed for the door.

"Wait . . . what about the photograph?" she barked. "I want it deleted! Immediately! I don't want you or anyone else using it!"

"No problem, lady," he mumbled as he crossed the living room. "They want a picture of a winner, not a crazy dame afraid of her own shadow."

"Excuse me?"

Hunter heard her stalking toward him but refused to turn around.

"I can't believe you just said that! You'd think a person with your celebrity status would have a little more decorum than to call someone crazy."

"Yeah, well . . ." He turned, but quickly took a step back as she stood toe-to-toe with him. He found the situation ironic.

Even though his six-six frame towered over her, this woman did not seem the least bit intimidated. It reminded him of the time when he was a teenager and cut across the neighbor's property on his way home from school. A pint-size terrier chased after him, nipping at his heels. The thing could not have weighed more than ten pounds. But that did not seem to matter to the terrier. His heart was as big as a Rottweiler, and he had the personality to match.

This pint-size woman was all Rottweiler.

"What's your problem, lady? I said I was leaving. I said I would get rid of the picture. Why are you making such a big deal out of this?"

"Not that it's any business of yours, but I have my reasons!"

Okay. That's it. He'd had enough of this woman yelling at him, clearly overreacting. "Let me guess," he snapped as he crossed his arms against his broad chest. "You're a mafia princess hiding from the family, slumming it here in *Hicksville* where no one would ever think to look for you. Or maybe you're royalty in hiding because you don't want to take your rightful place on the throne," he laughed. "Or better yet, maybe you're—"

"Hiding from a husband who repeatedly beat the crap out of me and threatened to kill me if I ever left him!"

Her words hit him like a blow to the gut, and seeing the tears that slid from her panic-filled eyes, he believed every word of it.

——— ● ———

Charlie covered her mouth with her hand, but it was too late. She had blurted out what she had never told a soul. *Oh, no! What have I done?*

"I . . . I don't know what to say," Hunter Jennings stuttered, looking at her with a horrified expression. "I'm sorry doesn't seem—"

"You don't need to say anything." She pinned him with

a stare. "Just make sure that picture is deleted and leave me alone." She took a step back. "You can see your way out."

She hurried down the hall to her bedroom, closed the door, and leaned against it before exhaling the breath she'd been holding. Slowly, she sank to the floor but could do nothing to stop the sob that rose from deep inside her.

———————— • ————————

Hunter stood in the woman's living room, stunned.

He wanted to go after her but figured it would only make matters worse. Raking his fingers through his hair, he stepped outside, and nodded toward the photographer. "Delete the picture."

"I already did."

Then he turned to the store owner. "You need to find yourself another winner."

Hunter climbed into the limo waiting curbside. He tried to put the whole fiasco out of his mind as they drove back to the event center, but all he could see were the tears rolling down the woman's face and the terror in her eyes.

Chapter Three

Charlie walked Goliath to the barn, feeling tired and listless. "Sorry, boy, I know you wanted to stay out longer, but I just don't have the energy."

Her night terrors were back, and she knew why. The ridiculous argument she'd had with Hunter Jennings yesterday. She must have replayed it a hundred times in her head. Country superstar Hunter Jennings was at her door—even in her house—and what did she do? Act like a raving maniac, saying things she had no business saying.

Walking Goliath to the stall door, she slipped off his bridle, looped a lead rope around his neck, then hooked the end over a post. Scratching his jowls and giving his shoulders a good rub, she spoke to her confidant as she reached for the curry comb.

"I'm such an idiot. I made a complete fool of myself." She scooted her ratty straw cowboy hat back off her brow. "Why couldn't I just keep my mouth shut? Why didn't I just tell him to get lost and leave me alone?"

Slowly she stroked Goliath's coat, first with the comb, then with her hand. "He just angered me so much. He thought he was so funny with his little Mafia joke. I just wanted to wipe the smug look off his face and make him eat his words. But how could I have been so stupid and—"

She stopped.

Hearing a shuffle behind her, she spun around and gasped. There stood Hunter Jennings, all six foot plus of him.

"I'm sorry. I didn't mean to startle you," he said in his award-winning bass voice.

Inwardly, she cringed. *This cannot be happening. Not again.*

"What are you doing here? Didn't I embarrass myself enough already? Or did you come back to see if I could top yesterday's performance?"

"Hey, that was my fault. I just wanted to make sure you were okay."

She crossed her arms defiantly. "Why wouldn't I be?"

"Well, you were pretty upset when I left. I just thought I—"

"You're right. I was upset. But how is that your problem?"

She watched as his clenched fists rested on the waist of his faded Wranglers, and the set of his well-built shoulders caused his chambray shirt to pull taut across his chest.

"Are you always this rude?" he asked, his piercing blue eyes glaring at her from underneath his black Stetson.

"Rude!" she laughed. "Are you kidding me? You barge into my house, call me crazy, are trespassing on my property as we speak, and you're calling me rude?"

"I'm not trespassing! For cryin' out loud. I just wanted to make sure you were okay."

"Well, don't waste your worry on me, Mr. Jennings. Neither my mob family or my royal court have found me yet."

"What about your husband?"

His words were like a knife to her chest. She quickly turned back to Goliath, not wanting him to see her fear. Just the thought of Daniel finding her was enough to make her want to puke. "That's none of your business, and I'd appreciate it if you would leave now." She stroked Goliath's coat, praying the man behind her would just go away.

"Look, I feel awful about how yesterday went down. So I brought a peace offering. My way of saying I'm sorry."

"Really, Mr. Jennings, that's not necessary." She continued to stroke Goliath, anything to hide the tremors in her hands.

"Call me Hunter."

"Goodbye, Mr. Jennings." Her tone was sharp as she spoke

16

over her shoulder, hoping he would get the message. She waited to hear the shuffle of feet. *Come on, leave already.*

"You know . . . I was wrong. You're not rude, just obstinate."

She swung around and saw him standing with his hat tipped back, a smug grin on his face.

"You know what, Mr. Jennings, I think I've had just about—"

"Come to my show tonight," he interrupted.

"What?" *He's crazy. That must be it because it's far too early to be drunk.*

"Come as my guest."

"I don't think so." She turned back to Goliath.

"Why not?"

"Because I don't want to. Besides, I . . . I already have plans."

"You couldn't change them?"

"Why would I want to do that?"

"Well," he cleared his throat, and she heard his boots shuffle closer across the scattered straw on the floor. "I don't mean to brag, but it *is* being touted as the hottest country tour in decades."

She stroked Goliath some more. "I can't. I'm working a late shift tonight."

"So, you're saying you would rather work the late shift than be my guest?" He crossed to the other side of Goliath and spoke to her over the stallion's towering back. "I don't know if my ego can take such a blow."

His self-deprecating comment caught her off-guard, causing the smallest smirk to crease her lips.

"Is that a smile?" he asked with a grin. "I must be wearing you down."

She quickly schooled her expression, locked her stare on Goliath's withers, and stroked him with the curry comb. "Look, Mr. Jennings—"

"Hunter, please. Mr. Jennings was my dad."

What is going on? This is crazy! Hunter Jennings is one

of the hottest country singers on the planet. He is the epitome of tall, dark, and rugged. He could have any woman he wants. Wait a minute. What am I saying? He's not here for me. She looked down at her tattered jeans, with the knees completely shredded and her paint-splotched John Deere T-shirt. *He's just trying to soothe his conscience and do some damage control. It wouldn't look good for his image if I decided to talk to the press and let them know how he had harassed me.*

"Look, I appreciate the offer, really I do. It's just that—"

"You're going to make me beg, aren't you?"

"No. That isn't what I'm—"

He stepped around in front of Goliath, pulled his hat from his head, placed it against his chest, and got down on one knee. "Miss Foster, will you do me the honor of gracing me with your presence this evening?"

She could feel heat racing up her neck, coloring her cheeks. "Please don't do that."

He obliged and got back on his feet, but that was even worse. He stood just inches away, his towering physique right in front of her.

"Why are you doing this?"

"Doing what?"

"Trying so hard. Surely you have better things to do with your time then scrounge up people to go to one of your sold-out concerts."

"I feel bad about the scene I caused yesterday. I just wanted to show you I'm not a complete jerk." His eyes were downcast, studying the rim of his hat while he spun it between his fingers. He glanced up but quickly looked away.

Why won't he look me in the eyes? He was smooth, charming, and incredibly handsome, but he was hiding something. She decided to go on the offense.

"You don't play cards, do you Mr.—"

"Hunter, please," he interrupted, "and what kind of question is that?"

"Because you can't bluff to save your life."

He smiled, as he glanced around the barn looking anywhere

but at her.

She tossed the curry comb into the nearby bucket and rested her hands on her hips. "I'll make you a deal. If you tell me the real reason why it's so important that I go to your concert, maybe I'll reconsider."

He stared at his boots for a few seconds, his hat still spinning in his hands. When he finally looked up, his gaze nearly melted her legs from beneath her.

"Because I owe it to my sister."

It wasn't the answer she was expecting. "What does your sister have to do with this?"

For the first time, he looked directly into her eyes, and instead of seeing humor or self-assuredness, she only saw grief.

"Amy's husband knocked her around. I knew something wasn't right, but by the time I did something . . . it was too late."

A chill raced through her veins as she remembered the headlines from a few years back, something about Hunter Jennings' sister being found dead. She did not know what to say. The pain on his face was palpable and raw.

"I'm so sorry."

"So am I." His tone was stoic.

Charlie stared at the toe of her boot as she pushed around soiled straw, the silence between them cold and awkward. "Look, I appreciate your honesty," she finally said, "but being nice to me isn't going to bring your sister back."

"I know that."

"Then I'll just accept your apology and call it even."

"Oh no," he said, the twinkle back in his cool blue eyes. "You said if I told you the real reason, you would go to my concert. I just laid it all out there for you, and you're still going to stand me up? That's not right."

"I said *maybe* I would reconsider."

Charlie's mind was mush. She couldn't think straight. She couldn't even comprehend the fact that she was carrying on a conversation with *the* Hunter Jennings, let alone that he was going to such lengths to persuade her to go to his concert.

Unhooking Goliath from the post, she led him inside the stall and dumped some oats into his trough. She was stalling, considering her options. After fumbling around for a few minutes, she exited the stall, latched the gate, and pulled off her hat to wipe the sweat from her brow.

Am I actually going to do this?

Putting her hat back on, she sighed as she looked up into his handsome face. "What time is the concert?"

The charismatic smile that had graced millions of CD covers illuminated the barn. "Seven o'clock. I'll have a car come and get you at six."

"No, that's okay. I can drive myself."

"But it's no problem. I can—"

Her cocked brow and crossed arms warned him not to push.

"Okay. Okay." He held up his hands in surrender. "Message received." Reaching into his back pocket, he pulled out a business card. "Here's my manager's phone number. When you get to the event center, call him. Once you hook up with Rob, he'll bring you backstage."

Charlie tried to hide her disappointment at being pawned off to his manager. He must have read her expression because he quickly explained.

"This is the best way to get backstage without causing a scene. I know it's not optimal, but Rob will take care of everything."

When his phone whistled a tune, he pulled it from his pocket, silenced it, then slipped it back inside. "That was Rob. I need to get going. I have a few obligations before sound check." He took a few steps backwards. "You're not going to stand me up, are you?"

"I'll be there."

"Good. I'll see you tonight."

As soon as he was out of view, she spun around, her hands covering her red-hot cheeks. "What in the world . . ."

Chapter Four

"Artie, it's Charlie." She sat on the edge of the bed, the cordless phone clenched between her ear and shoulder. "Hey, so something has come up. Would it be a huge inconvenience if I was a no-show tonight?"

"Wait a minute," he said, excitedly. "Did you actually win the contest?"

I knew it! It was Artie who filled out the contest entry.

"What contest would that be, Artie?" she asked, toying with him.

"You know . . . the one at the feed store. I kinda entered you in it."

"Artie, why would you do that?"

"Oh, I don't know. I just thought it would be fun. You've been such a big help to me. I thought you could use a night out on the town, and a brand-new saddle for that stallion you're always braggin' about. But I guess if I'm telling you all this, you must not have won," he chuckled. "Oh well, maybe next time."

"So, about tonight," Charlie nudged him back on topic. "How 'bout it, Artie? Do you think you can handle the shift without me?"

"Sure. Don't sweat it. I'm not expecting much of a crowd with that concert in town. You go ahead and take the night off."

"Thanks, Artie. The next double shift is on the house."

"Well, that won't be for a while."

"What?"

"Did you forget? We're closed all next week. I'm having the place exterminated and the hood replaced on the grill."

"That's right. You told me we would be closed."

Oh man, can I afford to give up my last shift for a week? Quickly, she went through a mental checklist. *I have a full tank of gas, enough groceries to make it by, and twenty dollars to get me through until my next payday.*

She could always tap into her emergency stash and put it back when she got paid, something she swore she would never do.

No. That money is for if I have to run. Not because I have to eat light for a week.

"So, I guess I'll see you next week?" Artie said, interrupting her thoughts. "And Charlie . . . if you need a little cash to tide you over, come by the house. We can work something out."

She smiled at the man with his fatherly ways. "Thanks, Artie, but I'll be fine."

Disconnecting the call, she set the phone in the charger on the bedside table, wondering if she had done the right thing. A shift with tips was close to a hundred bucks. And with only a few shifts a week, money was already tight. She thought a moment longer then shrugged. *I'll be fine.*

Walking over to her closet, she slid the door aside. "Now to find something to wear."

There wasn't much to look at. Jeans. A couple of summer dresses. A few blouses. "Well, it's just a country concert, not dining with the Queen." *And since I'll probably only see Hunter Jennings for a few minutes before I'm pawned off onto his staff, it's not going to matter what I wear.*

She pulled out her best jeans and tossed them on the bed. Shifting hangers from right to left, she shuffled through the few blouses she had but quickly gave up. Kneeling in front of her beat-up dresser, she rummaged through shirts until she found something decent. A black camisole and a sheer long sleeve gray T-shirt. "This could work."

Standing in front of the dresser mirror, she layered the two shirts, then held them up to her shoulders. "Not bad."

Happy with her choices, she headed back to the barn to finish the day's chores.

Her preoccupation with her plans for the night finally got the best of her. After looking at her watch for the umpteenth time, she propped the rake in the corner of the barn and headed to the house. She had plenty of time for a shower, a chance to do something with her hair, and still make the twenty-minute drive to the event center.

Chapter Five

Forty minutes later, Charlie looked at herself in the mirror, nervously turning from side to side. Though she decided to wear her hair down, she took the time to add a few waves. Nothing fancy, just enough to give her some style.

Her newest pair of jeans were slightly loose because of her stint with the flu, but she wasn't complaining, and the layered T-shirt and camisole actually looked nicer than she had expected. She smiled at the end result.

Digging around in the back of her closet, she grabbed her black Ariat boots. They had seen better days, but a quick polish would shine them up just fine.

Then she remembered what she was getting ready for and who she was going to see, and it hit her like a Mac truck. Sinking to the edge of the bed, she shook her head in disbelief. "What am I doing? This is ludicrous! I don't even know if I can go through with this."

She hurried to the kitchen and opened the cupboard under the sink. Sorting through the pile of plastic bags, she found the one from the feed store. Reaching inside, she grabbed the flyer with Hunter Jennings' picture on it—his drop-dead good looks and movie star smile staring back at her.

How can I not go?

After walking through the house one more time, making sure all the doors and windows were locked, she stopped and looked at herself in the hall mirror. Shaking her head, she stared at her reflection. "Here goes nothing."

Thirty minutes later—thanks to a fender-bender on the highway—Charlie turned her banged up, 1974 F-350 Ranger into the long line of cars funneling into the event center parking lot. It was slow going, bumper-to-bumper, three aisles deep, with car stereos blaring Hunter Jennings' classics. It was definitely a party vibe, and Charlie felt herself getting pulled into it. That is, until she got closer to the front of the line and saw the sandwich-board sign between the lanes.

Event Parking - $10.00

"That's just great!"

She looked over her shoulder, then at the truck ahead of her. She was sardined in. While keeping her eyes on the traffic in front of her, she pulled her purse onto her lap and rifled through it, hoping to find even a few extra dollars.

Nothing.

As she inched along, she looked through her wallet, but all she had was the twenty-dollar bill that was supposed to last her the rest of the week.

She thought about telling the parking attendant in the bright orange vest that she had made a wrong turn and accidentally got sucked into the line.

It probably happens all the time.

But her conversation with Jennings played in her head. *"You're not going to stand me up, are you?"*

She had promised him she would come. And somehow, Charlie knew if she did not show up tonight, she ran the risk of Jennings appearing on her doorstep tomorrow, demanding a reason or an apology. Then she would have to explain to a millionaire why she couldn't afford ten dollars for parking.

Resigned to the fact that she had to go through with it, she gave the attendant her last twenty, waited for her change, then followed the car in front of her until she was directed to a parking spot. Shoving everything back into her purse, she grabbed her hip-length denim jacket, and followed the throng of people headed across the street to the arena.

With the early evening winds kicking into high gear, she quickly slipped her jacket on—hoping it would be enough to ward off the unseasonable chill in the air.

Or maybe the chill running through her body had nothing to do with the weather at all.

Chapter Six

Hunter checked his watch.

She should be here by now.

Looking over the crowd of people milling around backstage, he spotted Rob. "Hey, have you heard from her yet?"

"Who?" Rob asked, angling to see around Hunter.

"Charlie Foster."

Rob looked at him with a blank stare. "Oh . . . right . . . the woman from the contest. No. I haven't heard from her yet."

"You're sure?"

Rob pulled out his phone and fiddled with the screen. "No missed calls. See." He turned his phone around.

"Rob . . . Rob Marshall?"

They both looked in the direction of the high-pitch squeal.

A buxom blond hurried toward them, then wrapped Rob in a hug.

Hunter watched as his manager stepped back and allowed himself a long, lingering stare at the woman whose figure was strategically poured into the proverbial little black dress.

"Stacy? Stacy Reynolds? What has it been, five years?"

"Closer to ten."

"Well, you look just fabulous. Time has certainly been good to you."

Hunter did not have time for his manager's blatant

27

pandering. "Look, Rob, I have—"

"Where are my manners?" Rob stopped Hunter mid-sentence and clamped his hand down on his shoulder with a friendly squeeze. "Hunter Jennings, this is Stacy Reynolds. Stacy, this is the one and only Hunter Jennings."

Out of courtesy, Hunter extended his hand. "Nice to meet you, ma'am."

"The pleasure is all mine." The blond smiled flirtatiously.

"I don't mean to be rude, but I have to give an interview in a few minutes." Hunter tipped his hat to the woman, then turned to his manager. "Don't miss that phone call, Rob," he warned.

"Don't worry, Hunter, I have it covered."

―――――― ● ――――――

Standing outside the arena, Charlie was beyond nervous. Groups of people clustered together trying to stay out of the swirling jet stream while mini mobs pressed toward the main doors. Standing so her hair wouldn't blow in her face, Charlie looked around at the sea of people spilling in from the surrounding parking lots. She could not remember the last time she'd been around so many people and had to work hard to keep her nerves in check.

Just a few steps ahead of her stood a group of giggling girls in their late teens or early twenties, each of them fiddling away on their phones. Charlie approached the group and smiled.

"Excuse me."

The girls turned toward her.

"I did the stupidest thing. I left my phone in my truck, and I'm parked all the way in the north forty. I was supposed to call my friends when I got here so I could get my ticket. Would one of you mind if I borrowed your phone, so I don't have to walk all the way back to my truck?"

The girls looked at her completely annoyed, all but the cute blond on the end. "Sure. You can use mine. I have unlimited everything."

"Thank you so much," Charlie said as the girl offered her a phone in a pink rhinestone-encrusted case.

Pulling the business card Hunter had given her from the back pocket of her jeans, she held it tight as she tapped in the number. Turning away slightly, Charlie listened as the girls went on and on about how gorgeous Hunter Jennings was and how they would just die if they couldn't get backstage.

"I already told you, it's not going to be a problem. I've done it a million times."

Charlie turned to see a tall redhead in a low-cut blouse, spike-heeled boots, and skintight jeans plant her hand on her hip as she continued to explain.

"We have floor seats right next to the soundboard. All we need to do is get in good with the sound crew—promise them a little *personal* reward—and they will get us backstage. No problem."

Charlie turned back around, shaking her head. The girls probably were not even old enough to drink. And if they were, they sure didn't look like they could handle themselves if they got in over their heads.

"Rob Marshall."

Charlie immediately turned her attention back to the phone in her hand.

"Mr. Marshall?"

"Speaking."

Charlie cupped her hands around the phone, dropping the business card from her grasp. Before she could bend to pick it up, it was swept away on a current of air.

"Hello?"

"Yes. Yes, I'm here. My name is Charlie Foster. Mr. Jennings told me to call you once I got to the event center."

"Yeah. Hunter told me to expect your call. So, this is what I need you to do. Go to the south side of the building and wait for me at the last set of double doors, all the way at the east end."

"Okay, thank—"

The phone went dead before she could even finish, leaving her with the impression Mr. Marshall wasn't too happy with this arrangement.

Handing the phone back to the blond, she thanked her.

"No problem."

The redhead was still talking about their plan to get backstage, and though it was none of Charlie's business, she could not walk away without saying something.

Clearing her throat to get their attention, she waited until all eyes were on her—specifically the redhead's. "I know you guys are just looking to have a good time, but a word of caution. Men don't take kindly to girls teasing them with promises of a little *personal* reward. Men take what they want, when they want it. And there's nothing *little* about a man's sexual appetite."

"What do you know about it?" The redhead challenged Charlie with a drop-dead stare.

"Enough."

Charlie looked at the rest of the girls, hoping they were getting the message she was sending, then smiled at the blond. "Thanks again."

As she walked around to the far side of the arena, she kept thinking about the group of girls.

If they only knew the kind of trouble their actions could get them into.

For their sake, Charlie hoped they didn't find any takers tonight.

Chapter Seven

Charlie waited at the last set of double doors on the south side of the arena. Unfortunately, no one came to meet her.

Walking to the far end of the building, she saw nothing but big rigs parked side by side with Hunter Jennings' picture plastered all over them. She stood and waited, looking at her watch every few minutes. After what seemed like an eternity, a man emerged from around the corner of the building. She sighed with relief, until she saw the uniform.

It was a security guard, not Rob Marshall.

The huge man with cocoa-colored skin walked to within ten feet of her.

"Miss, this area is off limits. I'm going to have to ask you to leave."

Glancing at his badge and side-arm, Charlie realized he wasn't just a security guard; he was a cop. "I . . . I was supposed to meet someone here." The tremble in her voice was not very convincing.

"And who would that be?"

"Rob Marshall, Hunter Jennings' manager." From the officer's annoyed stare, she could tell he didn't believe her. "I called him a few minutes ago, and he told me to meet him here."

"Call him again. I'll wait." He rested his hands on his sturdy black belt loaded down with all kinds of police paraphernalia.

"I . . . don't have a phone. I borrowed someone else's."

His stare was deadpan as he sighed. "Fine. Use mine." He reached into his side pocket without breaking eye contact with her.

When she went to retrieve the business card from her pocket, she cringed. The last time she saw it, the card was cartwheeling between cowboy boots and high-heeled shoes.

"I lost his number. I had his business card, but it blew away."

He raised a bushy brow and sighed. "Miss, do you have a ticket for this event or not?"

"No. I was going to—"

"Then I'm going to have to ask you to leave."

"But I was supposed to meet someone here."

"Meet someone or worm your way inside with a smile and a promise for a good time?"

Shocked by his statement, she just stood there with her mouth hanging open.

"Look, lady, either you leave, or I arrest you for loitering." He took a step forward and stood a little taller, as if he needed to look any more intimidating.

What choice did she have? No ticket, no phone, no number. There was nothing she could do.

"My truck is in the parking lot right across the street." She pointed over his shoulder where all of Hunter's buses were parked. "Can I go this way? Or do I need to walk all the way around?"

"You'll need to go around. That area is off limits."

He widened his stance, his hand resting atop his weapon.

Message received.

———— • ————

Hunter left the green room after finishing an interview with CMT. He expected to see Rob and Charlie, but they were nowhere to be found.

"Hunter."

He spun around to see the stage manager walking toward him.

"Hey, Jim, have you seen Rob?"

"Nope, but your meet and greet group is waiting for you in the northeast wing."

Hunter looked at his watch, then scanned the length of the south wing. The opening act would take the stage soon, and the crowd was getting amped up in anticipation. Heading toward the northeast wing, he kept his eyes peeled for Rob and Charlie, expecting to see them tucked in an alcove or dark corner away from prying eyes. But they were nowhere to be found.

When he walked into view of his fan club, they cheered with appreciation. He plastered on a smile, knowing these people were responsible for his success. And because of that, he would give them what they came for.

He did his best to stay in the moment, signing autographs, posing for pictures, and answering questions. The crowd, as usual, consisted of giddy females—young and old—squeezing in close to get a picture while telling him how much they loved his latest hit or music video. Of course, there were always the bolder ones in provocative clothing who asked for a kiss or for him to sign their shirts in inappropriate locations. And standing in the background was always a cluster of apathetic boyfriends and husbands glaring at him like it was his fault their female companions were fawning all over him.

Hunter always made a point of shaking the hands of the men in the crowd and including them in conversation. More times than not, he was able to win them over, and make them realize he really wasn't such a bad guy.

When a group of five circled around Hunter, wanting a group shot, he spied Rob out of the corner of his eye, the blond from earlier, still hanging on his arm. It took a minute for Hunter to get Rob's attention, when he did, he didn't like what he saw. He could spot Rob's *you're not going to like this* look from a mile away.

Chapter Eight

Charlie could not get across the arena parking lot fast enough. Unlocking her truck door, she threw her purse across the cab and slid in behind the wheel. Slamming the door shut, she rested her head against the steering wheel. "I can't believe I allowed myself to get talked into this! If I had just said, no!" Shoving her key into the ignition, she gave it a turn, only to be met with the horrible clicking sound, universally known as a dead battery.

"No!" She sat up straighter, pumped the gas pedal, and gave the key another twist. The same clicking sound mocked her. "Come on, you piece of junk!" She tried again and again, but the result was the same.

"This can't be happening!"

She collapsed against the steering wheel and willed herself not to cry. Crying would get her nowhere.

With her anger boiling and head spinning, she debated her options. *I could call Karen. She would come get me. But then I would have to explain why I'm here. No. Karen is out of the question.*

There was always Artie. *But he wouldn't be able to leave the diner, not right now.*

A harsh rapping on the door window startled her, causing her to scream. She turned to see a man in a yellow windbreaker, EVENT STAFF printed on it in bold black letters. She pressed her hand to her chest, hoping to catch her heart before it jumped out of her skin.

"Miss, is there a problem?"

She could barely hear the man over her pulse pounding in her ears. After taking a few deep breaths, she cranked the window down halfway. "My truck won't start. I'm pretty sure I have a dead battery."

The man took a step back and looked at her older than old truck. "Are you sure that's the only thing wrong with it?" he chuckled.

Charlie didn't find him the least bit amusing. "Yes! I'm sure it's the battery."

"Do you belong to an auto club?"

"No."

"Well, I could give you a jump." He flashed a roguish smile. "Your truck, that is."

She glared at him. "Is that what they teach you to say in rent-a-cop school?"

His playful smirk was quickly replaced with attitude. "How do I even know this is your truck?" he said.

"What?"

"I'm going to have to ask you to step out of the vehicle while I run the plates."

Now she had done it. Lover boy was going to make this hard on her. Realizing she needed to change her tactics, she gave him a sad smile. "Listen, I'm sorry about the rent-a-cop crack. I'm just a little upset. This evening hasn't gone at all like I expected."

He leaned against the door panel with a smug look. "So, is that why you're out here in the parking lot while everyone else is inside?"

It required all her self-control to tap down the anger brewing inside her. She took a deep breath and blew it out slowly before turning to him. "Look, I was meeting someone here. He was going to give me a ticket, but he stood me up. I guess the joke is on me. Now, could you just give me a hand so I can go home and forget about this whole miserable night?"

The way he stared at her, she was sure he was going to make things as difficult as possible. But after a few seconds, he smiled. "If it's just your battery, I can get someone over here to give you a jump, but there's a twenty-dollar service fee."

She closed her eyes and shook her head. *Will this night never end?* "I don't have twenty dollars. All I have is ten."

"Sorry. That's our policy." He pushed off the side of the truck and turned to walk away.

"But I don't have twenty dollars. Look." She yanked her wallet from her purse, opened it wide, and showed him how truly empty it was. He glanced at it, then back at her. She rifled through the center section, pulling the zipper open. "I have a ten-dollar bill, a button, a safety pin," she pushed around some coins, "and about forty-five cents in change. That's every penny I have to my name. I could give you every last cent I have, but it still won't add up to twenty dollars."

"Hey, rules are rules. I don't make them, I just enforce them."

She'd been strong up to this point, but felt her resilience begin to wane, tears stinging her eyes. *Don't you dare cry!* She bullied herself as she pressed her head against the back window and stared at the tattered ceiling of her truck. "Fine. I'll just wait here until the concert is over and have someone else give me a jump." She didn't dare look at the guy, because she knew if she did, she'd say something she would regret. Instead, she waited for him to walk away.

"Fine. Ten bucks."

She snapped to a sitting position and watched as he spoke into the radio mic attached to the shoulder of his jacket. "Yeah, I need a jump in lot 6E."

Someone responded with an ETA of five minutes.

"Thank you. Thank you so much." She looked at the guy and smiled. Unfortunately, it was all the encouragement he needed. With a creepy grin, he leaned against the side of the truck and said, "Well, if you really want to thank me, you could give me your number."

Play it cool, she cautioned herself. *Be nice. You'll be out of here in just a few minutes.* "Okay. I'll give you my number.

But the thing is, I lost my phone. That's why I couldn't call anyone to bail me out. I pick up my new phone tomorrow after work. So, why don't you give me a call around five o'clock. I should have it back by then. Maybe we could go to dinner sometime."

"That works for me." He smiled as he extended his hand through the half-opened window. "I'm Philip."

"Emily." She shook his hand and forced a smile.

Just as he was about to say something, a security truck pulled up in front of her parking spot. When an older guy got out, the two men exchanged a few words before Philip grabbed a set of jumper cables and the older man popped the hood on the service vehicle. It took Philip a couple tries before he was able to wrench open her rusted hood, then he attached the cables.

"Okay, give it a try," Philip said from under the hood.

"Please, please, please, let this work," Charlie mumbled under her breath as she turned the key. When her truck sputtered to life, she let out a little shout. "Yes!"

After disconnecting the cables, Philip let the hood of her truck drop into place then walked around to her window.

She reached into her wallet, hating that she was giving away her last ten dollars. *I'll worry about that later. Right now, I just need to get the heck out of here.*

"Thank you, Philip." She handed him the single bill. "I really appreciate it."

"Aren't you forgetting something?" he said as he took the cash.

"Of course." She faked a smile before digging around in her purse for a piece of scratch paper. After scribbling down a number, she handed him the old grocery receipt. "Here you go. But remember . . . give me until five or five-thirty. I should have my new phone by then."

"Or, I could just leave you a voicemail."

She cocked her head and flashed him what she hoped was a convincing smile. "Well, what's the fun in that? Voicemails are so impersonal."

He grinned. "You're right. I'll call you at five."

"I'll be waiting."

With her truck humming, she pulled forward and followed the arrows on the pavement to the nearest exit.

Chapter Nine

"What happened, Rob? Where's Charlie?"

"I don't know. When she called, I told her where to meet me, but when I got there, she was a no-show. Maybe she got cold feet. You said she was kind of skittish."

"Why didn't you call her back?"

"I tried, but she used someone else's phone. The girl who answered had no idea where she was. Come on, Hunter. This is probably for the better. You don't need the distraction."

He cocked his hip and crossed his arms. "You're not lying to me, are you? Because if I find out you—"

"Hunter, I'm telling you exactly what went down. When I went to the door, she wasn't there."

"But it doesn't make sense. Why would she bother to come here and call you if she had no intentions of sticking around?"

"Maybe she met some other guy outside and decided to spend her night doing something else."

"Shut up, Rob!" he snapped. A few stagehands turned around, but quickly went back to what they were doing. He changed his tone, but not his attitude. "She's not that kind of person."

"Oh really? You know what kind of person she is after talking to her for what . . . twenty minutes tops? I'm sure she was flattered with your unexpected visit. What woman wouldn't be? Even so, for all you know, some guy hit on her outside, she weighed her odds, and decided to go for

39

the sure thing."

"No." Hunter shook his head adamantly while his thoughts spun out of control. Rob didn't know the whole story. He didn't know Charlie's situation or what had gone down the day of the saddle giveaway. All Hunter had told him was there had been a misunderstanding, and that he wanted to pop in on the woman, offer her some tickets, and make sure there were no hard feelings.

Of course, Rob immediately assumed the worst and wanted to go with him to do damage control, but Hunter wouldn't let him. Rob had no idea about Charlie's past or why he felt an immediate attachment to her, and he wasn't about to disregard Charlie's privacy by telling him now.

"I don't think she would risk going off with some guy she didn't know. She's not that kind of woman."

"You mean the kind of woman who would meet a superstar singer backstage at one of his concerts, no questions asked, after knowing him for less than an hour?"

Hunter hated Rob's haughty, *I live in the real world while you live in a celebrity bubble* attitude.

"Look, I get it. Your ego is hurt. But don't make this out to be more than it is. You dropped in on the woman to make sure there were no misunderstandings. You were the bigger man. Now let it go."

Hunter stared out at the stage, watching the opening act do their thing while he debated if what Rob said was true. Was it just his ego that couldn't take being stood up? He knew Charlie was hesitant. She could have easily had second thoughts.

"Hunter . . . Hunter."

"What?"

"You're being straight with me about this Charlie person, right?" His cocky attitude had morphed into worry.

"What do you mean?"

"You said there was a misunderstanding at the prize giveaway, but you never elaborated. Is this woman going to cause problems for us? Tell me you didn't insult her or make a pass at her, or something she's going to take to the media and use against you. I mean, this little backstage set up wasn't your way of smoothing over something more serious, something that could get you into trouble, was it?"

He shook his head, his ego feeling a bit deflated. "No. It was nothing like that." He walked toward his dressing room, Rob in step beside him.

"You're sure?"

"I'm sure." He might have misjudged Charlie's integrity, but there was no mistaking the fear he saw in her eyes when she spoke about her husband. She definitely wasn't looking to get publicity out of their encounter or stir up the media. Unfortunately, the reality was . . . she just wasn't interested in him.

He had made the first mistake in the world of show business—believing his own hype. He just assumed, since he was *the* Hunter Jennings, Charlie would want to spend time with him, even though he was a total stranger.

Sitting down on the brown suede couch in his dressing room, he rested his head back against the cushions and closed his eyes.

"Come on, Hunter, shake it off. So she isn't attracted to the celebrity type. We're probably safer for it."

He didn't acknowledge Rob, he just tipped his hat forward over his eyes and said, "I'm going to catch a few Zs, and I don't want to be disturbed. Come and get me when my set is twenty minutes out."

When Hunter heard the door close, he peaked from under the brim of his hat to make sure Rob was gone. Sighing, he put his hands behind his head and stretched his long frame out in front of him, then replayed his conversation with Charlie in his head.

"You're not going to stand me up, are you?"

"I'll be there."

She said she would come. Did she feed him a line just to get rid of him? No. She *had* shown up. She even called Rob.

41

So what happened?

Immediately, his analytical brain went into overdrive. *What if her husband was here? What if he had come to the concert and spotted her?* Hunter didn't even know if her husband lived in Tennessee. *What are the chances?* After dwelling on the possibility that she'd had an encounter with the man she was running from, the voice of reason finally kicked in.

She stood you up.

It's just that simple.

Get over yourself.

Closing his eyes again, he decided his deflated ego was right. Though he thought he felt a spark between them—that little something that connects two people—he must've been wrong.

If he was honest with himself, it was probably the guilt he still felt over Amy's death. He hadn't been there for his sister, had not protected her from her abusive husband. When he found out Charlie was in the same situation, he transferred his guilt over Amy into a need to see Charlie safe. His knight-in-shining armor mentality saw a woman in need of protection, and his heart jumped in without a thought to what he was doing.

It was obvious Charlie could handle herself. She did not need him or his misguided guilt. She was a grown woman, dealing with life the best way she knew how. He just had to accept things at face value.

She wasn't interested.

End of story.

Chapter Ten

Charlie had tossed and turned all night, so when morning light filtered in through her bedroom window, she grabbed her pillow and pulled it over her head. She didn't have the energy to face the day. Not after such a disastrous night. What had started as a once in a lifetime experience, turned into a disaster of mega proportions.

It was bad enough she had spent ten dollars for parking, only to be stood up and treated like a criminal. Then, to give the last of her money to the creep in the parking lot made the night even worst. But . . . the proverbial *icing on the cake* was coming home to absolute silence.

Silence like she had never heard before.

It had taken only a few seconds for her to realize what it was she *wasn't* hearing.

The refrigerator.

While she'd been gone on her grand adventure, the refrigerator had decided to give up the ghost, and took with it her meager groceries—the ones she was counting on to get her through the next week. And even though her frozen foods were still salvageable, without money to buy ice, there was nothing she could do to save them. So, her last act of the night had been dragging a trash bag of wasted food to the curb.

She had crawled into bed emotionally exhausted.

Her life of solitude was getting to her.

Her lack of finances worried her.

And the uncertainty of her future terrified her.

She was barely hanging on, and for what? Her life would never be anything more than day to day living, with a shadow of fear always lurking over her.

But that was yesterday, and this is today.

Knowing she had to shake off her negative thoughts, and the fiasco from the night before, she threw back the bedcovers and swiveled her legs over the edge. She had chores to do and didn't have the luxury of staying in bed all day. And thanks to Goliath, she had a reason to get up each morning. If it hadn't been for him, and the routine she maintained to care for him, she was sure she would have given up a long time ago.

The first few months she spent running from Daniel were difficult and dark. She had even contemplated suicide on several occasions. Even though it was an oxymoron to be running for her life yet willing to end it at the same time, it was a control thing. Something she'd never had with Daniel. If she took her own life, she would have the satisfaction of knowing she had taken control away from him. To do what she had not allowed him to do. Many a night she thought about the very act of it. But in the end, she couldn't go through with it. And once she got Goliath, he cemented her need to get up each morning and put one foot in front of the other. So, Goliath was not only her friend, but her savior. And just like so many days before, it was Goliath's needs that convinced her to get out of bed, brush herself off, and forget yesterday's disaster.

━━ ● ━━

Hunter had been awake since dawn. Though Rob always arranged for him to stay in a luxury hotel when he was in the same city for more than a day, he had decided to crash overnight in his tour bus. After the letdown of Charlie's no-show, he needed time to himself, and his home away from home was the best place for that.

Though he had compartmentalized his feelings while doing his concert, afterward—even with the natural high that came from performing—his mind kept spinning, wondering what had happened to her. Try as he might, he just couldn't get Charlie off his mind.

Deciding a hot shower was in order, he got out of bed and walked the few steps to his private bathroom. When he saw his reflection in the small vanity mirror, he stopped and gave himself a good, hard look. He ran his hand down the whiskers on his face before turning around to the full-size mirror on the back of the bathroom door. With his briefs sitting low on his hips, he scrutinized his thirty-five-year-old physique.

He could thank the wonders of genetics for his broad shoulders, barrel chest, and long legs. He didn't have to spend hours in the gym for his well-defined body. It was an inheritance passed down from his father, the only good thing he'd gotten from the man. And though he occasionally hit a hotel gym, it just wasn't his thing. His solid biceps and muscular legs were the results from swinging an ax, splitting firewood, mending fences, moving hay, and riding the open range. That was his workout of choice. And he did it every chance he got on his Texas ranch, all thirty thousand acres of it.

Hunter continued to stare at his reflection, Charlie's rejection playing with his insecurities. He was a decent looking guy, with what most people considered a glamorous lifestyle. He had plenty of money and a soaring career. But none of that seemed to interest Charlie, and it perplexed him.

Though he always thought of himself as grounded, he had to admit, when he first hit the big time, his celebrity status went straight to his head. Feeling he deserved the fruits of his labor, he didn't hold back. For several years he lived an excessive lifestyle, buying lavish gifts for his family and friends, wining and dining women, and acquiring every toy imaginable for himself.

Thankfully, due to his mother's prayers and help from his brother, he eventually reined in his out-of-control living.

Now, what Hunter looked forward to most when he toured was a break long enough to go home for a few days, hang with his family, and spend time on his ranch, his most coveted possession. Not only had it been a great investment, but it was his crowning achievement, and where he planned to spend the rest of his life.

But obviously, fame and fortune did not matter to Charlie. Even with everything he had, none of it seemed to impress her. Not on their first meeting when she tried to slam the door in his face. Not on their second meeting when he had to beg her to join him at his concert. And not on their third—nonexistent—meeting when she chose to stand him up.

"But why?" he yelled at the mirror. "Why won't she even give me a chance?"

Hunter sounded like a spoiled child, throwing a fit because he did not get his way. But he didn't care. He wanted an explanation. He deserved that much.

"And I'm going to get it!" he said to the mirror as he balled his fists at his side.

He knew he was pressing his luck, but at least he would have closure.

With renewed justification, he stepped into the shower. He would go see Charlie one more time and give her a chance to explain.

Then he would move on with his life.

Chapter Eleven

An hour later, when Hunter pulled up in front of Charlie's house, he immediately noticed two things. One, her truck was in the driveway. That was a good sign. Two, there was garbage strewn everywhere in front of her house. Trash bags ripped open. Food littering the street and front yard. It was obvious animals had gotten to it.

But why hadn't she cleaned it up?

The haunting thought of Charlie's husband finding her flashed through his mind. His heart sank. Surely, that wasn't the reason she was a no-show.

He got out of his truck—the one he always trailered with him on tour—walked up to the front door and knocked. Then knocked again. But there was no answer.

Just like yesterday, he walked around to the back of the house, down the long drive, and out to the barn. Squinting in the darkness of the rickety structure, he stood for a moment to let his eyes adjust. Looking around he saw no signs of Charlie or her stallion.

Okay, so she's out for a ride.

Walking through the barn and out the other set of double doors, he strained to take in the extent of Charlie's property. He walked the fence line to the far side of the field, figuring it to be about three acres. He glanced back and forth down the common trail on the other side of the well-used gate, but there was no sign of the petite brunette or her mammoth horse.

Taking off his hat, he swiped his brow, not sure what to

do next. Turning back toward the barn, he walked slowly, trying to come up with a plan of action.

He could leave her a note, but what good would that do? *She probably wouldn't respond.*

He could wait in his truck. *And chance being spotted? No. That won't work either.*

He could come back later. It was probably his best option, but it didn't persuade him in the least. He didn't want to leave, not without talking to Charlie.

Back in the barn, he decided to wait for her, but not in his truck. He looked around, saw a few tasks that could be done, and decided to put his time to good use.

———— • ————

Charlie gently reined in Goliath. "Easy, boy."

Reluctantly, he slowed—his withers wet with sweat—and huffed in disapproval as she eased him into a leisurely pace.

"I swear your energy is endless. No matter how hard I push you, you always have more to give. You're a beast. You know that, right?"

Goliath let out a deep whinny and bobbed his head, as if he were answering her.

She laughed. Something she didn't do often. And it felt good. Especially after the disaster of the night before.

Continuing their mellow walk, Charlie looked up and squinted into the sun. She could not believe how inconsistent the weather had been the last few weeks. One day it was mild, even chilly by early evening, the next, it felt like summer all over again. Looping the reins loosely around the saddle horn, she pulled off her button-down shirt and tied it around her waist. Immediately she could feel the warmth of the sun on her shoulders.

And it felt wonderful.

Goliath loped along, seeming to forgive her for taking such a slow pace home. And even though she had a barn full of chores to do, her time with Goliath was the best therapy, so she didn't want to rush it.

When they reached the edge of the property, Charlie leaned down, unlatched the gate, and swung it wide. Goliath sauntered inside the fence and waited as she secured the latch behind them. As they walked toward the barn, she made a mental note of how many boards needed to be replaced on the fence. She'd been putting it off because finances were tight, but sooner or later she needed to get ahead of the curve before the whole fence decided to fall down. Besides, it was part of her lease agreement. She had negotiated the price down from fifteen thousand dollars for the year to ten thousand dollars cash, but all repairs and upkeep were her responsibility.

And now I have a refrigerator to replace and no money coming in for another week.

And just like that, the relaxation she had gained from her ride evaporated in the face of reality.

So much for therapy.

Outside the barn, she swung out of the saddle, her mind on her chore list. Sliding the reins over Goliath's mane and ears, she reached for the old, rusted door-pull on the barn. But, when she heard the telltale creak of the tack room door, she froze.

Someone's in the barn.

Her pulse immediately doubled, racing out of control.

The tack room door was stubborn and old. She had to yank it open and push it shut. There was no way it moved on its own. Which meant someone was definitely inside.

She tried to control her breathing, but it was no use. The fear inside her was stronger than her will. Goliath whinnied and pawed the ground, identifying with her agitation, as if to say, "I'm here; I'll protect you." But all he succeeded in doing was alerting whoever was inside the barn that she was just on the other side of the door.

Pulling the hoof pick from her back pocket, she flattened herself against the backside of the building. She only had one chance at the element of surprise. Hopefully, it would be all she needed.

Slowly, one of the barn doors swung wide, blocking her view of the assailant, but better yet, blocking his view of her. She took a slow measured breath, not sure if she would be able to do what she was planning. But as soon as she saw the tip of a cowboy boot clear the door, she charged the intruder, the hoof pick raised high overhead.

The towering figure turned at the last moment, and in that split second, she saw the surprise on Hunter Jennings' face as he blocked the forward motion of her arm. The thud of his forearm against hers knocked the pick from her hand, causing an electric shock of pain to shoot up her arm.

"It's me!" he shouted. "Charlie, it's me!"

Clutching her shoulder, she panted, her rage intensifying. "Are you crazy?" she hollered.

"Let me ex—"

"You jerk!" She shoved him, causing him to take a step back. "What is your freakin' problem?" She shoved him again, anger boiling inside her. When she lunged at him for a third time, he grabbed her wrists, pinned them behind her back, and pulled her to his chest.

"Let me go!" she shouted as she tried to squirm from his grip.

"Not until you calm down."

She thrashed some more, trying to wrestle free from his hold, but she was no match for his strength or his size. She looked up into his face, only inches from hers. "Let . . . me . . . go," she grounded the words between clenched teeth, "or so help me—"

"Are you going to give me a chance to explain?"

"Let me go!"

"I will, but you have to give me a chance to—"

"I don't have to give you anything!" she yelled in his face. "You have done nothing but harass me since coming to town. And for what? You beg me to go to your stupid show, and like an idiot, I go. And what did I get in return? I get stood up by your manager, I spend every last penny I have on parking and getting my battery jumped, while warding off the advances of a slimy parking lot attendant, and if that wasn't enough, I come home to a broken refrigerator after giving up my last shift for a week. So, now I'm broke, and I have no food. But you want me to give you a chance to explain? You're crazy! And I'm crazier still for letting you talk me into going to your stupid concert in the first place. Now, let go of my hands before I scream bloody murder!"

Chapter Twelve

When Hunter finally let go of her wrists, she marched toward Goliath, grabbed the reins that now hung on the ground, and walked him to the hitching post inside the barn. With her head resting against Goliath's sturdy shoulder, she covered her mouth with her shaking hand, and sobbed silently.

I could have killed him.

She pictured the hoof pick in her hand and how close she'd gotten to his head. If he had not stopped her, she would've buried it in his skull. She nearly passed out at the thought. White specks of light danced before her eyes, and she had to grab onto the saddle horn for balance.

"I can't leave until I know you're going to be okay."

She turned around and pointed at the door. "Get out!"

"I don't understand. Rob told me you were a no-show."

She shook her head in disbelief. "Are you for real? You attack me, and you still have the audacity to accuse me of lying?"

"I didn't attack you! You attacked me! I was only defending myself."

"And now you're defending your manager. You know what, *Mr. Hotshot Country Singing Star*, you're a real piece of work." She turned back to Goliath. "Now get out."

She waited for him to leave, but he just stood there. Knowing she couldn't call the cops, didn't leave her with many options.

Fine. I'll just ignore him.

Unbuckling the girth strap on Goliath's saddle, she pulled it toward her. But the pain radiating up her arm almost caused her to drop it. Taking a deep breath, she walked over to the tack room and swung the saddle over the rack. When she turned, she noticed the rake, shovels, hoe, and broom all leaning in the corner. *That's not where I left them.* She usually had them strategically positioned throughout the barn as improvised weapons of protection.

Whatever.

She walked back to Goliath, purposely avoiding Hunter where he stood twenty feet to her left. Pulling off Goliath's blanket, she flipped it over the sawhorse in front of his stall. That's when she noticed the new layer of hay on the floor and the trough filled with fresh water. Glancing around the rest of the barn, she saw the broken hay bales that had littered the floor were picked up and put in the wheelbarrow. The soiled hay from Goliath's stall and the rest of the barn was piled neatly to the left of the barn door, and the broken bin that held oats, was fixed and the oats that had siphoned onto the floor had been cleaned up.

With her eyes focused on Goliath, she stroked his neck. "You did all this?" she asked.

"I figured you were out on a ride, so I decided to make myself useful while I waited." His tone was sheepish, almost apologetic.

"You didn't have to do that."

"I know. But I wanted to see you. And I'm not one to just stand around."

What was she supposed to say? Thank you? *Thank you, Hunter, for doing my chores and scaring me to death. I really appreciate the way you have given me two nervous breakdowns in the last three days.*

No.

What he did was ludicrous. And she was not going to give him an easy out.

"If you're waiting for a thank you, you're going to be here a while."

"I can wait."

She closed her eyes at his persistence, feeling her anger coming back full force. Ignore him. That's all she could do.

She walked Goliath over to the area she had set up for bathing. Pulling the nylon harness over his muzzle and ears, she quickly unbuckled the leather harness and made the switch. She heard Hunter's phone whistle a tune and glanced over her shoulder. His manager was probably wondering where he was.

Good. Now he'll have to leave.

But he didn't move.

He just silenced his phone and put it back in his pocket.

Untying the shirt around her waist, she looped it over a rail and gave Goliath her full attention.

She tried to go about her normal routine and forget Hunter was even there. But every time his phone whistled, she was reminded today—just like yesterday and the day before—was anything but normal.

———— • ————

Hunter was still trying to process everything Charlie had said. No money . . . broken refrigerator . . . stood up. But what really bothered him was the thought of her having to fight off some guy in the parking lot.

He watched as she bathed her horse, wanting to say something but didn't know where to start. Had Rob lied to him? He said she was a no-show, but Charlie said she was the one stood up. It didn't make sense. And had she really spent all her money because of him? He wanted to ask but didn't want to give her another chance to send him away. He decided to wait, hoping he could wear her down.

———— • ————

Charlie worked on Goliath's coat with a sweat scraper, while glancing at her watch. Twenty minutes of silence.

How long is he going to keep this up?

She knew he had a temper. She'd seen it on their first encounter, and again when he refused to let her go without an explanation. What was his limit? How long before he blew a fuse?

I don't want to find out.

The yelling and screaming only dredged up memories from the darker times in her life. No. If she wanted him to leave, she'd have to indulge his questions. Maybe then he would finally go away.

With Goliath's bath over, she walked him back to his stall, took off the bridle, and gave him a scoop of oats. Latching the gate, she turned to where Hunter was leaning against a post, his arms crossed, his hat low over his eyes.

She hated herself for noticing how good he looked.

When he realized he finally had her attention, he pushed his hat back and walked toward her, his hands stuffed in his front pockets, shoulders slumped in defeat.

"Charlie, I'm so sorry. I can't tell you how horrible I feel. I've screwed up everything from the minute I met you. And every time I try to apologize, I just make matters worse."

She could not believe her heart was betraying her. She wanted to be mad at him and had every right to be. But seeing the sorrow in his eyes and hearing the regret in his tone, she felt her anger begin to melt away. "I don't know what to say, really I don't."

"Can you just explain again what happened last night?"

"Why?"

"Because I feel responsible."

When his phone whistled again, he quickly pulled it from his pocket, silenced it, and slipped it back inside.

"Your manager is going to send out a search party if you keep ignoring his calls."

"How'd you know it was Rob?"

She shrugged. "Same ringtone as yesterday."

Hunter smiled, rubbing the whiskers on his chin. "Do you think we could go inside and talk?"

Did she want to go inside and talk? She didn't think so. She stared at the toe of her boot, contemplating what to do next.

"Please. I promise to mind my manners."

She looked into crystal blue eyes that appeared to be sincere . . . and incredibly gorgeous. She sighed, "Fine. But only for a minute."

Chapter Thirteen

Hunter could not help but watch the gentle sway of Charlie's hips as she climbed the back steps of her 70s era ranch-style house. Once inside the mud room, he waited as she used the boot jack to pull off her riding boots. Wiggling the toes of her polka-dotted socks, she continued into the kitchen.

Following her lead, he set his size fourteen boot into the boot jack and pulled.

"Oh, you don't need to do that," Charlie said.

"Yes, ma'am, I do. If my mom found out I traipsed soiled boots through your house, she would take me to task." He smiled as he pulled his other foot from his boot, removed his hat, then looked around the sunny yellow kitchen.

A table for two sat against the wall across from the sink—a sink filled with an array of colored plastic containers, obvious casualties from her refrigerator fiasco.

Walking into the living room, Hunter browsed the room he'd been in once before. He didn't know much about decorating, but he knew what he liked, and he liked this. Earthy colors, comfortable furniture, nothing frilly. Charlie motioned for him to take a seat on the comfortable looking couch.

"I would offer you something to drink, but all I have is tap water or room temperature soda."

He smiled as he sat down, rotating his hat in his hands. "I'm fine but thank you."

She remained standing, hands in her back pockets, rocking on her heels.

"Could you sit down? Otherwise, I'm going to have to stand. Sorry, it's just my Southern upbringing rearing its ugly head."

She stepped in front of the overstuffed chair that matched the couch. Pulling her stocking feet up under her, she sat down.

He waited for her to say something, but she was obviously waiting for him.

Scooting to the edge of the couch, he put his hat on the coffee table, and rested his elbows on his knees. "Can you tell me what happened at the event center? Rob said when he went to meet you, you weren't there."

"That's because I had already been waiting twenty minutes when a cop walked up to me and told me to leave or be arrested."

Hunter hung his head. Rob told him the truth. He just didn't tell him the *whole* truth. "Why didn't you call Rob and have him vouch for you?"

"I didn't have a phone, and I lost his business card."

He remembered Rob saying something about Charlie borrowing a phone. "Why don't you have a phone?"

"I do. A house phone registered in my landlord's name."

"But why not a cell phone?"

She bent her head and fidgeted, looking uncomfortable. "I don't have anyone to talk to, okay? Besides, cell phones can be tracked."

"Not all of them. You could ge—"

"I don't need a cell phone," she interrupted sharply.

Hunter stopped, but only for a second. "But what if you had an emergency? You could fall while you're out riding. Or your truck could breakdown. Or what if your husb—"

"That's it!" She sprung to her feet. "I think we're done here." Marching to the front door, she flipped all three of the deadbolts, slid off the security chain, and pulled the door open wide. With her hand on her hip, she stood glaring at him.

He cringed. *How do I manage to keep getting on this woman's bad side?* "I'm sorry. I shouldn't have said anything."

She raised her brow. "Mr. Jennings, do you realize in the last forty-eight hours, how many times you've had to apologize for your actions? I don't think that's a good foundation for a friendship or acquaintance, or whatever it is you were hoping to accomplish by coming here. So, why don't you go back to your party-all-night, country music bad-boy, superstar-world, and leave me to my paycheck-to-paycheck, broken down pick-up truck, no-phone, life."

"I can't." He didn't budge. "Not until I make this right."

"Make what right?" she yelled, clearly frustrated. "What is with you?"

"I just want you to know there is more to me than what you see on stage."

"I've never seen you on stage," she said matter-of-factly.

"Okay, whatever you've read in magazines or seen on TV."

"This might surprise you, Mr. Jennings, but I'm not one of your fawning fans, and I don't follow your career."

"For cryin' out loud, woman," he jumped to his feet. "Are you always so unbending?"

"I choose to call it being a good judge of character."

"And me, coming to your house twi—"

"Uninvited," she cut him off.

"Coming to your house twice—"

"Scaring me half to death!" She crossed her arms, interrupting him again.

Taking a deep breath, he tried for a third time. "Coming to your house twice to *apologize*, makes me a person of bad character?"

"You know what, Mr. Jennings, since you're going to leave town, and we're never going to see each other again, it really doesn't matter what I think of you."

He scooped up his hat from the coffee table and grabbed

his boots from the mud room floor. Crossing the living room to the front door where Charlie still stood, he stopped just inches from her. "But it matters to me." Placing his hat on his head, he pulled his boots on, then looked her in the eyes. "Good night, Ms. Foster. I wish I could say it's been a pleasure, but my mom taught me never to lie, especially to a lady."

Chapter Fourteen

Charlie had stewed all last night, putting her in a funk that had followed her around most of the day. She tried to get Hunter Jennings out of her mind, but she kept remembering the dejected look she saw in his eyes when he walked out the door.

And I'm the person responsible for putting it there.

She had finished her outside chores in record time—thanks to the work Hunter had done in the barn the day before—and had used her pent-up energy to clean the house from baseboards to ceiling fans. Anything to defuse the guilt eating at her for being so "unbending."

Turning her attention to the kitchen, she decided to rearrange the cupboards. Currently, there was no rhyme or reason to where anything was kept. She had so few things when she moved in, and as she accumulated cups and plasticware, she had just kind of stuck them here and there. But today would be the perfect day to organize the kitchen.

Anything to keep her mind occupied.

Just as she opened the cupboard nearest the sink, there was a knock at the front door. *Of course.* Walking through the living room, she peered through the peephole and saw a man with an appliance store logo on his shirt.

Probably a wrong address.

Without removing the security chain, she opened the door slowly and spoke through the five-inch gap. "Can I help you?"

"I have a delivery for," he looked down at his clipboard,

"Charlie Foster."

She shook her head. "There must be a mistake. I didn't order anything."

"I was told to give you this." He pulled an envelope from his clipboard and slipped it through the crack.

She took it and watched as the delivery guy walked back to his truck. Closing the door, she quickly slid her finger under the envelope flap, and pulled out a folded piece of paper. When she opened it, something fluttered to the floor. Looking down, she saw a twenty and two hundred-dollar bills.

What in the world?

After picking them up, she turned her attention back to the handwritten note.

> *PLEASE ACCEPT THIS WITH MY SINCEREST APOLOGIES. MY INTENTIONS WERE NEVER TO HURT YOU OR MAKE YOU FEEL UNCOMFORTABLE. PLEASE DON'T REFUSE THE DELIVERY. I PAID CASH, AND THEY WON'T HAVE ANY WAY OF KNOWING WHO TO CONTACT IF YOU DON'T ACCEPT IT. I WENT WITH WHITE INSTEAD OF STAINLESS STEEL SO IT WOULD MATCH YOUR OTHER APPLIANCES. I HOPE THAT WAS THE RIGHT CHOICE. I INCLUDED SOME CASH FOR GROCERIES, AND A TWENTY SO YOU COULD TIP THE DRIVER.*
>
> *SINCERELY – H.J.*

Charlie quickly opened the front door, just as the delivery guy tipped his hand truck backwards and started rolling up her driveway, a picture of a refrigerator on the huge cardboard box. He stopped at the walk. "Which door should I use?"

"Umm . . . the back."

She hurried to the back door and pushed it all the way open, then watched as the deliveryman backed up to the porch and carefully pulled the hand truck up the three steps. With just enough room to squeeze through the doorway, he rolled the cardboard box to the center of the kitchen.

"Did you want me to dispose of your old refrigerator?"

"Sure. That would be great."

"Is it empty?"

"Umm . . ." She opened the door and grabbed the loaf of bread she had left inside, tossed it on the counter, then pulled the water-filled ice trays from the freezer and set them in the sink.

With skilled precision, the deliveryman pulled out the old refrigerator, strapped it to the hand truck, and disappeared through the back door.

Seeing the filth on the kitchen floor where the refrigerator had been, Charlie grabbed a dishrag and tried to clean the area as best as she could. When the man reappeared, she quickly moved out of the way, then watched as he fiddled with hoses and connectors on the backside of the fridge, her thoughts drifting to Hunter. *I can't believe he went to all this trouble.* She read his note again.

I WENT WITH WHITE INSTEAD OF STAINLESS STEEL SO IT WOULD MATCH YOUR OTHER APPLIANCES.

She was surprised by his intentionality. Choosing the color. Including money for groceries and a tip. *Making sure there was no way I could refuse it.* She grinned to herself. *He's thorough. I'll give him that.*

Closing her eyes, she remembered how he looked standing in the barn with his hat tipped back and a cocky grin on his face. Though he acted confident and self-assured, his words were humble . . . unassuming. Definitely not what she . . .

"Ma'am?"

She turned to the deliveryman, realizing she had zoned out for a minute. "I'm sorry. What did you say?"

"You should throw out the first few batches of ice cubes."

She nodded. "Sure."

"Well, that's about it." He picked up the remnants of tape and cardboard, then handed her the clipboard. "I just need your signature."

She signed next to the X, then offered him the folded twenty. "Thank you for your time."

"Sure thing."

She watched as he rolled through the mud room and out the back door. When she turned toward the new refrigerator, she couldn't help but smile. It was beautiful. She opened the side-by-side French doors and looked at all the drawers and special features, then slid open the freezer on the bottom and looked at a whole lot of nothing. Closing the doors, she pulled out Hunter's note once again.

MY INTENTIONS WERE NEVER TO HURT YOU OR MAKE YOU FEEL UNCOMFORTABLE.

A twinge of guilt stabbed at her. Had she been too hard on him? She thought about their conversations . . . more like confrontations.

But why is he being so persistent? She thought again about what he had said. *It must be because of his sister. Maybe he thinks helping me will somehow make up for what happened to her.*

But it wouldn't.

He couldn't help her situation. No one could.

She looked at the gleaming refrigerator, then pictured the towering cowboy.

With a smile, she whispered, "Thanks, Hunter."

Chapter Fifteen

Hunter plucked his guitar as he hummed a tune, words dancing around in his head. When he spun a phrase just right, he wrote it down on the mini notebook he always carried with him.

> *HOW DO I SHAKE THIS FEELING,*
> *WHEN I CAN'T GET YOU*
> *OUT OF MY MIND?*
> *OTHERS DON'T UNDERSTAND,*
> *THEY THINK I'M WASTING MY TIME.*
> *WHEN I CLOSE MY EYES,*
> *IT'S ONLY YOU I SEE.*
> *BUT YOU WON'T LET YOURSELF*
> *GET CLOSE TO ME.*

He continued to strum a brooding tune as he hummed along.

"Haunting."

Hunter looked up to see Rob standing in the bus doorway, leaning against the jamb.

"I didn't hear you come in."

"I gathered that." Rob walked over and took a seat across from him. "Working on a new song?"

"Just fiddling," he said as he set his guitar aside.

"Can I hear it?"

"It's not ready." Hunter always shared his tunes with Rob, but not this one. It was too personal. It wasn't just words. It was how he felt, and he didn't want someone critiquing his feelings. "Did you need me for something?"

"Just checking to see if you're ready for the meet and greet. We need to leave in ten."

Hunter knew the routine. New city, new promo. Of course, his thoughts had never left Tennessee. He stood and pulled his black T-shirt forward over his head. "Let me wash up and get a clean shirt."

"Sure."

In the bathroom, he splashed cold water on his face, trying to wash away the mood he was in. But it was no use. *Why am I so stuck on this woman? I blew every attempt to get to know her while she made it abundantly clear she had no interest in me. So why can't I get her out of my mind?*

Drying his face, he walked to his bedroom and grabbed another of his signature black shirts. His stylist had said the simple black T and black felt Stetson was sexy. He didn't feel sexy, but his wardrobe reflected his mood perfectly.

"Ready?" Rob asked when Hunter reappeared.

"Do I have a choice?"

"Man, what is with you? I haven't seen you this moody since Am—"

"Watch it!" Hunter snapped.

"I'm sorry. I didn't mean anything by it. I just don't understand how this woman has gotten under your skin."

"You know what," Hunter fired back, "I wasn't going to say anything, because it doesn't matter now, but how about you explain to me why Charlie waited over twenty minutes to meet you, but you never showed up?"

"Wh . . . what?" Rob glanced at his watch, ignoring Hunter's stare.

"Charlie told me she waited for twenty minutes when a cop hassled her and told her to leave or be arrested for loitering. Why did she have to wait so long?"

Rob shook his head sheepishly before finally making eye contact with him. "I'm sorry, man. There was just so much going on. You know how it is backstage. I have reporters to finesse, fan club members to appease—"

"And a blond with *easy* written all over her to entertain?"

"Come on, Hunter, that's not fair."

"Did you or did you not tell me you hooked up with that Stacy woman after the concert?"

"Well, yes, but—"

"Admit it, Rob. You were so distracted by what she was advertising, you completely forgot about Charlie."

Hunter watched as Rob readied his rebuttal, then dropped his shoulders in obvious defeat. "I'm sorry, Hunter. I screwed up. It wasn't as seedy as you make it sound, but I admit . . . I was a little distracted. By the time I got to the stage door, she was gone."

"And because of your screw-up, she was almost accosted in the parking lot."

"What?"

"Yeah, that's right. Her truck had a dead battery, and she had to fight off the advances of a too-friendly security guard. All because you were 'distracted.' "

"Hey, man, I'm sorry. I had no idea."

He knew he should cut Rob some slack, but he was ticked. Because of Rob's overactive libido, Hunter would probably never get the chance to see Charlie again.

"Hunter, I don't know what else to say."

Grabbing his hat from the hook by the door, he looked his manager square in the eye. "You lie to me again, you're fired. Now, let's go."

He stormed down the steps, refusing to let Rob have the last word.

Chapter Sixteen

Charlie had debated all afternoon whether she should or should not use the money Hunter had given her. On one hand, she felt guilty. She really didn't deserve the money or the refrigerator for that matter, not after the way she had treated him. On the other hand, she felt insulted he thought money could smooth things over between them. He'd been intrusive, meddling, and had terrified her to the point of violence. Did he really think a refrigerator, and two hundred dollars made them even?

Not hardly.

But since she could not return the refrigerator and had next to nothing to eat, she found herself cruising the grocery store aisles, picking and choosing between necessities and indulgences.

She felt like a kid at Christmas. With two hundred dollars in her pocket, she could get anything she wanted. Of course, her frugal side would not allow her to do that, but it was fun to pretend.

In the end, she only bought the basics: milk, cheese, eggs, some inexpensive cuts of meat, and a few pieces of fresh fruit. She made sure to keep it under a hundred dollars and had tucked away the other hundred-dollar bill, just in case she found herself in an emergency situation.

Which for her was always a very real possibility.

———— • ————

With a smile plastered on his face, Hunter waved his last goodbye before ducking into the backseat of the Lincoln Town Car Rob had rented for the event. Once inside, he slouched in his seat and groaned. Rob and Chet—Hunter's driver, pilot, and friend—slid into the front seat.

"That's it! No more meet and greets unless it's small and backstage. These larger events are a real pain in the butt."

Rob and Chet laughed.

"Come on, Hunter, do you really expect us to feel sorry for you?" Rob teased. "You have five hundred fans—mostly women—asking you to sign CD covers, shirts, their chest . . ."

"I don't care. Next time, I want security."

"Security? What for? None of the men hassled you. In fact, they love you almost as much as the women. You sing about the lives they wish they had."

"It's not the husbands and boyfriends I'm worried about. Those women are animals. They have no discretion whatsoever. Tugging and groping, sticking their chests in my face, it's ridiculous."

Rob laughed. "What do you expect? Your chart toppers are 'Honky Tonk Hookups,' 'Women & Whiskey,' 'Bar Flies & High Fives,' and 'Race Cars & Racy Women.' Do you really think you're going to attract the church crowd with songs like those?"

"But what about 'Memories in the Making,' 'You Can't Take It to the Bank,' or 'Stars, Stripes & Freedom?'"

"Well, those cuts are good too, but those aren't your brand." Rob's good-humored attitude turned serious. "Listen, Hunter, I know there's another side to you, and your family knows there's another side to you. But as far as the world is concerned, Hunter Jennings is a good ol' boy with a drink in one hand and a woman in the other."

"That's what bothers me. It's not the real me."

"Well, it didn't bother you when I took over your career and you landed at number one. Or, when the *Summer Days,*

Hotter Nights album went double platinum. Or when we revamped your country bumpkin style and turned you into one of country music's sexiest men. Like it or not, this *is* who you are. This *is* who your fans want to see when they come to your shows. This *is* who I expect to see when you show up to a meet and greet, and this *is* what you're selling when you work a room of industry insiders."

"So, maybe I should just throw in the towel. Take my good fortune and my investments and go back to Texas. There I could just be Aaron Jennings, ranch owner, instead of Hunter Jennings, superstar."

Rob looked at him with absolute shock. "What is with you? Ever since your run-in with that Foster woman, you've been a different man. You're obsessed with her even though she didn't give you the time of day. Are you telling me you would chuck it all, just so you could pursue a woman who clearly has issues?"

Hunter ignored him, turning his attention to the window and the passing buildings.

"Well, I hate to be the one to burst your *I'd rather settle down* mindset, but you are under a little thing we call *a binding contract,* which includes two more records and a greatest hits project. You can't just walk away from your legal obligations."

Hunter was ready to tell his manager exactly where he could stick his contract, but Rob cut him off.

"Come on, Hunter. You've got to let this go. You can't let that woman mess with your mind or your career. All she has been is a bad distraction. You need to get over her and move on."

Hunter pulled down his hat over his eyes, not wanting to hear anymore, because he knew it was all true. Rob had done a great job repackaging his image and getting his career off the ground. And he had gone right along with it. He had enjoyed the attention at first: the women, the hype, the sexy image. But somehow, seeing himself through Charlie's eyes had given him perspective, embarrassed him even. He wasn't the macho, uninhibited male he claimed to be. He was a country boy from the sticks with a mom who prayed for him every night. He'd been shy and awkward through his teen years and never really knew what to do around women. That is until someone put a drink in his hand. The party all day and bedroom nights persona were products of hard liquor and the need to be accepted

Well, he had finally arrived.

He was on top of the world.

Yet, he was all alone.

He could have just about any woman he wanted at the drop of a hat, but that wasn't the kind of woman he wanted, or the kind he would bring home to his family. He wanted a woman like Charlie. Someone not fazed by his mega-star status. At the very least, he wanted a chance to explore his feelings further. Unfortunately, she had made it extremely clear how she felt about him.

She wasn't interested.

Period.

Chapter Seventeen

Charlie walked through the mud room after her ride, took off her boots, and was greeted by the gleaming white refrigerator sitting in the corner. It was beautiful, and she loved it. But it was a mocking reminder of her bizarre encounter with Hunter Jennings.

He was now in Georgia, and she hated herself for knowing that. When she had gone to the feed store yesterday, she saw a leftover flyer regarding the saddle giveaway and noticed it listed Hunter's entire tour schedule. She grabbed one. Why? She didn't know . . . but she did. Of course, she also had to field questions from Gerald for her odd behavior when he tried to present her with the saddle. She gave the store owner a lame excuse about being incredibly camera-shy, before hurrying out of the store.

Now she stood in her kitchen, wondering about the handsome cowboy who had intruded on her already crazy world. Walking into the living room, she pressed the power button on her all-in-one stereo system, and picked up the CD cover with Hunter's picture on it. Sitting down with the remote, she clicked through to the sixth song on his second release, the same song she had played over and over again. "Memories in the Making" was a beautiful tune about the special events in life and the people who mattered. It was nothing like the country hits the radio stations played about partying, hooking up with women, and drinking the night away. It was about family and country and the simple pleasures of life.

Initially, she bought his new release, intending to use it to make her feel better about the way she had treated him. To prove all he cared about was getting lucky and getting drunk. That he was a shallow person who hopped from one woman's bed to another, something she'd have nothing to do with regardless if he gave her a refrigerator or a Ferrari. But instead, she found songs that touched her heart, songs that made her long for a family, a legacy, and a man who would love her above all else.

After listening non-stop to his current CD, she drove across town to the local retail store, pulled out the hundred-dollar bill she had squirreled away, and purchased three more of his CD's. And, just like his latest release, there were songs about girls, pickup trucks, and beer, but there were also songs that made her heart melt, songs that spoke about the important things in life.

And they were all written by Hunter.

She read each of the liner notes, enjoying the ability to get to know the man behind the music. She found out he had a brother, and he spoke about his mother, but nothing about a father. She was also surprised to find out he was nine years older than her, something she hadn't even thought about. But that wasn't the only surprise. When he doled out his thank yous to the multiple people responsible for his success, he thanked his manager, his fans, his band, and what she assumed were numerous people in the music industry. But something changed by his third CD. He spoke with more humility as he thanked God and his family for all their love and support. And his latest CD was dedicated to Amy, his guardian angel.

It caught her completely off guard, and before she knew it, tears streamed down her cheeks, her heart breaking for his loss.

She sat on the sofa, perplexed, feeling like she was reading about two different men. She didn't understand why he sold himself as an over-aged frat boy with no morals, when it seemed like the true Hunter Jennings lived for family, would die for his country, and knew the best things in life were free.

Fame.

That's what it was.

Fame and fortune.

He had sold out in order to make his millions, and in the end had sacrificed his character. Well, she thought he had sacrificed his character, but the millions of fans who bought into his party lifestyle hailed him as king of the tailgate parties. Guys used his tunes to get the girls, and girls used his songs to drive the guys crazy.

"Sad . . . that's what it is."

Charlie knew in her heart of hearts she could fall for the man behind the music, but not the performer. "Too bad." She talked to the picture on the CD cover. "You're off on your tour, selling empty promises and a shallow lifestyle, and I'm here asking myself, why do you do it?"

Chapter Eighteen

The concert high was still buzzing around the trio of groups that made up the After Party Tour. Everyone sat backstage long after the concert, feeding off each other's energy. The members of Arkansas Rain—the opening act—were elated their new songs were being so well received by the crowd. They had made one of their tunes available for download in anticipation of their coming release and were overwhelmed by the reaction. The Winchesters—the sibling trio that had been brought in as a special guest—were in stitches as Hunter and the lead singer from Arkansas Rain shared some of their best on-tour antics and behind-the-scenes stories.

They'd been reminiscing for about an hour when one of the road crew walked over to them, looking shaken.

"What's up, Darin?" Hunter asked.

"I just heard two people were shot and killed in the parking lot after the concert."

"What?" Several people exclaimed in unison.

"Yeah, I guess some chick was two-timing her husband, and he found out. So he staked out her car. When she and her boy-toy showed up after the concert, he shot them both, then waited for the police to arrive."

Everyone sat in horrified shock, except for Hunter.

He immediately got up and headed straight to his bus. Once inside, he couldn't sit down. All he could think about was Charlie, wondering if she was safe. It had been a month since he sent her the refrigerator. He thought about her night and day, wishing there was some way to contact her, to talk to her. Last week, when he went home on a break, he almost had Chet take a detour through Tennessee. He just wanted to go by her house and make sure she was okay. But he didn't. He knew he needed to respect her privacy.

Now this.

What if it had been Charlie? What if her husband found her? Would he really kill her?

His mind flipped to the night he found out about Amy. He had been in North Carolina on tour when the police called and informed him his sister was dead. They told him she had fallen down a flight of stairs and broken her neck. But he knew the truth.

Ray had killed her.

Plain and simple.

Just the night before, Amy had called him, and Hunter knew something wasn't right. She assured him she was okay, but when he suggested she join him on tour for a week or so, she jumped at the chance. She was supposed to meet up with him in Alabama at the end of the week. But she never made it.

People tried to console him, assuring him it wasn't his fault. But in his heart of hearts, he blamed himself for not doing something more.

Rob walked in while Hunter paced. "You okay?"

"No. No, I'm not." He tossed his hat on the couch and raked his fingers through his hair. "I need you to do me a favor."

"Sure. Anything."

"I need you to buy a phone and register it in your name."

"But why? I already have a phone."

"It's not for you."

"Hunter, you're talking in circles. What has you so twisted up?"

A battle waged inside him. *Am I betraying Charlie if I tell Rob what I know?* He thought a minute longer but didn't see that he had a choice.

"Listen, what I'm about to tell you can't leave this bus, you got it?"

Rob sat down on the edge of the couch, clearly confused.

"It's Charlie. I want—"

"I knew it!" Rob shot up from the couch, not allowing Hunter to finish. "You've acted like a crazy person ever since you met that woman. What is with you? What's going on?"

"She's in danger."

"What?"

"She's in danger from her . . ." Hunter hated the way this was going to sound. "She's in danger from her husband."

Rob's nostrils flared as he looked at him in disbelief. "You're kidding me, right? Tell me you're not infatuated with a married woman. Because the Hunter Jennings I know might sing about partying and hooking up, but he doesn't do that anymore, especially with married women. So, assure me, Hunter. Assure me you haven't gone and done something stupid."

"No. It's not like that."

His manager sauntered down the hall and back, doing nothing to hide his agitation or soften his raised voice. "So why don't you tell me what it *is* like."

"Okay. Just calm down and let me explain."

Rob stood with his hands plastered to his waist, his breathing nowhere close to normal.

"Charlie Foster is hiding . . . from her husband. I don't know all the details. I just know she told me he threatened to kill her if she ever left him. I don't even know if Charlie Foster is her real name."

Rob let his head drop back and stared at the ceiling. Taking a deep breath, he looked at Hunter. "You can't do this."

"Do what?"

"You can't get involved. This has nothing to do with

you. You stumbled across this woman because of some stupid contest. It's obvious she has taken care of herself this far. She doesn't need your help. Just let her be."

Hunter shook his head. "I can't do that. Those people killed in the parking lot, a crazy spouse seeking revenge. That could've been her."

"But it wasn't. Listen, her story isn't anything new. You hear about it all the time. That doesn't mean you can go around saving every woman who finds herself in a bad relationship."

"But I can't just walk away when I know she could be in danger. There has to be something I can do."

"This is about Amy, isn't it?" Rob whispered with compassion.

He turned away, feeling the sting of tears.

"Come on, Hunter," Rob said with a comforting hand to his shoulder. "Don't do this to yourself. Helping this woman isn't going to bring Amy back."

For a moment, Hunter couldn't breathe, couldn't speak. Emotions he had pushed deep down inside him came rushing to the surface. "But if someone had been there for Amy, if *I* had been there for Amy . . . maybe she would still be alive."

"Hunter, you *were* there for her. You tried to get her to come on the road with you. You did what you could. It's not your fault Amy never told you how bad things had gotten between her and Ray."

"But I knew something wasn't right. I knew it. When I asked her about her relationship with Ray, she got defensive and told me they were working a few things out, that I shouldn't worry. She downplayed their problems, probably because she didn't want to hear *I told you so* from me. I never liked Ray and she knew it. The night they planned to elope, I asked her to reconsider. She told me right then and there that she was in love with Ray, and if I didn't butt out, she would write me off. She was always so stubborn, so determined to be her own person. I knew if I kept grilling her, she'd end up pushing me away. So I let it go."

He sunk to the couch, his head drooping between his shoulders. "I let him kill her. I stepped out of the way and let Ray kill her."

"Come on, Hunter, don't talk like that," Rob said as he took a seat across from him. "You did no such thing. Amy wasn't straight with you. You can't blame yourself for something you weren't even aware of."

He looked up and pinned Rob with a stare. "Fine. But I know about Charlie. She told me she was running from her husband . . . a husband who threatened to kill her if he ever found her."

"So what does a phone have to do with any of this?" Rob said, getting back to the situation at hand.

"Charlie doesn't have a cell phone, remember?"

"Yeah. So what."

"The reason she doesn't have a phone is because she's afraid her husband could use it to find her."

"Come on, you hear about throw away phones on TV all the time. If she really wanted a phone, she could get one of those."

"Maybe. But for whatever reason, she hasn't. But, if I give her a phone . . . a phone registered in your name, traceable only to you, maybe she'd be willing to have one."

"And . . ." Rob looked at him like he was talking in circles.

"And," Hunter got to his feet, and resumed his pacing, "I could call her in situations like this, just to make sure she's okay."

"And what if we go to all this trouble and she still doesn't want a phone?"

Hunter rubbed his jaw in deliberation as he walked back to his bedroom. "I'll cross that bridge when I get there. Just get the phone," he said over his shoulder before shutting the door.

Chapter Nineteen

Charlie spied a man in a Courier Express uniform through the peephole on her front door. Making sure the chain was in place, she opened it slightly and asked, "Can I help you?"

"I have a delivery for Charlie Foster," he said as he looked up from his handheld computer.

"Can I ask who it's from?"

He looked at both the package and the handheld. "It's from a Courier Express store in Atlanta, Georgia."

Georgia? That's where Hunter is.

Charlie closed the door, removed the chain, then opened it again. The deliveryman passed her the handheld and showed her where to sign. She scribbled her name, illegibly, then handed him the minicomputer in exchange for the package. He pushed a few buttons, said goodbye, then walked away.

Charlie closed the door, twisted the locks, then sat on the edge of the couch. After wrestling with the packing tape, she removed the wrapper and held a cell phone box. Opening it, she pulled out a brand-new phone with a note taped to it. Unfolding the piece of paper—another one inside—she immediately recognized Hunter's handwriting.

HI CHARLIE
I KNOW THIS IS PROBABLY COMING OUT
OF LEFT FIELD BUT LET ME EXPLAIN. THERE
WAS AN INCIDENT THAT HAPPENED HERE LAST
NIGHT, AND I HAD A HARD TIME SHAKING IT.

He explained about a woman and her boyfriend shot by a jealous husband in the parking lot after his concert.

. . . I KNOW IT'S NOT MY PLACE, BUT IT BOTHERS ME THAT YOU DON'T HAVE A PHONE. YOU NEED ONE. JUST IN CASE YOU EVER FIND YOURSELF IN A SITUATION YOU CAN'T HANDLE.

Charlie thought back to their previous conversation about her not having a phone and sighed. She wanted to be mad at Hunter's continued interference in her life. But the fact that he seemed genuinely concerned and had obviously been thinking about her after all this time—*even though I basically told him to get lost*—tugged at a corner of her heart. She continued to read.

SO PLEASE, KEEP THE PHONE. IT'S REGISTERED TO ROB AND THERE'S ABSOLUTELY NO WAY ANYONE CAN TRACE IT BACK TO YOU. I PROMISE.

YOU NOW HAVE AN EMAIL, AMAZON, AND ITUNES ACCOUNT. THEY ALL HAVE A CREDIT CARD LINKED TO THEM SO PLEASE FEEL FREE TO USE THEM AT ANY TIME. I'VE INCLUDED ALL THE ACCOUNT NAMES AND PASSWORDS ON ANOTHER SHEET OF PAPER ALONG WITH THE CREDIT CARD INFORMATION.

IF YOU EVER FIND YOURSELF IN AN EMERGENCY, AND YOU DON'T HAVE CASH READILY AVAILABLE, YOU CAN USE THE CREDIT CARD AT ANY ONLINE STORE. AGAIN, NONE OF THIS IS TRACEABLE TO YOU. ALL BILLING WILL GO TO ROB. I ALSO TOOK THE LIBERTY OF PROGRAMMING ROB'S AND MY PHONE NUMBERS INTO THE CONTACTS LIST. MY NUMBER IS UNDER THE NAME AARON. IT'S MY GIVEN NAME. I FIGURED THAT WOULD

BE BETTER IN CASE SOMEONE GOT A HOLD OF YOUR PHONE. LESS QUESTIONS.

I'D LOVE TO HEAR FROM YOU FROM TIME TO TIME, JUST SO I KNOW YOU'RE DOING OKAY, BUT IT'S UP TO YOU. I WON'T COME BY UNEXPECTEDLY ANYMORE OR CALL YOU WITHOUT YOUR PERMISSION. I DON'T WANT TO BE AN INTRUSION IN YOUR LIFE. I JUST WANT TO HELP. I WASN'T THERE FOR AMY LIKE I SHOULD'VE BEEN. PLEASE ALLOW ME TO DO THIS FOR YOU.

GOD HAS BLESSED ME FINANCIALLY THROUGH MY CAREER, AND MY MOM ALWAYS TAUGHT ME TO SHARE WHATEVER GOOD FORTUNE THE LORD BRINGS MY WAY.
SINCERELY, H.J.

Charlie was stunned. She read and re-read the letter three times, flipping from Hunter's words to the list of accounts he had set up for her. Speechless did not even begin to describe how she felt. Who was this man? And why was he so hooked on her? She was a nobody. She wasn't an industry insider who could further his career, and she definitely had not given him any signals that a romantic relationship was even a possibility. They met by chance a month ago. Two out of the three encounters ending poorly. Why was he doing this?

Better yet, why did it bring a smile to her face?

Chapter Twenty

Charlie paced from the living room to the dining room, staring at the phone in her hand. She had spent the afternoon familiarizing herself with the screen and trying out all the bells and whistles. Now, she toyed with the idea of calling Hunter. It seemed only right to let him know she had received the phone and assure him—though she appreciated the gesture—she had no intention of using the credit card number he had given her.

She glanced at the clock over the fireplace. It was a little after seven. She thought about it. Hunter's concert started at seven, but he wouldn't be on stage yet, the opening band would be. So, if she called now, there was a good chance he would pick up. But did she want him to pick up?

No.

She didn't want to talk to him. She did not want to do anything he could misconstrue as a change of heart. But she did want to thank him. He deserved that much.

Plopping down on the couch, she tossed the phone on the cushion next to her and massaged her temples as she did some mental calculations.

The first band will probably play for twenty minutes to half an hour, the next band around forty-five minutes. With set changes and everything else that goes into a show, Hunter won't take the stage until at least eight-thirty.

After double checking her calculations, she decided to call around nine o'clock. That way, she could just leave a message on his voicemail. She would let him know she appreciated the refrigerator, the cash, and the phone. But she wouldn't actually have to talk to him. Glancing at the clock, she sighed.

Two hours to go.

She busied herself with chores. A little raking, a little mucking, nothing that really needed to be done, but stuff to keep her mind occupied while she waited to call Hunter. After fixing a few of the loose boards on the fence, she glanced at her watch for the hundredth time and decided it was close enough.

Taking off her boots in the mud room, she washed her hands, then took a seat on the couch. Picking up the phone from the coffee table, she tapped the contacts icon. Her list now totaled four entries, Artie and Karen's added to the other two.

She hesitated as her finger hovered over the name Aaron. Seeing Hunter's real name, not his stage name, made the call seem even more personal. Wavering—pros and cons running through her head—she took a deep breath, and before she could talk herself out of it, she touched the screen, then put the phone to her ear.

"You know who you're talking to, so go ahead and leave a message. I'll call you when I can."

Even though the message was vague, there was no mistaking Hunter's deep voice. But when the phone beeped, Charlie froze. For all the contemplating she had done, she was completely tongue tied.

Hang up. Just hang up.

No. That's immature.

Her conscience and rattled nerves argued back and forth.

You're an adult. Now act like one.

She cleared her throat.

"Hi. This is Charlie, Charlie Foster. I ahh . . . I wanted to let you know I got your package." She chuckled nervously. "I guess that's obvious since I'm calling you." She thought for a moment, the silence around her deafening. "I ahh . . . I also wanted to thank you for the refrigerator and the cash. It was totally unnecessary. It's not like it was your fault my old fridge died. I mean, if you were to blame for anything, it would be for me spending my last twenty bucks on parking and getting my battery jumped."

She cringed.

I'm supposed to be thanking him not blaming him.

"Not that I'm holding you to the twenty bucks. You more than made up for it with the two hundred dollars you gave me toward food."

That didn't sound right either.

"What I meant to say is you don't owe me anything. I'm doing just fine on my own. I'm not your responsibility, so please stop feeling like you have to take care of my problems. I'm sorry about your sister. Really, I am. But helping me is not going to bring her back. So, thank you again for the phone and the fridge, but please stop sending me things."

When she disconnected the call, she wanted to scream. She meant to sound appreciative and gracious, but instead, her thank you sounded more like an accusation from an ungrateful nag.

She set the phone down on the coffee table. "Why didn't I just say thank you, then hang up?" Marching into the kitchen, she pressed her forehead against the cool, sleek finish of her new refrigerator. "I sounded like a complete jerk."

I can't believe I brought up the twenty bucks when he clearly spent thousands between the refrigerator and the phone.

It was stupid and petty.

Without giving herself a chance to back out, she quickly walked to the living room, picked up the phone from the coffee table and tapped Hunter's number again. After listening to his message for a second time, she knew exactly what she wanted to say.

"Hunter, please accept my apology. What I meant to say is thank you. Thank you for the refrigerator and the phone.

I really do appreciate them. Hope you're having a good night. Goodbye." She disconnected and allowed herself a small smile.

"Better."

—— • ——

It was almost midnight when Hunter finally retired to his tour bus. Performing his nightly ritual, he hooked his custom Stetson on the hat rack by the door, stretched out on the couch, and reached for his cell phone where he always left it on the back edge of the couch. Scrolling to see if he had any voicemails from his mother or brother, he stopped when he saw Charlie's name on the screen.

Twice.

Snapping upright, he played the first message. The minute he heard her voice, and realized she was okay, he smiled. Her message was a bit blunt, in fact, Charlie's moxie made him laugh. But she was all right. That was what mattered. But when he played the second message and heard the softness in her tone, his heart twisted inside his chest.

He listened to the message three more times, while he thought about their encounter in the barn. Her petite features, her sable-colored hair, the fire in her eyes. *Man, she's beautiful,* he reflected, desperately wanting to call her back. He held his phone and stared at her name on the screen. All it would take is one touch.

No. I promised I wouldn't call without her permission. Besides . . . it's too late. If I called now, it would just freak her out.

Standing up, he pulled off his shirt while walking down the hall to the back of the bus. He collapsed across the bed, rolled over, and stared at the ceiling. Playing her message again and again—loving the sound of her voice—he wanted so badly to call her back.

But I promised I wouldn't call.

He smiled to himself. "But I didn't say anything about texting."

He glanced at the clock. It was too late now, but he could send her a quick message tomorrow. Nothing big. Nothing intrusive. Just a simple text thanking her for her message.

Feeling rejuvenated, he took a shower, stretched out on his bed, and fell asleep thinking about a certain brunette.

Chapter Twenty-One

Charlie and Goliath were cantering around the neighborhood rink when she felt a buzz between her and the saddle. She reined in Goliath and quickly dismounted, thinking a bee was on her backside. Twisting around, she swatted at her pocket, knowing any second she was going to get stung. That's when she felt the bulge in her pocket and realized her mistake.

The phone.

She expelled a deep breath and laughed out loud. Glancing around at the others using the rink, she hoped they didn't notice her frantic dance.

Come on, Charlie, it hasn't been that long since you had a phone. Get a grip.

When she pulled the phone from her pocket, she fumbled with the buttons, accidentally clearing the notification. But, before the message disappeared completely, she saw the name.

Aaron.

She stared at the phone, not knowing what to do. Thinking about the man on the other end of the message made her heart race. *Well . . . now isn't the time or place to exchange messages with him. I already thanked him for the phone, even if I did bungle it. I'm not going to start the back and forth thing. He said he wouldn't call or bother me, so I'm going to take him at his word.*

Goliath whinnied and bobbed his head, obviously annoyed his exercise routine was interrupted. Charlie stuck the phone back in her pocket and stroked Goliath's auburn mane. "You are one jealous horse, you know that?"

Goliath bobbed his head again and pawed the ground.

She laughed. "I swear you can understand me." Pulling herself back up into the saddle, she turned Goliath around. "Come on, boy, let's go home."

Taking a slow pace, she tried to think about anything or anyone other than Hunter Jennings. But it didn't work. After she'd left her disastrous phone message, she had listened to his music long into the night. She envisioned the rugged cowboy singing the songs that were quickly becoming her favorites, and found herself daydreaming about what it would've been like if they had met under different circumstances.

But who was she kidding? It was her circumstances that had captured Hunter's attention. She blurted out the abusive husband comment in order to wipe the smug look off his face. How could she have known it would be the catalyst that triggered his protective instincts? If it wasn't for the tragic fate of his sister, he probably would've written it off as a bad joke and left without giving it another thought.

He doesn't see me. He sees a cause. I can't get all Harlequin romance about this, and I certainly have no business involving someone in my twisted life.

She continued to reprimand herself as she unlatched the gate and walked Goliath into the barn.

Besides . . . Hunter will find a new project soon enough. I just have to give him time.

Charlie had tried to go about her day like it was any other. She did her chores and stayed busy, trying as hard as she could to keep her mind off the text waiting for her on her phone. She told herself she wasn't going to read it. If she didn't read it, she wouldn't feel obligated to respond. And, if she didn't feel an obligation to respond, Hunter would lose interest and move on.

She had the same conversation with herself several

times throughout the day. Never had she been so happy to have a shift at the diner, so it could eat up the rest of her night.

When she arrived at Artie's a few minutes before five o'clock, he was standing with a coffee pot in hand, debating politics with Frank, a dinner shift regular. He glanced her way with a good evening smile while he continued to banter with Frank.

Charlie walked through the swinging door, past the grill, to the kitchen office. Sliding her purse under the desk, she put on a black apron, criss-crossing the strings around her waist, and tying it off in front. After she washed her hands, she flipped two burgers sizzling on the grill.

Artie hurried through the swinging door and expelled a sigh of relief. "Thanks, Charlie. Frank does it to me every time." He crossed to the grill and threw a slice of cheese on each patty. "He gets me all caught up in conversation and then complains his burger is dry. I used to take a buck off his bill, but I'm wise to him now. He can talk all he wants, but he's paying full price. Dry or not dry."

Charlie just smiled because she knew Artie never charged Frank full price for anything. And as much as he blustered and complained, Artie had a heart as big as the moon. Frank's situation was sad. He lost his wife of fifty years to cancer just a few months ago, and even though he couldn't afford to eat out every night because of his fixed income, he did it anyway, just for the company. Ever since Artie figured it out, he always found a reason to discount Frank's bill.

The ringing bell over the front door signaled more of their dinner regulars had arrived. With order pad in hand, Charlie pushed through the swinging door and started her shift.

The steady crowd of weekly customers and a few stray visitors had made the last five hours go by like clockwork. Charlie tried to convince herself it was just another ordinary Thursday night. However, all she had to do is think about the text message from Hunter for her heart to race and her palms to turn sweaty.

This is crazy. I should've just read the message before I got to work. For all I know, it says, "you're welcome" and that's it.

Squeezing the mop head in the bucket ringer, Charlie hung it up, then rolled the bucket outside to dump the dirty water. When she walked back in, she noticed Artie staring at her from where he stood cleaning the grill.

"You okay?" he asked.

"Yeah, why?"

"I don't know. You seemed different tonight, like you were somewhere else. Jittery almost." He scrubbed the grill with the scouring brush, then looked at her with concern. "I hope you know you could come to me if you were in some sort of trouble."

She smiled, then walked over to where he stood and gave him a tender hug. "You're just an old softy, you know that?"

"I am not," he said as he squirmed in her embrace. "And you know I don't go for any of that mushy stuff. I just wanted to make sure you were okay, that's all. Geez, leave it to a woman to twist your words into something they're not."

She laughed as she pulled off her apron and grabbed her purse. "I'll see you tomorrow, Artie."

"Yeah, yeah. And make sure you're on time," he grumbled.

After climbing into her truck, Charlie squeezed her eyes shut, then turned the key in the ignition. Ever since her dead battery incident, she held her breath every time she started the engine. When it rumbled to life, she sighed with relief, wondering if Artie even realized she had completely avoided his question. Even though she was glad she had skirted that conversation, she felt a twinge of guilt.

Since the day she showed up at the diner and inquired about the *Help Wanted* sign in the window, Artie had been nothing but kind and considerate.

Well, at least after their first conversation.

She laughed, remembering how stern he'd been when he interviewed her for the job.

He let her know, no matter how hard she worked or how busy the diner got, he could not afford to offer her full-time hours or benefits. He explained that he would pay her in cash, and she would be responsible to file her own tax stuff. He made it very clear he wouldn't tolerate drinking, smoking, or chewing gum. And, if she didn't dress appropriately, or she flirted with the customers, she'd be gone.

Of course, she couldn't have asked for a better setup.

No tax forms.

No identification needed.

No having to avoid the usual questions.

But now that she had grown attached to Artie, she didn't like the fact that she wasn't being completely honest with him.

I could tell him. I know I could. But why should I put that kind of burden on him? He's protective enough already and has his own health issues to deal with. If I told him about Daniel, it might push him over the edge.

No. It was for his own good to keep him in the dark. Besides, there was nothing he could do to help her.

Of course, the Hunter Jennings situation was another story. If she told Artie about that, he would tell her she was crazy for not returning his message. The message he left on the phone *he* gave her.

Was she crazy?

Was she making a bigger deal out of it than it really was?

What would it hurt to return his call? Nothing would come of it. He was hundreds of miles away. Sure, they might call and text each other for a while, but sooner or later they would run out of things to say. Their phone calls would become fewer and farther apart, until Hunter's interest turned to someone else.

She chewed on that while she drove home, said goodnight to Goliath, and soaked in a nice hot tub. After pulling on the over-sized T-shirt she usually slept in, she tossed back the comforter and crawled on top of the bed. Sitting cross-legged, and leaning against the headboard, she reached for the phone where it sat on the nightstand and swiped the screen. She was surprised to see she now had two text messages and a missed call.

She smiled.

He's persistent. I'll give him that.

Chapter Twenty-Two

Charlie tapped the phone screen and read the first text message from Hunter.

> Hi Charlie. Thanks for the message. You sure have a way with words. LOL.

She winced, remembering the awkward message she'd left for him.

> I'm glad you like the refrigerator and are willing to keep the phone. I'll feel better knowing you have one, just in case there is an emergency. Of course, I have no doubt that you could go toe-to-toe with somebody if you had to.

Charlie pictured the grin she heard in his words.

> But I do have a question for you. How is your truck? I never got a chance to ask you about it. I'm assuming it was just a battery problem, but it's been nagging at me. Could you let me know if your truck is running all

94

right or if it needs any repairs? I know I said I wouldn't bother you, but a simple text saying "Yes, it's fine," would go a long way. Have a good day, Charlie. Don't ever hesitate to call if you need anything . . . anything at all.

What's going on? How is it I'm exchanging phone calls and text messages with Hunter Jennings? I don't get it. This is so surreal. Just last month I was living a quiet life— a life of secrecy and seclusion. And now I have a celebrity giving me a refrigerator, a phone, and asking if my truck is running okay.

She didn't know what to make of it or what to do about her racing heart. Shaking her head, she scrolled to the next text message and noticed the time it was left. A few minutes after five.

Hey, Charlie, it's me again. I know I said I wouldn't bother you, but I really would like to know if your truck is running okay. I keep picturing you broken down on a desolate road. Can you send me a quick text, just so I know? Hope you've had a good day.

No wonder he called. Great! Now he's probably going to think I'm ignoring him on purpose.

She tapped the phone screen and played his voicemail.

"Okay, Charlie, now I'm worried. If you don't want me contacting you, that's totally fine, just say so. But, if I don't hear from you by midnight, I'm jumping on a plane and flying to Tennessee."

"What!"

She looked at her bedside clock. *Eleven fifty-two.*

"Oh my gosh!" Immediately, she pressed the phone icon because texting would take too much time. On the second ring, Hunter answered the phone.

"Charlie, thank goodness it's you. Are you okay?"

She could hear the slightest hint of agitation in his voice.

"Yes. I'm fine. I just got done reading your messages and listening to your voicemail. I'm sorry I didn't respond sooner. I'm not used to having a phone, so I didn't pay attention to it until after work."

"That's okay."

Charlie could tell from his clipped tone he was suppressing his frustration. But what could she do about it? She didn't ask him to be her personal guardian. In fact, she didn't ask him for anything at all.

So why am I apologizing?

"Charlie, are you there?"

"Yep." Now it was her turn to be short.

There was a silent pause then a long, defeated sigh. "Hey look," the softness was back in his tone, "I didn't mean to sound so abrasive. I was just worried is all."

"But why?"

"Do I really need to answer that?" His tone flared once again.

"Look, Hunter, let me try to explain my situation." She stood and began to pace. "I left my husband over two years ago. I bounced around for a while before settling in Connor. I've been here about six months. I have no reason to believe he knows where I am or how to find me. I left my previous life behind along with my possessions and anything that could identify me as Charlotte Ful—"

She stopped, shocked she had almost divulged her real name, then continued. "Do I still look over my shoulder from time to time? Yes. Do I try to keep a low profile? Yes. Do I allow my picture to be taken for contests or local newspapers? No. But I also don't need a bodyguard or a babysitter. I appreciate the fact that you're trying to excise your own demons by doing for me what you weren't able to do for your sister. But, it's not necessary. I can take care of myself."

"So, you just pretend Charlotte no longer exists, is that it?"

She leaned against the wall and stared at the popcorn ceiling of her bedroom. "Hunter, please don't—"

"Okay," he interrupted. "But if we're putting all our cards on the table, allow me to show you mine. My interest in you is not purely of the protective nature. Granted, I would move heaven and earth if I thought you were in trouble or someone set out to hurt you. But, don't be mistaken, Charlie, I'm still a red-blooded, American male who appreciates a woman with jeans that hug her in all the right places, has long hair I can run my fingers through, brown eyes that are warm and mysterious, and just enough pluck to call me on my crap."

"But—"

"But nothing," he cut her off again, "don't sell yourself short, Charlie. When I look at you, I don't see a victim or someone who needs coddling. I see a drop dead, gorgeous spitfire who pushes the limits of my self-control. And, if I wasn't the polite Southern boy my momma raised me to be, I would've pulled you into my arms when we were in your barn and kissed you long and hard . . . or been slapped trying."

She was completely dumbfounded. Few things rendered her speechless, but Hunter's declaration had done just that.

"Come on, Charlie, don't tell me the feisty woman I met last month doesn't have a smart-aleck retort to put me in my place? Surely, you have a litany of comebacks prepared for when men hit on you or complement your finer assets."

He was right. She never had a problem handling herself when a customer got too friendly. But this was different. This wasn't a stranger at the diner trying to put moves on her or one of the regulars flirting with her. This was Hunter Jennings. Tall, incredibly good-looking, I-can-get-any-woman-I-want-with-a-wink-and-a-smile, Hunter Jennings.

She was utterly and completely speechless.

"Charlie . . . are you still there? Charlie?"

"Yes. I'm still here."

"Wow, I guess I have more power than I gave myself

credit for. Cat got your tongue?"

Her mind was reeling. She knew she needed to say something, but she couldn't get her lips to move.

"Charlie?"

"I . . . I don't know what to say."

"Okay. How about I speak for both of us? I have a break coming up at the end of next month. I would like to spend it getting to know you better. No photographers, no manager, no backstage fiascoes, no missed phone calls or texts. Just you and me. What do you say?"

"No." She started pacing again.

"No? That's it? No explanation? You're not even going to think about it?"

She heard the disappointment in his voice quickly morphed to frustration.

"What is there to think about? It won't work. People would ask too many questions. My neighbors aren't used to seeing a man around my place. If they got too curious it could mess things up for me."

"So, we'll go to my place in Texas. My ranch is thirty thousand acres of complete privacy."

"I can't. I have to work."

"You wouldn't be able to take time off?"

"No. Artie counts on me. I can't just ditch out on him. He's been too good to me."

"So, you work seven days a week?"

"No, just Thursday through Sun—" It was out before she could stop herself.

"Perfect! Monday through Wednesday it is. It's not a lot of time, but we'll make good use of it."

"Hunter, I can't . . ." she cleared the knot lodged in her throat. "I can't stay with you."

"Charlie, I'm not asking you to sleep with me. I'm asking to spend time together, to give us a chance to get to know each other better before you hand me my walking papers or give me the rehearsed *this isn't going to work* speech."

Pinching her brow as she massaged her forehead, Charlie

felt a spectrum of emotions pulling her in opposite directions. Fear, excitement, panic, attraction, terror, curiosity. With her heart racing, temples throbbing, and a tingling sensation rushing through her body, she sat down on the edge of the bed to catch her breath.

"Please say you will, Charlie."

"Hunter, I—"

"I know you have trust issues. But I promise, at the end of three days, if you still feel there's nothing between us, I'll respect your decision and leave you alone. The phone is yours to keep for safety reasons, and to call me if you ever need someone to talk to. But I promise, I won't bother you anymore."

She felt like she was going to pass out. With her head in her lap, eyes closed, she pictured Hunter—all six foot plus of him—in faded jeans, weathered boots, and a black tee stretched taut across his broad shoulders. His face sporting his signature stubble, penetrating blue eyes, and lips she had imagined more than once brushing up against hers.

So far, she'd been careful to keep her feelings in check. Of course, that wasn't too hard since each of their encounters had ended in arguments. But when she thought about Hunter at night, when it was quiet and still and the loneliness of her life closed in around her, she imagined what it would be like to feel the touch of a man who didn't paralyze her with fear. A man with a gravelly voice that sounded smooth as silk.

What am I thinking? I can't get involved with Hunter.

There was no way she could have a relationship with someone in the public eye. It was too dangerous.

She knew when she left Daniel, she was choosing a life of solitude, and that was the price she was willing to pay. She couldn't very well get involved with a man and then tell him, "Oh, by the way, Charlie isn't my real name, and I'm on the run from a sadistic man who threatened to kill me if I ever left him. Oh yeah, and . . . we're still married." Those weren't exactly words to build a relationship on.

But Hunter already knows my situation, and it hasn't deterred him in the least.

She was confused.

Saying yes to Hunter was opening a door she wasn't sure she was ready to walk through.

"Charlie, are you still there?"

She sat up straighter, realizing she had zoned out for a moment.

"Charlie?"

"I'm here," she whispered.

"Don't push me away. Just give me a chance."

Her hand was shaking as she held the phone to her ear. "Okay. I'll come."

Chapter Twenty-Three

The day was finally here. Charlie picked up her duffel bag and carried it to the living room. Her heart was beating so fast she sat down on the arm of the couch and took a couple of deep breaths.

What am I doing? This is crazy!

She had changed her mind a hundred times since telling Hunter she would spend a couple days with him on his ranch. And the few times she admitted to having second thoughts, he cajoled her into keeping her promise. She reminded him more than once that she had *agreed* to go, not *promised* to go, but he wouldn't let up until she gave in.

They had talked every night for a month, either while he was on his bus traveling to the next city or after his performance. And with each conversation, an easiness developed between them. She still got butterflies and sweaty palms every time her phone rang, but it only took a few minutes for her nerves to subside, replaced by an amazing feeling of calm just listening to Hunter's voice.

She really felt like she had gotten to know a completely different person than the Hunter Jennings the world knew. They talked about his music, his ranch, and the struggles he had with his public image. He shared stories about his brother, Jake, his sister-in-law, Diana, and their two kids, Cody and Courtney. And when he talked about his mom, he did so with such admiration in his tone, it made her jealous for the family she never had.

Of course, her side of their conversations she kept

vague, without too many specifics. She talked about her current routine, working at the diner, caring for Goliath, but shied away from giving information about her past. Hunter already knew the basics, and she saw no reason to go into detail. At least not yet.

Walking down the hall, she grabbed her overnight bag from where it was propped on the corner of the bathroom vanity and slung it over her shoulder. Catching a glimpse of herself in the mirror, she backed up and scrutinized her less-than-exciting wardrobe. She really didn't have much choice in the matter. Never one to be swayed by fashion or shifting trends, everything she owned was simple or practical. Since her time was either spent with Goliath or at the diner, she had no need for fancy clothes, and certainly did not have the income to acquire them.

Fingering the ties dangling from the scoop neck of her peasant blouse, she smiled. At least it was more feminine than the thrift store tees she usually wore.

I'm going to his ranch, not a red-carpet event. I look fine.

And even though she'd had this same conversation with herself a dozen times, she did break down and buy a new dress. A black and white haltered maxi she found on clearance.

But she left the tags on . . . just in case.

With one more analytical glance, she leaned closer and looked at herself in the mirror. "I sure hope you know what you're doing." When she heard a horn honk outside, she jumped.

"No turning back now."

She hurried to the front door, looked through the peep hole, and saw the cab waiting at the curb. Sliding the deadbolts and slipping off the security chain, she opened the door and signaled to the cabbie that she would be right there.

Taking a taxi had been a compromise. Even though Hunter had wanted to pick her up, she insisted that would raise too many questions with Karen, and he took the chance of being recognized. And though she was perfectly fine driving herself to the airstrip, Hunter had no faith in her truck and didn't want to think of her stranded for a second time on account of him. So, when he suggested a cab, she conceded.

With another honk from the cabbie, Charlie scooped up her duffel bag, closed the door behind her, and keyed the deadbolts into place. As she walked down the driveway, she pushed her shoulders back, raised her chin slightly, and whispered to herself, "Here goes nothin'."

The drive to the airstrip was quiet and uneventful. The cabbie attempted to make small talk, but her short one-word answers eventually deterred him. Twenty minutes later, they pulled onto the tarmac alongside a metal hangar. The cabbie hurried around to her door and helped with her bags.

"Have a good flight," he said as he tipped his hat, slid behind the wheel, and started to pull away.

"Wait a minute." She flagged him down as he was backing up. Coming to a stop, he rolled down the passenger window. She leaned in and asked, "What do I owe you?"

"Nothing. I was paid in advance, along with a mighty hefty tip. In fact," he reached for the dash and handed her a business card, "here's my number. If you ever need another ride, day or night, just give me a call."

She took the offered card, smiled, and watched as he drove away.

Turning to the tarmac, she focused on the small jet sitting parallel to the hangar, its engines already running. With her duffel over one shoulder, and her overnight bag and purse over the other, she walked the twenty yards or so to the foot of the jet's stairs.

"Hello," she yelled, looking up into the open hatch.

A middle-age guy in jeans and a brown plaid Pendleton stuck his head out the doorway. "Charlie?"

"Yes," she answered hesitantly.

"Good. I'm in the right place. Come on up."

She climbed the stairs, holding tightly to the handrail. When she got to the top, the man with the scruffy smile waved her in, then reached for her bags. "Welcome aboard. I'm Chet."

Thinking she was crazy for getting on a plane with a complete stranger, she eyed the man carefully. Mid-forties. Auburn hair and a thick mustache. He was tall like Hunter but lankier. And definitely more weathered. He looked like a mountain man. *Or an ax murderer.* Even so, she entered the cabin and watched as the stairs were drawn up behind her.

"Good morning."

Shocked, she turned around to see Hunter standing in the aisleway.

"What are you doing here?"

He walked toward her looking even better than she remembered. Gone was his custom black Stetson, replaced with a Texas A&M ball cap. And the simple white T-shirt he wore accentuated his sturdy shoulders and rock-solid chest.

Her heart flipped and fluttered.

With a gentle hand at her waist, he leaned forward and placed a peck of a kiss on her cheek. The warmth of his intimate touch took her breath away and sent heat radiating to all her limbs.

I don't know if I'm ready for this.

Though their conversations of late had felt a little more intimate, physical touch was going to take some getting used to. Not that she had not already allowed herself a daydream or two about what it would be like to be kissed by Hunter . . . or held by him. Even so, now that the time was here, she felt anxious, even panicky.

"I couldn't stay away."

"What?" She looked at him, not sure what she had missed.

"You asked me what I was doing here."

"Right. Right. Sorry. I guess I'm just a little nervous." She tried to smile but was sure it looked more like a grimace.

He reached for her hand. "There's no reason to be nervous."

"Are you telling me you're not even the least bit nervous?"

"Nervous, no. Excited, yes. I thought this day would never

come. That's why I'm here. Knowing you'd be in the air for two hours, I didn't want to waste any time when I could be spending it with you. So, I came along and kept Chet company. Here," he motioned to a beautifully upholstered chair, "have a seat."

Four swivel chairs of fawn-colored leather, and a high-gloss cherry wood table defined a meeting area. She imagined this was where Hunter and his manager hashed out record deals and strategically planned the next move in his mega career. Further back in the cabin was a cozy sitting area, complete with a couch in the same leather as the chairs, a richly carved coffee table, and a cabinet with a flat screen TV and wet bar accoutrements.

Hunter took the seat opposite her as she continued to look around.

"Did you get things worked out for Goliath?" he asked.

"Yeah. Karen was more than willing to take care of him, especially since she has done it before. She was a lifesaver when I had the flu earlier this year, and again when it hit me a month later. She's good with him."

"What did you tell her?"

"That I had some business to take care of out of town and would be gone a few days."

"I'm ready when you are," Chet said from behind Charlie's chair.

"We're more than ready." Hunter looked at her and winked, causing her skin to heat up all over again.

Reaching around for her seatbelt, she clicked it in place. Knowing her face was flushed, she glanced around the cabin, too nervous to look at Hunter. "This is a beautiful plane," she said, trying to get the attention off her.

"Thanks. I think it's a bit much, but Rob said I needed a tax write-off. I've only had it a year, but I have to admit, it does make traveling easier and a whole lot more comfortable."

"I thought you traveled by bus."

"Oh, I do, from show to show. But whenever I get a

couple days off, I hightail it back to the ranch. I get my hands dirty and sweat my way through some chores. It keeps me grounded."

When the plane lurched forward, Charlie grabbed the edge of the table. Hunter gently laid his hand on top of hers. "You're not afraid of flying, are you?"

"No. I'm afraid of crashing." She laughed nervously.

Hunter chuckled. "Don't worry, Charlie. I'm not going to let anything happen to you." He gave her hand a squeeze.

She looked into his eyes and knew he was promising her so much more than a safe flight.

When the plane began to taxi down the tarmac, Charlie clenched her fist even tighter. "Here, switch seats with me." Hunter unbuckled his seatbelt and stood. She looked at him dumbfounded. "Undo your belt, Charlie. We need to switch seats. You should be sitting facing forward if you don't like flying."

She fiddled with her belt and stood, trying to keep her balance. They quickly moved around the table, but Hunter never let go of her hand. They both sat down again, their joined hands resting on the table, the seat belts forgotten. Hunter brushed his thumb across her knuckles as the jet picked up speed and finally took on that weightless sensation, the kind that made her stomach swirl. But that was nothing compared to what Hunter's hand on top of hers was doing to her heart.

As soon as the plane leveled off, she slipped her hand from his and let it drop into her lap.

"I'm sorry. I didn't mean to make you feel uncomfortable."

"You didn't." She smiled, trying to hide her nervousness. First his kiss, then the way he stroked her hand. They were simple gestures, but she couldn't help wondering if she had made a mistake. It was easier on the phone with thousands of miles between them, but being with him, she was afraid things might escalate faster than she was ready for.

Stop. Give Hunter some credit.

She knew he wouldn't pressure her. She was sure of it.

Having learned so much about him over the last month, she knew he wasn't the kind of guy to take advantage of her, regardless of his party boy, lady's man reputation. He was a person of character, of morals, regardless of how the media portrayed him. She knew it from the songs he wrote and the conversations they had shared.

But I'm still married for heaven's sake.

Even if it was just a legal term—because she certainly didn't consider herself married—she shouldn't be getting involved with anyone, especially someone the Paparazzi enjoyed stalking. If Daniel somehow found her, he would not only kill her as he had threatened so many times before, but he would go after Hunter as well.

Oh my gosh. What am I doing? I can't allow that to happen.

"Hunter." She looked up at him. "I can't do this." Standing, she carefully headed toward the front of the plane. Knocking on the cockpit door, she waited for the pilot to answer. The door swung open just as Hunter gently squeezed her upper arm.

"Charlie, what are you doing?"

She didn't answer him but spoke to the pilot instead. "Excuse me, I'm sorry, but I need you to take me back. I need to go home."

He looked at her, then at Hunter.

"Give us a minute." Hunter gently took Charlie by the arm and led her to the couch in the back of the plane. He sat on the coffee table across from her, elbows on his knees, hands clenched. "Charlie, what's wrong?"

"I can't do this."

"Do what?"

"Involve you in my life."

"It's too late for that. I'm already involved."

"No you're not. Not really. I mean we've shared conversations, that's all."

Charlie was sure her accelerating heart was going to explode inside her chest. She was seeing points of light, and her fingers were going numb. She felt claustrophobic and was sure they were free-falling.

"I need to go home. You need to tell the pilot to turn around." She tried to stand but teetered before falling back against the couch.

"Charlie . . ."

"No, Hunter . . . I can't do this."

She tried to stand again but fell forward right into him. He braced her, then stood up. "Charlie, stop."

She was panting, gasping for air. Something was wrong. Terribly wrong. They were crashing, or the cabin was losing pressure, something. "Where are those little oxygen masks?" She looked up at the ceiling, arms flailing. "Why aren't they falling from the ceiling?"

Hunter gently grabbed her arms and pulled them down to her sides. "Charlie, you need to stop. Nothing is wrong. Everything is okay."

"But I can't breathe. Something is wrong. I can't breathe."

He wrapped his arms around her and pulled her to his chest. She held on for dear life as everything faded to black.

Chapter Twenty-Four

Charlie took a few deep breaths before opening her eyes. When she focused on Hunter, she cringed. Looking around, she realized she was lying on the couch at the back of the plane. *What a fool I made of myself.*

Again.

Hunter stared back at her from where he was perched on the edge of the coffee table, holding a cool washcloth against her forehead.

"Please tell me I passed out, and everything else I remember is just a horrible, horrible nightmare."

His eyes held no anger or frustration. Nothing but concern. "I think you had a panic attack."

"Is that what you call it when a grown woman goes completely psychotic?" When she tried to sit up, he pressed his hands to her shoulders.

"Just relax. We're almost there."

"Tennessee?"

"No. Texas."

"Why?" She covered her face with her hands. "Why are you doing this to yourself?" She wanted to be angry with him for not seeing how futile this thing was between them.

"Oh, I don't know," he said while pulling her hands away from her face and pinning her with a devilish grin, "I guess I'm just a sucker for a hot, sexy mess."

She couldn't hold back the smile that pulled at her lips. "You're crazy, you know that?" She swatted his arm.

"Crazy like a fox."

The landing was rocky, unsettling Charlie even more than she already was. Thankfully, she was back in her seat, the belt across her lap, offering her the tiniest illusion of safety.

"Sorry about that," Hunter said. "It's the drawback of having a dirt runway. I keep saying I'm going to pave it, but somehow I never get around to it."

She tried to smile, tried to relax, but it was useless as they bounced and rumbled.

"I take it you don't like flying?" he asked, with a slight chuckle.

"What gave it away? The panic on my face or the death grip I have on your hand?"

"The lack of feeling in my fingers is a pretty good clue."

Immediately she let go of his hand and ran her sweaty palms up and down her thighs. "Sorry."

"I wasn't complaining," he said, his voice low and oh-so-sexy.

Nervously, she turned to the small window on her right and studied the scenery. Then it clicked. "Wait a minute. Are you telling me you have your own landing strip?"

"Yep. Like I said, it's only dirt and a bit bumpy, but it sure beats having to fight a mob scene at the airport."

She watched as a large metal hangar came into view. The plane pulled alongside it before rolling to a complete stop.

"Well, here we are." Hunter stepped into the aisle and extended his hand. "You ready?"

Scooting from her seat, she took his hand and stood directly in front of him. "What if I said no?"

He took a step closer, leaving no room between them. "You'd be out of luck. Because like it or not, you're mine for the next few days. So, you can either enjoy everything Texas and I have to offer . . . or start walking."

Straightening her shoulders, she raised a resolute brow in challenge. "Oh yeah? If I said I wanted to leave, you wouldn't fly me back to Tennessee?"

"Of course I would." He walked toward the hatch where Chet had already lowered the stairs, then turned to her with a devilish grin. "First thing Thursday morning."

He disappeared down the steps leaving her with nothing but her racing heart and sweaty palms. She brought her hand to her cheek wondering if her complexion showed the heat she was feeling.

What have I gotten myself into?

Before she could take a step forward, Hunter stuck his head back through the doorway. "Well . . . are you coming or not?"

His smile was intoxicating, compelling her to move forward. "Ready or not," she whispered under her breath, "that is the question."

When she stepped from the plane, a warm breeze wreaked havoc with her long hair. Gathering it to one side, she carefully descended the metal steps. She looked around at the expanse surrounding them. For as far as she could see, there was nothing but beautiful sagebrush, massive oak trees, and amazing boulder formations. She did a complete three-sixty but saw no other buildings besides the hangar.

"So, what do you think of Colinas Pacíficas?"

"What?" She turned to him, while she pulled an errant strand of hair from her lips.

"Colinas Pacíficas. It means Peaceful Hills."

She looked around again. "It's breathtaking."

"Come on, let me show you around." Hunter grabbed her duffel bag from where Chet had set it at the bottom of the steps and led her toward a weird dune-buggy-looking vehicle parked just inside the hangar.

"What do you call this thing?"

"Technically, it's a Polaris RZR, but most people just call it a side-by-side, or a utility vehicle, or simply a UTV. It really has more power than I need to get around the ranch, but it's so fun to drive, I couldn't pass it up. And since it has four seats, Jake takes Diana and the kids out for a ride from time to time."

As Hunter backed out of the hangar, she took one more sweeping look. "This place is incredible."

"Are you kidding me?" He looked at her with a smile as he threw the vehicle into gear. "You ain't seen nothin' yet."

Chapter Twenty-Five

Charlie was in complete awe of Hunter's expansive property. They had been driving around for about an hour as he pointed out ancient caves, Indian carvings, and astonishing bluffs. Though they had not even scratched the surface of the thirty-thousand-plus acres, he promised they would go out again tomorrow and see more.

As they headed home, she rubbernecked from side to side while Hunter seemed content just to drive. When a flash of light in the distance caught her attention, she realized the reflection must have come from a windowpane on the house up ahead. The closer they got, the more details she could see. A red tile roof covered the modest home sitting atop a small bluff, while the foundation looked like it was hewn from the very rock it sat upon. With floor to ceiling windows, the view from his home had to be spectacular. However, even though she could see the house was quite beautiful, she was surprised it was so . . . small. Somehow, she had pictured Hunter living in something a little grander, but it was incredible, just the same.

"Your house is beautiful," she said as they got closer.

"Oh, that's not my house. It's my mom's."

Just then, as they veered around a small bluff, Charlie saw another structure of monumental proportions take shape on the other side of a stunning pool and backyard oasis.

"That's my house."

Charlie felt her jaw drop.

It was absolutely breathtaking.

She continued to be awed as they drove behind the house and around to the front. Two massive wood doors welcomed her as Hunter pulled up the circular drive. The house looked old, unique, and definitely masculine. Words could not describe how exquisite every detail looked, from the old-world light fixtures bookending the front walk, to the small Juliet balcony overlooking the circular driveway, complete with water feature.

She was speechless.

"Well, what do you think?" Hunter asked, as he killed the engine.

"It's . . . it's incredible. Absolutely amazing!"

"Well, I wish I could take credit for it, but I can't. I bought the place as is. I mean, the inside is all me, but I can't take credit for the architecture or the building materials. All I know is when the real estate agent showed it to me, I was sold before we even walked inside."

Circling the vehicle, he grabbed her bags from the back, slung them over his shoulder, then, with an extended hand, helped her out. As they crossed the driveway to the double door entrance, Charlie did not miss the fact that her hand was still in his . . . or that it felt so good.

Hunter gave one of the massive wrought iron handles a push, the weathered door creaking as it swung wide. Stepping into the front entry, Charlie's eyes wandered from one unique feature to another. Rugged slate tiles paved the entryway, and an iron-forged chandelier hung in the rotunda above them. The staircase to the right of the entrance was anchored by an intricate iron balustrade, and the stone archways lining the hallway looked like the passageway of an ancient abbey. She could not help but sigh in utter amazement.

Hunter dropped her bags onto the tile floor, then slipped his arm around her waist. "Are you okay? Come on, you need to sit down."

"No. I'm fine." She let go of the banister. "That wasn't a queasy sigh, it was an oh my gosh sigh."

"Are you kidding? We just got started."

She looked at him, surprised by his uncharacteristic arrogance.

"Hey," he tossed his hands in the air with a laugh, "I can brag all I want, because I had nothing to do with it. I was just smart enough to snap it up when it came on the market."

He walked her down the arched stone hallway, keeping her close to his side. She felt small next to his large frame, but incredibly safe. She savored the moment. It had been a long time since she felt so . . . protected.

He led them into a massive living room and smiled. "Welcome to my home."

A stone hearth of jagged rock was the centerpiece of the two-storied room. A prized elk was mounted above it, with five more impressive trophy heads displayed over each archway. Leather furniture in masculine proportions filled the room while a chandelier crafted from antlers descended from the twenty-foot high ceiling. She walked across the wide wood plank floors to where a large, glass-top coffee table sat in front of the four-cushioned leather couch. Encased in the table was a beautiful antique book. She brushed her fingers across the wood-framed surface.

"Our family Bible," Hunter explained.

She turned to him. "Really?"

"Um-hum. It has been in our family for over two hundred years."

Kneeling beside it, she stared at the yellow-tinged pages, the old English writing, and the cracked leather corners. "It's incredible." It spoke of history and heritage, something she knew nothing about. Something she had always longed for. She felt a knot form in her throat and was surprised to feel tears welling in her eyes. She stood, looking away from Hunter, not wanting him to see her emotions. She quickly swiped the errant tear from her cheek and meandered across the arched hallway to the most incredible chef's kitchen.

She couldn't help herself, she laughed out loud.

"What's so funny?" Hunter asked.

She walked the length of the kitchen, her fingers gliding across the expansive granite countertops. "You're not going to tell me you actually cook in this kitchen?" She turned to him from across the room and smiled.

"Of course I do."

"Oh, come on," she chuckled. "You don't have a staff that cooks for you?"

He planted his hands on his waist. "I do not," he said indignantly, then turned to the massive refrigerator camouflaged behind a rich paneled door. He mumbled then asked, "Would you like something to drink?"

"What was that?" she asked.

"I asked if you would like something to drink?"

"No, before that."

He turned to her, a bottled water in his hand. "How 'bout some water?" He extended it to her.

"Hunter, you're avoiding the question." She laughed as she accepted the bottle.

"What question?"

"You heard me."

He didn't make eye contact, but she could see the rosy color filling his complexion. She laughed again. "Aaron Hunter Jennings . . . do you, or do you not have a staff that cooks for you?"

He pressed the bottle to his lips and took a nice, long swig, clearly stalling. When he finally made eye contact, he looked like a little boy caught in a lie. "I don't have a staff." He slid his forearm across his lips to dry them. "My mom does most of the cooking . . . but only because she wants to, and because the guys eat with me when I'm home, just so I don't lose touch."

She grinned.

"What?" he asked, defensiveness in his tone.

"Nothing," she said, with a smile as she walked through another archway into the dining room, Hunter following behind her. Silently, she counted the chairs around the massive table. One, two, three . . . fourteen. Sipping her water, she walked the length of the dining room. "Where is everyone today?"

"I told them to make themselves scarce."

"Because of me?" She felt the sting of humiliation. Was he embarrassed to have her here? Did Hunter know she wouldn't measure up in the eyes of his family? Stepping to the floor-to-ceiling windows, she pretended to study the intricate pattern on the brocade drapes.

"I asked them to give us some space because I didn't want you to feel like you were on display."

"Whatever." She stared out the window as he moved closer.

"Charlie, look at me."

She took a silent breath before turning around. She glanced up, but quickly looked away.

"Charlie," he placed his index finger under her chin, lifting it until she had no choice but to look him in the eyes, "don't read in something that isn't there."

She just shrugged.

"I mean it, Charlie." He ran the back of his fingers down the side of her cheek. "I can't wait to introduce you to my family. I just didn't want to rush you."

She forced a smile, trying to shake off feelings of doubt. "That's fine."

"Good." He slid his hands up and down her arms, sending jolts of electricity through her body. "How about we continue the tour?"

"Sure." She followed him out of the dining room, wondering for a second time if she had made a colossal mistake by coming.

Chapter Twenty-Six

Shaking off her negative feelings, Charlie followed Hunter to the next room on the tour.

"This is my media room."

Stepping inside, he pressed a button on a programmable light switch. Immediately, wall sconces washed the room in an ambient glow.

Charlie took a few steps forward, feeling the slope of the floor. A loveseat and two rows of leather recliners sat in the center of the room, opposite a wall-size movie screen framed by crushed velvet drapes. Everything was red, just like an old-time movie theater. There was even an antique candy counter and nostalgic popcorn cart.

"This is so cool."

"It is, isn't it. Unfortunately, I don't use it as much as I thought I would."

"Why not?"

"I'm on the road too much. And when I'm home, I spend most of the day outdoors working with the guys. By the time I come in, shower, and eat, I'm too tired. But I promise we will definitely use it while you're here."

She smiled. "I'd like that. I can't remember the last time I went to a movie."

When he pulled her close, she flinched slightly, but it didn't discourage him. He slipped his hands around her waist and leaned in closer still. "I was hoping it could kind of be like our first date."

She took a step back, breaking the connection between

them. "Date?"

"Yeah, you know . . . two people . . . dinner, a movie . . . awkward conversation . . . maybe a good-night kiss, if I'm lucky."

She blushed like a schoolgirl and hated herself for it. She quickly turned and walked up the ramped aisle, but not quick enough. Hunter's low chuckle confirmed he had seen the redness in her cheeks. She fought the urge to turn around and give him an etiquette lesson on laughing at your house guest but chose to ignore him instead.

"So, what's this room?" she asked as she continued down the hallway.

"This will be your room." He stepped next to her and opened the double doors. Again, she was blown away by every detail as she walked inside. Cove ceilings, crown moldings, French doors to a private patio, a fireplace at the foot of the king-size, sled-style bed.

"And your bathroom is through here." He opened a frosted glass door to reveal a rather large bathroom. It was easily bigger than her bedroom at home and was decked out with the latest innovations. Jacuzzi tub, walk-in shower with multiple body sprays, a cedar-lined sauna in one corner and a small dressing area that led to a walk-in closet in the other.

"I don't know what to say." She peeked into the massive closet complete with drawers, cubbies, soft lighting, and a beautifully upholstered settee.

"I'll go get your things."

When Hunter disappeared down the hallway, she opened the French doors leading to the small enclosed patio. *Wow!* It was the perfect little sanctuary. Bistro table. Water feature. Every detail was flawless. She walked back into the bedroom as Hunter placed her bags on an antique trunk at the foot of the bed.

"So, you said earlier that the inside was all you. Does that mean you chose the room colors, the furnishings, and all the little details?"

He raked his fingers through his hair, a tell Charlie was beginning to realize usually preceded either frustration or an explanation. "Yes and no."

She cocked her head to one side, waiting for him to clarify.

"My mom and Diana helped a little."

"Ah, so what you're saying is they did it for you," she said as she walked back into the living room.

"No." He followed her. "They helped."

"Meaning?"

"Meaning, I was fine keeping the house the color it was, but Diana convinced me it needed some fresh paint. But there was no way I was going to go through hundreds of paint swatches or volumes of furniture catalogs. So, I gave Diana parameters."

"Parameters?"

"Yeah." He counted off on his fingers. "No pastels. No florals. Nothing frilly. I wanted to be comfortable in my own house. I didn't want to come home from touring to lace doilies and flower accents. And I definitely wanted furniture the guys and I could plop down on without ruining it. So, Diana narrowed the field by giving me a choice of three color schemes and a couple of different furniture styles. I chose what I liked; she did the rest. My mom added a few touches here and there—like the family pictures in the entry stairwell and the family Bible. I had the coffee table made for it and added my trophies." He glanced around the expansive room. "I'm satisfied with the end product."

"It's beautiful."

He looked at her with a frown. "Beautiful?"

"In a masculine, beefy kind of way," she clarified.

"That's better." He smiled. "So, let me show you upstairs."

"Sure."

They climbed a second stairway against the far wall. It led to an open balcony overlooking the living space below. The first room they looked at had a similar footprint to the room she would be staying in downstairs, complete with en suite and balcony. The next two guest rooms were smaller in size but still larger than her own bedroom at home.

It was funny. When she was with Daniel, she saw huge mansions, the best Miami had to offer. But she didn't think of them as homes. They felt more like museums, show places. Even her own house felt more like a gallery for Daniel's art or a high-end meeting place he used to impress his business associates. It was cold and lifeless. A home was supposed to be a place to celebrate holidays or gather as a family. Hers was a sterile exhibit hall that had to look perfect at all times.

"And this is where I spend a lot of my time when I'm home."

She snapped from her thoughts as Hunter led her to the far end of the hall.

"I guess you could call it my man cave, even though it's not in a basement."

A massive open loft was anchored on one side by a large overstuffed sectional, while the other wall was nothing but built-ins, filled with electronic gadgets and a huge flat-screen TV. There was even a wet bar.

"Wow . . . it feels so homey."

"And I have everything I need. The wet bar has a mini fridge and microwave. Through there," he pointed to a closed door, "is my office. That, over there," he pointed again, "is my home gym, and this," he walked toward a set of double doors, "is my bedroom. Everything I need is right here." He looked at her with his piercing blue eyes. "Well, almost everything."

Immediately she felt awkward and out of place. This was Hunter's private space, and somehow, she felt like she had crossed a line by being there. Taking a couple of steps back, she turned toward the balcony overlooking the living room. The panoramic view allowed her a glimpse of the pool and his mother's house on the other side.

"So, your mom lives over there?" she asked as she started back toward the stairwell.

"Yes," Hunter followed behind. "And Jake, Diana, and

the kids live a quarter mile down the road, closer to the stables."

"It must be great having your family right here whenever you get the chance to be home."

"It is. Jake toured with me in the beginning but stopped when he started putting down roots."

"That must have been fun, sharing your success with your brother."

"It had its moments. Jake and I have always had a love-hate relationship. We had some great times on the road, but other times we fought like cats and dogs. He took being head of the family a little too serious, and once I was an adult, I got tired of him telling me what to do. He toured with me until he and Diana got married. Now he takes care of the property."

When they reached the bottom of the steps, Hunter slid back one of the large panes of glass separating the living room from the outdoor space. They stepped outside onto the patio, a warm breeze brushing against her face. Seeing a large dining table and outdoor kitchen, she asked, "Do you eat out here much?"

"Yeah, when it's not too humid."

She walked the cobblestone path through the lush green lawn to the pool's edge. The water looked so refreshing, she wished she didn't have her boots on. She would've loved to dip her toes in it.

"Wanna go for a swim? The weather is just right."

"Sorry," she said as she continued to walk the edge, "I didn't bring a swimsuit." The truth was she didn't own a swimsuit. And even if she did, she certainly wouldn't prance around in it on a *first date*.

"Your house is beautiful." She turned to face him, shielding her eyes from the sun. "You should be very proud."

He smiled as he hooked his thumbs through his belt loops. "I don't take it for granted, that's for sure. I feel blessed to have what I do and to be able to provide for my family. But, if I had someone to share it with, I would retire tomorrow."

"No you wouldn't," she challenged.

"You're right," he looked at her, his expression stoic. "I have a contract for three more projects. But after I fulfill my end of the deal, I'm not signing my time away for nothing or nobody."

"But what about your fans?"

"Are you kidding?" he laughed as he pulled the ball cap from his head and wiped the sweat from his brow. "They'll follow the next big act that comes along."

"I think you're selling yourself a little short."

"No I'm not. I just don't believe my own hype."

"Then what do you believe?" She hadn't meant to be so blunt, it just kind of came out.

Hunter crouched down, plucked a blade of grass from the lawn, and split it between his fingers, then looked up at her, closing one eye against the sun. "You might find this hard to believe because of my reputation, but I believe in God . . . family . . . fighting for our freedom . . . the importance of supporting farmers, factory workers, the American auto industry, and not letting our jobs get outsourced to other countries."

She walked over to where he was crouched, her shadow falling over him. "I don't find that hard to believe at all. It's what you write about in your songs. Unfortunately, those aren't the songs you're known for."

"I thought you told me you didn't follow my career?" He grinned.

She smiled, slipping her hands into her back pockets. "I might've picked up a CD or two recently."

He stood, taking a step closer. "So, you're a fan?"

Charlie watched as his eyes focused in on her lips. "I wouldn't mind being friends with the real Hunter Jennings, but I'm not sure I like Hunter Jennings the celebrity."

Chapter Twenty-Seven

Her words were a subtle blow. Hunter took a step back and tossed the shredded blade of grass into the wind.

"I'm sorry," she said almost immediately. "I had no right to say that."

"Sure you did. It's the way you feel, right?"

"But I have no business judging the way someone lives. Me of all people. Every day I live is a lie."

"But what if there was another way to—"

"No." She cut him off. "There is no other way."

"But let me talk to some people. I could—"

She looked at him, her eyes turning cold and angry. "So . . . is that what this trip is all about?"

"What?"

"This was your plan from the beginning, wasn't it? To get me alone, so you could tell me how you're going to use your influence and wealth to free me from my life of seclusion. Or maybe you thought if you showed me this fortress of yours, I would come live with you and hide out here the rest of my life. We've talked about this, Hunter. I'm married and there's nothing you or I can do about it."

She marched into the house before he could respond. Turning around—anger igniting every fiber inside him—he pulled off his hat, flung it, and watched as it landed in the middle of the pool. He bit back the curse that so easily came to mind, growling instead.

What the heck just happened?

He walked to the far side of the pool, his hands laced on top of his head, trying to control his anger.

One minute she's telling me she listened to my songs and likes what she heard, the next, she's accusing me of an intervention?

Well, he wasn't going to let her get away with it. He walked back inside, and without even knocking, barged into the guest room. "You think you have me all figured out, don't you?"

She jumped and spun around. "I guess you don't feel like you have to knock in your own house?"

"No, as a matter of fact, I don't." He slammed the door behind him. "And just so you know, you have me all wrong. I didn't bring you here to have some sort of intervention. My intentions were a lot more selfish. I brought you here because I wanted to win you over. I've wanted to kiss you since that day in your barn when I convinced you to come to my show. And I've thought of nothing else since. So you see, I'm more man than saint."

"Well here, let me put you out of your misery."

In two strides she was in front of him, and before he knew her intentions, she reached her hand behind his neck and pulled his mouth down to hers. She kissed him. Not a peck, or a glancing blow, but full-on kissed him.

When she released her hold on his neck, she took a step back. "There! You got your kiss. Now you can take me home." She grabbed her bags from the foot of the bed and quickly stepped around him.

With his head still spinning from her kiss, it took a few beats before he could jump into action. "Wait! Charlie, don't go!"

"Yoo-hoo."

Great! Hearing his mother's high-pitched greeting, he cringed. *Not now.*

"You must be Charlie."

Hunter hurried into the hallway and watched as his mother pulled Charlie into a hug.

"I'm so glad to finally meet you, dear. You're all Hunter

has spoken about for weeks."

Charlie turned to him, a look of indecision on her face. He decided to work this awkward moment to his advantage.

"Hey, Mom," he leaned down and gave her a kiss on the cheek. "Let me introduce you. Charlie," he looked at her, challenging her to make a scene, "this is my mom, Irene. Mom, this is Charlie."

When it was obvious his mother was going to lean in for another hug, Charlie set her bags down and conceded.

"It's so nice to have you here. Have you met Diana and the kids yet?"

"Aah . . . no . . . but I don't think I'll be—"

"Mom," Hunter interrupted, "Charlie just got here. Let's give her a chance to get settled. We can do the family thing at dinner."

"But I thought we were all going to have lunch together?"

"No . . . Diana offered to have us over for lunch. I said we would play it by ear."

"But I thought I saw you drive in a while ago?"

"I did, I mean *we* did. I've just been showing Charlie around. Why don't you go ahead and have lunch with Diana and the kids. We'll have dinner here at six o'clock, like we planned. I can introduce everyone then."

"Okay. That sounds lovely. It's so nice to meet you, Charlie. I guess we'll have to wait until dinner to get better acquainted."

Hunter leaned down so his mother could give him another peck on the cheek, then watched as she walked out through the patio door.

Charlie grabbed her bags, tossed one over her shoulder and walked toward the front door, her boots clicking on the slate floor.

"Where are you going?" he yelled after her.

"Home."

"But what about my mother? She's expecting to see you at dinner."

With her hand on the front door handle, she turned to him.

"That's your problem, not mine." Heaving open the large wooden door, Charlie walked away, leaving him standing there.

"Where does she think she's going?" he said out loud even though there was no one there to hear him.

When he heard the roar of the Polaris' engine, he had his answer.

By the time he hurried outside, all he could see was the tail end of the RZR through a cloud of dust.

Chapter Twenty-Eight

Don't go left. Don't go left.

That's all Hunter could think about as he bolted toward the garage.

By the time he got to the multi-car structure he shared with Jake, and saw his quad wasn't there, he had no choice but to take his dirt bike. He tried several times to kick start it before remembering he had drained the gas the last time he used it. After he found the gas can under all the crud Jake had stacked in the bay, he filled the tank, rummaged around for his helmet, and took off after Charlie.

"Don't go left. Please, God, don't let her go left," he yelled inside his helmet.

He had to catch her before she came to the fork in the road. It wouldn't be such a big deal if she was in her right mind and out for a casual drive. But the way she took off like a bat-out-of-hell, she would never see the sharp turn that hugged the side of the bluff. Thinking about the possibility of what could happen made him go even faster, doing everything he could to keep his bike from flying out from under him.

———◆●◆———

Charlie had no idea where she was going. She just figured if she stayed on the rutted road, it would eventually lead her back to the airstrip, and once there, she would convince that Chet guy to take her home. That idea lasted only a few minutes when she came to a stop, a fork in the road ahead of her.

Looking at the position of the sun, she remembered it being on the backside of the hangar.

Do I go left?

Glancing at the rearview mirror, she saw a motorcycle kicking up dust behind her. She knew it was Hunter, and that she should just stop. *It's not like his friend is going to listen to me, anyway.* But it made her so mad that he thought he knew better than she did.

Daniel was not a man to be reasoned with. He was malicious and vindictive. It wasn't like Hunter could sit down with him, have a polite conversation, and negotiate her release. No one told Daniel what to do. And Hunter's money would mean nothing to him.

But that kiss.

Charlie brushed her fingers across her lips. It felt so good, so right. And if she was honest with herself—deep down in her soul—she'd like nothing more than to hide away with Hunter and never have to think about Daniel, or being found, or wondering what she was going to do when her money ran out.

The enormity of her situation weakened her resolve and stole what fight she had left. She took her foot off the gas, immediately feeling the energy drain from the vehicle. When she looked in the rear-view mirror, she saw Hunter quickly approaching, then watched in horror as the bike shot out from under him and sent him somersaulting to a stop.

Screaming, she turned off the ignition, jumped from the vehicle, and ran back the twenty or so yards to where Hunter laid motionless.

"Hunter! Hunter!" She collapsed alongside his body, face down in the dirt. She pressed her cheek to the ground in front of him. "Hunter, can you hear me?"

"Yeah."

She sat up, shocked.

He rolled over and pushed back the visor from his

helmet. "I'm okay."

"Are you sure? Should I go for help?" She pressed her hands to his chest, to his abdomen. "What if you broke something?"

He tugged at the chin strap on his helmet, pulled it off, and let it roll to the side. Charlie sat back on her heels, tears running down her cheeks, staring at his eyes for signs of . . . of what she wasn't sure.

"Charlie," he reached for her hand and clutched it, "I'm okay. I laid the bike down on purpose."

"You what?" she snapped.

"It was the only way I could think of to get you to—"

She jumped to her feet. "You did it on purpose? Are you crazy?" Angry beyond words, she hauled off and kicked him with the toe of her boot.

"Ouch!" He flinched. "Why did you do that?"

"Because you're an idiot." She kicked him again.

"Knock it off!" he yelled. "You're hurting me."

"Good! You deserve to be in pain after a stunt like that."

"I *am* in pain, dang it!" He clutched his side. "Now knock it off!"

"What?" Her heart stopped as she crumpled beside him. "But you said you were okay?"

"I am, considering I just fell off a motorcycle. But those boots of yours are going to put me in the hospital."

"I'm sorry." She watched as he grimaced in pain. "I didn't mean—"

"It's all right." He held his hand up to silence her. "I'm all right. Just give me a second to take inventory."

She sat with her hands twisted together in her lap and watched as Hunter closed his eyes and took a couple of deep breaths. Rolling over, he gradually got onto his hands and knees, then paused for a moment before standing.

Getting up, she tried looking into his eyes. "Are you sure you're okay?"

He half smiled, half grimaced as he brushed the dirt from his arms and chest. "I'm fine, but those boots of yours are lethal."

Unable to control her emotions, she burst into tears, covering her face with her hands.

———————— ● ————————

Hunter felt horrible but justified.

If Charlie had gone another hundred yards, he'd be dealing with a major tragedy not just a few scrapes and bruises. Wrapping an arm around her shoulders, he pulled her close, cradling her head against his chest. "I'm fine, Charlie, I'm fine." Wrapping his other arm around her, he stroked her back, trying to console her. She molded perfectly to his body, his arms all but swallowing up her petite frame.

When her shoulders stopped shuddering, he dipped his head close to hers and whispered, "Are *you* going to be okay?"

"Me?" She looked up at him. "What about you?"

"I've been worse." With his thumb, he swiped at the wet dirt streaks on her cheeks. "Come on, let's take a little walk."

"What?"

"I need to show you something."

With his arm still around her shoulders, and a small catch in his step, they started walking.

"You're limping."

"Yeah, because someone kept kicking me."

She stopped.

"Come on," he chuckled, "I'm fine."

Hunter could tell he was going to be sore. Not only did he hurt where Charlie had kicked him with the point of her boot, but his right hip and shoulder took the brunt of the fall and were definitely letting him know there would be a price to pay.

They walked a little further, then stopped. "This is what I wanted to show you." Three more steps and the road took a dramatic turn to the left. Ahead of them . . . nothing but a sixty-foot drop. "You would've never seen it coming. Not at the speed you were going." He watched as the color drained from her face, and her breathing accelerated.

———— • ————

Charlie felt like she was going to be sick. The thought of driving off a cliff—possibly being thrown from the vehicle—made her legs turn to jelly. She held onto Hunter a little tighter. "I didn't know."

"Of course you didn't."

Quietly, they walked back to the vehicle. When they got there, Hunter leaned against the hood and pulled Charlie close. "Look, this is *not* how I envisioned our time together. So, I'm going to put it all out there, no mixed signals. No unspoken expectations." His hands came up to frame her dirt and tear-stained face. "I want to be with you, Charlie." He looked directly into her eyes. "Do you hear what I'm saying? I . . . want . . . to be . . . with you. Don't try to dissect, overanalyze, or read something into my intentions that isn't there. You're an intriguing woman, and I want to spend time getting to know you better. But not if I have to defend or explain every word I say. I know we have some obstacles to overcome, some more difficult than others. But let's see how things go before we get too far ahead of ourselves. When you see my day-to-day living, you might decide I'm a real bore and lose interest. Or when you find out about my less than saintly past, you might see me differently."

She looked like she was ready to say something, but he quickly continued.

"On the other hand, I could find out you can't cook your way out of a paper bag or that you hate children. Those would be real deal breakers for me." He chuckled, trying to lighten the mood. "So you see, we have a lot of discovering to do in the next few days."

Stroking her face, he smiled but made sure she knew he

was serious. "Let's put what happened today, and the things we've said behind us, and just enjoy the time we have left. Can you do that? Can you give us a chance? Because if you can't, if you don't feel the same way about us as I do, I'll have Chet fly you home. I'm not going to force you to stay somewhere you don't want to be. It's your call."

Chapter Twenty-Nine

Charlie looked at Hunter, sincerity mingled with concern in his eyes. She knew what her heart wanted, but also knew the painful truth. The "what ifs" in their future were bigger than Hunter realized. She had to be honest with him. Covering his hands with hers, she brought them down away from her face, but didn't let go.

"Nothing you could tell me about your past would scare me away. And I don't hate kids." She smiled timidly. "But our obstacles are bigger than that, and you know it."

"But they don't have to—"

"Hunter, let me finish."

He held back his argument and looked ready to listen.

"You're a public figure with the media around you wherever you go. That means we could never be seen together. We could never chance a photographer snapping a picture of us. I could never be backstage while you're on tour or accompany you to an awards ceremony, a friend's wedding, or even something as simple as going out to dinner."

"So, we keep our relationship private. I haven't dated seriously for over a year. The press is used to me showing up at functions solo or with my mom."

"You could handle that?"

"To keep you safe, absolutely."

"What about your family and your staff? They couldn't tell anyone about us."

"That's not a problem. Everyone who works for me has signed a confidentiality agreement. Besides, the guys here on the ranch, in my band, and on my crew, they're my friends. They would never sell me out to the media just to make a buck."

"But what about my neighbors, or the people at the airstrip, even Artie? What if they get curious? Even Karen could pose a problem. She's just a neighbor who's willing to watch Goliath. What if she gets curious and asks more and more questions about the time I spend away from my place?"

"So we board Goliath instead." Hunter stroked her arms and smiled. "See, we can work these things out."

"And what happens when your mother finds out I'm a married woman?"

His smile disappeared. "Come on, Charlie, that's only a legality, and you know it. You're married on paper, that's all. It might take some explaining, but when she knows the truth, she'll understand. Besides, it's been two years since you left. How do you know your husband still wants to harm you? Maybe he's moved on, found someone else."

She shook her head. "You don't know Daniel. It's not about moving on for him. It's about exacting revenge." She stepped away from Hunter, breaking their connection, and took a deep breath. The thought of Daniel—of the pain she had endured the last time he warned her about leaving— caused her body to shudder. At times, she could not control the anxiety that overtook her. Her heart would accelerate uncontrollably, and her limbs would turn weak. She would have to block out everything around her so she could work to control it.

"Charlie?"

"I'm okay," she said with a raised hand, stopping him from touching her. She paced a few steps away, put her hands on her head, and took several, deep cleansing breaths. After a minute, when her breathing return to normal, she walked back to where Hunter was anxiously watching her every move. She could see the questions in his eyes and the anger in the set of his jaw.

"It was never about love with Daniel. I was a possession to him, something to show off to his business partners or the other slimy people he had dealings with. He's not going to let me go just because I tell him I've moved on."

"Why didn't you go to the police?" Hunter asked, as he tucked a wayward strand of hair behind her ear.

"I was too afraid. Daniel always bragged about his friends in high places and the powerful connections he had. He told me if I ever went to the police, he would know."

"So what did you do?"

She looked off into the distance, trying to decide how much she wanted to tell him, how much she wanted to relive. "I don't want to talk about it. Not now."

He reached out and squeezed her hand. "Okay. But know that I'm here and ready to listen when you do." He let go of her hands and slipped his fingers around her neck, gently tipping her head back so she would have to look at him. "We have three days. Three days we can spend together doing whatever we want. We don't have to worry about the media or the neighbors. And you don't have to keep looking over your shoulder for shadows from your past. So . . . what do you say?"

She looked into his eyes and saw hope, something she hadn't felt in a very long time. And even though she knew their obstacles were bigger than Hunter might be willing to accept, she wanted nothing more than to pretend her life could be more than it was, even if it was only for the next few days.

With a deep breath she looked at him, sternness in her expression. "On one condition."

He smiled. "Anything. Just name it."

"No more motorcycles."

"Deal." He leaned in to seal it with a kiss, but she playfully stepped out of his reach. That's when she saw the red stain on his shirt. "I thought you said you were okay?"

"I am." He glanced at his shoulder, stretching the neck of his shirt.

"Hunter, that doesn't look good." She stepped up on the

bumper of the vehicle to get a better look at his shoulder. "My gosh, Hunter, you have a whole chunk of skin missing."

"I'm fine. I'll clean it out when we get back to the house and put a bandage on it." He reached out for her hand and pulled her down from the vehicle. "Come on, let's go."

"What about the bike?" Charlie asked as she walked around to the passenger side.

"What about it?" he said as he walked slowly past the vehicle.

"Hunter," she yelled after him, "you're not going to ride it back, are you?"

"Why, did you want to?"

"You can't. You're limping and your shoulder is messed up."

"I can still handle a bike. Just take it slow."

She watched as he put on his helmet and muscled the bike to an upright position.

"Are you sure you're all right?" she yelled, as she walked around to the driver's side.

He waved at her, then tried to kick-start the bike. It took several attempts but finally it revved to life.

Turning the vehicle around, she followed Hunter back to the house, wincing and gasping every time he bounced over a large rut. She knew his shoulder had to be hurting him, and the pummeling she gave him probably didn't help.

He drove past the house and continued down the dirt road. After driving over a small rise, she saw a couple of large structures. Hunter drove the bike into a multi-door garage and killed the engine. She pulled up in front and watched as he slowly swung his leg over the back of the bike, stood, removed his helmet, and set it on the seat. He limped his way to the passenger side of the vehicle and climbed in.

With his head back against the cushioned seat he closed his eyes. "Follow the road to the left," he said in a casual tone, like this was an everyday occurrence.

After parking in the circular driveway, she pulled her bags from the back. Hunter kind of rolled out of the vehicle and waited for her to walk around to his side.

"Here, let me take those." He reached for her bags.

"I've got them. You just worry about yourself, gimpy."

"Wow! Maim a guy, then call him names."

She shot him a drop-dead look.

"I'm kidding, I'm kidding." He chuckled as he pushed the front door open.

Chapter Thirty

Hunter limped upstairs, Charlie following slowly behind him. She looked at the pictures that stair-stepped up the wall, allowing her a glimpse into Hunter's past.

Him as a kid playing with a dog.

As a teen riding a horse.

As a decked-out cowboy wrestling a steer.

Pictures of him with his mom, and with a man his height and built. *Must be Jake.* And of him with a beautiful young woman who shared Hunter's crystal blue eyes. *Amy.*

When Charlie got to the top of the stairs, she continued to follow Hunter into his bedroom.

She looked at the king-size bed with its carved-wood headboard, then spied a pair of crumpled jeans and a shirt tossed on a chair in the corner. The setting seemed too private, too intimate, and she immediately felt awkward and out of place.

"Okay . . . so, I . . . I guess I'll go put my bags away." She turned to make a hasty exit.

"But I'm going to need your help with this," he said as he disappeared around the corner.

She stopped, not sure what she should do, her eyes drifting around the room. Beamed ceiling. Flat screen TV. A leather upholstered bench tucked against the foot board of the bed.

"Are you going to help me or not?"

"What?" Charlie turned around to see a shirtless Hunter standing on the far side of the room. Her pulse quickened.

"What . . . sure . . . I mean . . ." she cleared her throat, trying to swallow past the knot in it. "What do you want me to do?"

"Come help me get the dirt out." He turned back around and disappeared into the bathroom.

Setting her bags on the leather bench, she mumbled to herself. "Stop acting like a child. You're going to embarrass yourself. It's not like you haven't seen a man with his shirt off before."

She followed Hunter into the bathroom, awed by its cavernous size. It had all the same amenities as hers, but in larger proportions. The Jacuzzi tub was the size of a backyard spa. The shower, with its multiple shower heads and sprays, looked like it belonged in a high-end locker room.

"This is insane! You could fit a whole baseball team in here." She continued looking around, anywhere but at Hunter.

"The owner who built this house was a really large guy. He definitely bought into the *bigger is better* mentality."

Charlie walked over to the vanity area and watched Hunter's reflection in the mirror. As he reached for something deep in the linen cupboard, the corded muscles in his back and shoulders flexed and rippled. *Wow! How does he stay in such good shape when he's on a tour bus for weeks at a time?*

When he turned and set a large rectangular box on the granite countertop, she saw for the first time the angel tattoo on the left side of his chest, and the screaming red scratches running down the side of his torso.

"Hunter!" She reached for his right arm and pulled it away from his side.

"It's just a little road rash."

She shook her head. "There's nothing little about it."

"Come on. It's no big deal. I can take care of that later." He untucked the ends of the box and pulled back the lid.

"What's that?"

"My first-aid kit."

"In a boot box?"

"Hey, it works." A myriad of bandages, gauze pads, and ointments littered the bottom of the box.

"But we need to wash it first."

"I know." He turned back to the cupboard and pulled out a plush brown washcloth. Tossing it at her, he laughed. "You might want to use it on your face first."

She glanced in the mirror and leaned in closer. "Oh my gosh! Why didn't you tell me I had dirt all over my face?"

"I thought you would've seen it for yourself, but I guess you were too busy ogling me in the mirror to see your own reflection."

She spun around to defend herself, but his devilish grin and laughing eyes silenced her. Without a word, she turned back to the sink, wet the corner of the washcloth, and wiped at the dirt streaks on her face. Glancing in the mirror, she watched Hunter watching her. He was doing it again, making her heart race and her head spin.

When she was done washing her face, she made sure to rinse the cloth well before turning to Hunter. "Okay, *Mr. Smart Mouth*, are you sure you want my help? I could cause you a lot of pain."

He took a step closer, his stare moving from her lips to her eyes. "I trust you," he whispered.

When he stood this close, his presence was intoxicating and completely scrambled her senses. Never had a man wielded such power over her, at least not without instilling terror at the same time.

She took a step back. "If I'm going to be able to see what I'm doing, you need to sit down."

Hunter walked over to the side of the tub and sat on the edge of the marble surround. Charlie positioned herself on his right side, and inspected the bloody gash, peppered with bits of dirt and gravel. She leaned over the tub and turned on the infinity spigot, soaking the washcloth in her hand. Ringing it out, but leaving a fair amount of water in it, she pressed it to Hunter's shoulder. He flinched as water drizzled down his chest and back.

"Sorry." She quickly pulled back the cloth.

"Don't be."

Wetting the cloth again, she decided to use a different approach. Without wringing it out, she held it above Hunter's shoulder and squeezed, allowing the water to overflow the gash. But that just made a mess. Water ran down his chest, back, and arm, then onto the floor.

"I can't do this, Hunter!" Frustrated, she backed away from him and tossed the washcloth in the sink. "I'm going to end up hurting you, and I don't want to do that. Take a cold shower. I'm sure it will do you a world of good."

Smiling, he stood. "I guess you're right. I could use some cooling off."

She caught his double meaning but refused to give him the satisfaction by acknowledging it.

"Fine. You do that. I'm going to put my stuff away." Hurrying out of the bathroom, Charlie walked into Hunter's bedroom, shocked to see a man standing there.

Chapter Thirty-One

Charlie didn't know what to do or say.

The man standing in front of her—obviously Hunter's brother—did not look happy.

"You must be Jake." She smiled nervously.

He looked her up and down, his expression like stone. "And you must be Charlie."

"Ahh . . . Hunter is taking a shower."

"So I heard."

She realized he was getting the wrong impression. After all, she was in Hunter's bedroom, her bags at the foot of his bed, Hunter taking a shower. It didn't look good.

"Umm . . . this isn't what it looks like."

He glanced at her bags, then back at her. "Looks pretty self-explanatory to me."

She took a step forward. "But that's what I mean. It's not like that at all. I can explain."

He leaned against the dresser, ankles crossed, hands clutching the edge, and looked at her with disdain. "By all means. Explain."

"Well, umm . . ." Charlie clasped her hands behind her back so he wouldn't notice how badly they were shaking. "Hunter had an accident on his motorcycle and got a pretty nasty gash on his shoulder. I was trying to help him get the dirt out, but I was only making it worse. So . . . he's taking a shower . . . to clean it out."

He glanced at her bags again.

"I'm not staying in Hunter's room, if that's what you're

thinking. He showed me where I'd be staying downstairs. It's just that I had my bags with me when I followed him into his room—"

"Because you didn't want to stay downstairs, is that it?"

"No." She shook her head quickly. "I mean, that's not how it is. I was going to leave, so I put my bags in the vehicle, but Hunter convinced me to stay."

"In his room," he reemphasized, disgust coloring his tone.

"No. You've got this all wrong."

"No, sweetheart," he came up off the dresser and crossed the room faster than she could blink, "*you've* got it all wrong." He pointed his finger, stabbing the air inches from her face. "I'm not some back-road idiot, so don't treat me like one. I've dealt with this kind of garbage from Hunter ever since he hit the big time. He told me he changed, that he was no longer doing the party scene or the one-night stands. I wanted to believe him. But this . . ." he waved his hand at her and her bags, "this has the old Hunter written all over it. The only difference is the *old* Hunter wasn't stupid enough to bring his groupie fling home with him."

He sauntered a few steps away, then turned back to her.

"Well, I'm not going to stand for it. I'm not going to let him parade his lifestyle around in front of my kids. They think their Uncle Hunter hung the moon and stars. They're too young to know the truth. One day they'll understand, but until then, Hunter is not going to bring his cheap thrill home and play house in front of my family."

His words were like a slap across the face. "Cheap" was exactly how she felt, even if he was completely off base with his accusations. But it didn't matter. When he found out about her true circumstances, he would be just as protective of his family. Knowing it would do her no good to try to explain further, she did the only thing she could do.

Concede.

"I would never do anything to hurt Hunter, you, or your family. I was wrong to come here, and I'm more than willing to go." She walked over and picked up her bags. Can you drive me to the airstrip? I'd do it myself, but I already got turned around once."

"It would be my pleasure."

His sarcasm felt like another invisible blow.

Picking up her bags, she walked down the hallway and took the stairs one at a time. Her legs trembled so badly, she was afraid she would fall, so she clung to the banister with every step she took. As she passed the pictures on the wall, she looked at the one of Hunter astride a beautiful Palomino, arms crossed, leaning on the horn of the saddle, his roguish smile staring back at her. She sighed. A part of her had wanted to believe she could love again. But the choices she'd already made in life had sealed her fate.

Her life would never be more than it is now.

Feeling like she could not get out of there soon enough, she hurried toward the off-road vehicle, stumbled, and went down on all fours. Feeling beyond humiliated, she sat back on her heels, brushed the dust from the front of her jeans, and felt the sting of her scraped-up palms.

Jake picked up her bags and offered her a hand, but she ignored him. She would not give him the satisfaction. Slowly, she got to her feet and walked the last few yards to the utility vehicle.

"Hey, wait a minute, what's going on?"

Charlie and Jake turned to see Hunter leaning against the railing of the second-story balcony. Having nothing to say, she turned back to the vehicle while Jake rounded the bumper and put her bags in the back.

"Charlie . . . what are you doing? Where are you going?"

She heard the confusion in his tone. But still, she didn't dare turn around. As Jake climbed into the driver's side, Hunter came running from the house, barefooted, bare-chested, hair wet, buttoning his jeans.

"What's going on?" he asked as he hurried to the side of the vehicle and grabbed onto the door frame.

She didn't dare look at him.

"Charlie wants me to drive her to the airstrip."

"What are you even doing here?" Hunter asked his brother.

"Diana sent me to check on you, to see if you were coming for lunch. Charlie and I got talking, and she decided she made a mistake by coming here. I offered to drive her to the plane."

Jake glared at her, challenging her to disagree.

"Bull! I know that self-righteous look of yours. You gave it to me every time you pulled me out of a bar. Charlie, look at me." He reached in the vehicle and squeezed her hand. She flinched, pulling away. "I don't understand. We talked this all out. You said you would give us a chance . . . that you would give us the next few days."

"Hunter, just stop it!" Jake hollered. "Stop screwing up your life! She's smart enough to know a train wreck when she sees one, why aren't you? Just let it go."

"No way! You have no idea what you're talking about. You have no business interfering with my life."

"I do when it affects my kids!" he snapped back. "I will not have you cavorting around, showing off your barfly girlfriend to Cody and Courtney."

Lightning fast, Hunter rounded the front of the vehicle, grabbed Jake by the collar, and yanked him from the driver's seat. They both went down in a heap.

"Stop it!" Charlie hollered as she leapt across the gearshift and out the driver's side. She tried to pull Hunter from on top of his brother, but his arms were still wet from his shower, and she couldn't get a strong enough hold. "Stop it!" she screamed again, tears streaming down her face, as the two men rolled in the gravel.

Hunter got the upper hand, pinning his brother with a forearm to his neck. Blood was running from Jake's nose, and the gash on Hunter's shoulder was a mixture of blood and gravel. Again.

Charlie tried to untangle the two men. But when Jake pulled back to sucker punch Hunter, he missed his mark completely, his fist landing on the side of her face.

She crumpled.

Chapter Thirty-Two

On her knees, her head in her lap, Charlie held her cheek, stunned by the blow.

"Are you okay?" Hunter squatted next to her.

She didn't answer because she wasn't sure. Opening her mouth, she worked her jaw, wincing at the pain.

Hunter held her by the shoulders and pushed her to an upright position. "Let me see."

But she refused to look at him.

"Come on, Charlie, let me see." He reached to pull her hand from her cheek, but she swatted his hand away.

"Just take me home, please."

"Not until you explain to me what just happened. One minute we're fine, the next you're on your way out of here with my brother."

"It doesn't matter." She slowly got to her feet, Hunter alongside her.

"It does matter!"

"Hunter, please . . ." Charlie chanced a look at Jake, to see if he was going to say anything, but Hunter saw her.

He spun around to face his brother. "This is all your fault. What did you say to her?"

"What are you talking about?" Jake said as he wiped the blood from under his nose.

"You said or did something to make Charlie want to leave. What did you do?"

"I simply told her the facts! The cold hard facts! You told me you changed. You told me you turned over a new leaf. I believed you, and then you pull a stunt like this."

"What are you talking about?" he yelled. "You knew I was coming home; you knew I was bringing Charlie with me."

"You also said your relationship was platonic, that she was recovering from a difficult situation, and needed a place where she could regroup."

"Yeah. So?"

"Regroup? Is that what you call a hook up these days? I'm not stupid, Hunter. She was in *your* room, while you were in the shower, her bags at the foot of *your* bed. It doesn't get much clearer than that. She's an opportunist, just like every other woman who ended up in your bed."

"No. You have it all wrong. I had to convince Charlie to come. She didn't want to. In fact, she wanted nothing to do with me the first two times we spoke. I've been pursuing her, not the other way around."

"Boy, does she have your number," Jake laughed. "She's a freeloader, Hunter. Can't you see that? She gave you some sob story, made you feel sorry for her, and is playing with your emotions. You're worth millions. Don't tell me she's not interested in you. How stupid can you be?"

"Why you son of—"

"Stop it!" Charlie shouted, then coddled her cheek. "Stop talking about me like I'm not even here." She turned to Jake, wanting to hate him for the things he had said about her, but knowing she couldn't. No matter how misguided or hurtful his words were, he was only trying to protect his brother. She admired that kind of love.

"No matter what you think, Jake, I'm not an opportunist. I've seen firsthand what money can do to a person, and I want nothing to do with it. As for Hunter, he's been nothing but a complete gentleman. He just wanted to bring me here to give me some space to think, to allow us some time together without being seen."

"Give me a break. What woman wouldn't want to be seen with Hunter Jennings, country's sexiest man alive?" he said sarcastically with air quotes.

"A woman like Amy," Hunter answered before she could respond.

Jake looked at her, then to Hunter. "What are you talking about?" A renewed anger fueled his words.

"Charlie is in hiding. Her husband is just like Ray. He beat the living crap out of her. Repeatedly. And threatened to kill her if she ever left him. Just like Ray did to Amy. That's why Charlie is afraid to get involved with me, why she doesn't want to be seen with me. Your screw-up brother isn't trying to take advantage of someone. I'm just trying to help Charlie see she has options, that she doesn't have to live in fear the rest of her life."

Hunter moved to her side and gently tipped her chin up. "Do you think anything is broken?" he whispered. She shook her head. "Then let's get some ice on it."

With his arm around her waist, Hunter led her toward the house.

"Wait!" Jake barked. They both turned around. "I'm sorry things got out of hand. What else can I say?"

"Nothing," Hunter said, clearly disgusted. "I think you've said enough for one day."

Chapter Thirty-Three

Charlie sat on a barstool in the kitchen while Hunter grabbed an ice pack from the freezer. "This is probably going to hurt," he said as he handed it to her, scrutinizing her swelling cheek.

She looked at him, then looked away. "I've had worse."

Hunter watched as she gingerly pressed the pack to her cheek.

She flinched.

He cringed, contorting his face.

"That's not helping," she said as she held the pack in place, working through the pain.

"Sorry." Looking dejected, he walked over to the sink and turned on the spigot. Scooping up a handful of water, he swished it around in his mouth, then spit it out. He repeated the process a few more times before drying his face.

When he turned back around, she saw dirt was stuck to his bare chest and blood oozed from his shoulder. She felt guilty for scolding him, knowing he had to be in a fair amount of pain, especially after going down on his motorcycle. "You need to take another shower and get that gash looked at."

He glanced at his shoulder, then at her. "I don't care about my shoulder, especially if you're just going to bolt again."

She thought for a moment, looking at the clock hanging over the stove. *Is that what I want to do?*

It was only a little after one o'clock. If she left now, she could be home in just a few hours, and pretend today had never happened. She looked at Hunter, hurt and defeat evident in his sagging shoulders and wounded eyes.

"Do you believe in signs, Hunter?"

"What?"

"Signs. Omens."

He shook his head. "No, I don't."

"But look at all that has gone wrong since I got here. I have a panic attack on the plane. You crash your bike. Jake walks in on us and gets the wrong impression, then coldcocks me. You're hurt. I'm hurt. And I've already caused problems between you and your family. Maybe it's a sign. Maybe we just need to cut our losses and admit this isn't going to work out."

"No. Only quitters give up. And I'm no quitter."

She sighed, too exhausted to argue. "Go take your shower."

He pinned her with a look, and she knew exactly what he was asking.

"Don't worry. I'll be here when you get out."

She watched as Hunter disappeared around the corner. When she was sure he was gone, she tossed the ice pack on the countertop and allowed the tears she had held back to fall. The punch to the jaw was nothing compared to the things Jake had called her. Barfly. Groupie. Cheap. She couldn't blame him, because he didn't know anything about her.

Until now.

Looking down at her dirty jeans and blouse, she decided she needed to shower and change, then she would figure out what she was going to do next.

Realizing her bags were still outside in the vehicle, she groaned, not having the energy to move. Taking a couple of minutes to gather herself, she wiped the tears from her left cheek and gently blotted them from her right, then slid from the barstool.

With her ankle tender from her little stumble, she walked slowly to the entryway, using the wall for balance. When she reached for the handle of the front door, it burst open. She barely got out of the way before Jake walked in carrying her bags.

Their eyes met.

"Umm, I figured you would need your things." He sat the bags down.

"Thanks."

Tipping his head to the side, he looked at her cheek. "Are you okay?"

She shrugged. "Sure."

"Diana is a nurse. She could take a look at it for you."

"That won't be necessary. I've had a lot worse." She ignored the pity on Jake's face and continued. "But I think she should look at Hunter's shoulder. The gash is pretty deep, and if he doesn't clean it out right, it will get infected."

He nodded, his hands in his pockets.

They stood, a very loud silence between them. Not having the energy to go another round with him, she reached for her bags.

"I'm really sorry about what happened," Jake blurted out.

"You were protecting your brother; I get that." Slinging her duffel over her shoulder, she swayed.

Jake reached out to steady her, but she took a step back.

He shoved his hands into his pockets. "Are you going to stay?" he asked.

She spoke over her shoulder as she walked away. "At least for now. But don't worry, I won't come anywhere near your kids."

Jake said something as she walked away, but she didn't hear what it was, nor did she care. Locking the bedroom door behind her, she carried her bags to the bathroom and plopped them on the closet floor. Making sure the bathroom door was locked as well, she leaned over the marble counter and examined her cheek in the large mirror. It was already turning shades of purple and blue.

With a groan, she used the boot jack in the closet to remove her boots, then undressed. Turning the shower on, she got the temperature just right before stepping into the therapeutic flow. With body sprays and a rainfall showerhead dousing her from above, she leaned against the wall and sobbed.

Emotionally, she was spent.

Physically, she ached.

Being home in her own environment sounded so good. No questions. No fights. No misunderstandings. But she barely had the energy to step from the shower and dry off, let alone get on a plane and fly home.

After sitting on the settee—for how long, she wasn't sure—she dug through her bag and pulled out some black yoga pants and a vintage Ariat tee. Getting dressed and dragging a comb through her wet hair zapped her of what little energy she had left, so she curled up against the king-size headboard, and closed her eyes.

Chapter Thirty-Four

Hunter felt like a caged animal as he paced the living room.

After his shower, he threw on some sweatpants and a tank top, then hurried downstairs to be with Charlie, but she had locked herself in the guest room. He was relieved to hear the shower running when he pressed his ear to the door, but when she didn't materialize an hour later, he was concerned.

Hating himself for doing it, he felt around on the top of the door frame until his fingers touched the spare key. Slowly and quietly he turned the key in the lock and pushed the door open. As soon as he spotted her curled up on the bed, he sighed with relief.

Thank God she's still here.

Silently, he closed the door, put the key back where it belonged, and walked into the kitchen.

Feeling beat-up from his bike crash and his run-in with Jake, he grabbed a bottle of water from the refrigerator and a couple of ibuprofen from the cupboard. Tossing the pills to the back of his throat, he drained the bottle dry. Crushing it, he tossed it into the recyclables and grabbed another one from the fridge before walking into the living room.

Stretching out on the couch, he decided to close his eyes until Charlie woke up. He was just short of falling asleep when he heard someone at the front door. Opening his eyes, he watched as Diana quietly slipped into the living room.

His sister-in-law was the best thing to happen to his brother. She was beautiful, and strong, and ferociously protective of those she loved.

At first, Hunter didn't think the two would last. He figured she wouldn't put up with Jake's exploits and would be gone in a week or two. But Diana was different, and that difference had been life-changing for Jake.

Hunter watched their relationship play out, his doubts soon turning to envy. So much so he began to change his own ways. Partying no longer held its allure. Women throwing themselves at him night after night became annoying and pathetic. He became more introspective to what was important in life. Family, country, values he wanted to pass down to kids one day. His songwriting changed. His lifestyle changed. But since Jake wasn't on the road with him anymore, his brother was skeptical.

Jake turned his life around because of the love of a good woman but didn't think Hunter could do the same. So to Jake, Charlie just looked like another woman in a long line of dalliances who played with Hunter's affections in exchanged for a little fun and funds.

Diana sat down on the couch opposite Hunter, interrupting his thoughts. Setting a red backpack on the floor beside her, she spoke in a quiet tone. "Jake told me what happened."

"And what did he say?" Hunter was doubtful his pig-headed brother admitted any wrongdoing.

"He said you two got into a fight, and he accidentally hit Charlie."

"Did he tell you *why* we were fighting?" he challenged.

Diana hung her head. "Because he said some pretty nasty things about her."

"He was a complete jackass! That's what he was!"

"He said as much." She moved over to the cushion next to him. "Mind if I take a look at that?" She pointed to the swatch of gauze sticking out from under his tank top. He shrugged then sat up a little straighter.

Moving the shoulder seam aside, Diana peeled back the gauze, and wrinkled her nose. "It doesn't look good, Hunter. It really needs to be irrigated."

155

"Do what you have to."

"Okay, then let's move to the kitchen sink."

Hunter followed Diana into the other room and watched as she rifled through her medical bag. She pulled out a large syringe and a couple tubes of solution.

"Your first aid kit is a lot nicer than mine," he chuckled.

"Yeah, well, it's a little more than that."

"Once a nurse always a nurse."

"And it's a good thing with the stupid stunts you and Jake are always pulling."

Hunter slipped his arm through the neck of his tank top while Diana watched.

"Wouldn't it be easier just to take your shirt off?"

Hunter didn't want her to see the road-rash on his side. She would make a big deal out of it, and he wasn't in the mood. "This is fine," he answered.

"Have it your way," she mumbled as she gently peeled off the gauze pad. "Lean over the sink."

Hunter set his elbows on the edge of the counter and leaned over the sink. Diana hopped up on the granite countertop and positioned herself where she could see what she was doing. Snapping off the top of one of the plastic tubes, she inserted the end of the syringe into the solution and pulled back the plunger.

"Okay, this is going to hurt, but I need the pressure to get the dirt out and push it away from the wound."

"Go for it."

Hunter turned his head and grimaced. He flinched and groaned a few times while Diana continued to squirt the solution into the gash. Just about the time he had reached his limit, Diana put the syringe down and started dressing the wound.

"There. That should do it. No shower tonight or in the morning. I'll check it again tomorrow afternoon and see how it's doing." She jumped down from the counter, scrunched up the bandage wrappers, picked up the solution tubes and threw it all into the compactor. Tossing a few things back into her bag, she zipped it up, then turned to Hunter.

"So, is her cheek bad?"

"Yeah," Hunter said as he slipped his arm back through his sleeve. "It's swollen and is going to be pretty bruised, but she insisted nothing was broken."

"Do you think she'll allow me to look at it?"

"I don't know. She's sleeping right now, and when she wakes up, I wouldn't be surprised if she insisted I take her home."

"Jake feels horrible. You've got to know that."

"He should. He had no right doing what he did—barging into my house, insulting my guest. I mean, where does he get off?"

"I'm not going to defend him, because we both know Jake has an exceptionally short fuse. Even so, he was only trying to protect you because he loves you."

"Well, I don't need his protection. I'm a big boy. I can handle myself just fine."

"But there was a time when you didn't always make the right decisions."

"And there was a time when Jake was right alongside me when I made those decisions. Until you came along, Jake could party with the best of them."

His sister-in-law hung her head, making him feel like a heel.

"I'm sorry. I shouldn't have said that."

"No. You're right. I know all about Jake's past. He wasn't a saint by any stretch of the imagination. And I think it's because of his past and the choices he made that he feels like it's his fault you spiraled when you hit the road."

"But he changed, big time. Look at him now. He has you and the kids. He's the epitome of a family man. Why can't he believe I've changed too?"

"He wants to believe you, Hunter, I know he does. But you have to admit, from what he told me, the situation he walked in on looked pretty compromising."

"And he chose to believe the worst instead of giving me the benefit of the doubt."

Diana nodded. "You're absolutely right. And he feels horrible. But don't shut him out. He's your brother and he loves you."

"Yeah, well, he has a heck of a way of showing it."

When she stepped forward and wrapped him in a hug, her arm pressed against the road rash on his side, and he had to swallow back a grimace.

"I'm sorry this happened, Hunter. And if Charlie is the woman in your life, I want to meet her and get a chance to know her, so I hope she stays."

"Me too." He stepped back. "So, how much did Jake tell you? About Charlie, I mean?"

She looked at him. "That she's a lot like Amy."

Hunter raked his fingers through his hair. "You know what she said when Jake hit her? That she'd had worse. Can you believe that? It made me want to puke to think some guy used her for a punching bag. It makes me sick to think about the pain she has endured. What possesses a man to hit a woman? What satisfaction does a guy get from knocking a woman around?"

"I don't know, I really don't. But I saw my fair share of abused women in the ER. Daily. Of course, some of them wouldn't admit to the abuse. They would say they fell down the stairs, or tripped, or fell off a ladder even though their injuries weren't consistent with their stories. They would actually protect their abuser. It's an odd dynamic. But for some women, it's their only hope for survival."

Hunter shook his head, feeling ill. "Men like that deserve to be taken out into a field and shot, but only after someone beats the living daylights out of them."

"But you're not going to do that, right?"

Hunter could see what she *wasn't* saying by the worry in her eyes. "No. You don't have to worry. I'm not going to go off half-cocked. I don't even know who the guy is. But Charlie said something . . . something I'm going to have to ask her about later. That is if she ever talks to me again."

"She will. Have a little faith. Look, I'm going to go, but call me if you need me. And don't worry about dinner tonight. If Charlie decides to stay, she'll need some down time. Not the chaos of a family dinner."

"But what about Mom?"

"I'll talk to her. She doesn't need to know what happened, only that Charlie took a spill. Don't worry, I'll run interference for you."

He walked her to the front door. "Thanks, Diana."

She stood on her tip toes, gave him a kiss on the cheek, and smiled. "It's what family does for each other."

Holding the door open, he watched as she walked down the steps. "Hey, Diana . . ."

She turned around. "Yeah?"

"How did you know Jake was the one for you? I mean, you did the whole long-distance thing, and back then, he wasn't the man he is today. How did you know?"

She shrugged and smiled. "My heart just knew. Even though my friends were telling me he was just another smooth-talking cowboy, I knew there was something more. Something different. Behind the Jim Beam and the swagger was the man I wanted to spend the rest of my life with."

"And you knew that after only three months?"

She grinned. "I knew after only three days."

Chapter Thirty-Five

Hunter walked back into the kitchen and stopped abruptly when he saw Charlie standing there. He wanted to go to her, wrap her in his arms, convince her to stay, but wasn't sure what kind of reception he'd receive.

"How are you feeling?" he asked, wondering if she had overheard his conversation with Diana.

"Okay."

"Were you able to sleep at all?"

"A little."

"Do you feel like eating something?"

She brought her hand up to her cheek and worked her jaw from side to side. "Maybe something soft."

Hunter opened the refrigerator and studied the contents. "How about some yogurt? Or I could cut up some fruit and make you a smoothie."

"Yogurt sounds good."

He grabbed two containers from the refrigerator and put one on the bar where she was sitting. Getting two spoons from the kitchen drawer, he handed her one.

"Thank you." She pulled back the foil from the container and took a small scoop.

He watched as she carefully slipped the spoon into her mouth and slid it out from between closed lips.

They ate in relative silence while Hunter watched her, trying to get a vibe for what she was thinking.

"Wow, if your fans could see you now."

"What do you mean?"

160

"Rough and rugged Hunter Jennings, eating lite yogurt instead of swigging a beer."

He chuckled, taking Charlie's poke at humor as a good sign.

"How is your shoulder?" she asked.

"Diana cleaned it out, and believe me, she did not hold back." He finished his yogurt, tossed his spoon in the sink, and the small carton into the trash. He stood across from Charlie, leaning on the counter. "She also came to tell me how bad Jake feels about what happened."

She lifted another spoonful of yogurt to her lips and swallowed. "I understand his gut feeling to protect you, but why is it when people jump to conclusions, they always assume the worst?"

"Jake has always been that way. It came with the responsibility of being the head of the house at an early age."

"What happened to your dad, if you don't mind me asking?"

"He didn't like being tied down." Hunter shrugged with indifference. "He was a salesman who liked the road instead of traditional family life. When my mom was pregnant with Amy, he found himself another woman who wanted to travel with him. No strings attached. That's when he checked out for good."

"Has he tried to contact you since you hit it big?"

"Yeah. He tried a few times. But I have no desire to see him. When he walked out, I was only three years old. As far as I'm concerned, I don't have a father, even though I have his name."

"What?"

"Aaron Hunter Jennings . . . II. But everyone just called me Hunter. I thought about using Aaron when I got older, but I didn't want to give my dad the satisfaction. I will never forgive him for what he did to my family. After Amy was born, my mom held down a full-time job, and kept us all together. She's the reason I'm here, not him. I don't even think of him as my dad. He's just a man who slept with my mom."

He noticed Charlie's surprised reaction.

"I know that sounds callous, but it's how I feel. He forced my mother to live a very difficult life. She didn't deserve to be treated like that, so I'm not going to waste my time on him now." He paused, wondering if Charlie would be willing to share as well. "How about you? You haven't mentioned your family."

"No dad," she said firmly, "and my mom . . . she was pretty much a free spirit. We wandered a lot, hooked up with her friends, did a lot of camping, but never stayed in one place for any length of time. But, when I was seven, a truant officer came knocking at the door where we were staying and asked my mom why I wasn't in school. Thinking I was helping, I piped up and said my mom taught me all kinds of things. Well, that was all he needed to hear. He reported my mother to Child Protective Services, but by the time they came looking for me, we were already gone.

We moved in with my aunt, and I was enrolled in school. Luckily, my mom had taught me basic math and how to read. So, when she was asked why I hadn't been enrolled in school earlier, she just gave a sob story about a difficult life. Since I was bright and seemed well-adjusted, nothing much came of it."

"So you stayed with your aunt?"

"I did."

Hunter didn't miss the past tense or the emotion in Charlie's eyes. "What happened?"

"Like I said, my mom was a free spirit. She stuck it out the first year, got a job as a receptionist at a car dealership, and tried to be a traditional mom."

"But . . ."

"But, when I came home from my first day of second grade, my aunt sat me down and explained to me that while my mother loved me very much, she wasn't cut out for the conventional lifestyle we'd been living. From that day on, my mom would float in and out of my life, stick around for a week or two, then disappear again. My aunt was my mother. She's the one who took care of me when I was sick, made sure I had braces when I needed them, helped me with my homework, and dreamed with me about which colleges I should apply to. She sacrificed everything for me."

"You're talking in the past tense," he said softly.

"When I was sixteen, we found out she had stage four breast cancer. It was too advanced for most treatments, so instead of putting energy into her health, she used it to prepare me for what lay ahead. I graduated from high school early, was declared an emancipated minor, and got a good job at the local racetrack. She wasn't happy about the job, since she wanted me to go to college, but I convinced her it would be a good place to work since I was interested in veterinary medicine. She died two weeks before my seventeenth birthday."

"And your mom?"

"I haven't seen her since I was fifteen."

Hunter hung his head, imagining the weight of the world put on the shoulders of a sixteen-year-old girl.

"You know what?" Charlie looked at him with a bit of a smirk. "If this is your idea of a date, you're pretty lousy at it."

"What?" He stood up straighter, shocked by her statement.

"Well, I thought you brought me here to wine and dine me. So far, all I have to show for this shindig is a panic attack, a dressing down, a left hook, and a not so pleasant stroll down memory lane."

"And an hour ago, you were hightailing your way out of here. So, I guess the real question is . . . are you going to stay?"

———— • • ————

Charlie sighed. She could tell Hunter she wanted to go home. And after all that had happened, especially how Jake had treated her, she knew he would do the gentlemanly thing and concede. But deep down, she wanted to stay. She wanted her date—dinner and a movie. She wanted to spend time with him and pretend she was normal, even if it was just for a few days. She wanted to believe Hunter found her attractive, and that they had real chemistry. She didn't want to think about his celebrity status or if his family liked her or not, or about Daniel. She just wanted to live in the moment.

"How about we set some ground rules?"

He crossed his arms, an intrigued smile on his face. "I'm listening."

"You're not Hunter Jennings, superstar, and I'm not Charlie Foster, woman in hiding."

"We're not?"

"Nope. We're just Hunter and Charlie. You're not trying to save me from myself, and I'm not going to tell you why this won't work out. We are just two people spending time together. No prying questions about the past or strategies about how we will handle the future. We'll just enjoy our time together and worry about life on Thursday."

Hunter walked over to where she sat on the barstool. He stood as close to her as he could get and looked at her with overconfident eyes. "I have only one addendum to that."

"And what would that be?"

"I'm not losing the ground I've already made."

"What does that mean?" she said, feeling intoxicated by his closeness.

He slipped his hand up and cupped the left side of her face. "I would never do this with a woman I just met." He bent down and gently pressed his lips against hers.

Her head spun while her pulse raced. She leaned back, breaking the connection between them. "Okay . . ." she cleared her throat, hoping it would help her clear her mind as well. "Now that you . . . I mean we have established the ground rules, what do we do next?" she asked.

NO SECRETS NO LIES

He stepped back, his cheeks slightly blushed. "We have all afternoon. You name it. We could go for a ride or we could—"

"Oh no. We already agreed. No more motorcycles." All she had to do was look at the bulge of gauze on his shoulder to know that was the last thing she wanted to do.

"I meant horseback. We could tour the west side of the property. I'll even take you to see the original homestead from the 1800s."

"Are you sure you feel up to it? You're still limping."

"That's why I'm going to let the horse do the walking," he teased.

"And your shoulder?"

"Believe me, I've ridden with worse injuries than these."

She smiled, knowing there was no place she would rather be than in the saddle. "I'd like that, if you're sure you're up to it."

"Then it's settled." He reached out and slipped his hand around her elbow, so he could help her down from the barstool. "Go change your clothes and prepare to be amazed."

Chapter Thirty-Six

Hunter stood by the front door waiting for Charlie. As she walked toward him, he couldn't help but stare.

Man! She's gorgeous.

There was just something about her. She was petite and had the greatest little shape, but she walked with such confidence, defying anyone to think she was weak. He was sure it was a protection mechanism, her way of making sure people didn't mess with her. But her eyes told the rest of the story. They were the richest shade of brown . . . but held such pain.

She was afraid to trust.

Afraid to open up.

Afraid to let go.

It pained him to think about the life she had led, but he quickly shook off the negative. They had just a few days together, today being nothing less than disastrous. The only good thing that had happened so far was her willingness to put it all behind them and try to enjoy what time they had left.

"Ready?" he asked.

Putting on a ratty cowboy hat, she smiled. "Ready."

He playfully tugged at the splintered straw on the crown of her hat. "Looks like this is on its last leg."

"No it's not. It's broken in just right."

He chuckled. "If you say so."

———— • ————

They had been riding for little over an hour when Hunter

suggested they rest the horses and let them drink from a nearby stream. He pulled two water bottles from his saddle bag and handed her one. "It's not too cold, but it's wet."

"It will do," she said as she unscrewed the top and carefully took a sip.

"So, what do you think of Lois Lane?" he asked, after taking a long swig.

"Besides her name?"

"Hey, I didn't name her. She and Superman were already named when I bought them, and I wasn't about to pass up two incredible specimens just because someone got cute in the naming process."

Charlie patted the mare's withers. "She's beautiful and has a smooth gait."

"And she has power. Don't let her fool you. She can sense you're a seasoned rider, so she hasn't given you any grief. If you weren't, she would've thrown you by now."

"Really?" She looked at the beautiful brood mare finding it hard to believe.

"Really. Just ask Diana," he said with a grin.

"No!"

"Yep. First time she rode her. Diana and Jake decided to take Superman and Lois out for a ride, for a little one-on-one time. Now, the owners warned us Lois could be quite spirited, but Jake failed to pass that bit of information on to his wife. Diana had been around horses all her life, but since having the kids, she had pretty much stopped riding. She cantered Lois around the rink a few times without any problems, but when she came to a halt and carelessly slacked the reins, Lois sent her over her shoulder and right onto her butt."

"Oh no," Charlie gasped. "Was she all right?"

Hunter chuckled. "Yeah. Let's just say her pride wasn't the only thing bruised."

Charlie laughed but only for an instant before bringing her hand to her cheek and whimpering. "Well, she's a beautiful horse. And though no horse could ever top

Goliath, she's still a wonderful mount."

After a few minutes, they saddled up to resume their ride. Silently, she took in the amazing landscape, loving the fact that they were riding on open land, not a trail, or a path, just undeveloped property for as far as the eye could see.

"It's just a little further to the homestead," Hunter said as they rode slowly, side by side.

With the heat of the day intensifying, Charlie removed her hat and pulled her hair into a ponytail. After putting her hat back on, she looked over at Hunter and caught him staring.

"What?" she asked.

"I didn't say anything."

"But you have a look on your face, like you're thinking something."

He grinned. "Just enjoying the view."

She scanned their surroundings. "It's beautiful."

"Oh yeah, the property is great too."

She shook her head and tried not to smile. "Aren't you the smooth-talking cowboy."

"No, ma'am. Just speaking the truth."

"Oh my gosh." She rolled her eyes. "Do those lines really work on other women?"

He sat up straighter. "I don't know what you're talking about."

She couldn't help but laugh, even though it was painful. His playfulness was charming. Fun. Different from anything she'd experienced before.

"Well, there it is."

She looked where Hunter was pointing, amazed by what she saw.

After tethering the horses to a hitching post, she quietly approached the small, moss-covered log cabin, afraid she would disturb something sacred if she hurried her steps. Awed by the glass pane windows and the sturdy front door, she loved how it was nestled in a grove of oak trees, shading it from the Texas sun. Pulling down on the old metal chain, she listened as the latch on the inside released. The door slowly opened, its old hinges squeaking in protest. Charlie was struck by how cool it was inside. And the musty smell that enveloped her wasn't an assault to her senses but welcomed . . . like she was inhaling history.

Everything about the homestead was still in place. A log-framed bed draped in a hand-stitched quilt sat opposite a large cook stove. A table with two chairs hugged the front window, and a beautifully carved rocking chair was nestled in the far corner.

It looked as if time had stood still.

"Hunter, I don't know what to say." She touched the tabletop and allowed her fingers to skim the back of one of the chairs. Glancing up on the wall, she saw three extremely weathered wood crosses hanging next to each other. "It feels like the owners just stepped out and will be back any minute, wondering why we're in their home."

"I know. It's pretty incredible, isn't it?"

"Was it like this when you bought the place?"

"Yes and no. The stove and furniture were here, except for the rocking chair. They just weren't in this good of condition. The windows were all broken out, and the door hinges were barely holding on by a thread."

"So, you did all this?"

"Jake and I did."

"Why? I mean, it's wonderful," she said as she turned her back to him and examined the stove top. "But what made you want to restore it instead of tearing it down?"

"It's . . . special."

Charlie heard something in his voice. Like there was more to the story. She turned and saw him looking out the window, longingly.

"Does anyone use it?"

"I do."

"You?"

"Yeah. When I want to be alone," he said as he walked to the rocking chair and sat down. "Now, don't get me wrong, I love my family. My mother is amazing, and I have a great time with Cody and Courtney, even Jake when he isn't being a pain in my side. But sometimes, I just need to be alone. No phones, no interruptions, no noise from a TV, nothing but silence." He rocked with a smile on his face. "This is where I do most of my writing."

She didn't know what to say. This was a side of Hunter she never even imagined.

Nostalgic.

She studied him as he rocked in the chair, elbows on the arms, hands clasped, eyes closed. He didn't need an alluring smile or a fitted shirt and jeans to look sexy. Right now, in the middle of this old log cabin he looked sexier than ever.

"What are you thinking?" he asked, opening his eyes.

She smiled. "Just enjoying the surroundings."

———— • ————

The ride home was faster, more direct. Superman and Lois knew the way and needed little encouragement to get them there. He warned Charlie that Lois liked to jump, so if she saw an impediment in her way, she would likely choose to go over it instead of around it. Through it all, Charlie kept her seat like a pro. She was a true equestrian.

They had a pseudo-race back to the stables. Charlie won, but only because he was too distracted watching her ride. While he admired the way she looked in the saddle, she pulled away, leaving him in the dust. He tried to catch up to her the last fifty yards, but it was no use.

All four of them were panting heavily by the time he and Charlie dismounted alongside the practice rink.

"That was incredible," she said between short labored breaths.

"Man, I can't remember the last time I rode like that," he said, flipping the reins over Superman's ears.

"Hi, Boss."

Hunter turned around. "Hey, Evan. How you doin'?"

"Good." Evan gave a sideways glance to Charlie, then back

to him. "And yourself?"

He smiled when Evan arched his brow. He was a good kid, in his early twenties and an excellent horseman. "Evan, this is my friend, Charlie. Charlie, this is Evan. He's a big help around here."

She took a step forward to shake his hand. Hunter didn't miss the way she turned her right cheek from view.

"Pleasure to meet you, ma'am."

"You too, Evan."

"Did Lois treat you right?"

"She did. She's an amazing animal." Charlie stroked the mare.

Evan looked at Hunter. "Lois behaved herself? That's a first."

"She had a seasoned rider on her back," Hunter explained. "She might be cagey, but she's smart."

"Here, I'll take care of them for you." Evan reached for both sets of reins. "It was nice meeting you, ma'am."

"You too."

Evan walked away, Superman and Lois on either side of him.

Hunter walked beside Charlie, sliding his hand into hers as they headed to the UTV. "How is the cheek feeling?"

She raised her other hand to it and worked her jaw from side to side. "It's not too bad."

"Good. After we get cleaned up, I'll fix you dinner."

"You're going to cook?"

"I just said that, didn't I?" He put his hand on the small of her back as she got into the vehicle."

"I thought you said your mom did the cooking?" Charlie asked as she watched him walk around and climb in the driver's side.

"No. I said my mom does *most* of the cooking, and only because she wants to. I am more than capable in the kitchen when I want to be."

"Then by all means, dazzle me with your talents."

"Oh . . . believe me . . . I plan on it."

Chapter Thirty-Seven

After taking a quick shower, Charlie slipped back into the T-shirt and yoga pants she'd had on earlier, then stared at her reflection in the bathroom mirror. Her cheek was swollen, and the sun she had gotten on their ride had added a nice red glow to the already blue and purple bruise. She leaned in closer and grimaced.

"I look like a rainbow-colored chipmunk."

Feeling discouraged and definitely less attractive, she thought about changing her shirt to something a little nicer but decided it really wouldn't matter what she wore. Nothing would draw attention away from her puffy, multi-colored cheek.

She walked into the kitchen where Hunter was already hard at work. He had steaks on the massive indoor grill, along with corn on the cob. He stopped mid-stride to the refrigerator when he saw her standing there.

Watching as his eyes traveled from her head to her toes and back up again, he smiled, her knees almost turning to Jell-O.

"You sure clean up nice."

"Yeah. And if purple and blue weren't enough, my cheek now has red highlights."

"You look great," he said. "It's going to take more than a little bruise to detract from your natural beauty."

"Oh, brother. You must have been working on that line all afternoon." She quickly brushed aside the compliment and took her place on one of the barstools so she could observe.

Watching Hunter as he worked on dinner, she had to admit

she was impressed. Though she had teased him about his cooking skills, he definitely knew his way around the kitchen. She watched as he seasoned the steaks and rolled the corncobs on the grill. Normally, she loved corn on the cob, but with her jaw bruised and swollen she wasn't sure she'd be able to tackle it.

I'll just have to cross that bridge when I get there.

Hunter mixed a salad of fresh greens and spinach. After crumbling feta cheese on it, he tossed in some candied walnuts and dried cherries.

"Fancy," she teased. "I guess you do know a little something about cooking."

He returned to the grill and rolled the corncobs. "I can handle a meal or two," he said as he flipped the steaks.

She found herself watching him intently. Not his culinary skills, just him.

He was too good to be true.

This was too good to be true.

When she left Daniel, she knew she would be on her own forever. She would never allow another man to get too close to her, because caring for someone would only put them in danger. But here she was, with a man who sent her heart racing, among other things she wasn't willing to admit, even to herself.

Her eyes traveled from his broad shoulders to his muscular back, and to the way his jeans fit him so well. But it wasn't Hunter's incredibly good looks or feisty charm that made him so sexy. It was something else . . . something she had a hard time putting her finger on.

Maybe it was the way he made her feel safe, or the way he made her believe that this thing between them could work. She wasn't sure, but she did know this: She was falling for him like a ton of bricks and breaking every rule she had lived by for the last two years. And she seemed powerless to do anything about it.

And that was what scared her the most.

"Charlie?"

She jumped.

"You okay?" he asked, looking a little concerned.

"Yeah . . . sure . . . I guess I just kind of zoned out for a minute. What did you say?"

"Where would you like to eat?"

"I don't know. How about you?"

"Outside should be nice."

"That sounds great."

"Then here." He handed her a towel. "Why don't you go ahead and wipe down the table outside while I get everything served up."

She took the towel and walked outside, thankful for the chance to regroup. Closing her eyes, she slowed her breathing, and tried to shake the tingling sensation squeezing her heart.

The patio area was shaded, but the warm breeze still danced across her sun-kissed skin. She wiped down the table as she stared at the pool with its azure water sparkling in the sun. It looked so crisp and refreshing.

Maybe if I jump in it, the shock of the cold water will knock some sense into me. She laughed to herself. *Oh, sure . . . and then I'll just explain to Hunter that I jumped into the pool—fully clothed—because I'm falling for him and was hoping the shock from the water would give me some clarity.*

Luckily, when she walked into the kitchen, Hunter had his back to her and was working on something on the far counter. He glanced over his shoulder. "Why don't you pour us something to drink. I'll take cranberry juice. Glasses are in that cupboard." He nodded to the right.

After icing both glasses, she filled them with juice, and carried them outside to the table. When she returned, Hunter was still working on something on the far counter.

"There are placemats and napkins in the drawer by the toaster and silverware to the right of the sink," he said without turning around.

"Okay," she walked up alongside him, "but what are you working on over here?"

"I'm cutting the corn off the cob. There's no way you're

going to be able to eat it straight from the cob, but I didn't have any frozen. Besides, it always tastes better grilled."

She smiled at his thoughtfulness. "Thanks. I was wondering how I was going to pull that off without hurting your feelings. It's not like I could hide the cob under my napkin like a piece of broccoli."

He laughed.

Reaching for the salad bowl, the butter dish, and the raspberry vinaigrette, She carried everything outside and placed them on the table. When she walked back into the house, Hunter had both plates in his hands and was walking toward her. "Anything else?"

"No. I think that covers it."

"Do you need steak sauce, ketchup, or a steak knife?" she asked as she followed him back outside.

"Bite your tongue," he gasped, acting appalled, as if she had committed a cardinal sin. "These fillets are so tender you'll be able to cut them with a butter knife, and their flavor needs no doctoring."

"Oh, well, pardon me." She pressed her hand to her chest with exaggerated flair. "Please send my apologies to the chef."

"Yeah, well, I'll forgive you this once, but don't let it happen again."

Chapter Thirty-Eight

The first several minutes of dinner were silent and awkward. Hunter seemed to be enjoying his meal, while she took small bites and chewed slowly. But it wasn't her swollen jaw or the discomfort she felt when she opened her mouth that occupied her thoughts, it was Hunter and the way he sent her emotions into overdrive.

She glanced at him over the top of her glass as she sipped her juice. He looked so good. He was rugged and sexy, yet tender and compassionate. He had the muscular physique of an athlete, his build exuding real strength, but when he held her, his touch was soft and sensitive. To say he was every woman's dream was such a cliché. But that didn't make it any less true.

"How's your steak?"

"It's good. Just like you said, it melts in your mouth."

"And your salad?"

"Everything tastes wonderful." She looked at him and smiled. "Just wonderful."

"Are you sure? Because it looks like you're just pushing things around on your plate."

"No, really, everything tastes great. I just haven't had much of an appetite lately. Added to the heat, my jaw, and the leftover jitters from flying, I'm really not that hungry. Besides, we just had yogurt a few hours ago."

"So, it isn't my cooking?"

"No. Not at all." She smiled as she slipped a piece of steak into her mouth, just to prove her point.

They ate in quiet.

But it was an awkward quiet.

And the look on Hunter's face was perplexing.

She needed to say something before the conversation turned too serious.

"It's not as hot as I thought it would be. I mean, I just always thought Texas temperatures were well into the 100s." *The weather? Really?* But that's all she could think of to break the silence.

Hunter swallowed the bite in his mouth and took a swig of juice. "Only record days hit the 100s. It's the humidity that makes it feel hotter. It's not much different than Tennessee."

She nodded as she played with the kernels of corn on her plate, her appetite a thing of the past.

She used to be a big eater, thinking nothing of devouring a double cheeseburger and a basket of fries on her dinner break. Now, a couple of chicken tenders and a handful of fries were all she could handle.

Initially, she chalked up her diminished appetite to a weakened immune system. She'd had a pretty nasty case of the flu in January, and a couple of smaller bouts with it since then. At first, she saw no reason to be concerned or to complain, especially since she'd been able to lose the extra weight she put on since working at the diner. But in the last several weeks, a nagging pain had developed in her stomach. It wasn't constant, and it didn't flare up every time she ate, but it was getting harder to ignore.

That's all I need, to get sick while I'm here. Maybe the punch in the mouth was for the better.

Looking up, she noticed Hunter staring at her, a question perched on his lips. She wasn't about to share what she was thinking, so she blurted out the first thing that came to mind. "So, tell me about life on the road?"

His fork stopped midair. "Where did that come from?"

"Well, it was either that or more stimulating conversation about the weather."

He chuckled and proceeded to eat the piece of steak on his fork. After washing it down with some juice, he wiped his mouth and leaned back in his chair. "What do you want to know?"

"What do you like best about being out on the road?"

He stared at the overhead beams of the pergola while stroking his chin. "Of late . . . I would say watching the way the new bands connect with the audience."

"Really?"

"Yeah. It can be rough for an opening act. The crowd is there to see the headliner, and if you don't pull them into your music in the first few minutes, the audience can get pretty restless. So I love watching from the wings, seeing how the crowd responds."

"Who are your openers?"

"Arkansas Rain and The Winchesters."

"The Winchesters, they're pretty new, aren't they?"

"Yeah. They started getting radio play late last year. We picked them up for the second leg of the tour."

"A brother-sister act, right?"

"Yeah. A trio. Two brothers and a sister. And they're all incredibly talented. Between the three of them, they can play any instrument imaginable."

"That should keep costs down, not having to hire a back-up band."

"You would think so," Hunter said, taking another swig of juice. "But the two brothers are heartthrob material, so Rob doesn't want them hiding behind drums and a keyboard. He wants them out front where the girls can see them. So, they have a decent size band backing them up while they play bass and electric guitar out front. And Carrie plays acoustic guitar and banjo."

"So, are they holding the crowd's interest?"

"Oh yeah. They aren't going to be featured artists for long. Mark my words, by this time next year, they will be co-headliners."

"Is that what Arkansas Rain is, a co-headliner? Because

they have been around for a while, right?"

"Yeah. They are definitely more than just an opening act, but they kind of hit a rough patch a few years ago. They lost their lead singer, had some substance abuse problems, and an album that went nowhere. But once they got going in the right direction again, Rob decided a tour would be the boost they needed to put them back on top, so we teamed up."

"And is it working? For them, I mean?"

His expression changed as he shook his head. "For now, but it isn't going to last long. Too many egos and addictions. They're going to self-destruct, it's just a matter of time."

"And what about you? Where do you see yourself going?"

"Three more years and I'm out. Maybe sooner." His response was quick, like it was well rehearsed.

"You sound pretty sure about that."

"Like I told you, I have three contractual commitments left to fulfill. But when my contract is up, I'm done."

"You don't think you'll miss it?"

"Nope."

"So that's it? You're just going to hang it all up? The world will never hear from Hunter Jennings again?"

"No, they'll hear from me, but it will be the real me. Not the rebel rousing, party-all-night, live like the devil persona Rob has created."

She wanted to ask him why he pretended to be something he wasn't but didn't want to say anything that would ruin the mood. They were talking like real people, getting to know each other like a real date. It felt so right she didn't want to do anything to spoil it.

"What are you thinking?" he asked, as he scooted his plate out of the way and rested his elbows on the table.

"Nothing."

"Yes you are. I can see the wheels turning."

She twisted the napkin in her lap. "It's nothing, really."

"Come on, Charlie, what were you thinking?"

She took another sip of juice and gazed out over the pool, sensing Hunter's eyes on her. She knew he was waiting for her to say something, but she didn't want to rock the boat.

When the silence got to be too much, she blurted out, "I just don't understand why you let people think you're something that you're not. When the real you is so much more than the person who takes the stage."

Stretching back in his chair, he sighed. "Because, that's who I was when I started out in this business." He looked at her with regret. "I struggled in beer shacks and roadside bars for years, and then all of a sudden, I'm topping the charts. I'm not going to sugarcoat it. Success went straight to my head; I was out of control. I had money, fame, and beautiful women coming on to me. I thought I had it all. Jake and I were living the high life, but when he met Diana things changed. Pretty soon Jake was bowing out of after parties and flying to Alabama to see Diana every chance he got. When he told me he was done with the partying, I thought he was crazy to give up all we had for just one woman. I told him he could do his own thing but not to infringe on my good time."

He sighed, his look introspective.

"But things started to change when I realized what Jake had was the real deal . . . something lasting. And all I had each morning was an empty bed and a headache that took most of the day to get rid of it. After every show, after every one-night stand or drunken stupor, I felt as empty as I had when I was dirt poor, digging ditches, roping cattle, and playing roadside bars for tips. The only difference was when I woke up the next morning, I felt a little less like a man and a lot more like an opportunist. I took advantage of a lot of women back then. I was a complete jackass."

Charlie didn't know what to say. She knew Hunter had been a partier. The tabloids were full of his antics. But she didn't expect him to be so transparent. She stabbed at her salad and pushed a dried cherry around on her plate. She could feel Hunter staring at her, but she didn't know what to say.

"Surprised?" he asked.

She just shrugged, feeling embarrassed she had asked.

"Too blunt?"

"No," she answered quickly. "Not at all. I appreciate your honesty."

"It's not honesty, Charlie. It's me coming to grips with the mistakes I've made. I'm not proud of what I've done, but I'm not going to pretend it didn't happen either. I was a screw-up through and through. I hurt people and let others down. Worst of all, I've disappointed and embarrassed my family."

He hung his head.

She could almost see the weight of degradation on his shoulders. *Great job, Charlie. You've succeeded in ruining dinner.* She set her fork down and played with her napkin once again. "I'm sorry, Hunter. I didn't mean to ruin—"

"Hey, hey," he sat up straighter and took a deep breath, "you didn't ruin anything. I'm done with that life. Hunter Jennings might still croon about honky-tonks, beer, and women, but Aaron Jennings knows what's important. What's real. Now I know what I want out of life, and it isn't in a bottle or a one-night stand."

She sat silently, not knowing what to say.

"So, enough about me." He looked across the table at her plate. "Are you done or are you going to keep rolling that cherry around on your plate?"

She looked up ready to argue when she was met with one of his killer smiles.

"What do you say we take a walk?" He stood, laid his napkin on the table, and picked up his plate. "I can walk off my dinner, and you can walk off your salad."

"Hey, I ate more than just salad. In fact, the corn was great. But to answer your question, a walk sounds great."

181

Chapter Thirty-Nine

Walking Hunter's property felt like the most natural thing in the world. Their pace was leisurely because of Hunter's sore hip and her tweaked ankle, but their conversation skills improved immensely. They covered a gamut of subjects, from the music industry to livestock, to Texas history, even the stock market. They laughed and teased and bantered, but even when there were long moments of silence, it felt good.

More than good, it felt right.

As they headed back to the house, the sinking sun streaked the sky with hues of burnt orange and blazing gold. The rolling hills were mere shadows, and the brush swayed in the light breeze. Hunter reached for her hand and slipped his fingers between hers. She looked at their joined hands, then up at him.

"Do you mind?" he asked, a low, sultry timbre in his voice.

"No."

He smiled. "Good. I want to show you something."

They walked hand in hand as Hunter led her up a craggy knoll. It wasn't that steep, but they took it slow because of the uneven surface and the fading light. The last step was easy for Hunter's large stride, but a little more difficult for her to maneuver.

"I gotcha. Just step there." He pointed to a crevice with a flat surface. "I'll pull you up."

Charlie did what he said, and in one quick tug, she was not only on top of the knoll but firmly in Hunter's embrace. She rested her hands against his biceps and grinned. "That was a pretty fancy move, cowboy. Looks like you've had a lot of practice."

He laughed. "Nope."

"So . . . I'm supposed to believe you've never shared a sunset with another woman here?"

"No ma'am."

"Are you sure?" She looked up at him. "It has all the elements for the perfect make-out spot. Sunset. Tranquil breeze. Beautiful surroundings."

"Really?" He pulled her closer. "Then I guess we should test your theory."

Slowly, Hunter captured her lips with his. His kiss was tentative, gentlemanly, and patient. Charlie felt her resistance fade away. She feared commitment, she feared having a relationship. But she wasn't afraid of Hunter. She decided to take a chance, even if it was only for a few days. Wrapping her arms around his neck, she returned his kiss, a kiss that told him exactly how she felt.

Her pulse was swooshing in her ears, her limbs weak and tingling. She was sure Hunter could feel her heart beating through her shirt.

Even after he pulled away—breaking the intensity of their embrace—she was breathless, little stars dancing in front of her eyes.

Hunter looked down at her with a smirk and bent close to her ear. "I guess you were right," he whispered, his voice husky with emotion.

"Right?" She didn't even remember what she had said. "Right about what?"

He pulled her close, crushing her against his chest. "It is the perfect make-out spot."

After proving her theory again, they worked their way back to the house. But the minute she walked into the well-lit entryway, she felt self-conscious. The kisses they had exchanged on the knoll were under the cover of dusk. The atmosphere romantic, their actions bold and passionate. But now, she felt awkward, wondering what Hunter was thinking.

I've put him off for so long and then bam, I'm all over him.
Nervously, she tucked her hands into her front pockets. *Well, he certainly didn't seem to mind.*

Hunter leaned over her shoulder and pressed a kiss to the nape of her neck. "There's no reason to be embarrassed, Charlie. We are adults."

She spun around. "Embarrassed? That's ridiculous! Who said anything about being embarrassed?"

He laughed as he headed toward the kitchen. "You're blushing."

"I am not!" She hurried behind him. "I . . . I just got too much sun."

He chuckled, glancing her way. "You didn't get *that* much sun." He grabbed a bottle of water from the refrigerator and offered it to her.

"No thank you. But you go ahead. You could use some cooling off."

"Oh really?" He uncapped the water, took a long swig, then stared at her with a knee-melting smile. "Are you saying I'm too hot to handle?"

"Oh . . . I see how it is." She stood, hands on her hips. "You finally wear me down and now you're going to go all egomaniac on me."

He stepped alongside her, slipped his arm around her waist, and pulled her close. "Don't worry, sweetheart, if anyone can handle me, I'm confident you can."

"Are you kidding me?" She pressed her hands to his chest, trying to push away, but he only held her tighter.

"Come on, Charlie," he laughed while she squirmed. "I'm only teasing you."

"Teasing me?" She looked at him, her hands still resting on his chest. "What part? The part about me being embarrassed because you kissed me, or you letting your enormous ego show its ugly face?"

"Well, correct me if I'm wrong, sweetheart, but I wasn't the only one doing the kissing."

She felt her complexion flame again as Hunter gently framed her face with his large, calloused hands, and ran his thumb across her moistened lips. She raised her hands to his forearms, intending to push him away. But the electricity ignited by his gentle stroking was stronger than her irritation. Leaning into his touch, Charlie felt her objectivity wane. But when she looked up into Hunter's eyes, she was terrified by what she saw.

"I love you, Charlie," he whispered as he lowered his lips to hers.

She turned her head sharply before their lips touched. "Don't say that." She pushed away from him and walked briskly into the living room. Standing in front of the large sliding glass doors, she crossed her arms against her chest to keep her heart from exploding.

"Why not?" Hunter's voice was elevated, and she could tell by his heavy footfalls on the wooden floor he was agitated.

"It's just not right," she bristled. "We have only known each other a couple months, and in that time, we've spent less than twenty-four hours together. You're confusing lust for love. Let's just take it—"

"Don't you dare!" Tugging on her arm, Hunter turned her around, and glared. "Don't you dare tell me how I feel or reduce the way I feel about you to nothing more than sexual urges."

He looked at her, not allowing her to break his stare. "You're right. We haven't known each other long, or spent a lot of time together, but I know how I feel. If you're not ready for that, fine. But don't insult what we have by cheapening it to nothing more than sexual attraction."

"Okay, then tell me this," she said, her eyes riveted on his. "If it isn't sexual, what is it? It can't be because we have so much in common because we don't even know if we like the same foods, the same music, or if we even share the same faith, or politics. So, what is it about me that makes you so sure it's love?"

"That!" he said, pointing to her crossed arms and defiant stance. "That hellcat, I-don't-take-no-crap attitude."

She quickly uncrossed her arms and let them drop to her sides.

"The fact that my celebrity status means absolutely nothing to you. And that you're more at home boot deep in manure than letting a guy wine and dine you just to get what you think you deserve out of life."

"So, you're saying you're in love with me because I argue with you, I don't take any of your crap, I'm not impressed with your money, and I can shovel horse manure? Nothing else?"

"That," he stepped closer, "and the way your doe-eyes are windows to your soul." He brushed a strand of hair away from where it rested on her lashes. "Eyes that show me you're not as closed off as you want everyone to think." She looked down, but he caught her chin with the crook of his finger and raised it up, so she had to look at him. "I can also see how tired you are of looking over your shoulder and pushing others away."

"And what if I told you the only reason I came here was because I was looking for a physical, no-strings-attached relationship? The proverbial roll in the hay, no commitment weekend."

"I would say you're lying through your teeth, because if that was all you wanted out of this, it probably would've already happened."

"Ahh!" She pointed her finger at him with a smirk. "But you said this had nothing to do with sex?"

"No, I said my attraction to you was more than sexual." He gently rested his hands on her hips. "Come on, Charlie, don't keep trying to find reasons to sabotage our time together."

She wanted to argue with him but couldn't. He was right. She was trying to find any reason she could to put distance between them. "I'm sorry." She looked up at him. "I guess I overreacted. I'm just so used to keeping people at arm's length."

He pulled her close, pressed a kiss to the top of her head, and rocked her slowly. "It's okay. Just forget it even happened. Besides, we have a movie to pick out."

With Hunter's arm still wrapped snuggly around her waist, they walked to the media room. Charlie closed her eyes and took a silent breath, her thoughts a jumbled mess. She was falling so hard for Hunter; she didn't know if she would have the emotional strength at the end of the weekend to tell him goodbye. Subconsciously, she knew that was why she kept picking fights. She wanted him to get angry enough to throw in the towel, but it wasn't happening.

She thought she could do this. Indulge him for a few days, let him figure out for himself this wasn't going to work. But she was only fooling herself. Her feelings ran so much deeper than that. And now, with Hunter thinking he was in love with her, she was in major trouble and felt powerless to do anything about it.

He led her to the media room, and to the shelf of DVDs behind the bar. "So, what will it be? Comedy? Action? Horror? Or maybe something more on the Rom-com side?" He grinned.

Just enjoy the moment. Don't overthink it. Curl up with him. Take one day at a time. You'll know what to do when the time comes.

And that was two days away.

She cleared her thoughts and looked at the shelves of movies, noticing they were all in alphabetical order, that is, all except the ones starring Sandra Bullock. Her movies had a shelf of its own. "Someone has a crush on Ms. Bullock," she teased, trying to lighten the mood.

"Guilty," Hunter said, not the least bit apologetic.

"Then let's watch one of hers."

"Okay, you pick."

Charlie fingered the slim boxes as she read each title. "This one," she said as she handed him *Hope Floats*.

She remembered the first time she saw the movie. She

was twelve when her mother had blown into town. She'd been there a week and had promised her a girl's night out. So, they went to the mall, got their nails done, and her mom even bought her a new dress and shoes. After going home and getting all dolled up, they went to the neighborhood steak house and ended the night at the dollar movie theater.

Hope Floats was playing.

They had popcorn, Milk Duds, and a huge soda between them. Her mom went on and on about how she wished some cowboy would come along and sweep her off her feet. But all Charlie thought about was the little boy who dressed up like a frog. She felt sorry for him because his mother had run out on him, just like her mother had done to her.

She handed the case to Hunter.

"This is one of my favorites," he said as he pulled out the DVD and put it in the player. "Have you seen it?"

"Um-hum. A long time ago."

Hunter flipped a button causing the popcorn machine to light up. He filled the popcorn and butter dispensers, then opened another drawer filled with candy.

"Name your poison."

She looked at her array of choices. There was everything imaginable, even her favorite Pay Day bar. But she took the Milk Duds instead. It was the only real choice with movie house popcorn.

She continued to peruse the movie titles while the popcorn popped, and Hunter fiddled with the DVD player. When everything was ready, he passed her a glass bottle of Coke and led her to the loveseat. With arms loaded down with the popcorn bowl, king-size candy cartons, and soda, he sank into the luxurious leather upholstery and she took a seat beside him. Passing her the popcorn bowl, he flipped up the armrest on the loveseat and pulled out a remote from a hidden compartment. As the DVD cued up, the lights dimmed, just like a real movie theater would do.

Hunter slid his arm around the back of the couch allowing his hand to rest on her shoulder.

It felt good.

Authentic.

Like a real date should.

It was the only real thing she had felt in an incredibly long time.

Chapter Forty

Though Charlie watched the movie, her thoughts were elsewhere. All the highs and lows of the day vied for her attention. A panic attack, a motorcycle crash, a run-in with Hunter's brother, and a swollen cheek—definite lows.

An afternoon ride, kisses at sunset, and Hunter saying he loved her—unthinkable highs.

And it all happened in less than a twenty-four-hour period. Now she sat next to Hunter, like a normal couple, on a normal date.

But how could that be? He wasn't just a good-looking guy she had met at the diner or the feed store; he was Hunter Jennings.

Celebrity-status, media-following, paparazzi-fodder Hunter Jennings.

If he wasn't famous, if he was just an average Joe, maybe this could work. Maybe she could take a chance on love again. However, as much as she wanted to ignore the circumstances, they were right there in front of her, her conscience choosing to remind her at every turn.

Daniel had constantly reminded her she was his. His possession to do with what he wanted. He had told her over and over again she would never have a life apart from him. And even though she had escaped, left that life behind, his threats still rang true. She hated him. She hated him for what he'd done to her. But she hated him even more for what he was doing to her now—the hold he continued to have on her.

Something had to change.

She could not continue to live in fear.

Not anymore.

She felt a surge of confidence build inside her.

This is where it stops.

She would not allow Daniel to control her any longer. Hunter knew what they were up against and had told her it didn't matter, that he loved her and would help her. And even though she was scared to death, even though she knew what Daniel was capable of, she wanted to try.

She *had* to try.

It was time she took Hunter at his word. Otherwise, she would never have a life worth living.

"Earth to Charlie." Hunter gave her shoulder a squeeze.

"I'm sorry. What did you say?" She turned to him, realizing she had daydreamed through most of the movie.

"I was teasing you for studying the closing credits so intently. But I guess you had something else on your mind." He reached out and gave her hand a squeeze, his expression immediately changing from playful to serious. "You okay?"

She smiled at him, ready to take charge of her life. "Yeah. I think I am."

He studied her but didn't say anything, he just smiled. "Then how about a double feature?"

"I'd like that. A lot."

As Charlie watched the credits scroll on the second movie, Hunter pulled her closer. "This was great."

She looked up at him. "No . . . this was perfect."

"I wish we could stay like this all night," he sighed as he stroked her arm.

"Maybe we can," she said softly.

He slid to the edge of the couch cushion and turned to look her in the eyes. "What are you saying?"

"Well . . ." She stood and started to pace, feeling as skittish as a new foal. "I don't know what it will look like—you and me—and I know it's not going to be easy, but I want to try."

She sat back down next to him. "I care for you, Hunter. I care for you a lot, and I'm ready to see where this takes—"

Before she could even finish her declaration, he pulled her close, and pressed his lips to hers. His kiss was slow and intimate but soon turned to searching and consuming. Wanting to feel more of him, Charlie wrapped her arms around his neck and pressed against his chest. In one easy motion, Hunter lifted her into his lap, making their connection even stronger. A jolt of electricity coursed through her body like nothing she had ever experienced before. She deepened her kiss, ignoring the pain in her jaw, and felt Hunter respond like a thirsty man desperate for water.

Explosions of heat warmed her flesh from head to toe, and Charlie knew, at that moment, she wanted Hunter more than she had ever wanted anything in her life. Right up until the second when he slid her off his lap and got to his feet.

She was shocked, confused, and when she saw the look of discomposure on his face, she felt embarrassed. Immediately, the warm sensation heating her from the inside out turned to ice.

She'd been willing to give herself to Hunter.

Completely.

Only to be rejected.

"Charlie, I'm sorry." He shoved his hands in his pockets and paced in front of the movie screen.

"I don't understand. I thought this is what you wanted? Us. Together."

"I do, but not like that."

Hurt and anger catapulted her to her feet. "So, you're saying you don't want to sleep with me? Even though you just told me you love me?"

"I'm saying," he pulled her close, "if we're going to do this, I want to do it right."

She tried to step back, but he tightened his hold. "Charlie, look at me."

She steeled herself to see the perplexity in his eyes that had been there just seconds before, only to see eyes lit with passion.

"We're both adults, Charlie, so I'm not going to beat around the bush. I'd like nothing more than to wake up each morning with you by my side. But we can't. It wouldn't be right."

"Even though you've done it dozens of times with other women?" She didn't mean to sound combative, but at the moment, she was hurt and confused. She had just put herself out on the farthest limb only for Hunter to snap it off.

"No. That's not true."

"Don't lie to me, Hunter," she pushed away from him, this time breaking his hold. "You told me yourself you—"

"No!" he shouted. "What I had with those women was sex. It had nothing to do with love. And I'm not saying what I did was right, but in my alcohol-numbed days I justified my actions by convincing myself the women who followed me back to my tour bus or my hotel room knew exactly what they were doing. They wanted to sleep with a superstar. So, I gave them what they wanted, and I refused to feel guilty. But that was a lifetime ago, Charlie. I'm not the same person anymore."

"So, you never even considered sleeping with me this weekend?"

He hung his head, looking embarrassed. "Thought about it, yes. Considered it, no."

He reached out for her hand and tugged her close. "I'm not a choirboy by any stretch of the imagination, but what we have is special, something I've never felt before. And I don't want to do anything to screw it up."

"But—"

"Uh-uh," he interrupted. "I'm not blind, either. I know we have some major obstacles to overcome, but we can do it. I know we can." He pulled her closer still. "Come on, Charlie, I want to spend tomorrow, and the next day, and the day after that with you." He looked into her eyes, his lips a breath away from hers. "Tell me you want the same thing."

She stared at him, selfishly wanting everything he was offering her. Safety. A future. Love. But knowing in her heart of hearts, it wasn't fair to him. That sometime . . . down the line . . . Hunter would realize the sacrifices he was making and the limitations he was putting on himself. He was buying her freedom at the cost of his own.

"Don't do it, Charlie."

She looked at him. "Do what?"

"Don't fill your mind with all the reasons this won't work. Don't deny us the chance to be together."

Chapter Forty-One

Charlie lay in bed, watching the shadows and patterns on the ceiling change with the rising sun. Sleep had eluded her for most of the night, her racing heart keeping her awake.

She had finally convinced herself a relationship with Hunter was worth the risk. And somehow, they would make it work. They had to. Because by the end of the second movie she realized living without Hunter was not an option.

She loved him.

And as hard as she'd tried to keep him at arm's length, to treat whatever it was they had as a fling, she had failed. She opened her heart to him, and now it was his completely.

Throwing back the comforter, she swung her feet over the side of the bed and stretched as she stood. She slid the sheer curtains aside, opened the French doors, and allowed the morning sun to flood the room. Tipping her head back and closing her eyes, she felt the sun warm her face in reward.

The start to a wonderful day.

After taking a shower and slipping on a blue V-neck, she pulled on a pair of jeans that just kind of hung on her. She turned around in front of the mirror and eyed the loose-fitting denims. *It has to be stress.* Her emotional highs and lows were working as quite the appetite suppressant.

When she turned to the mirror to brush her hair, she cringed. Not only was her cheek still swollen, but the colors had deepened. No amount of make-up would be able to hide the sickish purple and deep blue, which coincidently matched her shirt.

Rifling through her bag, she pulled out a pink Henley. It was faded and worn, but at least it wouldn't highlight the blue tinge of her cheek. Yanking off one shirt and pulling on the other, she looked in the mirror again and shrugged.

Well, it's better than the battling blues.

Ignoring her swollen reflection, she smiled. Today was a new day. And hopefully it would be free of motorcycle wrecks, flying fists, and explosive confrontations. If it was all she dreamed about last night, it would be the start of a whole new life.

When she opened the bedroom door, her senses were immediately overwhelmed with the wafting aroma of breakfast. Bacon sizzling. Coffee brewing. It smelled incredible. Hunter was working over the stove top when she stepped into the kitchen, so she silently watched as he flipped pancakes, a dishtowel lapped over his shoulder. He looked so good standing there barefooted, his T-shirt rumpled, and flannel pants slung low on his hips. When he pulled a plate stacked with pancakes from the oven, he saw her out of the corner of his eye and smiled. "Good morning."

"You're up early," she said as she leaned against the wall, hands in her back pockets. "I thought superstars slept until noon?"

"I would, but I hate to do things alone."

His devilish grin and innuendo-laden comment caught her completely off guard. He laughed at her obvious loss for words as he set the plate of pancakes on the counter. "What? No snappy comeback?"

She just shook her head. "Are you always this cocky in the morning?"

He winked. "I guess you'll just have to stick around and find out."

Stepping forward, he brushed the back of his hand gently across her cheek and frowned. "This looks pretty bad. I would still feel better if Diana took a look at it."

She covered his hand with hers and tucked it in the crook of her neck. "It's not pretty, that's for sure." She looked into his crystal blue eyes. "But I'm okay."

"I don't know . . ." He took a step closer. "I think I should make sure nothing is broken." His eyes dipped to her lips.

"And how are you going to do that?" she teased.

He stared deep into her eyes. "I'll show you." Slipping his hands to her waist, he pulled her against him, and kissed her softly.

Charlie could feel his hesitance, so she kissed him with a little more enthusiasm, just to assure him she was really okay.

He got the message.

Hunter *examined* her bruised cheek thoroughly, and though it ached, Charlie did nothing to discourage him. But, when smoke started to rise from the stove, she took a stepped back."

"Hunter, I think something is on fire."

"You ain't kidding," he said, as he pulled her back toward him.

She pressed her hands to his chest, giggling. "No. Seriously. Something is on fire."

When he turned and saw the griddle ablaze, he hurried to the pantry cupboard, grabbed a box of baking soda, and smothered the flames. He tossed the box in the sink and stood staring at the stove top. "Oh well, everyone knows bacon isn't good for you."

Charlie hid a smirk behind her hand while he dumped the skillet into the sink and grumbled. "Go ahead and say it."

"Say what?" she giggled some more.

"Come on, I know you're dying to say something."

"I was just going to applaud you on how capable you are

in the kitchen. You're a man of many talents, Mr. Jennings: singer, songwriter, chef, firefighter."

He cocked his head. "Very funny."

She couldn't help it. She burst out laughing, then quickly reached for her swollen cheek and moaned.

"That's it," he said, all humor gone as he picked up his cell phone from the counter. "Good morning, Diana. Did I call too early?"

Charlie hurried around the counter and grabbed for his phone, but Hunter swiveled out of reach.

"Hunter, don't. I'm fine," she whispered.

He ignored her and continued his conversation. "Yeah, I was wondering if you could come take a look at Charlie's jaw, just as a precaution."

"Hunter, please!"

"Okay, see you in about twenty minutes."

"That wasn't necessary," she said as he set his phone on the counter. "Yes, it's painful, but that doesn't mean it's anything more than a bruise."

"Well, it won't hurt for Diana to give her professional opinion. Now . . . since she won't be here for another twenty minutes, why don't you go ahead and see if you can eat some pancakes before they get cold."

They took their plates out to the patio and enjoyed the quiet of early morning. Charlie ate her pancakes while Hunter watched her every move like a hawk. When she put her fork down and set her folded napkin on the table, he eyed what was left on her plate.

"You're not done, are you?"

"Yeah. I'm not much of a breakfast person unless it's being served for dinner."

"You're sure that's the only reason?" he asked, as he shoveled the last of his pancakes into his mouth.

"I'm sure."

"Knock, knock."

Charlie turned to see a beautiful blond in jeans, boots, and a sleeveless shirt standing behind her, a red backpack slung over her shoulder.

"I didn't mean to intrude," she said as she continued across the patio, "but no one answered the door. I figured you might be out here."

Hunter got up and stepped around the table. "Hey beautiful." He gave the woman a quick hug, then turned to Charlie. "Diana, this is Charlie Foster. Charlie, this is my sister-in-law, Diana."

The woman stuck out her hand and smiled. "Nice to meet you. Sorry it couldn't be under better circumstances."

Charlie shook Diana's hand, feeling awkward at the way she was scrutinizing her cheek. "Wow, Jake didn't hold back, did he?"

"That's because he was aiming at me," Hunter snapped.

Pulling out a patio chair, Diana sat down next to Charlie. "Jake feels awful about what happened."

"Not as awful as Charlie."

"Okay, Hunter, I get it. I'm not here to defend Jake. I'm here to see Charlie." She turned to her with sympathetic eyes. "How does it feel?"

"It's fine, really," Charlie answered as she fiddled with the hem of her shirt, never really making eye contact. "Hunter's the one you should be examining."

"Don't worry, I'll get to him next." Diana scooted forward in her chair and brought her hands up under Charlie's chin. She gently ran her fingers the length of her jaw, up to her ears, and across her cheekbones. "How does that feel?" she asked as she pressed a little firmer.

"It's sore, but I don't feel any sharp pains."

"Don't let her fool you," Hunter butted in. "She winced and grabbed her cheek this morning when she was laughing."

"Well of course she's going to wince, dummy. She got coldcocked. What do you expect?" Diana gave her a wink. "In fact, if I remember correctly, the last time you and Jake got into it, you ended up with a shiner and moaned and groaned for days."

"Hey," Hunter threw his hands up defensively. "I just want to make sure you have all the facts. You can't blame a guy for caring."

Charlie enjoyed the easy banter between Hunter and his sister-in-law, the levity relaxing her a little as Diana continued her exam. "How about your teeth, any problems there?"

"No. Really, I'm fine."

"Well, all kidding aside, Hunter was right to be concerned." Diana looked her in the eyes as she scooted back in her chair. "The bruising is pretty extensive. An x-ray wouldn't be a bad idea. Just as a precaution."

"I appreciate your advice," Charlie leaned closer and lowered her voice. "But I've had my jaw broken before. I know what it feels like, and this is nothing compared to that."

"Oh wow, how did you do that? A riding accident?" Diana asked.

"No."

Charlie watched Diana's expression turn from a question, to realization, and then to compassion. "I'm sorry," she whispered.

Charlie just shrugged. What could she say?

"Well, you should probably eat soft food until the soreness is gone. If you have any centralized pain in your gums rather than your cheek, I suggest seeing a dentist. Other than that, ibuprofen is about all I can recommend."

"What about ice?" Hunter asked.

"That would've helped last night, but it really won't do much good now. It will numb the soreness if the ibuprofen doesn't work, but it won't help with the swelling. That will just take time." Diana stood, moved her bag over to the other side of the table and walked around to where Hunter was sitting. "Now, let me see your shoulder."

Charlie watched as Hunter pulled his shirt over his head and sat back in his chair. She tried not to ogle his muscular chest, but she was having a hard time looking anywhere else.

"What's this?" Diana asked as she moved Hunter's arm away from his side, giving her a better view of the angry scratches on his ribcage."

"Just a little road rash," he said. "It's no big deal."

"Why didn't you show me this yesterday?" she said, squatting down to get a better look.

"Because my shoulder was the bigger problem."

"Mm-hmm." Diana grabbed her bag and set it down on the cement next to her. Rummaging through it, she pulled out a small square packet, ripped it open, and quickly stroked up and down Hunter's side, causing him to flinch.

"What the he—" Hunter pinched his lips closed, muffling his choice of words.

"Oh, come on, Hunter," she leaned back on her heels with a chuckle. "This is Benzalkonium Chloride. It doesn't even sting."

"Who said anything about stinging? You're scrubbing to beat the band."

"Well, I wouldn't have to scrub, if you had shown it to me yesterday. I just want to make sure it's cleaned properly."

He winced but held his tongue as she continued. When she was done, she stood and pulled back the gauze from his shoulder wound.

"I'm telling you right now," Hunter said, with a raised finger pointed directly at her, "if you start scrubbing my shoulder like you just did my side, I'm going to toss you into the pool."

Charlie grinned. "Most people use their pool for relaxation and fun, not leverage."

"Well, if she was a guy, I would just deck her. But since I was taught never to hit a woman, I have to resort to other resources."

"I guess Jake didn't get that memo," Charlie said, jokingly.

Diana turned to her with shame-filled eyes. "I can't tell you how sorry he is, Charlie."

"And you shouldn't have to," Hunter chimed in. "Jake should've come over here himself, not have you do his bidding for him."

"Jake already apologized."

Hunter turned to her. "When?"

"Yesterday. While you were in the shower. He brought my bags in from outside and apologized for hitting me."

But not for his choice of words.

An awkward silence filled the air while Diana finished the bandage job on Hunter's shoulder. When she scrunched up the wrappers and dropped them into her bag, she smiled hesitantly. "So, will you guys be coming over for lunch? Courtney made your favorite cookies and Cody's been dying to challenge you to horseshoes."

Hunter looked at her for the answer.

"I don't think that's such a good idea," she said. "I know Jake apologized for what happened, but I don't think it changes the way he feels about me." Standing, she picked up her plate and cup. "I don't want him to feel uncomfortable in his own home."

"Wait a minute, why would he feel uncomfortable in his own home?" Hunter looked at her or at least tried to as she avoided his stare. "What else did he say to you?"

"It doesn't—"

"Look, Charlie," Diana said, "I know you and Jake got off on the wrong foot but give him a chance to redeem himself. He really isn't a bad guy, just a little overprotective. Besides, Cody and Courtney are dying to see their Uncle Hunter."

Charlie looked at Diana then at Hunter.

"It's your call," he said as he slipped his shirt over his head. "But don't feel like you have to. I brought you here so *we* could spend time together. Now . . . I know I've screwed that up all by myself, but I definitely didn't count on my family being such a liability."

"Hey!" Diana snapped. "I take exception to that. I'll admit Jake overreacted, but don't throw the rest of us under the bus. Mom and the kids will be so disappointed if they don't get a chance to spend some time with you."

"Oh well, they'll just have—"

"It's all right, Hunter, we can go."

Though Charlie had no desire to see Jake again, she certainly did not want to put a wedge between Hunter and his family.

"We don't have to," he reiterated.

"No, it's fine. I don't want to give your mom the wrong impression, that I'm controlling or antisocial or something. It's just lunch. It will be fun." She forced a smile.

What could be more fun than sitting under a microscope?

Chapter Forty-Two

The day was off to a wonderful start.

After doing the breakfast dishes, Hunter showed her more of the ranch. They took off in the four-wheel drive vehicle and drove for miles. Every so often, they would park and explore further on foot, Hunter taking every opportunity to reach for her hand or wrap his arm around her shoulder. And the best part was . . . it felt so right.

Hunter showed her Indian ruins and pointed out animal dens, anything of interest. And whenever he got the chance, he would steal a kiss. Well, it wasn't really stealing since she put up no resistance.

So far, it had been the most magical day she'd ever experienced.

Walking hand-in-hand along a dried creek bed, Hunter lifted their hands to look at his watch. "We had better head back. It's almost noon." He gave her hand a squeeze. "Are you still good with having lunch with the family?"

"Sure," she answered quickly, trying to sound upbeat.

"You're going to love the kids. Cody's six and Courtney's three. Cody is all boy, a cowboy through and through, while Courtney is just the cutest little thing. She's going to be a real heartbreaker when she gets older. I can't wait to see what Jake does when she hits the teenage years. I bet he'll lock her away until she's twenty," he laughed.

"Diana seems nice."

"Yeah. She's great. Jake is a lucky man."

Lucky . . . not the word I would use to describe him.

She thought about the things he'd said and the names he'd called her. Even though he had apologized, she was pretty sure his opinion of her hadn't changed.

Hopefully, since the whole family will be there, he'll have the decency to keep his opinions to himself.

After going back to the house to freshen up, Charlie and Hunter rode over to his brother's house. She was fiddling with the hem of her shirt when Hunter reached for her hand and smiled.

"Relax. Everyone is going to love you."

Not everyone.

As Hunter reached for the front door, it swung open wide. Two shrieking kids ran out and attached themselves to his legs. Charlie just took a step back.

"Uncle Hunter, I made your favorite—"

"Ah, he doesn't care about stupid cookies," the little boy grumbled. "Will you play horsesh—"

"He does so like cookies!" The sassy little girl with blond pigtails, perched her hands on her pint-size hips and scowled. "Don't you, Uncle Hunter?"

"Cookies are for sissies, and Uncle Hunter is no sissy!"

"Okay, now both of you calm down," Hunter said with a chuckle.

Diana came to the door obviously hearing Hunter's gentle reprimand.

"Okay you two, give Uncle Hunter some space. The poor man can't even get through the front door without you two ambushing him."

"But Cody said cookies are for sissies," Courtney said with crocodile tears threatening to fall.

Hunter scooped her up into his arms and stared at her nose to nose. "Well, he's wrong. I love cookies," he said with a smile. "And I'm going to have me a whole passel of them after we are done with lunch."

The little girl smiled from ear to ear as she wrapped her little arms around Hunter's neck and gave him a squeeze.

Charlie's heart melted as she watched the two interact.

Courtney turned to her, smiled shyly, then whispered loudly in Hunter's ear. "Who is the pretty lady with the purple makeup, Uncle Hunter?"

Hunter smiled as he set her down. "This is my friend, Charlie."

"Charlie?" The girl scrunched up her nose in dislike. "That's a boy's name."

"Courtney!" Diana snapped. "Apologize for being rude. Miss Charlie is Uncle Hunter's guest, and you need to use kinder words."

"I'm sorry," Courtney hung her head.

Charlie knelt beside her. "That's okay. And I'm not wearing purple makeup. It's just a nasty old bruise."

Courtney gently touched her cheek. "Does it hurt?"

"Just a little."

Courtney reached for her hand, her eyes sparkling again. "Want to see my room? Daddy built me a trailer for Barbie's horsies. It lights up and everything."

"Now, Courtney," Diana said, "Uncle Hunter and Miss Charlie are here for lunch and to visit with *all* of us. She can see your room another time."

"Ahh, mommy."

"Courtney . . ."

The little girl stomped into the house while the adults did their best to hide their snickers.

Charlie looked at Cody, his arms crossed against his small chest, dejected. Hunter ruffled his blond hair and squatted down. "I'm sure we can find time for at least one round of horseshoes while I'm here. But first, you need to apologize to your sister for hurting her feelings." The little boy lit up like a Christmas tree. "Okay, Uncle Hunter." He ran into the house yelling for his sister.

"Well, now that you've staved off a miniature uprising, are you ready for some lunch?" Diana asked.

"Absolutely," Hunter answered as he pressed his hand to the small of Charlie's back and guided her through the door.

Jake and Diana's house was much like Hunter's, just on a smaller scale. It was obvious Diana had a real flare for interior design because every piece of furniture, every knick-knack, every picture, complimented each other perfectly.

"Your home is beautiful," she said as she continued to look around.

"Thanks. We like it. The hardwood and tile floors can take the punishment my kids dish out."

Diana led them into the kitchen where Hunter's mom was waiting. She immediately got up from where she was sitting and wrapped her arms around Charlie. "I was beginning to think I wasn't going to get a chance to talk with you at all." She gave her a squeeze, but when she stepped back, she noticed her swollen cheek. "Oh my goodness, how did that happen?"

"Your son—"

"Your son," Charlie spoke louder, interrupting Hunter, "was showing me around, and I took a little tumble. But I'm fine."

"What?" Hunter said with exasperation when she stabbed him with a stare. He pressed his lips together silencing his rebuttal.

"Hunter, you need to be more considerate of your lady friend," his mother said in a disciplinary tone. "The terrain around here is rugged. You need to be more careful."

"Yes, mother," Hunter said, forcing a smile.

"Now come here and greet me properly."

Hunter stepped forward, giving his mom a hug and a kiss on the cheek. He glared at Charlie over the top of his mother's head and mouthed *you owe me big time.* She turned to Diana, the both of them doing their best not to laugh.

The patio door opened and in stepped Jake with a platter in his hand. "Burgers and dogs are done."

"Perfect." Diana turned to them. "I figured it would be easier to assemble our plates in here before going outside to eat."

"Sounds good to me," Hunter answered as he stepped forward and grabbed a plate.

"Manors, Hunter. Charlie is our guest," his mother reprimanded.

"I was getting the plate for Charlie," he said, the hint of agitation in his words. He passed her the plate, then bent to whisper in her ear. "Maybe this wasn't such a good idea after all."

She smirked as she stepped up to the kitchen island and filled her plate, then waited by the patio door until Hunter was done piling food on his.

Walking outside together, Hunter asked, "What was all that about? Taking a tumble?" He pulled out a patio chair for her. "Why are you protecting my brother?"

"I wasn't protecting Jake," she said as she sat down. "I just didn't want to have to explain to your mother how I got caught in the middle of a fist fight between her two sons."

He took a seat beside her. "So instead, I get scolded by my mother for not treating you right."

"Come on, Hunter, you're a big boy, you can take it." She grinned.

"Oh really?" he smirked. "Okay, sweetheart, but you owe me, and I plan to collect later tonight."

"And how exactly are you going to do that?"

"I'm going to—"

"I get to sit next to Miss Charlie." Courtney hurried across the patio, Diana carrying her plate for her. "Can I, Miss Charlie?"

She turned to Courtney. "If it's okay with your daddy," she said as Jake approached the table with Cody beside him.

"Can I, Daddy, please?"

Jake looked at his daughter as he took a seat at the head of the table. "What is that, sweetie?"

"Miss Charlie said I could sit next to her as long as it was okay with you."

"Actually, Courtney asked me," she clarified. "But I told

her she had to check with you first. I didn't want to presume anything where your kids are concerned." She looked at Jake and saw the rise of his chin. He got the point she was making.

Diana set Courtney's plate down next to Charlie's, clearly missing their conversation. "Of course you can. Just mind your manners and no spills."

"Okay, Mommy." Courtney beamed at Charlie as Hunter's mother took her place at the table followed by Diana.

Charlie felt Courtney reach for her hand for the second time. She looked at the little girl with the bright blue eyes. "What is it, sweetheart?"

"We need to hold hands so Daddy can pray."

"Oh." She took Courtney's little hand, then laced her fingers with Hunter's, smiling at him. But when she turned to Jake, he was staring directly at her.

"Ready?" he asked with a raised brow.

She nodded, then bowed her head to pray.

Chapter Forty-Three

Jake's prayer was soft-spoken, eloquent, humble even. So unlike the man who had told her exactly what he thought of her just the day before.

"I don't know about anyone else," Hunter's mom said as she slid her napkin onto her lap, "but I'm dying to hear how you two met. I bet sparks flew the moment you laid eyes on each other."

Hunter chuckled. "That's a fact. Sparks flew all right, but only because Charlie wanted nothing to do with me. But my bull-headed self wouldn't take no for an answer. So, I continued to pursue her until I finally wore her down."

"Okay, that's the Reader's Digest version. I want the details," his mother persisted.

Charlie locked eyes on Hunter, not wanting him to explain to his mother the whole picture taking debacle. Hunter gave her knee a gentle squeeze, his eyes assuring her everything would be fine.

He proceeded to tell them about the saddle giveaway, the concert fiasco, and the hoof pick incident, omitting a few things here and there about her situation. Irene and Diana ate up every morsel. And even though Jake tried to look disinterested, by the time Hunter had finished, Charlie could tell he had listened to every word. When all was said and done, Courtney looked at her with an inquisitive expression. "But you like Uncle Hunter now, right?"

She smiled. "I do, Courtney. Your Uncle Hunter is a very special guy."

"Are you going to marry him?"

"Courtney!" Diana snapped. "It's not polite to ask that sort of question. Now apologize to Miss Charlie and Uncle Hunter."

The little girl hung her head. "I'm sorry I asked . . . but are ya?"

"That's enough, Courtney," Jake said sternly. "Of course they're not getting married. Charlie is just a friend Uncle Hunter is helping out. Wanting to help someone isn't reason enough to marry them. Now finish your lunch." Jake flicked a steely glance in her direction, as if to ask if she got the point he was making.

Message received.

Hunter was about to say something to Jake, but she squeezed his knee under the table. He looked at her, his jaw clenched. "Let it go, Hunter," she whispered.

"But—"

"Please," she whispered again.

She could tell Hunter was irritated with his brother, but instead of causing a scene, he made small talk with the kids. And as Charlie listened to Diana and Irene talk about their favorite design show on HGTV, she tried to eat her lunch as best she could with her sore jaw, but her appetite was gone.

Unfortunately, the relaxed mood was gone as well.

"Mommy, I'm done with my lunch. Can I take Miss Charlie to see my room now?"

"But she isn't done with her lunch, sweetie."

"Yes I am." She draped her napkin over her half-eaten lunch then stood. "I would love to see your room."

"Yippee!" Courtney slipped out of her chair and reached for her hand.

Charlie glanced at the adults around the table, all but Jake. "Excuse us. We have a horse trailer to inspect."

Charlie sat on Courtney's pink polka-dot comforter, thankful for the reprieve. The little girl showed her all her stuffies, told her their names, and explained when she got them. Charlie made sure to look interested, even though she was replaying their lunch conversation in her head.

Courtney showed her dolls from all over the world—gifts from Uncle Hunter, and some of her favorite toys. Just when she thought the little girl was running out of things to show her, Courtney stood and asked, "Do you want to see my castle?"

"You have a castle?" she asked, matching Courtney's enthusiasm.

The little girl nodded her head vigorously.

"I would love to see it."

Courtney squealed with excitement before darting out of the room and down the stairs. Charlie followed, ending up in the kitchen where Diana and Irene were finishing up the dishes. "Miss Charlie and I are going to play in my castle," Courtney explained as she hurried to the French doors across the room.

Diana glanced at Charlie, her eyes asking if she needed to be rescued. She just smiled back, shaking her head slightly.

"Okay, Courtney, but you can't keep Miss Charlie to yourself all day. Grandma and I would like to visit with her too."

"Okay, Mommy," she answered as she swung the door open wide.

"Charlie," Diana stopped her before she reached the patio door, "don't feel like you have to entertain Courtney all day."

"It's all right. I don't mind."

"Okay. But save some time for Irene and me."

"Sure thing." She walked outside, glad for the escape. Truth be told, she would rather hang out with the accepting three-year-old than be on the receiving end of any more scrutiny.

Crossing the yard, she caught up with Courtney, and saw Hunter, Jake, and Cody tossing horseshoes across the way. When she reached Courtney's castle, she stood in awe. It was enormous. But what struck her wasn't only the beautifully detailed accents that looked like something out of a fairytale, but the fact that when she walked to the other side of the castle, the façade turned into a fort, complete with a camo paint job and gun tower.

"This is amazing. Did your daddy build this for you?"

"Um-hum, and Uncle Hunter. Cody wanted a fort, but I wanted a castle. Daddy said he wouldn't build anything until we agreed on one thing, but Uncle Hunter said we could have both, as long as we shared."

Courtney disappeared inside. A second later, her head popped up in the turret at the top. "Come on, Miss Charlie, come inside and play."

———————◄ ● ►———————

Hunter watched as Charlie and Courtney crossed the yard to the playhouse. He wanted to go to her, make sure she was doing okay, but spending time with Cody was important as well.

"House rules?" Hunter asked as Cody handed him two green horseshoes.

"Yep. Closes color gets the point," Cody said as he handed his dad two yellow horseshoes and kept the blue ones for himself.

They didn't play by traditional rules. They had shortened the distance and adopted the color horseshoe system when Cody was big enough to toss a shoe. That way, all three of them could play at the same time.

Allowing Cody to go first, Hunter stood next to Jake, noticing the scowl on his face.

"What?" he asked defensively.

"Just wondering where you think this thing with her is going."

"What's that supposed to mean?" he asked as he tossed a shoe, careful to keep the irritation out of his voice for Cody's sake.

"Come on, Hunter, you're playing with fire."

"Uncle Hunter plays with fire? I want to see." Cody

said, staring at him with astonishment.

Hunter turned to his brother and cocked a brow in challenge.

Jake squatted down next to his son. "He doesn't really play with fire, buddy. It's just an expression grownups use sometimes."

Cody wrinkled his nose. "Is that what people mean when they say someone is hot?"

Hunter turned his head and laughed.

"Yeah, something like that," Jake replied. "Now come on, are we going to play horseshoes or not?"

After everyone threw their two shoes, Jake sent Cody to retrieve them, explaining that they were only going to toss in one direction so the sun wouldn't be in their eyes. When Cody rushed down the course to get the shoes, Jake picked up the conversation where he had left off. "She's married, Hunter. How can you just ignore that?"

"And she would've gotten a divorce a long time ago if her husband hadn't threatened to kill her."

Jake just shook his head. "I can't believe you're justifying it. Do you realize the kind of scandal this will be if the celebrity rag magazines get a hold of it?"

"They're not going to, but even if they did, I wouldn't care. I love her, Jake. And I'm going to do everything in my power to convince her we can make this—"

"Wait a minute," Jake snapped. "What do you mean *convince her*? Are you telling me she isn't sure about you two? That you're putting your butt and your career on the line for a woman who isn't even committed to whatever it is you think you have?"

Before Hunter could answer, Cody was back with their horseshoes. He divvied them out, oblivious to the tension between them.

"Your turn to go first, Uncle Hunter."

Hunter and Jake quickly took their turns, the game no longer holding their attention. When Cody went to retrieve the shoes again, Hunter answered his brother's question.

"She's afraid, okay? She's had a rough life. Her father was non-existent, her mother abandoned her, and her husband abused her. So she's a little shaky in the commitment department."

"*Shaky?*" Jake huffed louder. "You're ready to throw away everything for *shaky?*"

"Come on. She needs someone. She needs someone who can protect her and take care of her. She deserves that."

"Yeah, well, and what about your family? What do we deserve?"

Hunter watched as Cody hurried toward them with their horseshoes, a smile on his face. But when he heard his father's clipped tone, his steps slowed, and his smile faltered.

"Listen, Jake," he whispered. "let's not talk about this right now."

"Why? Because you know this is bull—"

"Uncle Hunter! Uncle Hunter!"

He spun around to see Courtney running toward him, tears streaming down her face, Charlie nowhere to be seen. Instantly, his heart was in his stomach.

Jake bent down and scooped up his daughter, "What is it, sweetheart?"

She turned to Hunter. "Something is wrong with Miss Charlie."

He didn't wait for an explanation he just bolted toward the playhouse. When he got there, he saw Charlie slumped against the backside of the fort, one arm wrapped around her middle, the other braced against the wood frame, her lunch in the dirt in front of her.

"Charlie, what is it? What's wrong?"

She looked at him, eyes red, skin pallid. "I don't know. I just feel—" she squeezed her eyes shut, obviously fighting off another wave of nausea.

He stepped closer and pressed the back of his hand to her forehead. "You're burning up. What can I do?"

"Just get me outta here."

He turned to see his brother being dragged along by a worried Courtney and an inquisitive Cody. "Jake, bring the Polaris around," he yelled.

Jake hurried his pace, actual concern creasing his face. "What's wrong?"

"Charlie. She's sick. I need to get her to the house."

What ensued was momentary pandemonium as Jake tried to assure a distraught Courtney that Charlie would be okay, got the kids into the house, and pulled the UTV next to the playhouse. In the meantime, Hunter tried to comfort Charlie through another round of retching.

Once in the vehicle, he turned to her and spoke softly, "I can do this one of two ways." He reached over and squeezed her knee. "I can drive like a bat-out-of-hell and get you there fast, or I can go slow, avoid the potholes, and take the easy way. You pick."

She turned to him, her eyes swollen with unshed tears. "I learned a long time ago there's no such thing as an easy way."

Chapter Forty-Four

About an hour later, Hunter heard the creak of the guestroom door. Springing to his feet, he crossed the living room and met Charlie in the tile hallway. "How are you feeling?"

"Humiliated," she said dryly. "How many bad impressions can one person make?"

He pulled her into a firm embrace, thankful to feel she was no longer feverish. "I don't care about that. I care about you. So, I'll ask again. How are you feeling?"

"Okay, I guess. Just sore. But it's so weird. It just strikes out of nowhere."

"*It?*" he asked, pulling away from Charlie, so he could look into her eyes.

"The flu. I've had it on and off since the beginning of the year."

"What do you mean on and off? How many times have you been sick?"

"It's hard to say. Sometimes it's full-blown puking, other times it feels like a stomachache."

"So, you've been sick all year?"

"No. Not completely. I mean, I've just had a hard time bouncing back, that's all." She stepped out of his embrace and walked toward the sliding glass door in the living room. "I can't believe I got sick in front of your entire family. I didn't think me being here could get any worse. What else could possibly go wrong?"

He chuckled slightly as he slipped his arms around her

217

from behind. "You're being a little melodramatic, aren't you? The only person who saw you puke is Courtney."

She rested her head back against his chest. "Still. Meeting your family has been a complete bust."

"Well, that wasn't the point of you being here. The point was for *us* to be able to spend time together, to relax and get to know each other better."

"Okay." She turned around inside his embrace and smiled. "Let's change the subject. What do you say to another movie?"

He brushed a loose tendril of hair behind her ear. "But we can't talk if we're watching a movie."

"What's left to talk about? Haven't we pretty much covered it all?" She took a step back. "Let's see . . . you have a great family, and I have none. You're a public figure recognized wherever you go, and I'm a loner just trying to avoid being seen. You're mega rich, while I work at a diner. And even though you are tired of the rat race and I'm tired of running, it's what we do and who we are." She shrugged. "I don't know about you, but I think we've covered a lot of ground."

"And where does God fit into your life?"

He saw a momentary flicker of surprise cross her face, but just as quick it disappeared behind indifference.

"He doesn't," she said curtly, as she stepped around him and headed toward the kitchen.

"Why not?" He followed.

"I don't know. Why don't you ask Him? We're not exactly on speaking terms anymore."

Her cavalier attitude surprised him.

"Why is that?"

"Because I got tired of a one-sided relationship."

He watched as she opened the refrigerator and grabbed a bottle of water. But when she turned to him, he could see hurt in her eyes. He realized her tone wasn't disrespect as much as it was defeat.

"So, you believed in God at some point in your life?"

She took a sip of water. "Sure I did. My aunt took me to

church every Sunday. I loved the worship and the image of a father who cared for me and loved me, something I had never experienced. But when Aunt Bev got too sick to go to church, I stayed home with her."

"So is that when you gave up on God, when your aunt died?"

"Nope. Even though God had taken everyone from me, and I was angry with Him, I was still naïve enough to believe all I'd been taught about Him. So, I gutted it out and prayed. I had my job at the track and prayed I wouldn't lose it. I had Aunt Bev's beat-up Pontiac and prayed it would keep running. I got a small hole-in-the-wall apartment a block away from the track and picked up as many side jobs as I could juggle. I was hit on by handlers, owners, even the general manager, but I made it very clear I was there to work with horses and nothing more. I refused to sell myself to get a leg up in the world. I worked my butt off, all while putting myself through school. It was tough, but I was doing it."

She chuckled slightly and took another swig of water. "That was before I met Daniel." She glanced at him, then quickly looked away. "It's ironic, really. I actually thought he was a knight in shining armor God had sent to take care of me."

She quieted for an instant, and he could tell she had lapsed momentarily into the past.

"Boy, was I wrong," she whispered, as she walked back to the living room and curled up in the corner of the couch.

"So is that why you don't believe in God anymore?" he asked as he sat down on the couch next to her.

"Oh, I believe in Him," she said emphatically. "He just isn't someone I want to have a relationship with. My prayers were nothing more than one-sided conversations with a cruel Creator. Being ignored by Him was more devastating than Daniel's abuse. Daniel terrorized me, but God abandoned me. Just like everyone else."

"So, was Daniel one of the owners who hit on you?" he

219

asked.

"No. Daniel was too smooth for that."

"Then how did you two meet?"

"I was the resident guru on hydrotherapy at the track, and Brian, Daniel's barn manager wanted to give it a try. Daniel wasn't interested, so Brian decided to conduct his own experiment. I worked with two of their horses for a month while Daniel was out of the country. When he came back, Brian ran the horses for him. Their best times were improved by more than three seconds. That was the day I met Daniel."

Charlie swigged her water and fell silent.

Hunter waited, not wanting to rush her.

"That first meeting was pretty intense. Daniel was angry with Brian for going behind his back and threatened to have me removed from the track permanently for *tampering* with his horses. But I wasn't about to stand there and take the fall for Brian, especially when the therapy proved to be a success. I told Daniel he was nothing more than a pompous jerk who knew nothing about horses. I also told him if I as much as heard a whisper from other owners that he was maligning my name, I would sue him for every penny he had."

"What did he say to that?" he asked, loving the fact that Charlie stood up to the degenerate.

"He laughed, said he admired my spunk, then backed me up against the wall and—with a well-manicured finger pointed directly in my face—let me know if I ever spoke to him like that again I'd be out on my can."

"Obviously that didn't happen."

"Nope. In fact, I started working with Brian exclusively. Daniel offered me double what the other owners were paying, so I couldn't afford to turn him down. Soon after that, Daniel started coming to the track more regularly. He watched me as I worked with the horses, asked questions about the therapy, about my school classes, and what my plans were for the future."

"But he never hit on you?"

"No. He never did. In fact, he apologized on more than one

occasion for yelling at me. For six months he was nothing but a gentleman."

"Then what happened?"

She took another sip of water and tensed noticeably.

"I showed up to work one day to find Brian yelling at the kid who maintained the stables. Rumor had it that a couple of horses in other stalls the kid was responsible for had come down with thrush. Brian wasn't about to take any chances with our horses, so he fired the kid on the spot.

"Unfortunately, Brian took out his frustration on me. He insisted I clean all the stalls. He said he didn't care if it took me all night, and if I didn't like it, he would fire me too." She shrugged. "I couldn't afford to lose my job, so I stayed. It was about ten o'clock at night when I was finishing the last of the stalls . . . that's when someone grabbed me from behind." She shuddered, reached for a throw pillow on the couch, and clutched it against her chest.

Hunter didn't like where this story was headed, but silently waited for her to continue.

"The guy pushed me to the ground, covered my mouth so I couldn't scream, and began grabbing at my clothes. I tried fighting him off, but he was twice my size. I even tried scratching his face, but with work gloves on it was no use. He tore my shirt open and started pulling at my jeans when out of nowhere Daniel showed up, grabbed the guy from behind, and threw him against the opposite wall. They exchanged punches and Daniel was knocked to the ground. The guy took off, but instead of going after him, Daniel stayed with me."

She quickly stroked a tear from her cheek.

"I was crying hysterically and trying to cover myself with what was left of my shirt. Daniel draped his jacket across my shoulders, asked me if I was hurt, and tried to comfort me. After a few minutes, he helped me to my feet and told me I needed to go the hospital. I pled with him not to make me go and assured him—other than being terrified and having a few scratches—I was okay. But he insisted I get checked out. When I burst into tears, he wrapped his arms around me and conceded. He held me until I stopped crying."

Hunter hated that Daniel had been a decent guy at one time. "So . . . he was your knight in shining armor after all."

Charlie looked at him, her eyes ablaze. "It was staged."

"What?"

"I found out later the whole thing had been staged. The rumor about the thrush, Brian firing the stable boy, making me stay late, the attack, everything. Just so Daniel could swoop in and be the hero. You see, Daniel would never allow himself to be vulnerable. He was infatuated with me but couldn't take the chance I might turn him down. He needed a sure thing. So, he fabricated the perfect scenario for me to fall for him. And it worked. We were married six months later."

Chapter Forty-Five

Charlie watched as Hunter processed everything she had said. He got up from the couch, his hands clenching and unclenching at his side, a curse slipping from his lips as he paced. "So . . . did the abuse start right away?" he whispered through gritted teeth.

"Physically, no."

"Verbally?"

"It wasn't verbal abuse as much as it was intimidation and control. Daniel was extremely possessive, and had to know where I was, who I was with, and what I was doing at all times. After we were married, I wasn't allowed at the stables, unless I was with him. I no longer worked with the horses because he said it wouldn't look right for him to be married to a stable hand, even though that's what I was. And the only friends I had were the wives of his associates, but they didn't feel like friends . . . not really. They were more like eyes and ears for Daniel. In the beginning, I tried to convince myself he was just being protective—that he really loved me. But I soon realized I was nothing more than a possession to him."

"When did the physical abuse start?"

"We were on a cruise celebrating our first anniversary. He accused me of flirting with the cabin steward. When I told him I was merely being nice, he slapped me and insisted I was lying. He apologized later and acted like he truly regretted it. But soon, I realized what a mistake I had made. I didn't know Daniel at all, at least not the real

Daniel."

She sighed, remembering all she had endured.

"After that first incident, Daniel's behavior went from bad to worse. His mood swings intensified. His drinking was out of control. His words and actions were more abusive. It was like a switch had been flipped and he no longer felt the need to hide his temper from me. When business was good, he stayed out late with his associates, went to expensive clubs, and flaunted his money. But when business was bad, he came home drunk and sullen. I would break out in a cold sweat whenever I saw his car pull into the driveway or heard the front door slam shut. Some nights it wasn't so bad. He'd go straight to his home office and continue drinking until he passed out. Other nights, he came looking for me to work out his frustration."

Charlie chanced a look at Hunter. The set of his jaw, the way he gripped his left hand in his right, and the red rimming his eyes told her he knew exactly what she meant.

"One night, about six months after our anniversary, everything blew up. Daniel came home ranting and raving because one of his business partners had cheated him on a major deal. When he found out the business partner's wife had been at the house that same afternoon for lunch, he accused me of being in on the scam. I told him I had no idea what he was talking about, but he wouldn't listen. Each time I denied any knowledge of the deal, he hit me."

Hunter winced as if feeling the blows himself.

"I tried everything I could to calm him down, to assure him I would never do something like that to him, but it didn't matter. He was on a rampage, and I was terrified. I tried running from him, and got as far as the upstairs landing, and then everything went black. When I came to, I was in the emergency room with two broken ribs, a concussion, and . . ." she cleared her throat and swiped at an errant tear, "a miscarriage."

She watched Hunter deflate before her eyes.

He sunk to the edge of the couch, elbows on his knees,

head hung between his shoulders. After what felt like an eternity, he finally asked, "Did you know you were pregnant?"

"Yes," she whispered.

"Did Daniel?"

"No. Not until the doctor told him I had miscarried."

Hunter reached across the distance between them, grasped her hand, and gently stroked the back of it with his thumb. "I'm so sorry. That had to be terrible for you."

She nodded, wiping more tears away. "I felt like a murderer."

"But it wasn't your fault."

She shot to her feet. "Of course it was my fault!" She walked in circles, remembering the struggle she felt when she found out she was pregnant. She wanted to believe the baby could be the one thing to bring Daniel and her closer together, but in her heart, she knew it wasn't true. "I should've left Daniel the moment I found out I was pregnant. But I didn't. I was too afraid."

"What did the police do?"

She sat back down, weighted with shame. "The police were never called."

Hunter's expression turned from silent horror to indignant anger. "What do you mean the police were never called? Daniel pushed you down a flight of stairs! He tried to kill you! And you're telling me the police never got involved?"

"Daniel told the doctors I *fell* down the stairs."

"But you told them the truth, right?"

She just looked at him, her stomach twisting all over again. "It wasn't that easy, Hunter."

Again, he was off the couch and pacing. "What do you mean? You were in the hospital. He beat you to a pulp! How could they not see that?"

"When I came to, Daniel was an emotional wreck, being consoled by the doctor. I didn't even know where I was or how I had gotten there. My mind was a scrambled mess, I was having a hard time breathing, and every bone in my body ached. When I finally found my voice enough to ask what had happened, the doctor explained that I had suffered a serious fall. Then, in an extraordinary display of emotion, Daniel took my hand and told me I had lost the baby. He kept saying how thankful he was that I was going to be okay; that he didn't know what he would've done if something had happened to me. He assured me everything was going to be fine, and we could try again to have a baby."

She didn't dare look at Hunter, she just continued.

"The doctor offered his condolences for our loss and went on to explain how lucky I was that my injuries were not more extensive. Then he left, so Daniel and I could have some privacy to grieve."

A tremor shook her, but she took a deep breath and continued.

"When I asked Daniel what happened, he asked me what I remembered. I knew we were arguing, and that I had run out of the bedroom, but that was all. He said he followed me to the stairs, and that I turned around and took a swing at him, losing my balance. He said he reached for me, but I was already falling."

"You didn't believe him, did you?"

"I didn't know what to believe. I was confused and in pain, and still a little scared. But Daniel looked genuinely distraught over losing the baby and kept telling me how sorry he was. He promised things would be different, that he wanted to try to have another baby right away. I wanted to believe him."

"So you stayed."

"Yes." She sighed, wrapping her arms around her raised knees.

Hunter just shook his head, obviously not understanding the emotional battle she struggled with.

"I know. I was stupid to think Daniel could change, but you have to understand where I was coming from. I never had a father, was an inconvenience to my mother, and felt abandoned by God. I was convinced there was something wrong with me and struggled with feelings of worthlessness. The psyche is a powerful thing, and Daniel was a master manipulator. Even so, he *chose* to be with me. Not out of obligation, but by choice. I was hanging on by a thread, and I didn't want to be alone in the world. So, I weighed the balances and decided to stay. Even though I wanted to believe Daniel could change, I knew I had to take precautions."

"What do you mean?"

"I talked to the doctor privately and told him Daniel wanted to try for a baby right away, but I wasn't ready emotionally. He gave me a six-month supply of birth control pills and told me I would know when the time was right. He then explained to Daniel that my body needed to rest and heal. He suggested we wait a few months before trying to conceive again."

With hands fisted on his hips and a chip on his shoulder, Hunter asked, "So how long was it before he took another swing at you?"

She looked up at him, then turned away. "A month."

Plopping down on the couch next to her, Hunter scrubbed his head in frustration and muttered something under his breath. Finally, he asked, "What happened?"

"Daniel found the birth control pills and snapped. He told me the only reason he kept me around was so I could provide him with a son—a successor—and that I had betrayed him by using the pills. He knocked me around pretty bad that night and threatened to kill me if I ever tried to leave him. That was the night I finally convinced myself Daniel would never change, and if I wanted to live, I needed to come up with a plan to get away from him. So, the following week I enlisted the help of the only person I thought I could trust."

Surprised, Hunter asked, "Who?"

"Cherie, our housekeeper."

"But she worked for Daniel."

"Yes, but she helped me that night. After Daniel left,

Cherie found me in the bathroom trying to clean myself up, but I was in rough shape. Without a word, she took over. She got me into the shower and washed the blood from my face and out of my hair. She dressed me, applied compresses to my welts, and sat with me the rest of the night. She cried as she apologized for not stepping in sooner. I assured her there was nothing she could've done to stop Daniel, that she was just as powerless as I was. Even so, that night I realized I had an ally."

"What did you do?"

"I spent the next seven months doing everything I could to stay on Daniel's good side, to earn his trust. I was the perfect, submissive wife."

Hunter's eyes asked what he could not verbalize.

"It was survival. I did what I had to do. But there was no chance I would get pregnant again, I made sure of it."

"How?"

"Cherie slipped me birth control pills every morning."

"How did Daniel handle it? You not getting pregnant?"

"Not well. He blamed me. Said I was defective. He even made me go to a fertility specialist."

"What did you do?"

"Before he ran a litany of tests, I told him I wasn't ready to get pregnant again, but I didn't have the heart to tell Daniel. Though the doctor did not agree with my tactics—and felt I should be honest with my husband—he couldn't tell him due to patient-doctor confidentiality. Instead, he explained to Daniel how traumatic a miscarriage could be both emotionally and physically. He encouraged him to relax and give it a few more months and that I would get pregnant when the time was right."

"How did Daniel react?"

"He was annoyed, but since the doctor assured him there was nothing wrong with me physically, it was enough to keep me in his bed, and for him to stop using me as a punching bag. He still slapped me around from time to time, but the vicious beatings stopped."

"How did you get away?"

"Cherie and I strategically planned my disappearance. She had a second cousin with shady business practices. Falsifying records, bogus identities, credit card fraud—he dabbled in a little of everything. When I was ready to leave, I had a new identity, a car with a legitimate pink slip, and twenty thousand dollars cash. All I had to do was wait for an opportunity to present itself.

"That opportunity came nine months to the day from my trip to the hospital. The security system at the house was getting a major overhaul. All the surveillance cameras were being replaced and would be down for the day. I simply slipped out the service entrance and hunkered down in the backseat of Cherie's car while she drove away. Once I was out, she took me to where she had stashed the car, and I just started to drive. The next morning, I traded the car for another one, and did the same thing the next day in another state."

Remembering those frantic days made her break out in a cold sweat. It had been two years, but it felt like it was just yesterday.

"Hey, are you okay?" Hunter laid his hand on hers.

She nodded but needed a second to regroup. After taking a few deep breaths, she continued.

"Those first few weeks were terrifying. I barely slept. I hardly ate. I just kept driving. For a long time, I didn't go into restaurants or markets because I was afraid someone was following me, and I would be trapped. Instead, I would stop at roadside fruit stands or food trucks but always ate in the car."

"Did Daniel ever figure out it was Cherie who helped you?"

"I don't know. I never spoke to her again."

"So why Tennessee?"

She shrugged. "I drove from state to state for almost two years, staying in motels, getting part-time jobs where I was paid under the table. I knew I could never stay in one place too long. But then I ended up in Connor. I was at Artie's diner, reading the newspaper left on the table by a previous customer. When I glanced at the classifieds, I saw an ad for a ranch-style house with property. I sat there and dreamed what it would be like to stay in one place, to have a home, and a steady job. For whatever reason, I decided then and there I didn't want to run anymore."

She took a sip of water, remembering that day like it was yesterday. She'd been so weary, so tired.

"My fleece was the ranch-style house. If I could get it, I would stay. So, I negotiated a deal with the owner, and he accepted. I went back to Artie's the next week and took the part-time job he was advertising. Shortly after that, I bought Goliath. It was a fluke really. I got him for next to nothing. Even so, I debated about spending the money, knowing I was adding to my monthly expenses and making it more difficult if I had to disappear again. But in the end, I went for it. And I'm so glad I did. There have been times when Goliath was the only thing that kept me going. Anyway, I've been in Connor ever since."

She could tell Hunter was trying to take it all in, to absorb everything she had said. Seconds, maybe minutes passed in silence.

"So that's my life. Sounds like a bad Lifetime movie, doesn't it?" Her nervous laugh did nothing to disguise the emotion in her voice. Sitting with her legs pulled tight to her chest, her chin on her knees, she looked at Hunter through blurred eyes.

"You're amazing." He reached forward and brushed his thumb across her cheeks, catching her tears.

"An amazing mess you mean."

"No. I mean amazing, as in incredible."

"You're so full of it." She laughed, then stood and dried her face with the hem of her shirt.

"Why do you say that?" He looked up at her as she paced nervously in front of the fireplace. "I'm being honest with you. I think you're incredible. You've been through so much, but here you are determined not to give up on life."

"Determined?" she laughed. "Is that another way of calling me stubborn?"

Crossing the room, he reached for her, pulled her close, and grinned. "Maybe. But only in the most flattering sense of the word." He bent to kiss her, but she ducked her head. "I wouldn't do that if I were you. I have minty throw-up breath." He tipped her chin up until their eyes met. "I'll take my chances."

Chapter Forty-Six

The phone rang just as the movie credits began to roll.

Because of her emotional storytelling and upset stomach, Charlie had asked that they stay in and watch movies for the rest of the afternoon. But just like before, her symptoms went away as quickly as they had appeared. Other than a lingering pain in her stomach, she felt okay.

Not great, but okay.

"Hey, Mom," Hunter answered the phone. "Yeah, she's doing fine." He looked down where she was nestled against his side—his arm draped across her shoulders—and gave her a squeeze. "Well, I don't know if she feels *that* fine. Let me ask." He muted the phone. "She wants to know if you're feeling up to having a family dinner?"

"Ahh . . ." she hesitated.

"That's okay, I'll just tell her no." Before he could un-mute the phone, she stopped him. "How about we have dinner here?"

"We don't have to. Remember, this time is meant for *us*, not my family."

"But your family is a big part of you, and that's the *you* I want to get to know."

He quickly brought the phone up to his ear. "Mom, can I get back to you? Yeah, just give me a minute." Disconnecting the call, he asked, "What do you want to do, Charlie? It's up to you."

"I want to spend time with them, really I do. But, if we have dinner here, and I start to feel poorly again, I can just

232

excuse myself and go to my room. I'd rather do that than have your family think I'm purposely avoiding them."

"They're not going to think that. It was obvious you were sick earlier. They'll understand."

"But I want to. Really, I do. I don't want to leave here and their only impression of me is Jake thinking I'm an opportunist, Courtney being scarred for life because Uncle Hunter's lady friend threw up all over her castle, and your mom and sister-in-law thinking I'm trying to alienate you from your family."

He sighed. "That's not going to happen. Besides, I don't want you to feel like you have to win them over. I love my family to death, but who I see is my decision. I don't need their approval."

"But I want to have dinner with them." She quickly glanced at her watch. "It's four-thirty now. You said your mom likes cooking for you, right?"

"Yeah."

"So, why not have everyone come here? Your mom, Diana, and I can work on the meal together. That will give them a chance to get to know me while you spend quality time with Cody, Courtney, and Jake. Maybe if Diana sees I'm not a crazy woman or a groupie, she will put in a good word for me with your brother."

"I don't care what Jake thinks," he snapped.

"Yes you do, and you know it. You might be mad at him now, but deep down, you care what he thinks."

He shrugged in indifference.

"I want to do this, Hunter." She looked into his eyes. "If you want me to be a part of your life, that means being a part of your family's life too. If the ranch becomes my home someday, I want to know I'm accepted, not just tolerated. I want to do this for us."

Charlie watched the change in Hunter's expression as the meaning of her words sunk in. His calloused hands came up and gently framed her face. "Are you saying what I think you're saying?"

She nodded, her heart racing a million miles a minute, her smile quivering with emotion. "I don't know how we are going to make this work, or what the next step will be, but I *do* want to take that next step . . . with you."

The heat of his lips pressed against hers felt amazing.

Miraculous.

Extraordinary.

Words were not strong enough to express what she was feeling. His kiss was passionate and overflowing with joy. Her jaw throbbed slightly, but she didn't care. Closing her eyes, she drank in Hunter's touch, his scent, his love. Though doubt and fear still lingered in the recesses of her mind, she refused to give into them. She needed to break their foothold if she was going to move forward. And as terrifying as it was, this was her chance to be loved.

Truly loved.

Deeply loved.

And she was going to take it.

Chapter Forty-Seven

Charlie stood back, looking at her reflection in the full-length mirror, knowing Hunter's family would be there any minute.

She hated the purple tinge on her cheek but liked the feminine silhouette the maxi dress gave her. The black halter top and black-and-white geometric skirt looked classy, sophisticated even. She debated wearing it, afraid it would look like she was trying too hard, but she didn't feel yoga pants or tattered jeans were appropriate for a family dinner.

Gently, she pressed on her abdomen, trying to decide if it was swollen or just her imagination. She turned sideways, gliding her hand down the flowy dress, scrutinizing her shape. Her stomach was tender, something she had noticed of late whenever she ate too much or after she'd been sick. But at least it wasn't noticeable.

Taking one more look in the mirror, she decided to leave her hair down. Since the dress was backless, she didn't want to show too much skin and give anyone the wrong idea.

Besides, this looks more casual.

Hearing loud conversation coming from the living room, she took a deep breath and swallowed back her racing nerves.

Okay, God, here is Your chance to prove to me You are the God I believed in as a child, not the God who takes pleasure watching me screw up my life.

She walked out of her room and into the chaos of two children vying for a piggyback ride from their favorite uncle. When Hunter saw her, he stood up straight and silently mouthed, *Wow!* His eyes traveled from her bare feet poking out from under her skirt to her bare shoulders and back to her eyes. It made her blush.

"I'll just go see what I can do in the kitchen," she said as she scooted by the giggling kids and a speechless Hunter.

"Miss Charlie!" Courtney exclaimed. "You look so beautiful." The little girl turned and tugged on Hunter's arm. "Doesn't she look beautiful, Uncle Hunter?"

"She sure does, Courtney."

They exchanged a second glance, causing the heat in her complexion to intensify.

When she walked into the kitchen, both Irene and Diana looked up from what they were doing and smiled. "How are you feeling?" Diana asked as she washed potatoes in the prep sink.

"Better."

"What a lovely dress," Irene said. "Are you sure you want to work in the kitchen? I would hate for something to happen to it."

"It's okay. I got it on sale." Feeling the muscles in her stomach contract slightly, she willed her body not to embarrass her again. It took a second for her to realize she was pressing her hand to her abdomen, but it was obvious from Diana's quick glance, she had noticed too.

"Hunter mentioned you've been battling some kind of bug," Diana said as she dried potatoes and punctured them with a fork.

"It's nothing." She smiled, shrugging off her concern.

"It doesn't sound like nothing."

Charlie fidgeted, certain she didn't want to spend the time it would take to fix dinner talking about her health problems.

"Diana, you're making Charlie feel uncomfortable," Irene said.

"I'm sorry. I didn't mean to give you the third degree. It's just the nurse in me. How about your jaw? It's pretty bruised, and I noticed you didn't eat much at lunch."

"It's a little sore, but it will be fine." She forced another smile. "Now, what can I do?"

Working side by side, Charlie helped them prep the meal while they asked a litany of questions: about her parents, where she grew up, where she lived. She kept her answers vague and stretched the truth when she needed to.

"But I still don't understand why you and Hunter butted heads over that saddle giveaway," Irene said as she gathered ingredients from the refrigerator to make a Caesar dressing.

The stress of answering Irene's questions was causing her insides to twist and tighten. She wasn't mad at her. How could she be? Irene was asking questions any mother would have of the person in her son's life. Deciding she might as well tell the truth and get it out in the open, she cleared her throat. "It's kind of complicated. The reason I didn't want my picture taken was—"

"Hey, Mom," Diana interrupted. "Would you do me a favor and check on the kids? Jake is supposed to be watching them, but I don't want them horsing around near the pool."

Grandmotherly concern immediately creased Irene's face as she wiped her hands on a dish towel. "I know they know better, but I'll check on them anyway." Irene hurried from the kitchen.

Charlie looked at Diana. "Thank you. I didn't want to lie, but I wasn't sure how much to divulge."

Diana's smile was thin. "I knew you were ready to come clean, which I applaud. But Amy's death was incredibly difficult on Irene. Knowing you've suffered some of the same things Amy did might be a little too much for her to digest. She blamed herself for a long time. It was tough on all of us. We struggled with the what-ifs, and the I-should-have-knowns. But knowing you're still in danger might be a bit much for Irene to handle."

Charlie looked down and continued to chop the chives she was working on. "So, you don't think I should've come?"

"No, I didn't mean for it to sound like that," Diana assured her. "I'm glad Hunter brought you home, and I can already tell you have just the right amount of spunk to keep him in line."

Charlie slid the chives into a small bowl and set the knife on the drain board. With her back to Diana, she pressed her palm to her stomach and tried to massage away the tightness. When she turned around, Diana glanced at her then continued what she was doing.

"So how bad is the pain?" she asked matter-of-factly.

Charlie looked at her, not sure what to say.

"Like I said, I'm a nurse. I notice these things."

"It's not too bad."

"But it's recurring?"

She nodded.

"What are some of your other symptoms?"

"Normal flu stuff. Nausea, vomiting, sometimes a fever."

"And the pain in your stomach, is it a sharp pain or does it just feel tender?"

She shrugged. "Tender, I guess. I just figured my muscles were sore from puking."

"What about your appetite? You didn't eat much at lunch, or was that because of your jaw?"

"My jaw isn't helping matters, but I haven't had much of an appetite lately. I think I'm just leery about putting too much food in my stomach when it feels queasy all the time."

"So it's all the time?"

"That's not what I meant." She hated herself for using such a definitive word. "Just lately."

She watched as Diana tidied up the counter, putting ingredients back where they belonged. When she was done, she wiped her hands on a dish towel and leaned back against the counter. "Charlie, I know it's none of my business, but your health is nothing to fool around with. If these symptoms are recurring, you should see a doctor."

"A doctor? For the flu?"

"That's just it. I don't think it's the flu. If you're having symptoms you can't seem to shake, it could be something bacterial or viral. Something a round of antibiotics could take care of. But left unchecked, it could get worse."

"I appreciate your concern, Diana, really I do, but I don't feel like it's that serious. I just think the first time I got the flu, it really took it out of me, and I haven't given myself enough time to recover. And with the stress I've been under lately . . . I just need some time to bounce back."

"Okay," she said with a conciliatory smile. "But listen to your body. You need to be careful that—"

"Be careful about what?" Hunter said as he walked through the kitchen to the refrigerator.

Charlie looked at Diana and shook her head subtly.

Not now.

Chapter Forty-Eight

Hunter closed the refrigerator, Worcestershire in hand, and asked again, "Be careful about what?"

Charlie looked at Diana, eyes pleading with her not to say anything.

"Aah . . . I was just telling Charlie to be careful . . . about what she eats until her jaw feels better."

"Well, don't discourage her too much. She already eats like a bird."

Poised to issue a rebuttal, Hunter silenced her with a quick kiss. Surprised by his show of affection in front of his family, she just stood there as he winked, then disappeared back through the living room. She chanced a look at Diana who was grinning from ear to ear.

"Thanks for not saying anything."

"But he knows you've been sick, right?"

"Kind of. I mean, after today, he knows I haven't been feeling my best. But it will pass. I know it will."

"Well, he seems to know how to apply just the right kind of medicine." Diana grinned.

Desperate to change the subject, she looked around the kitchen for something she could do. "Would you like me to make a hollandaise sauce for the asparagus?"

Still smiling, Diana shook her head. "Sure. That would be great."

Irene returned several minutes later apologizing for leaving the cooking to them while she played poolside with the kids.

Seeing the spark in her eyes when talking about her

grandkids, Charlie tried to keep the conversation on Cody and Courtney, anything to deflect questions away from her. Unfortunately, that lasted for only a few minutes.

"So, I heard you rode Lois Lane," Diana said while putting the asparagus on to steam. "Did Hunter tell you what happened the first time I rode her?"

She smiled as she stirred the simmering hollandaise. "He did."

"I swear that horse had it in for me since day one. Did she give you a hard time too?"

"No. But Hunter warned me she was a little high strung, so I kept my guard up."

"Do you enjoy riding?" Irene asked.

"I do. I have a retired thoroughbred named Goliath. I spend as much time with him as possible when I'm not working."

"And what line of work are you in?"

Charlie froze. *I stepped right into that one.* Even though she knew it would come up eventually, she'd been dreading it. Seeing the disappointment on Irene's face when she found out her wildly successful son was seeing a waitress—a part-time waitress at that—was going to be tough. *Just blurt it out! Rip off the Band-Aid.*

"I'm a waitress, Mrs. Jennings." She tried to sound proud, unashamed, but she still felt embarrassed.

"Well, that must be why you're in such good shape. I was my skinniest when I was waitressing. Of course, I was also running after three little ones at the time. But I'll tell you, that job kept me in tip-top shape. Between balancing plates, wiping down tables, and doing laps from the booths to the kitchen, I worked every muscle I had. I learned two things back then: Don't take your body for granted and invest in a good pair of shoes. Wouldn't you agree?" Irene said with a chuckle.

"Yes, ma'am."

"Now, Charlie, none of that ma'am or Mrs. Jennings hoo-ha. Call me Irene. It makes me feel younger."

"My pleasure, Irene."

Just as the microwave dinged, Hunter walked into the kitchen. "Steaks are done. Everything else ready?" he asked as he grabbed a platter from the cupboard above the refrigerator.

"The potatoes and asparagus need a few more minutes, but after we toss the salad and set the table, we should be ready."

"I'll set the table," Charlie offered since she knew where everything was. Removing the sauce from the burner, she did a mental head count, then gathered enough silverware and placemats before going outside.

Hunter looked at her from where he stood next to the grill and gave her a wink. She smiled but kept walking. After putting the placemats down, she was laying out the silverware when Hunter snuck up from behind and startled her. "What are you doing?" she scolded in a hushed tone. "I nearly jumped out of my skin."

He leaned in close and whispered into her ear. "You look amazing." Then, brushing his lips against her bare shoulder, he sent chills racing down her spine.

"Hunter!" She quickly looked around, thankful Jake's attention was on the grill, and the kids were too busy playing.

He reached for her elbows and pulled her closer. "What?" he chuckled.

"Someone will see you." She turned back to the table, fumbling with the rest of the silverware.

"Oh no," he whispered once again in her ear. "Heaven forbid someone sees me kissing my girlfriend. What will they think?"

Charlie quickly stepped around to the other side of the table and continued laying down forks, knives, and spoons. "Come on, Hunter," she spoke softly as she glanced toward the barbecue. "Your brother already hates me. Let's not stir things up."

He grinned. "If you didn't want to stir things up, you shouldn't have worn that dress."

Immediately, she looked down at her dress, feeling embarrassed. "Why? Is it inappropriate?" She dropped the rest of the silverware on the table and walked toward the open patio door.

He laughed as he caught her arm and turned her around. "I didn't say it was inappropriate." The look in his eyes, along with his playful grin was way too sexy. It rattled her nerves from head to toe. "I just said you were stirring things up . . . with me."

"Well, toughen up, cowboy. This is a family dinner, with five sets of eyes on us. You might not care what your family thinks, but I do. I have a lot of damage control to do. Now, tell me the truth. Should I go change?"

"Absolutely not. You look amazing!"

"But is it appropriate? I wasn't trying to stir things up. I just wanted to look nice, and I didn't think yoga pants or jeans were going to cut it."

"You look great." He pulled her into a quick hug and kissed her on the forehead. "Now, relax and stop trying so hard."

Just then, she felt a tug on her hand. "Miss Charlie, can I help you set the table?" She took a step back from Hunter and bent down next to Courtney. "I would love for you to help me. How about I finish with the silverware while you go inside and ask your momma for the napkins." The little girl nodded with enthusiasm as she ran inside. Charlie stood up and looked at a smiling Hunter. "What?"

"Nothing." He winked again, then went to help Jake with the steaks.

With the table set and the food in place, everyone took a seat around the table and bowed their heads as Hunter said the evening prayer. He thanked God for his many blessings: his family, his career, his health to enjoy them, and Charlie—the woman he loved. When everyone said amen, Diana and Irene smiled at her, but Jake just shook his head, clearly irritated as he stabbed a piece of steak and put it on his plate.

Conversation was light. Irene and Diana helped the kids with their plates while everyone complemented each other on their contributions.

The guys had grilled the steaks to perfection, the Caesar dressing had a zing to it, which Charlie learned was one of Irene's signature dishes, and everyone raved about the hollandaise sauce. Everyone but Cody. He made a face and said it was yucky, which Diana quickly scolded him for.

Charlie quietly took it all in. This was what it was like to sit at a family dinner table. The kids chattered about the barn cat, guessing when she was going to have her kittens, Irene described to her and Diana the new window treatments she was thinking about getting, and Jake talked with Hunter about the ranch. Everything was great . . . until Jake raised his voice.

"But Hunter, we've talked for years about developing the north-east section. To drill wells, so we could expand the herd."

"I know we have, but I've been thinking lately that might not be the direction I want to go. In fact, I'm considering selling it off."

Diana and Irene stopped talking and turned their attention to Hunter. Charlie could tell from the looks on everyone's face this was a monumental decision.

"What are you talking about?" Jake's tone was controlled, but she got the impression that was only for the children's benefit. "You've never once considered selling that land. Why the one-eighty all of a sudden?"

Hunter took a swig of tea before looking at the adults staring across the table at him. "I'm thinking about buying out the remainder of my contract. I figure it will cost me between ten and twelve million if I negotiate it right. Selling a section of the undeveloped portion of the ranch will allow me to hold onto my other assets."

"But you only have three years left, maybe less than that. Why now?" Jake asked matter-of-factly as he looked at Charlie. "As if I didn't know."

"Knock it off, Jake. This has nothing to do with Charlie."

"Yeah, right. Why do I find that so hard to believe?"

Charlie stared at her plate, knowing all eyes were on her.

"Well, believe it," Hunter continued. "I've been thinking about this for a while now. I didn't say anything because I wanted to figure it out for myself, and I decided not to make a decision until this tour got underway. I wanted to see if it reignited the excitement and the energy I used to get from being on tour, but all it has done is confirm what I've known for a long time. I'm done."

"You're done. Just like that?"

"Jake . . ." Diana laid her hand on top of her husband's while glancing at the kids. "Maybe you two can discuss this later, after dinner."

"There really isn't anything to discuss. I've made my decision. This is my last tour, and I'm going to talk to Rob about getting everything in motion for a buyout."

"Uncle Hunter," Courtney looked at him, her eyes sparkling with excitement, "does that mean you'll be home for ever and ever, and never go away again?"

He smiled. "Well, I'll still be gone every so often, but I will definitely have more time at home with you and Cody."

"Yippee!" Courtney flung her arms over her head, spilling her juice in the process. Both Diana and Irene jumped to their feet and hurried to mop up the spill.

Jake stood, tossed his napkin on his plate, and shook his head. "Well, I guess I know where I stand. I'm nothing more than a hired hand." He turned to leave.

"Jake, stop. You know that's not true."

He spun back around. "Then why didn't you discuss this with me sooner, let me know what you were thinking? You used to talked to me about everything, but I guess that was before you got your high-priced manager and your entourage of advisers. I mean, after all, I'm just your brother." He walked away, leaving tension in his wake.

"Why is Daddy so mad at Uncle Hunter?" Courtney asked, looking at Diana.

"He's just a little upset, sweetie, like you and Cody get sometimes with each other."

"Well, he has no right to be," Hunter said belligerently. "It's my life."

Diana looked at him directly. "And until today, you always made him feel like he was a part of it."

Hunter hung his head, and Charlie could tell Diana's words stung.

"Look," Hunter turned to Diana, "I didn't mean to cut Jake out of the decision-making process, and just so you know, I haven't discussed this with Rob either. This decision is personal, not business. It's my future. I need to do what's right for me. I'm sorry it came up now. I wasn't going to say anything until I had all the bases covered, and I certainly did not mean to ruin dinner." He pushed back from the table. "I'll go talk to Jake." He reached for Charlie's hand and gave it a squeeze. "I'll be right back."

Irene nervously blotted her lips with her napkin. "Those boys. They're just so pig-headed. Have been since the get-go."

"Charlie, I swear we aren't usually this dysfunctional," Diana said with a nervous chuckle. "It's just that Jake is very protective of Hunter. Unfortunately, his protectiveness has a way of coming across as hostility. I'm sorry we haven't made a better impression on you."

Even though Irene and Diana tried to put the blame on simple sibling rivalry, she knew the truth. "I'm the one who should be apologizing. If I hadn't come here, none of this would've happened."

"That's not true," Diana said. "Please don't blame yourself. Hunter shouldn't have brought up selling the ranch. It was poor timing on his part."

"Please, dear," Irene said with a warm smile, "let's just go ahead and finish our dinner. The boys will work this out between themselves. They always do."

Charlie pushed her food around on her plate while she listened to Diana, Irene, and the kids carry on a normal conversation. She didn't dare take another bite. Because there was no possible way she'd be able to keep it down.

Chapter Forty-Nine

Hunter hurried to catch up with his brother as he power-walked home.

"Come on, Jake, slow down and let me talk to you."

He whipped around, his pointed finger lashing the air. "You never once talked about selling off that land, even when we knew there was a possibility it was dry. You said you didn't care if it sat empty or barren. It was your land, and you were not going to sell it. Now, suddenly, it's a done deal? You're selling it so you can buy your way out of your contract? What's this all about, Hunter? What is this woman doing to you?"

"This isn't about Charlie! This is about me! My life! My future!"

"And she has nothing to do with it? Nothing at all?" Jake challenged.

Hunter sighed, his hands on his hips. "Not to start with, no. But I won't lie. Meeting Charlie, being with her, has made the decision easier."

His brother just shook his head.

"Come on, Jake, don't tell me you don't understand what I'm feeling. When you met Diana, your world consisted of wherever we were on the road and a small apartment in Alabama. If you were away from her for more than four days, you were unbearable to be around. That's what I've found with Charlie. Someone who is interested in me for me. Not my celebrity status or my money. Just me."

Jake looked at him like he was going to unload. Hunter

squared his shoulders and prepared himself for the *you're throwing your life away* speech.

"You really love her, don't you?"

His brother's softened tone took Hunter completely by surprise. He relaxed his shoulders and sighed. "I do."

Jake rubbed his face, looking exhausted. "And you're sure this isn't your way of excising your demons over Amy?"

"That's not it at all. I'll admit, the first time Charlie blurted out she was running from an abusive husband, I wanted to do everything in my power to ensure her safety. And maybe, in some strange way, I wanted to protect her as a way of making up for the fact that I wasn't there for Amy. But the more I've gotten to know Charlie, the more I want to be with her. We started talking on the phone after concerts or when I was traveling from town to town, and it felt like the most natural thing in the world. This is love. I'm sure of it."

"But you're not even sure she feels the same way. You said yourself that you needed to *convince* her."

"I admit, she's still scared. And no, she hasn't said the exact words, *I love you*. But I know she does. I feel it. Even when she's pushing me away, I know she is doing it to protect me. She doesn't want me to get hurt or to ruin my career. I just have to make her understand none of that matters to me. All I want is her. And I know we'll find a way to make this work."

"Even though she's still married?" Jake said, irritation creeping back into his words.

"Legally, yes. She's still married. But that's just a piece of paper shackling her to a man who beat her, put her in the hospital, and threatened to kill her. If there isn't a safe way for Charlie to break ties with him, we will have our own ceremony here, where we commit ourselves to each other before God."

"Mom will never go for that, and you know it."

"And I will *not* put Charlie in danger. Not for you. Not for anyone. So if that means she stays in hiding here on the ranch, and we never get the chance to legalize our marriage . . . then that's just the way it will have to be."

Chapter Fifty

When Hunter returned to the house, his mom was scraping leftovers into plastic containers while Charlie did the dishes.

"Did Diana and the kids go home?" he asked as he leaned against the granite island.

"Yes," his mom said, while putting items into the refrigerator. "She thought it was for the best."

Charlie turned around and gave him a guarded smile.

"I'm sorry. I didn't mean to ruin dinner."

"It's not your fault, dear," his mom said in a reassuring tone. "We all know how Jake gets. He has taken care of you since you were a kid, and hasn't been able to let go yet, even if you are all grown up. Change is hard for him."

"But any decision I make in the future that he doesn't agree with, he'll blame on Charlie. And that's not fair."

"Life isn't fair, sweetie. You know it and I know it, and Jake will just have to get over it."

Hunter watched as his mother turned to Charlie and gave her a hug. "Like we said, sweetheart, we might be a dysfunctional bunch, but only because we love each other fiercely. Give Jake time. He'll come around." She gave Hunter a firm embrace and a peck on the cheek. "Now, I'm going to get out of the way so you two can enjoy the rest of your evening. But, Charlie," she said over her shoulder as she walked away, "I'm going to expect some quality gal time on your next visit."

After they watched his mother disappear through the

patio doors, Charlie smiled at him.

"Well, that was fun," he said, tossing a dishtowel into the sink, totally frustrated. She just laughed, catching him completely off guard. "What's so funny?"

She shook her head. "I've never seen so much love and need to protect each other in one room."

"That's what you see?" he asked, his fingers laced on top of his head. "I see a pain-in-the-neck brother who doesn't seem to realize I'm not a little boy anymore. I no longer have to follow his rules or abide by his decisions. I'm an adult who can make mature choices all by myself. I do not need his permission."

"You're right. You don't." She moved closer and circled her arms around his waist. Looking up into his eyes, she smiled. "And that's why he's acting the way he is. I don't think Jake wants to admit you're all grown up and no longer need his help, at least not on everything."

He wrapped his arms around her and waited for the other shoe to drop. But she just continued to look at him, smiling. Tipping his forehead down to meet hers, he whispered, "I thought this was going to be the last straw. I figured I would come back to find you packing your bags."

"But if I run, I'll only prove Jake right. I decided I'd rather stick around and prove him wrong."

Hunter smiled then kissed her, knowing this was it.

He was head over heels in love.

Chapter Fifty-One

The next morning, when Charlie heard the shower running upstairs, she slipped out of the house while the sun barely peaked over the distant mountains. She left a note for Hunter, explaining that she went for a walk to clear her head, assuring him she was fine and would be back in time for breakfast. After working her way toward the stables, she waited.

It wasn't long before Jake appeared. When she stepped out of the shadows, it stopped him in his tracks. "I was hoping we could talk."

Without a word, he led her to a secluded place where no one would see them. Jake motioned toward a tree stump. Even though Charlie would've rather stayed standing so she would be on an even playing field with him, she knew she didn't have the strength to. She was terrified to talk with Jake and needed all her energy just to keep her composure.

She took a deep breath but could not bring herself to look at him. "I will sign an—" Her words stuck in her throat, causing her to cough, making her want to cry. But she was determined to sound strong . . . confident . . . not weak and fragile. Clearing her throat, she started again. "I will sign anything you want, to prove I have no claim to Hunter's estate, and I'll tell you whatever you want to know about my situation. I will do anything you ask," she looked him in the eyes. "Anything . . . except leave Hunter."

She could feel her legs shaking, and her heart was racing so fast, she thought she might pass out.

Jake stared at her blankly, giving away nothing about what he was thinking, but she refused to look away. She was fighting for her future here and refused to concede.

He finally sighed and switched his weight from one foot to the other. "This could ruin him, you know that, right?"

"No it won't. And you would know that too if you listened to the songs he's written."

"What is that supposed to mean?" he asked as he crossed his arms and stood ramrod straight. "I know every one of his songs, even the unpublished ones."

"Then you should know what matters to him, and it's not the fame or the money."

"Well, *that* fame and *that* money is what bought all this," he said with a sweep of his arm. "It has made him who he is today."

She shook her head vehemently. "No. It has given Hunter *things*. *Things* people measure success by, but it didn't make him into the man he is today. You did. You, Irene, Diana and your kids, and God. Don't you get it? In Hunter's eyes, *you* are the one living the American dream. Family. Love. Faith. You're living the life he wants."

"But—"

"Let me finish," she interrupted. "I know you don't trust me, and that's okay. You have a right to your opinion. But if you think it's Hunter's money I'm after, I'll sign anything you put in front of me. If things don't work out between us, I will walk away and only take what I brought with me."

"Hunter would never allow that."

She pushed her shoulders back. "He doesn't have to know. This can be just between you and me."

"So, you're willing to be deceptive to get what you want." He raised a brow as if he had scored a point in his favor.

"I'm willing to do whatever it takes to prove I have no intentions of hurting Hunter. I love him too much for that, and I know you do too."

"What about your husband? Do you realize Hunter is ready to move you here and set up house with you even though you're still legally married to another man? Do you have any idea what that will do to our mother?"

It took her a minute to formulate what she wanted to say.

"I ran away from Daniel over two years ago because he threatened to kill me. I have no doubt if I had stayed, that's exactly what would've happened. And you're right, I'm still married to him. The courts still have a piece of paper that says he is my spouse. But we were never husband and wife. I was a possession, and he was the possessor. I . . ." Closing her eyes, she fought off the nausea stirring inside her. Just thinking about Daniel caused dizzying bursts of light to dance before her eyes.

"Are you okay?" Jake asked, actually sounding concerned.

She ignored his question—not believing he cared—and quickly gathered her composure. "Hunter and I have talked about this, what our options are. I will do whatever I can to dissolve my relationship with Daniel, but if at any time that puts Hunter or anyone in your family in jeopardy, I'll pull the plug. But I won't leave Hunter. I will not allow Daniel to take just one more thing from me. I deserve to have a life without fear and abuse. I can't imagine God wanting me to step forward, to come out of hiding, and give Daniel the chance to do what he threatened for so many years, just so I can get a piece of paper negated. I can't believe God would want me to do that. I won't do it for Him, and I won't do it for you. However, if at any time it gets to be too much for Hunter, I'll walk away. But that will be up to him. Not you."

She sat in silence, waiting for Jake to say something . . . anything, but he just paced back and forth. Finally, she asked, "I have an offer on the table. Are you going to take it or not?"

He paced some more, than stopped. "So, you want me to

write you a prenup behind Hunter's back, then welcome you with open arms?"

"No. A prenup assumes we'll get married, and since that might not be possible in the eyes of the law, I want you to write something that takes place immediately, regardless of our relational status. And as for welcoming me with open arms, I don't expect you to do that. Not unless you mean it. So, I'm not asking for your blessing. I'm just asking that you not be the obstacle that keeps Hunter and me apart."

He cocked his head. "So how do you think Hunter will feel if he finds out about this little negotiation of yours?"

She thought for a moment, knowing she had taken a risk, that Jake could turn this around and use it against her. But it was a chance she'd been willing to take to prove to him she wasn't after Hunter for his fortune. "I think he'd be disappointed with me for going behind his back, but I think he would be devastated if he found out you purposefully set out to destroy our relationship."

Jake's shoulders sagged. "I don't want to hurt Hunter. I just don't want him to make a life-altering mistake. I already lost a sister to circumstances that, had I interfered sooner . . . might still be alive. I don't want to lose a brother too."

"The only way you're going to lose Hunter is if you keep trying to run his life for him. He loves you, Jake, and respects you more than anyone he knows. Don't make him choose."

Chapter Fifty-Two

Walking back to the house, Charlie's whole body shook from her conversation with Jake. Thinking she could slip in through the French doors off her bedroom, she hurried across the patio. That's when she saw Hunter sitting under the pergola, a coffee mug in his hands, the rising sun streaking his face with both shadow and light.

He looked so good with his jean-clad legs stretched out in front of him, his bare feet crossed at the ankles, a cornflower blue V-neck matching his eyes perfectly. Eyes that were trained on her.

She felt overwhelmed.

Not because of her discussion with Jake, but because she realized no matter what obstacles or struggles they would inevitably have to face, she loved Hunter. Something she was afraid to admit—even to herself—just a few days ago.

"So, where did you run off to so early?"

His tone was solemn, tentative even. She stepped closer and smiled, but he didn't return it. Seeing his scruffy face, mussed hair, and a hint of uncertainty in his eyes, she realized she couldn't lie to him. The story she had fabricated was on the tip of her tongue, but she couldn't do it.

Nervously, she sat down next to him, clasping her hands together to prevent them from shaking. "I wanted to talk to your brother before I left, give him a chance to speak his mind, get it all out in the open."

"I thought he already did that when he tried hustling you

off to the airstrip?"

"Yeah, well, he was pretty upset yesterday, so I thought I would . . ." She watched Hunter glance toward the pool, as if looking at her was too painful. She sat up straighter. "I told him I'd sign anything he wanted me to, so I could prove to him I wasn't after you for your money."

Hunter turned toward her, looking crushed. "So, you offered to sign a prenup . . . to appease my brother . . . without talking to me?"

Hearing the disappointment in his voice, she slouched back in the chair and closed her eyes. Her motives had been so pure. All she wanted to do was reassure Jake and the rest of Hunter's family. She never meant to hurt him.

Opening her eyes, she saw that Hunter was waiting for an answer. "Only because I knew you wouldn't go for the idea."

"But you did it anyway."

Hunter started to stand, but before he could, she scooted to the edge of the chair and took his hands in hers. "Hunter, listen to me. You and I know what we have, know what we feel, but your family doesn't." He looked at her with glossed over eyes, and it was nearly her undoing. "They don't understand what this is between us. Heck, a few days ago, I didn't even understand it myself. But you have to believe me, I didn't mean to hurt you. My intentions were to put Jake at ease about our situation. I thought if he knew I was willing to sign away any claim to your holdings, maybe he'd give me half a chance and not be so negative."

"So, you were willing to sign whatever he put in front of you?"

"I told him I would agree to anything he put in writing, as long as he didn't ask me to leave you."

But now she was wondering if she could do this.

She knew her feelings for Hunter were real. But the problems she brought with her had the potential to blow up in his face. He would be the one to suffer public scrutiny and a firestorm of media attention. Hunter would pay for her mistakes. Just like Jake said.

Maybe . . . if she *really* loved him . . . the best thing she could do *is* walk away?

"You went behind my back, Charlie."

She shot to her feet confused and overwhelmed. "I'm sorry, okay? I was wrong. I admit it. But I thought if I could talk to Jake on my own, show him how serious I was about us, he'd give us some space."

"You don't know Jake."

"You're right, I don't." She dropped back into the chair, weighed down by hurt and disappointment. "It's wrong of me to think I know how this will affect anyone in your family. It's not fair to them."

"What about me?" He stared at her intently. "What's fair for me? That my family has the right to run the woman I love off my ranch and out of my life? Does that sound fair?"

"Hunter," she reached for his hand, "I've been looking over my shoulder for more than two years, and I'm tired of it. But it won't be any different here if I have to deal with Jake bird-dogging me around, waiting for me to do or say the wrong thing."

"But, Charlie, it would be different here. You'd be safe. Jake can think what he wants because *I* know the truth. Over time, he'll see he was wrong. But at least you would be out of danger and out of Daniel's reach." He brought his hand up to her cheek, caressing it softly. "I love you, Charlie, please tell me that's reason enough to try."

She melted under his touch. Closing her eyes, she brought her hand up and laid it on top of his. She was so sure when she woke up this morning, so determined she could do this and ignore the consequences.

Now she needed time to think.

But being this close to Hunter, hearing the emotion in his voice, was making it difficult for her to think rationally. She needed time to herself to process everything, to weigh what would be a life-changing decision for both of them.

For all of them.

Was she really ready to live a life of *complete* seclusion? Because that's what it would be. She couldn't take the chance of being photographed with Hunter or associated with his ranch, which meant she wouldn't be able to come and go as she pleased. Even simple things, like grocery shopping or grabbing a bite to eat would be off limits. Going to a gas station or a feed store would be out of the question too. Which meant never leaving the ranch.

Ever.

And what if Hunter's family never warmed up to her? What if Jake continued to see her as the enemy? And Irene never got past the fact that she was still married to another man? Would they have family dinners? Would Courtney and Cody be allowed to spend time with her? Or, would she be responsible for the estrangement of Hunter's family? Could she really do that to him?

It was all so overwhelming.

"What are you thinking?" he asked.

"I think I need some time to think things through."

"But yesterday you said you wanted to make the ranch your home. Now you need more time? What did Jake say to you?"

"It's not what he said. It's what he made me realize. This decision isn't just about you and me. It affects your entire family. I just need some time to figure out the logistics."

"Then you're not giving up on us?"

"Absolutely not."

At least not for the next few days.

Finally, a smile crossed Hunter's face. He moved to the edge of his chair, and with his hand molded to the back of her neck, pulled her closer and kissed her like only a man in love could.

Chapter Fifty-Three

For lunch, they decided to ride out to the old homestead and have a picnic. Packing up the leftovers from last night's dinner, they took the long way around so they could enjoy a leisurely ride.

When the cabin came into view, Charlie was once again struck by a feeling she could not put her finger on . . . as if the cabin came alive in their presence.

It welcomed them.

Pushing the strange vibe aside, she draped a gingham blanket over the rustic table and unloaded the picnic basket. When they sat down, Hunter reached for her hand, then said a quick prayer of thanksgiving for his family, his prosperity, and her. His words were simple, but they washed over her like a cleansing tide. Enjoying the companionable silence while they ate, she looked around the cabin, soaking it all in.

"What are you thinking?" Hunter finally asked between bites.

"This cabin, there's something about it. I can't explain it, but it just feels so . . . I don't know . . . I mean, I'm not a person who believes in spirits or ghosts or anything like that, but it makes me feel . . . at peace, calm, loved even." She laughed at herself before looking at Hunter. "I know that makes me sound like a crazy person, but I don't know how else to explain it. My heart just feels touched somehow."

Hunter wiped his lips with his napkin, then stood.

Silently, he crossed to the bed and the rustic nightstand that sat beside it. Opening the weathered cabinet door, he pulled out a tin box, old and rusted, then handed it to her as he sat down.

"What is this?"

"Open it."

Lifting the lid, she found several sheets of paper folded together. They were old, brown, and slightly brittle. She looked at him.

"Read it."

Carefully, she unfolded the papers, began to read, then gasped and looked up. "Is this what I think it is?"

He smiled. "Read it out loud."

> To whomever finds me-
> My name is Sarah Muster, and I fear I will not survive the winter. I am writing this now, while I still have energy and my mind is clear. My dearest Samuel struck out on his own weeks ago to gather game. I believe something has happened to him, and he has gone to be with the Lord. I know this because though my heart aches for him, the Almighty gathers me to Himself each night and gives me strength for the coming day.

Tears slid down her face as she continued.

> I would ask of the soul who finds me, to bury me where Samuel and I have laid to rest our only two children. This is where Samuel will look for me if I am mistaken, and he is still on this earth.

She looked up at Hunter. "This is so sad."

He nodded. "Just keep reading."

If you look out the front window, you will see a hill with two crosses on it.

Quickly, she looked through the windowpane, shocked to see three white crosses on top of a small hill. "Oh my gosh, Hunter, there are three crosses up there."
"I know," he smiled again.
Awed, she turned back to the letter.

Samuel and I have had a very full life. We have laughed and cried and grieved many things, but always had the love of the Lord, and the love of each other to see us through every trial and circumstance. Burying our Sadie when she was just ten days old was wrought with many tears, but we knew God, in His mercy, did what was best. She struggled since the day of her birth, and we felt powerless to help her in her fight. There was nothing the doctor could do for her. So, we held her and loved her for those few precious days before releasing her into the arms of Almighty God.
When our Seth died from the fever at the age of twelve, I cursed God. I argued with Him and hated Him. He already had my little girl; now He was taking my precious boy. I didn't understand it. I didn't want to. But slowly, with the help of my Samuel, my sorrow was turned into peace. And somehow, I found comfort knowing our children were in heaven and would be waiting for us to join

them.

    Samuel and I have had a wonderful life—a passionate love affair. After experiencing such loss, we learned to love deeper, hold each other tighter, and wasted not a single day on pettiness or strife. We treasured each moment, never letting the trials of life rob us of our joy.

    I pray, whoever finds this cabin, this letter, and my departed body will learn from what I have written here. God is love, and love—though not without its sorrows—is worth far more than any earthly treasure. Whoever finds this cabin and this letter will also find a deed to this property. I know God will lead the exact person to this land to care for it and give it life once again. It is now yours. I pray you see it for what it is. A testimony to an Almighty Creator.

In a faint, hard to read scribble, Charlie finished reading.

    I've made it to spring, but I am tired now and feel the Lord calling me home. I am anxious to go, to be with my children and my beloved Samuel. I commend my body to this land, and my spirit to the Lord, this glorious 5th day of April—

She gasped, covering her mouth.

"What's wrong?"

"April fifth," she looked up at him, "that's my birthday."

She held the letter, reread sections at a time, looked out the window at the white crosses on the hill, then at the ones hanging on the wall.

"Those are the original crosses, aren't they?"

He nodded. "I found them after reading the letter. They were knocked down and weathered, covered by years of growth, but I found them. If you look closely, you can still see the carvings on them."

She got up and studied the crosses, touching them gently. The tears in her eyes made it hard to see, but she could make out each name and the year of their birth. The year of their deaths were no longer there, the length of the cross having disintegrated over time. "They're amazing."

"I know," Hunter said as he stood behind her. "Jake and I thought so too. We all did. That's why we didn't tear the place down. There was too much life yet to be lived in it. I come here when I want to think or just need time away. As crazy as it sounds, I feel the love and the life this place held, and it ministers to me and has allowed me to have some incredible conversations with God."

She turned to him, shaking her head. "It doesn't sound crazy at all. I feel it too."

"Do you want to hike up the hill and see the new crosses?"

"I'd love to."

Silently, holding hands the whole way, Hunter led her to the top of the hill where the three crosses stood. When they got there, she saw not only the crosses, but an engraved plaque in the ground. Kneeling in front of it, she brushed the dirt and weeds away, then read:

Here lies Sarah, Sadie, and Seth Muster.
They have gone to be with the Lord,
and to join Samuel Muster, husband and father.
We wish we could have known them in life,
because we have learned so much from them in death.

Charlie just sat there, on her knees, tears streaming down her face.

"Come here." Hunter said as he helped her to her feet and wrapped his arms around her. "This is why I know we can make it," he whispered in her ear as he slowly rocked her side to side. "Like Sarah said in her letter, there's no obstacle or circumstance too big for God. We just need to have faith and know God will be there with us every step of the way, even if the steps are difficult to take."

She couldn't speak.

She just nodded and held on tighter.

Chapter Fifty-Four

Charlie zipped closed her duffel bag and slung it over her shoulder. Walking through the bathroom one last time, she made sure she had everything, then grabbed her overnight bag from the counter before meeting Hunter in the hall.

"Here, let me take those."

With her bags in one hand, Hunter wrapped his other arm around her shoulders, then walked with her out to the driveway. She was shocked to see Hunter's entire family waiting there for them. Even Jake.

Irene immediately stepped forward and pulled her into a hug. "Hunter said you'll be back soon."

Charlie turned to Hunter then back to Irene and smiled. "When he's done with the tour."

Irene gave her another squeeze, then whispered in her ear. "You're good for him, Charlie. Thank you for making my son so happy."

Working to control her emotions, she smiled at Irene, afraid if she tried to speak, she would break down and cry.

Courtney was next. Charlie squatted down as the little girl wrapped her arms around her neck and held her tight. "I'm sorry my castle made you throw up, Miss Charlie. Maybe next time you could just read me a book."

Hunter chuckled while Diana cringed.

"I would love that, Courtney." Charlie gave her another squeeze, then stood.

When she stepped toward Cody, he quickly stuck out his

hand. She shook it and said, "Maybe when I come back, we can play some horseshoes. It's been a while for me, so I could use some pointers."

He smiled up at her. "Sure thing, Miss Charlie."

Diana gave her a hug and casually slipped her a piece of paper. "This has my phone number on it," she whispered. "I know you don't want to see a doctor because of all the information they ask, but you can call me anytime if you're feeling bad, or you just have a question, okay?"

"Thanks, Diana. I appreciate that."

Jake stood next to his wife, his hands in his pockets. With a nudge from Diana, he offered Charlie a hand. She shook it. "My offer stands. If you write up an agreement, I'll sign it."

Hunter wrapped his arm around her, resting his hand on her hip. "That won't be necessary."

"Maybe not for you, but if it would make Jake feel better, I'd like the opportunity to put his mind at ease." She never broke eye contact with Jake. She watched as he looked at Hunter, then back at her. With a slight tip of his hat, he said, "I guess we'll see you in a month." Then turned and walked away.

The sun was just setting as they made their way to the airstrip. Charlie looked out across Hunter's ranch, soaking it all in, actually feeling excited to know she would be back soon. She thought about Sarah and Samuel's little cabin, the grief that touched their lives, and the love they shared.

A love so strong, so fierce.

She wanted that.

She wanted that with all her heart.

"What are you thinking?" Hunter asked.

"What?"

"You look like you're a million miles away."

She reached for his hand on the gear shift and smiled. "No. I'm right here. Exactly where I want to be."

When they boarded the plane, Hunter pointed to the back. "Go ahead and take a seat. I'll be along in a minute. I just need to talk to Chet."

She took a seat on the couch and watched as the men bantered back and forth. They both glanced at her and smiled, then Chet disappeared into the cockpit.

When Hunter finally sat down next to her, she curled up and snuggled close to his side. Kissing the top of her head, he asked, "Tell me again why you need to go home?"

"Come on, Hunter, we've been over this. I can't just pick up and leave. I might not have a lot of loose ends, but I do have some. I need a little time to make sure I've covered all the bases. The month will go fast."

"Why wait that long? Tie up your loose ends and come back when you're done. It shouldn't take you more than a week."

"Hunter, you still have the final leg of your tour. I don't want to sit on the ranch all by myself. I want you there."

"But you won't be by yourself. You'll have Diana, my mom, the kids, and—"

"Jake."

"Forget about Jake. And forget about that prenup garbage. You don't have to sign anything."

"But I would feel better if I did."

"Charlie . . ."

She turned so she could see him better. "What harm is there in doing it? If it puts him at ease, maybe he won't be so antagonistic around me."

"But it torques me that he still feels like he knows best, and I'm just some stupid kid who can't take care of himself. I'm a man, Charlie. I don't need Jake running my life for me."

"He's just trying to pro—"

The plane chugged forward, causing her to jump. Hunter chuckled and pulled her closer. "Come on, I'm not going to waste what little time we have left arguing about my brother."

She looked up into his beautiful, crystal-blue eyes and smiled. "Okay, what do you want to talk about?"

"I don't want to talk at all." He leaned down and pressed

his lips to hers. She enjoyed his kiss, but only for a second before the plane began to roll forward. She quickly put her feet on the floor and pushed her head back against the couch cushion, her eyes squeezed shut, Hunter's hand clutched in hers.

He laughed. "Charlie, relax."

"I will."

"When?"

"When we land."

Once the plane was in the air and leveled out, she finally eased her death grip on his hand and opened her eyes.

"Wow, you did great."

She looked at him. "How can you say that?"

"Well, I still have feeling in my hand, and this time you didn't lose consciousness," he teased.

"Thanks."

"I know what will take your mind off of flying."

"What's that?"

"Here, I'll show you."

He kissed her soundly, setting off aftershocks throughout her body. Soon, they were stretched out on the couch, her arm across his chest, her hand feeling every beat of his heart.

With her eyes closed and feeling so safe, she wished they could stay this way forever. That is . . . until she remembered where they were.

Pressing her hand to his chest, she tried to sit up, but Hunter held her tight.

"Where do you think you're going?" he asked, opening one eye.

"I know planes have autopilot. Chet could walk back here at any moment."

"But we're not doing anything wrong."

"I just don't want to give him the impression we are."

He kissed the top of her head then closed his eyes. "He's not coming back here."

"How can you be so sure?"

"Because I told him to give us our privacy."

"Hunter!" Exasperated, she tried to push away, but with his arm locked around her, she didn't get far. "Why would you say that? What if he thinks we are . . . you know . . ." she tried pulling away again.

"Relax." He looked at her and smiled. "Chet knows me better than that." When he pushed a wayward strand of hair behind her ear, his gentle touch stirred powerful feelings inside her.

"So . . ." he whispered, "are you really going to make me wait until the end of the tour before you move in with me, I mean, move to the ranch?"

She looked at him and smirked. "A Freudian slip?"

"I caught myself."

"But Hunter, you realize even if I—"

"*If?*" he questioned loudly.

"Okay, *when* I move to the ranch, I can't live with you. Not until we figure out what we're going to do. I would never disrespect your family like that."

"That's ridiculous! Just because you'd be living in my home, doesn't mean you would be sleeping in my bed. And if my family can't handle that, it's their problem not ours. I have a huge house with bedrooms on two different levels. There's no reason for you to live somewhere else."

"Yes, there is. There are two very good reasons. Courtney and Cody." She saw a flicker of understanding in his eyes. "I don't want Diana and Jake to have to explain to them why we are living together even though we aren't married. And, I don't want the rest of your staff getting the wrong idea either."

"Okay, you have obviously given this some thought. Which is good. But, if you're not planning on living at the house, then where? With my mom? Or maybe you planned on bunking at Jake's house? That would be fun. You could wake up every morning to a healthy dose of disapproval."

"Actually, I thought I could stay at the homestead."

"What?" Hunter propped himself up on one elbow and looked at her square in the face. "You can't live out there.

It's too remote."

"No it's not. It's an easy walk. And I could use a quad to get back and forth at night, or we could put up a temporary corral for Goliath around back. The cell reception might not be perfect, but it's there."

"And what about electricity, food, hot water?"

She looked into his eyes, patted his chest, and smiled. "I didn't say I would be exiled there. I still would be spending most of my time with you, but I definitely would be sleeping at the homestead. Besides, I'm used to solitude. It's not that big of a deal."

He continued to play with a few loose strands of her hair. "It just sounds like such a hassle, having to go back and forth every day."

"Are you kidding me?" She smiled and sighed. "It sounds like a vacation. Wake up when I want, ride when I want, for as long as I want. Make meals in a completely stocked kitchen instead of having to ration everything until my next payday. Go for long walks without having to look over my shoulder. Be able to lie by the pool whenever I want. It sounds perfect."

"So, why wait until after the tour? Move now. Since none of your scenarios included me, it's obvious I'm not needed for you to enjoy yourself. Wait a minute . . . maybe you are after me for my land."

Her mouth hung open in utter shock. "I can't believe you just said that!" She tried to sit up again, but Hunter tugged her back in place, laughing.

"Come on, I was just kidding."

She was ready to read him the riot act when he pressed his lips firmly against hers.

Her protests easily forgotten.

Chapter Fifty-Five

The plane had been idling on the tarmac for several minutes. Chet had already opened the cabin door and taken her bags down to the waiting cab.

Hunter stood with his arms wrapped around her. "This is going to be even harder than I imagined," he whispered in her ear.

She pulled back, looked into his eyes, and smiled. "Come on, Hunter, with the crazy schedule you have for the next month, you won't even have time enough to miss me."

"But I miss you already, and I haven't even let you go." He held her a little tighter. "So, you'll work on your loose ends?" he asked as he placed a kiss on top of her head.

Even though they had a plan to move Goliath to the ranch without involving Hunter's name, she still had other things to do: pack, give notice to Artie, say goodbye to Karen, and make arrangements with her landlord.

Hunter insisted she could get it all done in a week. He even used her own words against her, reminding her how much she enjoyed her *solitude*, so there really wasn't any reason for her to wait until he got home.

"I'll do what I can," she said. "I just don't know how I'm going to explain to my landlord that I'm leaving five months earlier than agreed upon."

"What's there to explain? It's not like you're asking for a refund."

"But don't you think that will make him even more

suspicious? It's a lot of money to walk away from without a fight. Plus, I never made the property improvements we agreed upon."

"So tell him you feel bad that you didn't get to the improvements and that's why you're not asking for a refund. Besides, he's getting a brand-new refrigerator out of the deal too. It will all work out—you'll see."

———— • ————

When Hunter finally let Charlie go, he watched as she walked down the steps and to the waiting cab. He couldn't take the chance of the cabbie recognizing him, so he had waited inside the jet, just out of sight.

Watching the cab pull away, his heart clenched. When the taillights disappeared around a cluster of trees, he stepped back from the stairs, allowing Chet to pull them up. He paced to the back of the plane and forward again. "Chet, is your brother-in-law still a private investigator?"

"Yeah."

"And he's good, right?"

"Very good. In fact, he's worked at one time or another for every government agency with an acronym. But you didn't hear that from me," he chuckled.

Hunter took a seat, and steepled his hands in front of him. "I need him to find out everything he can about a Daniel Fuller."

Chet nodded. "Do you have anything else other than a name?"

"Only that he's had success in the horse-racing industry. I just don't know how much success."

"Good enough," Chet said. "I'll give Jerry a call while we're in the air." He headed for the cockpit.

"Oh, and Chet," Hunter waited for him to turn around, "this is between you and me. No one else needs to know."

"Sure thing, boss."

Charlie thanked the cab driver again after he insisted on carrying her bags to the front door. He thanked her profusely for the generous tip both on Monday and this evening, and offered another one of his business cards, making sure she knew he was available night and day.

After putting her bags in her room, she made a beeline down the back steps, straight to the barn. The minute she slid the large door open, Goliath poked his head out of his stall and nickered.

"Did you miss me, boy?" she asked as she rubbed his chin and the sweet spot between his ears. She crossed to the feed bin, grabbed a bucket, and filled it with a couple of handfuls of oats. "I know Karen has already fed you, but I can still give you a late-night snack."

He made short order of the treat and nodded a thank you. "You're welcome, big guy." She stretched to massage his neck, and as always, Goliath lifted his head over her shoulder and soaked up all the spoiling she was willing to give him.

"I've got a surprise for you, boy," she said as she continued her ministrations. "We're going to be moving soon. And though I know you hate being cooped up in a trailer, it will be worth it in the end." She backed up and looked into his rich, chocolate eyes. "You'll get to run as far as you can see, and we will have more time to ride. It's going to be amazing." She hugged his neck and closed her eyes. *It's going to be amazing,* she thought, trying to convince herself she was doing the right thing.

Chapter Fifty-Six

The next morning Charlie was out in the barn bright and early.

"Welcome home."

She jumped and spun around, her hand pressed to her chest. "Karen, you scared me half to death."

"Sorry about that. I just wanted to make sure—" Karen walked toward her, a look of worry on her face.

"What is it? Did something happen while I was gone?"

She didn't answer, she just raised her hand to Charlie's chin and turned it slightly. "What happened to you?"

She forgot about the bruise on her cheek. Not the pain of it, since it reduced her breakfast to a carton of yogurt. But that it was visible enough that she would have some explaining to do. "It was an accident."

"What kind of accident?" she asked directly.

"Ahh . . . two friends of mine got in a scuffle. I tried to break them up and ended up in front of a flying fist."

Karen looked at it closer. "Did you have it checked out? It looks pretty bad."

"Yes. I had a nurse look at it. It's not broken or anything. Just really sore."

"And you're sure the person who hit you was a friend?"

"What's that supposed to mean?" She didn't like the look on Karen's face, like she was hiding something. "What's wrong? Did something happen while I was gone?"

Finally, Karen looked her in the eyes. "I know you're running from something or someone. And from the looks of

274

that bruise, I'd say that someone found you. You can tell me the truth. I won't judge you. I just want to help, especially if you're in some sort of trouble."

She chuckled, hoping to conceal her panic. "I told you, it was an accident. What would make you think I was in some kind of trouble?"

"It doesn't take a genius to put two and two together. You show up out of nowhere. You live alone. You have no friends. You never go out, except for work. You paid your lease with cash, and Artie pays you in cash. No paper trails or forms to fill out. You keep your blinds drawn almost all the time, and you jump at every little noise. You're a beautiful woman, yet you never go out on dates or do anything social. It all adds up to someone in hiding."

"Wait a minute, how did you know I paid my lease in cash?"

"Are you kidding me?" she laughed. "You gave Mr. Duffy ten thousand dollars cash. It was like winning the lottery for him. He couldn't keep that kind of information to himself any more than Gerald at the feed store kept his mouth shut about the ruckus you threw over winning that saddle."

"People know about that?" She felt her heart begin to race.

"Well yeah. Someone turning down a five-thousand-dollar prize definitely gets tongues wagging."

"What? People are talking about me? What are they saying? Do they think I'm running from somebody? They don't think I'm a criminal, do they?" Her head was spinning.

I thought I'd done such a good job of blending in.

Karen reached out for her. "Relax. No one thinks you're a criminal. Actually, the rumor going around town is that you are some sort of heiress in hiding."

"An heiress? What on earth?"

She shrugged. "What can I say, people think you have money."

She shook her head. "I can't believe people have been wasting their time talking about me."

"Hey, it's the beauty of small-town living."

"But if that's what everyone else is thinking, why do you assume I'm in some sort of trouble?"

"Because I know you aren't rich. If you were, you wouldn't be driving a beat-up old truck, you'd have fixed your fence instead of chancing Goliath getting hung up on a rickety rail, and the saddle you use wouldn't be secondhand."

"How do you know it's secondhand?"

"It's hand-tooled leather with the initials T.J. on the fender. So, you either changed your name or bought it secondhand. I'm betting it's the latter because if you were hiding from someone, you wouldn't be careless enough to keep things from your former life."

Charlie chuckled and smiled, trying to act amused. "I think you've watched too many crime dramas on TV. You're letting your imagination run wild."

"Am I?" Karen asked, looking genuinely concerned. "I'm not a threat, and I've never pried or asked questions. I just want to make sure your past hasn't caught up with you."

She was ready to bluff but decided she needed to trust Karen. "No. My past hasn't caught up with me."

"Thank God. When I saw that bruise on your face, I immediately thought the worst." They stood silent for a few awkward seconds before Karen asked, "So, are you safe?"

She smiled. "I will be soon."

"What do you mean?"

"I'm moving."

"Moving or running?"

"Moving." Charlie could not keep from smiling. "I met someone. Someone who knows all about my past and still thinks we can make things work."

"And do you think it will work?"

For an instant, she panicked but quickly pushed her fears aside, refusing to let her nerves get the better of her. "I do." She smiled. "I think this is my chance at real happiness."

"And you're sure you know him? I mean, *really* know him. Because, men will say or do just about anything to get a woman into their bed. He could be prince charming now. But once the thrill of the hunt is over, he could turn into a real frog."

"First of all, I just spent three days with him, and not one of those nights was spent in his bed. Second, even though we haven't had a lot of time together because of his job, I feel like I've known him my entire life. He makes me feel safe, and that's something I haven't felt for a very long time. Third, I met his family, so I know he has a strong foundation. He's definitely more prince than frog."

"That's wonderful, Charlie. I'll be sorry to see you go, but I'm so glad to know it's for a good reason. Congratulations."

"Thanks, Karen."

Chapter Fifty-Seven

Charlie had been throwing up in the storeroom bathroom for the last fifteen minutes. Leaning over the yellowed porcelain sink, she squeezed her eyes shut hoping it was over.

What's going on? It can't be the flu again, and it can't be food poisoning.

She had shared a Denver omelet with Artie when she showed up this morning. Right after he gave her the third degree about her bruised cheek.

All she could think about is what Diana had said, suggesting that what she had was more than the flu.

But if it wasn't the flu, then what?

When she was pretty sure there was nothing left in her stomach, and the queasiness had passed, she stepped from the bathroom not only feeling horrible physically, but beyond embarrassed. "Artie, I'm so sorry."

"Nothin' to be sorry about, sweetie, you can't help it if you're under the weather. But I gotta ask ya . . . your sour stomach has nothing to do with drinkin' a little too much, does it?"

She stood up straighter shocked he would even ask her such a thing. "Artie, you know I don't drink. Why would you say something like that?"

He shrugged, looking a bit awkward. "Well . . . bar fights and sour stomachs are known to go hand in hand. I just thought maybe that bruise of yours has more of a story than you're tellin' me."

"Artie, I didn't get drunk, and I certainly did not get in a bar fight."

"Okay, okay. Sorry I asked, but it's only because I care and don't want to see you gettin' hurt, or in trouble. I wouldn't be doin' my job as a friend if I didn't ask."

She wanted to give him the "what fors" but didn't. She could tell from his demeanor he didn't mean to insult her, he was just concerned.

"If you don't mind, I'd like to go home and lie down for maybe an hour or so. If I don't have any more stomach troubles, I'll come back in time for the lunch crowd."

"No. Just go home and take care of yourself. I'll call Kay. She's been wantin' more hours. I'm sure she'll be happy to fill in."

Smiling briefly, she knew it wasn't the hours Kay wanted. She just needed an excuse to spend more time with Artie. Kay was in her mid-fifties, and not especially good as a waitress, but Artie didn't seem to mind. It actually made Charlie feel better knowing when she left, Artie wouldn't be so alone.

She hurried home, afraid she would get sick again. Thankfully, she made it without incident, but felt completely wiped out. Lying down, she reached for the clock on her nightstand and set the alarm for six—Goliath's feeding time—then quickly fell asleep.

Startled awake by the buzzing of her alarm, she reached for the off button, then dropped back against her pillows. She felt hot, sweaty, and miserable but knew she needed to get up.

Swinging her feet over the side of the bed, she sat there for a moment. When her stomach didn't protest, she stood and took inventory of her aches and pains. She always felt about the same after a round of vomiting. Her stomach was tender to the touch, and she felt hot and sticky from sweating.

When she caught her reflection in the dresser mirror, she stepped closer. *Yuck!* As if her pallid complexion wasn't enough, the blue and yellow bruising on her cheek, coupled with the perspiration shining on her forehead, made her looked about as good as she felt, maybe worse, if that was even possible.

Taking her time, she walked slowly to Goliath's stall. He was his cheery self, knowing it was feeding time, not caring how she looked. She gave him a smile as she crossed over to the hay bale and pulled off a flake of hay. She immediately dropped the bundle and pressed her hand to her midsection, trying to buffer the pain.

It could be something bacterial or viral. Once again, Diana's words played through her mind.

"No," she said out loud. "It's nothing but stress. It's thinking about the move, what Hunter's family is going to think, and if I'm really ready for this. That's all it is."

But the pain and sickness started before I met Hunter.

Her conscience wasn't allowing her to brush off how she felt. But she chose to ignore it. Two weeks. Everything would be fine in two weeks. And if she still hurt after she was safe on Hunter's ranch, she would know it had to be more than stress.

Once the pain subsided, she gingerly carried the hay to Goliath's feed holder. Knowing she didn't have the energy to lift a bucket of water, she fastened the hose to the spigot, looped the end over Goliath's water trough, and turned it on. Waiting for it to fill, she rested against Goliath's stall.

"Sorry boy. I know I've been a real downer lately, but just hold on. Everything will be better soon." Goliath looked up at her and neighed. She couldn't help but smile.

Dragging herself back to the house, she didn't do much of anything the rest of the night. She just listened to Hunter's CDs, waiting for him to call. It was almost midnight when her phone vibrated on the nightstand. She eagerly snatched it up and pressed it to her ear. "Hey there, cowboy."

"Hey there, yourself," Hunter answered in a sexy whisper.

She smiled. Just hearing his voice was all the medicine she needed. "How did it go tonight?"

"It was awful."

She pushed herself up a little straighter against the headboard. "What do you mean by awful?"

"It had to be the worst night of my career."

Pressing the phone against her ear, she asked, "What happened?"

"I just couldn't get into it. All I could think about was you and how the days can't go by fast enough."

"Hunter," she exhaled. "You scared me half to death. I thought something really horrible happened."

"It *was* horrible. You weren't there."

"Okay, okay, enough of that. How did the show *really* go?"

She heard him groan, imagining him stretching his long muscular legs out in front of him, his custom cowboy boots crossed at the ankles, his head back against the edge of the couch cushion.

Man, I wish I was there beside him.

"It was good," he finally said. "The Winchesters really got the crowd going. With their single at number ten and climbing, they're getting the respect they deserve. On the other hand, Arkansas Rain held their own but are beginning to unravel. Rob told them to get their act together. If they bring any negative press to the tour, he's going to hit them with both barrels."

"And you?" she asked.

"I gave the crowd what they wanted. As far as they're concerned, Hunter Jennings is a good ol' boy with a beer in one hand and a babe in the other. I'm just livin' the dream."

She could hear the sarcasm in his tone and tried to think of something positive to say. "Did you talk to Rob about buying out your contract?"

"Nah. I'm not going to hit him with that until the end of the tour. If I ask him now, he'll be on my case day and night. I'll tell him when I can put some miles between us. That way, he can only berate me over the phone. So, enough about me. How about you? You sound a little tired."

"I guess I am. I was up early for the breakfast shift." She wasn't about to tell him she was sick again. She would just try to sound a little more upbeat.

"Oh . . . well . . . if taking my phone calls late at night is tiring you out, I can—"

"I'm not complaining," she cut him off and laughed. "You're the one who asked why I was tired. I just figured I'd be straight with you. But, if you would rather I lie . . ."

"No, no, no," he chuckled. "No secrets. No lies. There's no need for that."

No secrets. She closed her eyes and felt the sting of guilt. She should say something. Tell him how she was really feeling. But she couldn't. Not now. She knew he would overreact and blow it out of proportion.

I'll be on the ranch soon enough. If I still feel bad, I'll talk to Diana. There's no reason to concern him about it now.

She heard him muffle a yawn. "Okay, so who sounds tired now?"

He sighed. "Guilty as charged. It's just another reason I know I'm done with this. I used to get a huge adrenaline rush after a show. Stay up for hours. But now . . . all I can think about is you and me." He sighed again, but this time she could tell it had nothing to do with fatigue. "Man, I wish you were here." His words were hungry and filled with desire.

"From the sound of it, it's a good thing I'm not."

"You're probably right. But I keep thinking about how it's going to be when it's just you and me."

Heat crept into her every pore. "Okay, cowboy, I think we both better say goodnight before—"

"Before what?" he challenged.

"Before your thinking gets out of hand."

He sighed again.

Charlie closed her eyes fighting to keep herself in check. "Good night, Hunter."

"Good night, babe."

Chapter Fifty-Eight

The next morning Charlie woke up but didn't move. She cautiously took inventory of her body. No pain. Getting to her feet, she waited for her stomach to seize, but nothing happened. "Thank God."

She shocked herself. She hadn't thanked God for anything in a very long time. It felt foreign, but somehow it felt right. She thought about it long and hard throughout the day and into the night.

When Hunter called later that evening, she was closing up shop at the diner. She had insisted on working an extra shift to make up for stranding Artie the night before.

"Hey, you didn't mention you had a late shift tonight."

"I didn't. But it was busier than usual, so I told Artie I would stick around." She cringed. *No secrets. No lies.* She hated the way the lie rolled off her tongue so easily. But there was no reason to worry Hunter needlessly, at least that's what she kept telling herself.

"Then call me when you get home. I don't want you distracted while you're closing up or driving."

"Okay. I will. Talk to you soon." Slipping the phone back into her pocket, she turned around. Artie was staring at her with a Cheshire grin. "What?"

"Someone has herself a gentleman friend."

She smiled at Artie's old-fashioned term.

"Ooh wee, must be serious." He turned off the lights in the backroom and joined her by the front counter. He was beaming. "So, when are you going to bring him around?"

"Bring him around?"

"Heck yeah! You don't think I'm going to let you go out with just any ol' Tom, Dick, or Harry, do ya? I might not be your father, but you can bet I think of you as my own. I want to meet this guy. Make sure he's good enough for you."

His words touched her heart, especially since she'd never had a father to look out for her. "He's away on business for the month, but you have nothing to worry about. He's an amazing guy, and I know he cares for me very much."

He looked at her, his eyes searching. "Tell me he had nothing to do with that bruise on your cheek or your weak stomach yesterday."

She smiled, trying to reassure him. "He didn't hit me, if that's what you're thinking."

He grasped her hands firmly, his heart on his sleeve. "Nothing is worth staying with a man who treats a woman poorly. Nothing."

"Believe me, Artie, I know that. And he isn't like that at all. I promise."

"Because, if he's pushing you around now, it will only get worse. No matter what."

It was like he wasn't even listening. He just kept squeezing her hands and staring at the apron tied around her hips. Then it dawned on her.

"Artie, I'm not pregnant, if that's what you're thinking."

He looked at her, doubt obvious in his stare. "I'll help you anyway I can, you know that, right? You have options, Charlie. You don't have to stay with him."

"Artie," she tugged on his hands with a smile and kissed his knuckles, "you're not listening to me. Hunt—umm . . . Aaron is the best thing to ever happen to me. He's loving, caring, and protective. He would never raise a hand to me. Ever. He has a great family and a relationship with God. A strong one. We haven't even slept together."

He pulled his hands free and wiped at his eyes, making the tears in her own fall all the more easily.

"Do you love him?" he asked with a slight sniffle.

She nodded slowly. "Yes. I do."

"And he loves you?"

"He does."

"So why haven't you brought him around? Why is it this is the first I'm hearing about him?"

She couldn't help but smile at his fatherly interrogation. "It's complicated. But it has more to do with me than Aaron."

"On account of you runnin' from another man?"

His words shocked her, leaving her speechless.

First Karen, now Artie.

She thought she'd hidden her past so well. Obviously, the only person she was fooling was herself.

"Come on, Charlie, I've worked this diner my entire life. You learn how to read people after a while. You came in here a little over six months ago, as jittery as a long-tailed cat in a room full of rocking chairs. Every time the bells on the front door jingled, you jumped, like you were afraid of who might be standing there. You're a natural beauty, but you do nothing to draw attention to yourself. No makeup, no fancy clothes, no flashy jewelry. You don't flirt with the fellas who come in here even though a couple of them would be considered a good catch. They fall all over themselves to get your attention, but you just smile and walk away."

She wanted to stop him—try to explain—but he just shook his head and continued.

"It was obvious some man did you wrong, leaving you frightened and scared. But something has changed in the last few weeks. Your smile is brighter, your shoulders more relaxed, your eyes warmer. And if this Aaron fella is responsible for that, I'm glad. But Charlie, if things go south with this guy, I want you to know I'm here for you. I won't judge. You can trust me on that."

She couldn't help but wrap her arms around him and hold him tight. "Thank you, Artie. You don't know how much that means to me." She stepped back and looked him square in the face. "And I promise, you'll be the first person I come to if things don't work out." She hugged him again, but he quickly bristled at her show of affection.

"Okay, okay, enough of that touchy-feely stuff," he said. "It's late, and you gotta get home, or you'll be worthless to me tomorrow."

He tried to sound cantankerous, but she saw right through it. "See you tomorrow, Artie."

"You better. No more of this namby-pamby sick stuff."

She saluted. "Yes, sir."

Chapter Fifty-Nine

It was happening again.

Charlie rushed through the door and dropped her groceries on the kitchen table, before tossing the contents of her stomach into the kitchen sink. She had gone a whole week without feeling sick, but here she was, bent over, heaving up everything she'd had for lunch. Turning around, she slid to the kitchen floor and stared at the empty boxes in the corner, questioning herself once again.

Two days ago, she decided to go for it, to move up her timeline.

She was going to take the leap and move to Hunter's ranch as soon as she could get everything taken care of. She had done the whole pros and cons thing and convinced herself the good far outweighed the bad. She hadn't told Hunter yet, wanting to surprise him with a text and a picture of her boxes all packed up. Now she didn't know what to do.

After her queasiness settled, she picked up her phone and gently curled her aching body into the corner of the couch. She could feel the heat emanating from her skin as she scrolled her minimal list of contacts.

Her finger hovered.

If she did this, there would be no turning back. She'd be admitting it was something more than the flu plaguing her. But she didn't see any other way.

"Hello?"

"Diana . . ."

"Charlie, what's wrong?"

"I need your help." She closed her eyes and explained what the last few days had been like.

"You really should tell Hunter. He would want to know."

"Diana, I trusted you. Telling Hunter isn't going to help. At least not yet."

I knew I should've handled this on my own.

"Okay. Just give me a minute to think."

The silence on the phone was deafening, causing Charlie to get antsy. "Diana?"

"I'm still here. I'm just considering some options."

She continued to wait, hating herself for saying anything at all.

"Okay, Charlie. Tell me again, how long has this been going on?"

"Since January. The first time I got the flu."

"How many times has it occurred since then?"

She didn't know what to say. She hadn't felt a hundred percent for so long, but that didn't mean she had been sick the whole time, or did it? "You mean actually throwing up?"

"Not just throwing up, but anytime you felt nauseous or sick, even if you had a loss of appetite."

"It's hard to say. I haven't felt a hundred percent for a while."

"What about weight loss? Have you lost any weight?"

"Well, yeah, but I figured that was from being sick. I've also been cautious about eating too much when I haven't felt well. Nothing sounds good when you think you're going to throw it back up."

Diana was silent.

"You said it could be bacterial or viral. Is there something I can do to find out if that's what I'm dealing with?"

"I don't think it's viral. At least not anymore. Your symptoms have hung on for too long. But that doesn't mean it can't be some type of parasite."

"A parasite? How would I have gotten that?"

"There are a few different ways. Meat that isn't cooked

properly is very common. It happens to people more often than you might think."

It was what Diana *wasn't* saying that bothered Charlie. "And what are some other ways I could've gotten it?"

"It really doesn't matter. We just need to find out what's making you sick and take care of it."

"What else?" she asked firmly.

Diana cleared her throat. "Well, sometimes parasites can come from areas with large infestations of rodents, even dogs. The parasite is passed through fleas and cockroaches."

She immediately took offense. "I might not be living in the lap of luxury, but I'm certainly not living with fleas and cockroaches."

"I didn't mean to suggest you were. I was just answering your—"

"Is that it?" Charlie asked, feeling more irritated by the minute.

"It doesn't matter what you have or how you got it. What matters is that you get tested right away so we know what we are deal—"

"How else?" she snapped, knowing Diana was holding something back.

"Charlie . . ."

"How else does someone contract a parasite? It's not like I can't look it up on the internet."

"Fine. Sexual contact would be—"

"Wow!" It was like a physical blow. "You must really think I'm a piece of work. Just forget it, Diana. I'll figure things out on my—"

"Cut the attitude, Charlie!" Diana's voice was sharp. "And don't put words in my mouth. I didn't say what you have was sexually transmitted. I merely answered your question. Believe it or not, I'm not judging you. I just want to help. You're sick. And if you don't get treated soon, it could get a lot worse. So, let's save the bickering for later, okay?"

She wanted to throw her phone across the room and scream. But that wouldn't do her any good.

"Listen, Charlie, there's a test you can take. It's to detect blood in the stool, but it can also test positive for parasites and other things."

"But I can't go to a doctor. It raises too many red flags."

"You don't have to. You can pick it up at a pharmacy and administer the test yourself. Then you send it to a doctor for analysis."

"What good will that do me? I would still have to use a doctor. They'll want my name, my history, my social—"

"No. They won't. I'll have you send it to the doctor I used to work for in Alabama. He'll think it's mine."

Charlie was shocked. *She* knew there was zero chance she was battling a sexually transmitted disease, *but* Diana didn't. "You would do that for me? I mean, you have no idea what the results are going to say."

"I told you, Charlie, I want to help. Especially if this can be solved with a simple round of antibiotics."

"And what if it's not a parasite?"

"Let's not get ahead of ourselves."

"And you promise not to say anything to Hunter or Irene, even Jake?"

"As a medical professional, I'm HIPAA certified. The minute you divulged information to me in confidence, I considered you a patient seeking medical help. I took an oath. An oath I take very seriously."

"Thank you, Diana. Sorry for jumping all over you earlier."

"Don't worry about it. Just take the test as soon as you can and follow the directions precisely. There are certain foods you can't eat before taking the test."

"I will. I promise."

"Okay. What's the name of the pharmacy in your town?"

There was no way she would use the local pharmacy. People were already talking about her. "Just choose a pharmacy in Nashville. I'll pick it up there."

Chapter Sixty

Charlie stared at her phone, waiting for Hunter to call. When it finally vibrated it was like an electric shock. She dropped it and hurried to pick it up but when she swiped the screen, she fumbled it again. "Dang it!"

"Charlie? Charlie?"

She quickly pressed the phone to her ear. "Yeah, I'm here."

"Hey, babe, what's wrong?"

"Nothing. I just dropped the phone." She took a couple of silent breaths, to clear the edginess in her tone. "How did everything go tonight?"

"Like clockwork."

"Good."

"How about you? How did your shift go?"

"It was a little hectic, but good overall."

"Why was it hectic?"

"A baseball team's bus broke down up the street from us. While their coaches arranged for a second bus to pick them up, the team hung out at the diner."

"What are we talking here, little league, high school?"

"Actually, they were a minor-league team from Nashville."

"Really? And how long were they there?"

"A couple hours."

"Artie must've made a killing."

"He sure did, and the tips were great too. The team had won in extra innings, so they were already fired up and hungry. I don't think I've ever served so many burgers in one day."

"Did they give you any trouble?"

"Not really. Like I said, they were fired up over their win, but they never got completely out of hand."

"What do you mean by fired up?"

She wasn't sure, but she thought there was a slight edge in Hunter's tone. "You know . . . they were amped. A little rowdy. But Artie warned them if they didn't behave, he would kick them to the curb."

"So . . . did they hassle you?"

Now she was positive she heard a hint of belligerence in his voice. "I know how to handle myself, Hunter."

"That's not what I asked," he snapped. "Did anyone hassle you?"

"A couple of them were a little forward, but they were basically harmless."

His silence bothered her.

"Hunter, men have made passes at me before."

"Is that all it was? Or did they expect a little something extra in exchange for a generous tip?"

She was doing her best to ignore his barbed comments. Her day had started way too early with her round-trip to Nashville to pick up her test kit. Then, she had to deal with the busiest day ever at Artie's, terrified her stomach was going to revolt on her at any minute. And if that wasn't enough, she had to spend two hours dodging frisky hands and suggestive comments. After all that, she certainly did not feel she should have to defend herself to Hunter.

"You know what, I'm tired. So before I say something I'll regret, I'm going to hang up. Goodnight, Hunter."

"Hold on, hold on. Why the attitude?"

"Why the third degree?"

"I was just asking about your night."

"No you weren't. You were insinuating that I don't know how to handle myself around a few obnoxious guys."

"No I wasn't. It's just that I can tell when you're holding

something back. I wanted to make sure nothing happened that I should know about."

She leaned against the headboard and thought about the test kit sitting on her bathroom counter.

How does he do that? How can he read me so well over the phone?

She sighed, gathered her composure, and got to her feet. "Actually, there is something I think you should know." She hurried to the kitchen.

"I knew it. I could hear it in your voice. What is it, babe? What's wrong?"

"Hold on a minute. I'm going to send you a picture." She quickly snapped a shot of the moving box with Texas or Bust written across the side, then pressed Send.

"Come on, Charlie, talk to me. What's wrong? Did something happen?"

"You'll se—"

"Wait a minute, here it comes," he said.

She waited for it to sink in, but she didn't have to wait long. Hunter let out a howl that nearly pierced her ear.

"You're really going to do it?" he asked.

"If the offer still stands."

"Are you kidding me? I can pick you up tomorrow."

She laughed, loving the excitement she heard in his voice. "Now, now. You can't rush a girl, cowboy. In case you didn't notice that box was empty. I still have to pack up and tell Artie."

"Okay, what are we talking about here? Next week? The week after?"

"I was thinking next week if that's okay with you. It will give me a little time to get adjusted before you come home." She burst out laughing at his cowboy holler. "I guess that means yes?"

"You bet it does! Aw man, just knowing you're on the ranch will make it a whole lot easier on me. Oh . . . I guess I need to get the ball rolling for Goliath."

"Yes. But you have to make sure whoever you get to

transport him understands he hates trailers. He's very temperamental and gets extremely agitated when he feels penned in. And if I'm not there he could get pretty difficult to handle. Maybe I should just do it myself. I mean, who's going to pay attention if an old beat-up truck and trailer shows up at your ranch?"

"Babe, that's a fifteen-hour drive. There's no way I'm going to let you do that by yourself. Especially in that truck of yours. Don't worry. I'll find someone who is used to working with temperamental horses. Would Monday work for you?"

She thought about it for a second. "I guess that would be all right. It will give me a couple of days to get his gear packed up."

"And when can *you* be ready?" he said with such joy in his words, it nearly brought tears to her eyes.

"I'm not sure. I was going to tell Artie yesterday, but he was in a sour mood. And then today was too hectic with the baseball team showing up."

"Well, you had better get on it, sweetheart, or I'll just kidnap you and whisk you away."

"Oh, you will, will you?"

"Yes, ma'am."

"Well, it won't come to that. I'll tell him tomorrow. He already has my replacement, so it won't be a problem. It's just going to be hard to leave him. He's been so good to me."

She headed back down the hall toward her bedroom but stopped at the bathroom door, the kit on the counter stealing her attention.

"How does he already have your replacement, if he doesn't even know you're leaving?"

"Remember I told you about Kay working a few hours here and there?"

"Yeah."

"Well, she has it really bad for Artie, and I think he's a little smitten with her too. She'll jump at the chance to take over my shifts. She isn't as fast as I am, but she and Artie will get along just fine."

"I can't wait for us to start doing life together, Charlie. It will be great. Just wait and see. Nothing will be able to come between us."

She stared at the kit by the sink.

I hope not.

Chapter Sixty-One

The week had been a whirlwind of activity, but Charlie had everything on her to-do list crossed off.

She had loaded Goliath and his tack on Monday, which had been quite a feat. His keen senses had warned him something wasn't right, so he'd been a real pain over the weekend. Then, when the trailer showed up, he acted out something fierce. It took her a while to calm him down with gentle strokes and soothing words, but she was finally able to coax him into the trailer. After instructing the driver of Goliath's likes and dislikes, he was on his way to his new home.

Their new home.

Monday night, she had carefully followed the instructions on her test kit and had dropped it in the mail on her way to work on Tuesday. Even so, she was beginning to think she might have overreacted. She had felt better than usual the last few days, even under all the stress of goodbyes and packing. She thought about calling Diana and apologizing for getting her involved but decided it would be easier to do it in person when she got to the ranch.

Her landlord had been more than amiable when she told him she was leaving, but that she didn't expect any kind of refund. She apologized for not completing the work that was outlined in their agreement, but he was easily appeased when she informed him that she'd be leaving some of her furniture behind, including a brand-new refrigerator.

By far, the hardest thing she had done was tell Artie she was leaving. He took it well and admitted he'd seen it coming after their conversation about her "gentleman friend." But he still gave her the third degree, needing the reassurance her new man wasn't bullying her. He even offered her a raise and his slightly used car, thinking financial trouble was why she was moving in with her mystery man. She assured him her plans were carefully thought out and that they had nothing to do with money troubles.

After convincing him she was truly happy and excited about her future, he wrapped her in a hug. With emotion-filled words, Artie admitted how much he would miss her, but that he was thankful she had someone special in her life.

Now here she was, the sum total of her life packed up into just a few boxes.

I'm really doing this.

I'm moving to Hunter's ranch.

She would finally be out of Daniel's reach, and starting a new life with an incredible, amazing man. It was overwhelming.

In a good way.

A knock on the door pulled her from her thoughts. She peaked through the peephole to see Karen standing on her porch. Disengaging the locks, she swung the door wide.

Karen walked in and glanced at the boxes in the corner. "That's all you're taking?"

"Yep." she said, shutting the door and throwing the deadbolts. "The rest is up for grabs, everything but the refrigerator."

Karen slowly looked around the living room. "I can't believe you're leaving all this stuff behind."

"The place I'm moving into is already furnished." She thought about the homestead with the log-framed bed, wood table and chairs, and old rocker. "This stuff would just look out of place."

"And you're sure you don't mind me picking through it?"

"Not at all. I told Mr. Duffy I was leaving some stuff

behind, but I didn't tell him what. I also told him he could pick up the keys from you on Sunday. That gives you a couple days to go through the place and take whatever you want."

"But what about your truck? I know it's old, but I bet you could still get a couple hundred bucks for it from some high school boy looking for his first set of wheels."

"I don't have time. Besides, I've already signed the pink slip over to you." She reached for the piece of paper on the dining room table and handed it to Karen. "If you want to sell it, go for it. I just thought it would be perfect to haul hay and supplies to the far end of your property."

Karen looked at the piece of paper in her hand, her eyes glossy and red. "I'm going to miss you."

"I'll miss you too."

Karen hugged her. "Call me when you get there, so I know you're safe?"

"I will."

"And you'll call me from time to time just to let me know you're doing okay?"

"Sure."

Karen pulled back and looked her in the eye. "And if things don't work out with this guy, and you need a place to regroup, promise you'll call me."

"I promise, but you don't have to worry. I'm going to be okay. Better than okay."

Karen hugged her again. "I'm happy for you, Charlie. I'm so glad you found someone good."

"And Karen, if anyone ever comes looking for me, you'll call the number I gave you, right?"

"You really think someone is still looking for you?"

"I don't know. My ex was never the type to give up. But even if he managed to trace me here, he'll never find me where I'm going."

Never.

After a tearful goodbye with Karen, Charlie nervously paced the house, waiting for the cab to show up. Karen had offered to drive her to the UPS store and the airport, but she politely declined. Even though she trusted Karen completely, she didn't want her knowing about the private airstrip and jet. The less she knew, the less chance she had of accidentally divulging too much information to the wrong person.

Twenty minutes later, a white pick-up pulled into the driveway. She opened the back door and watched as Rudy, the cab driver, walked around the front of the truck.

"You said to pull down the driveway, right?" he asked hesitantly.

"Yes. That's fine. I figured it would be easier to load the boxes this way instead of walking them all the way to the curb."

And the neighbors won't see and get curious.

Rudy followed her through the kitchen and to the stack of boxes in the living room.

"Thanks again for getting a truck. I didn't think all of this would fit in your cab."

"No problem," Rudy said with a groan as he lifted the first of six boxes. "I borrowed it from my brother. He owed me a favor. As long as I bring it back gassed up, we're square."

She grabbed a box and followed Rudy out to the truck. After he hefted his into the back, he turned and took the box from her. "You don't have to do that," he said. "I can get them."

"It's okay. It wasn't too heavy. But I'm afraid the bottom two are," she said as they walked back into the house.

"No problem. I'll get the rest. For the amount you're paying me, I should've come over and packed them for you." He laughed.

It was true. She had offered him three hundred dollars to take her and her boxes to the airstrip. Actually, Hunter had sent her five hundred dollars to give to him, but she thought that was a bit excessive. She was afraid if she offered Rudy too much money, he would get the impression they were doing something illegal. Instead, she offered him three hundred dollars to rent a truck and drive her to the airstrip. He told her it wasn't necessary, that he would borrow a truck, but the price remained the same. Borrow or rent, either way, she would pay him three hundred dollars.

While Rudy loaded the truck, she walked through the house for the umpteenth time, opening drawers and closet doors, making sure she wasn't leaving anything personal behind. When Rudy picked up the last box, she glanced at her watch.

Right on schedule. We might even beat Chet there.

The drive was relatively quiet. She asked Rudy about his family, his schooling. Benign subjects. However, when he started asking her questions like: Where are you going? And how long are you going to be gone? She panicked, mumbled some ambiguous answers, then reached for the radio dial, anything to deter his line of questioning. "Do you mind some music?"

"Not at all."

A Luke Brian party anthem filled the silence. Not wanting to take a chance one of Hunter's songs would come on, she reached to change the station.

"What, you don't like country music?"

"No. I like country. I was just turning it up a little."

"So, did you go to the Hunter Jennings concert when he was here a couple months ago?"

She turned toward the window. "No. I missed it."

"Ahh, that's too bad. It was epic. I waited in line sixteen hours to get tickets, and it was worth every minute. That guy is livin' the dream. Travelin' from town to town, singing his music while hundreds of women throw themselves at him. Making millions. That's a lifestyle I could certainly get used to."

She didn't trust herself to say anything, so she just nodded in agreement.

By the time they got to the airfield, night had swallowed the sunset. Flashing lights were blinking at the far end of the airstrip, and she could just make out the silhouette of the jet.

"Right on time," Rudy said as he got out of the truck and watched the approaching plane. Standing by the passenger door, she held onto the handle to steady herself as the jet taxied into position. But this time, she knew the light-headedness she felt had nothing to do with her stomach issues. It was panic, clear and simple. Her heart was racing, and her hands were shaking. She closed her eyes and took a couple of deep breaths to calm herself, thankful Rudy was distracted by the oncoming jet.

Don't do this to yourself. This is the right thing to do. Hunter loves you . . . and you love him. Don't blow it now.

By the time the stairs were lowered and the tires chalked, she had her breathing under control. Chet tipped his hat at her then helped Rudy load the boxes into the jet. When they were done, she handed Rudy an envelope and thanked him again.

"I'm sure sorry to see you go," he said as he peeked into the envelope. "You are by far the best customer I've ever had. Enjoy Peru." He waved, got in his truck, and drove away.

Chet pulled the chalks from the wheels and chuckled as she approached the plane. "Peru?"

"I panicked."

Chapter Sixty-Two

When Charlie entered the cabin of the plane, she immediately looked around, even though she knew Hunter was in Seattle.

"He wanted to be here," Chet said as he boarded the plane. "But getting into a jet and flying *away* from a city you have a sold-out concert to perform at, would raise suspicions. Hunter couldn't take the chance that the paparazzi would get curious."

"Of course," she said flippantly. "I knew he wouldn't be here. I'm just nervous is all."

"Do you want to sit in the cockpit with me? I can talk you through everything from takeoff to landing."

"I don't know if that would be more comforting or more terrifying."

"Come on, it will be a good distraction."

She followed Chet into the small cockpit area. He took his seat and immediately started messing with buttons and switches. She slid into the co-pilot seat, her eyes transfixed on the instrument panel.

"How on earth do you keep all these buttons straight?"

"When you've been doing it as long as I have it's no big deal."

"Shouldn't you have a co-pilot to help you?"

"Most times I have Hunter. He's a licensed pilot and usually sits up here with me when we're flying. But I've logged plenty of solo miles."

She continued to look around in front of her, behind her, above her, while Chet talked into his headset.

"Okay, Charlie, we're clear for takeoff. Go ahead and fasten your seatbelt."

She quickly pulled on the belt and shoulder harness, closed her eyes, and held her breath. When she felt the jet lurch forward, she gasped, opening her eyes. She quickly turned to Chet and saw a big grin on his face.

"If you're going to laugh at me, maybe I should sit in the back." She started to undo her belt. "That way, I only have to worry about being terrified, not humiliated too."

He stopped her from getting out of her seat. "Sit down. I'm not going to laugh. I promise. Come on, I'll give you a step-by-step of what I'm doing. You have nothing to be afraid of."

She survived the takeoff and the sharp pull as they rose to the proper elevation. At first, she stared out into the inky black sky, then turned her attention to the control panel. Chet explained the job of the altimeter, navigational system, and a few other things she didn't quite grasp. She had to admit it was all very fascinating and went a long way in calming her nerves.

After Chet had explained every button, switch, and toggle, an awkward silence filled the cabin. She didn't know what to say to fill the void, so she just stared out the window at utter darkness. She stole a few glances at Chet, watching him as he worked. He didn't seem to mind the quiet.

They had been in the air for about an hour when she finally spoke up. "So how long have you been with Hunter?"

"Goin' on ten years," he said as he continued to monitor the control panel.

"Wow. So you've been with Hunter since the beginning?"

"Yep."

"I guess you two are pretty close then?"

"Like brothers."

"So . . . what has he told you about me?"

Chet offered her a quick glance. "He didn't have to say anything. It's written all over his face whenever he talks about you. He loves you, Charlie."

"But still . . . he must've told you something."

"Sure. A little."

Talk about pulling teeth. "Like what?"

Chet was so quiet, she figured he was ignoring the question, but he finally spoke up.

"Hunter told me you had a husband who used you for a punching bag and threatened to kill you if you reported him. He said you can't be seen in public because your husband is vengeful, and you're afraid he'll come after you if he knows where you are."

"And . . ."

"And what?"

"You believe all that?" she asked.

Chet turned to her, a confused expression on his face. "Why wouldn't I?"

"Come on, you have to admit it all sounds pretty soap opera-ish. The whole damsel in distress scenario. Maybe I saw a unique opportunity when Hunter Jennings showed up on my front porch, and I decided to take advantage of it."

She waited for him to read her the riot act, or give her the third degree, but he didn't.

In fact, the quieter he was, the guiltier she felt.

What am I doing? Why am I trying to plant seeds of doubt in one of Hunter's closest friends?

Because I'm an idiot!

"I'm sorry. I shouldn't have said those things." She nervously twisted and untwisted the strap of her seatbelt. "I'm just freaking out a little bit. And since Jake already thinks I'm an opportunist, I figured you might too. I guess I just want to know where I stand with everyone."

He glanced her way and then back to the panel in front of him. "Jake has his reasons for being so protective. Cut him some slack. He'll come around eventually."

"Sure . . . of course. I'm just afraid something is going to go wrong. Someone is going to find out I'm here and cause trouble for Hunter and his family." Tears welled in her eyes. "I just don't want to see Hunter get hurt. I love him too much for that. Really I do."

Chet reached around and pulled something from alongside his seat. Handing her a tissue box, he grinned. "Apology accepted."

Chapter Sixty-Three

"Okay, Charlie, we're going to start our descent and prepare for landing."

She watched Chet manage the controls, but when she knew the landing was near, she braced herself, clutching the armrests and squeezing her eyes shut. She didn't allow herself to exhale until the plane rolled to a complete stop. When she let out a large gasp, Chet laughed while he flipped switches and pushed buttons.

"Good thing it was a quick landing. I thought for sure you were going to pass out."

Her chest heaved as she took a couple of deep breaths. When Chet unfastened his belt, she followed his lead. "I don't think I'll ever get used to flying."

He patted her on the shoulder as he got up from his seat. "Sure you will. Just give it time."

When he lowered the steps, she saw Diana waiting for her next to the Polaris. Feeling off-balance, she took the steps one at a time. When she made it to solid ground, Diana rushed forward and gave her an emotional hug.

"Welcome home," she whispered into her ear.

Home. What a wonderful word.

"Are all the boxes going to the house, or do you want some of them at the homestead?" Chet asked, stacking one on top of another.

She turned to Diana for clarity. "I don't understand. Why would they go to the house?"

Diana smiled hesitantly. "Because Hunter wants you to stay

there until he gets home."

"That's silly. I'll be fine at the homestead."

"I'm sure you would be, but those are his instructions. He doesn't want you out there alone, at least until you're familiar with the property. Besides, this will be easier. Not only will you be closer to Goliath and us, but you'll have a fully stocked kitchen, and a spa tub to relax in at the end of the day."

She couldn't help but smile. It sounded amazing.

After sorting the boxes into two stacks, she climbed into the UTV next to Diana while Chet followed in a pick-up truck.

"Here," Diana said as she handed her a phone. "Hunter wanted you to call him the minute you landed."

She took the phone, seeing that it was all cued up and ready to go. All she had to do was tap the screen.

"Hey there, cowboy, you must have your phone plastered to your ear to be able to pick up on the first ring."

"You've been on the ground fifteen minutes. I was beginning to worry."

Having a hard time hearing, she plugged one ear and ducked her head. "Diana and I were just discussing my living arrangements. It seems they have changed since we last spoke. You know . . . I would be perfectly fine at the homestead."

"I'm sure you would, but for my own peace of mind, I'd prefer you stay at the main house until I get there. No driving off cliffs. No getting turned around."

"But Hunter, I don't see—"

"Please, Charlie, just humor me, okay? I'm thousands of miles away. I don't want to be worried about you riding back and forth every day for meals and a shower, or not be able to reach someone because of the shoddy cell reception."

She rolled her eyes at his over-protectiveness, but in her heart, she smiled. It had been so long since someone cared for her, looked out for her well-being. How could she refuse? "Okay. The main house it is."

Not hearing a reply, she pressed the phone harder against her ear. "Hunter. I can't hear you." She heard half words and cut off sentences. "Hunter, you're cutting out."

"Can you hear me now?"

"Yes. That's better," she relaxed her hold on the phone slightly. "But I missed what you were saying."

"I said, convincing you to stay at the house was easier than I thought it would be. I figured I'd have to do some major begging and pleading."

"No begging. You'll just have some making up to do when you get here."

"Oh, believe me, I will make it up to you." Hunter said in his sexy tone, the one that always sent chills down her spine. "I love you, Charlie."

"I love you too, Hunter." *Shoot!* It slipped out before she could stop herself. She had wanted the first time she told him to be face-to-face, intentional, not over the phone while their reception cut in and out. "I'm sorry. That didn't sound very romantic. I had it all planned out how I was going to—"

"Are you kidding me? That was the most beautiful thing I've ever heard. I love you so much, Charlie . . . there are no words."

She could almost hear the tears in his voice, it tugged on her own emotions. "Will you call me when you're done tonight?"

"Absolutely."

When Charlie disconnected the call and handed the phone back to Diana, she was grinning from ear to ear.

"What?" she smiled, a blush warming her cheeks.

"Nothing. Nothing at all." Diana kept driving, a silly grin on her face.

Chet and Diana helped her carry the boxes to the first-floor guest room. When they were done, Chet excused himself while Diana hung back.

"Did you take the test?" Diana asked as soon as Chet closed the front door.

"Yes. I mailed it Tuesday."

"And how have you been feeling?" she asked as they walked into the kitchen.

"Umm . . . I've felt okay most of the time."

"That doesn't sound very convincing," Diana said as she grabbed two bottles of water from the refrigerator and passed one to Charlie.

"I've been sick twice since I got home."

"Okay, Charlie, I'm just going to be blunt. Are you sure there's no way you could be pregnant?"

She choked and hacked, a mouthful of water going down the wrong pipe. She tried to answer, but every time she opened her mouth, she coughed and sputtered.

"Sorry. Bad timing on my part."

When she was finally able to regain her composure, she cleared her throat. "I can't believe you just asked me that."

Diana raised her brow. "Is it out of the realm of possibility?"

"Yes. Because Hunter and I are not sleeping together."

"But you know what they say. It only takes once."

"Then let me be abundantly clear. Hunter and I have *never* slept together." She shook her head. "You know, it's one thing not to trust me—I'm a complete stranger. But to insult Hunter like that . . . I guess neither you or Jake thinks he can change."

"You're right; I'm sorry." Diana said with an exasperated sigh. "I'm not being fair to Hunter, and I certainly didn't mean to offend you. I'm just grasping at straws."

"Well please, grasp somewhere else." She offered Diana a smile and tried to make light of her assumption, but it still stung.

"Well, there's no reason to speculate. We'll have your test results soon enough." Diana took another swig of water, then asked, "Can I help you unpack? Or I could make you something to eat."

"I'm really not hungry. I'm afraid flying doesn't agree

with me." *Liar.* "I think I'll just go lie down for a little while. Get acclimated. Maybe we could do lunch tomorrow."

"That would be great. Courtney would love to come too if that's okay with you."

"Of course." At least that would keep the conversation from getting too personal.

She walked Diana to the front door and waited for it to shut before hurrying to the guestroom bathroom. Flipping up the toilet seat, she gathered her hair to one side and hunched over. Closing her eyes, she pleaded.

Not again.

Chapter Sixty-Four

Charlie lay awake in bed, staring at the ceiling. She glanced at the clock on the nightstand, waiting for Hunter to call. He was going to ask her how things were going, and she wasn't sure what to say.

After her conversation with Diana, Hunter's mother called to see if she was all settled in. Taking the call from where she sat on the bathroom floor alongside the toilet, she tried her best to sound pleasant. Before hanging up, she had a breakfast date with Irene for the next morning.

Once her stomach settled, she had gone to the stables to check on Goliath. The walk by flashlight creeped her out, so by the time she saw Goliath, she was a stressed-out mess. He was clearly agitated when she got there, but after twenty minutes of brushing and stroking, they both had calmed down. Evan saw her as she was leaving and assured her Goliath was doing fine. Though he was still acting a little high strung—something Evan attributed to the anxiety of the move—Goliath had been eating and drinking just fine.

If only she could do the same.

Glancing at the clock again, she tried to formulate what she was going to tell Hunter when he called. "Everything is fine. The flight was fine. Goliath is fine. Your mother is fine. Oh, by the way, Diana accused us of sleeping together. Other than that, everything is fine."

Of course she wouldn't say that. Because if she did,

she'd have to explain how they had gotten on the subject in the first place. And she certainly had no intention of telling Hunter about her health issues, at least not over the phone. She turned to the clock again and did some quick math.

He should've called by now. Maybe he had a meet and greet Rob forgot to tell him about.

She closed her eyes, deciding to rest while she waited.

The vibration from her phone made her jump. Half asleep, she felt around on the bed next to her, finally locating her phone. She quickly shook the cobwebs from her mind and tried to sound alert. "Hey, cowboy," she said, forcing a smile into her words. She glanced at the clock and realized she had been asleep for hours.

"Charlie," he sighed, "you have no idea how good it is to hear your voice, especially knowing you're home safe and sound."

"Yep. Safe. Sound. Asleep."

"Sorry. There was something I had to do after the show."

"I figured it was something like that."

"So . . . did Diana interrogate you?"

"Interrogate me?" *What does he mean by that? Did Diana tell Hunter I was sick? Or, had she already questioned him about their sex life?*

"Yeah. I just figured she'd have you all to herself and would grill you a little more about us. Diana is all about details. I guess it's the nurse in her. She likes facts."

She thought a moment, wanting to choose her words carefully. "Diana had a few questions. Just girl stuff. So how was tonight?" she asked, quickly changing the subject. "Better than last night, I hope."

"It was definitely better. Knowing you were on the ranch made all the difference."

"I'm glad."

"But you know what would be even better?"

"What's that?"

"Seeing you for myself."

"You will. Two more weeks and you will." She closed her eyes, knowing the days could not go by fast enough.

"I can't wait that long."

"Come on, Hunter, you knew this was going to be the hardest stretch. Rob has you booked back-to-back-to-back, with personal appearances sandwiched in-between. He barely left you enough time to sleep."

"Sleep is highly overrated. Besides, I'll have plenty of time for that later. Right now, all I want to do is see your face."

"Hunter, you know Skype and Facetime creep me out. I don't like the thought of a camera being on me. I know it is just a phobia but I—"

"Who said anything about Skype or Facetime?"

"Then what are you suggesting?"

"Go to the living room. You'll see."

"What?"

"Go on."

Charlie got up from bed, curious what Hunter had up his sleeve. She hadn't notice anything different in the living room when she arrived. Of course, after her conversation with Diana and being sick, all she cared about was checking on Goliath and going to bed.

With her phone pressed to her face, she opened the bedroom door and walked out into the dark living room. She moved by memory to the wall on the far side of the room and groped around for a light switch. "I can't see a thing, Hunter. Where is the light switch in the living room?"

"Behind you."

"What do you mean be—" When she turned around, she saw Hunter walking towards her, the glow of his phone against his cheek.

Her heart raced, and her eyes stung. Trying to show some control, she propped her hand on her hip and asked, "What are you doing here?"

He clicked off his phone, slid it into his pocket, and

closed the distance between them. "I wanted to welcome you home properly." He slipped his arm around her waist and pulled her close, his kiss definitely welcoming.

When they finally came up for air, she looked into his eyes, a sliver of moon-glow their only light. "I'm not sure if your mother would consider that a proper welcome."

"Then I guess it's a good thing she isn't here."

He dipped his head for another kiss, but she pressed her hands to his chest and stopped him. "Hunter, what are you doing here?"

"I told you."

"But how?"

He smiled. "After Chet dropped you off, he came and got me."

"But you have a Fan Club signing tomorrow afternoon at two o'clock."

He glanced at the clock over the mantel and squinted. "That gives us at least eight hours before Chet picks me up and takes me back."

"But Hunter, you need your sleep. You have another show tomorrow."

"I told you, sleep is overrated. It won't be the first time I've done a show after pulling an all-nighter. The only difference is this time I won't have a hangover." He pulled her tight against him. "Now, are you going to spend the next eight hours telling me why I shouldn't have come, or are you going to let it go and just be glad I'm here?"

She let her kiss do the talking.

Chapter Sixty-Five

Hunter more than appreciated Charlie's warm welcome but knew they needed to turn down the heat. Even though her over-sized tee had all the bases covered, he didn't trust himself to keep his hands where they belonged. Brushing his lips against her cheek, he whispered in her ear, "You should probably get dressed. I only have so much self-control."

Charlie pulled back, and even though it was dark, Hunter could see the mischief in her eyes. "You surprise me in the middle of the night, and you're going to scold me for being under dressed?"

He laughed. "Oh, it's not a scolding, it's a warning."

"And what if I choose not to heed your warning?" she taunted.

"I guess I'll have to call Chet to fire up the jet." He tried to pull away, but Charlie held on tight.

"No need," she said with a peck to his cheek, "I'll be right back."

Hunter watched her walk away, enjoying the scenery just a little too much. "Phew." He walked over to the sliding glass door, opened it slightly and inhaled some fresh air.

Get a grip cowboy.

———— • ————

"Will this do?" Charlie asked as she walked back into the living room, interrupting Hunter mid-yawn.

He crossed to the end table and switched on the lamp while she did her best runway model impression, flaunting her baggy black sweatpants and a worn-out tee with Brad Paisley's faded image on it.

"Really? You don't have a different shirt you could put on?"

She looked down at her shirt. "I thought it would work as a mood killer, to keep us safe. You know . . . seeing me with another man."

"You've got that right."

He plopped down on the couch, and she curled up next to him.

"Man, this feels good." He pulled her closer and tipped her chin. Brushing his thumb across her cheek, he smiled. "Beautiful as ever."

"I wouldn't go that far. I can still see shades of yellow."

"Well, you know what they say, love is blind." He winked, then rested his head against the back of the couch and closed his eyes. "So tell me, how is Goliath doing?"

"Are you kidding? You came all this way to see me, and you want to talk about Goliath?"

"Okay, let me ask you this. What was the first thing you did when you got here?"

I fielded questions from Diana and had to convince her we weren't sleeping together, but I'm not going to mention that. She sighed. "I went and checked on Goliath."

"My point exactly." He stroked her arm as he spoke. "Is he doing okay?"

She nodded. "Evan said he has been a little feisty but is doing well."

"He'll calm down now that you're here."

Hunter's tone was soft, and he sounded so tired. She couldn't believe he flew all the way home, just to be with her for a couple of hours.

"Have you talked to my mom, yet?" he asked, yawning again.

"Yep. We're having breakfast tomorrow, and then I have a

lunch date with Diana and Courtney. But I can reschedule with them."

"No need," he said, eyes closed. "I have to be out of here by eleven, noon at the latest."

"Are you sure?"

"Yep."

"Okay, but I'm supposed to meet your mom at nine o'clock. Is that a problem?"

"Uh-uh."

She looked up to see that Hunter was fading. She watched as his chest contracted, his breathing slow and steady. Snuggling closer, she draped her arm across his chest, feeling every beat of his heart. Not allowing her anxieties to get the better of her, she enjoyed the simplicity of just being together. "I love you, Hunter," she whispered.

Stroking her arm, he gave her a squeeze. "I love you too, Charlie."

Chapter Sixty-Six

Charlie turned to look at the clock over the mantel. It was already eight-thirty. She was supposed to meet Irene for breakfast in half an hour, but she didn't want to move. With Hunter stretched out next to her, she could not imagine being anywhere else.

"Don't you have a breakfast date?" he asked even though his eyes were closed.

"I thought you were still asleep."

"It's hard to sleep when you keep twisting around to look at the clock every five minutes." He grinned, opening one eye.

"Oh. I'm so sorry," she said, a sarcastic tease in her tone. "I didn't realize I was being such a bother." She pushed away from his chest, but he quickly wrapped his arms around her.

"Come on, I was only kidding." He laughed as he tried to steal a kiss. She wiggled and squirmed, avoiding his lips. "What, no morning kiss?"

"You had your chance . . . right between calling me a bother and laughing at me."

"I did no such thing." He nuzzled her neck, his heated breath tickling her skin.

"Let me go. I have to get ready," she laughed.

"Not until you give me a kiss." He stretched, but she continued to dodge and weave.

"No. Besides, I have morning breath."

"So do I."

"Nope. Not gonna happen," she said resolutely.

"Oh really?"

Before she could respond, Hunter flipped her on her back, pinned her against the couch cushions, and leaned in close.

Laughing hysterically, Charlie twisted her head from side to side, eluding Hunter's every attempt.

"Give it up, Charlie. I'm not going to stop until you give me a kiss."

"Aaron Hunter Jennings! You stop that right now!"

Hunter flipped around so fast at the sound of his mother's voice, he fell to the floor between the couch and the coffee table.

Charlie quickly sat up, seeing Irene standing near the entryway, a picnic basket hanging from her arm. "Mrs. Jennings, wha . . . what are you doing here?"

"Yeah, mom?" Hunter asked as he got to his feet, visibly annoyed.

"It's so beautiful outside; I thought Charlie and I could have breakfast on the patio."

"Well, you should've knocked," Hunter huffed.

"You're right. That was very rude of me." She turned to Charlie. "I'm sorry. I should've knocked, but I certainly did not expect to find my son assaulting you in the living room."

"Come on, Mom, we were just messing around."

"Obviously." Irene disappeared into the kitchen.

Charlie looked at Hunter, the blush in his cheeks making her giggle. "Oooh . . . you just got busted by your mom," she taunted.

With his hands planted on his waist, he looked at her unamused. "Good one, Charlie. Teenagers get busted. Adults get interrupted."

"I would apologize for *interrupting* you," Irene said as she walked back into the living room, minus the basket, "but from what I could tell, it's a good thing I did." She raised a scornful brow.

"Come on, Mom, we're adults. I'm not going to have this conversation with you."

"Be happy it was me who walked in, not Jake, or Diana with the kids."

"Mom! We were just having fun."

Charlie snickered. Everything he said seemed to indict them even more. "Quit while you're ahead, Hunter. The more you talk, the worse it sounds."

"Smart girl." Irene said as she stepped forward with a smile and pressed a sweet kiss to her son's cheek. "Now, what are you doing here? I thought you weren't coming home until the end of the month. Did something happen?" Suddenly, her irritation was replaced with concern. "Are you all right?"

"I'm fine, Mom. I just wanted to spend a little time with Charlie."

Irene grinned. "Well, now that you have, why don't you go get showered and join us for breakfast. That is, if Charlie and I still have a date?"

Irene turned to her, looking slightly disappointed. "Absolutely. Let me just freshen up. I'll be right back."

Chapter Sixty-Seven

Even though the morning got off to an awkward start, breakfast with Hunter and Irene felt so normal. After he entertained them with a few anecdotes from the road, the three of them discussed the weather, politics, and a host of other topics that had peppered the headlines in the last few weeks.

Just like normal adults would.

Normal.

Something she hadn't felt in such a long time.

After a bit more ribbing about their morning tussle, mixed with a hint of motherly concern, Irene said her goodbyes so she would not monopolize the little time Hunter had before he needed to leave.

As soon as Irene swung the door shut, Hunter scooped Charlie up in an amorous embrace and indulged in a world-tilting kiss. When he finally pulled back, he smiled. "Man, I thought she would never leave."

She was spellbound, her heart racing out of control. On her tiptoes, with her arms wrapped around Hunter's neck, and her lips just inches from his, she looked into his eyes. "Oh, I don't know, after a kiss like that, I'm thinking it's probably not safe to be alone right now. Just you and me, that is."

His grin was anything but chaste as he slowly stroked her back. "Are you saying I'm irresistible?"

"I'm saying your kisses are wreaking havoc on my senses."

The look in his eyes turned from mild vexation to intense sensuality. She could see the battle waging in his stare. She could feel the heat from his body. Sexual tension was getting the better of them, and Charlie wasn't sure she was strong enough to ignore it.

Her mind told her their circumstances were special.

Complicated.

Out of the ordinary.

That the act of love in their case wouldn't be a blatant dismissal of what they knew to be right. However, her conscience told her truth was truth. And to disobey God at this juncture in their relationship would do nothing to bring them closer together. It would only serve as a constant reminder of their lack of faith in God and His plan for them.

She looked away, embarrassed by what she was thinking. But Hunter tipped her chin back so he could look into her eyes . . . into her soul.

"Don't worry. I've got this. I love you too much to ruin things now."

She couldn't speak, emotion getting the better of her. She just nodded, thankful for Hunter's strength. Framing her face with his large, sturdy hands, he pressed a firm yet gentle kiss to her forehead. "We don't have much time before I have to leave, but I don't think we should spend it indoors. How about we go for a walk? We can check on Goliath."

"I'd like that."

———— • ————

Their time together had gone faster than Hunter expected. He was tempted to cancel the meet and greet but thought better of it. Now was not the time to raise a red flag with Rob. He was already going to have to face an interrogation about his banzai trip home.

Just gut it out. This is almost over.

The next time he came home, it would be for good, and nothing or no one was going to come between him and

Charlie.

With her hand in his, they walked out onto the patio. Chet was waiting for him in the driveway, but Hunter wanted his goodbye with Charlie to be a little more private.

"This is so hard." He stroked away a tear from her cheek.

"I know," she said as she rubbed his back and offered him a reassuring smile. "But Rob has you so busy, it will go by fast."

"Not fast enough."

"Then I guess we'll just have to take it one day at a time." She pressed her cheek into the palm of his hand.

"Charlie . . . I was thinking . . ." he looked into her eyes, praying she would listen to what he had to say. "When I get home, when the tour is over, I think you should file for divorce from Daniel."

She stiffened. "Why would you bring that up now?"

"Because I think it's doable. Florida is a no-fault state. Daniel doesn't have to agree—"

She took a step back, clearly shocked. "How did you know Daniel was in Florida?"

Crap. He didn't mean to tip his hand, but now that he had, he might as well tell her what he found out. "Chet's brother-in-law is a P.I. I asked him to look—"

"What? You gave Chet Daniel's name? What for?"

He took a step forward, but she took another step back. "I just told him to have his brother-in-law check out Daniel Fuller. To find out what he could. He found him in Florida."

He watched as Charlie paced away and back again, rubbing her forehead, her complexion noticeably paler. "Why would you do that?"

"Because I want us to be able to move forward."

"And you think I don't? Did you forget I'm the one who took the punches? Had the broken bones, the bruises, the miscarriage?"

"Of course not. I was just trying to put together a game

plan for when I get home. When I found out Florida was a no-fault state, I thought it was a good thing."

"But that doesn't change anything. Sure, I can file for divorce without Daniel's signature and have him served, but if he doesn't respond to the petition, I have to go before a judge—in person—and ask for a contested divorce. Once I'm out in the open, Daniel will hunt me down." She paced like a caged animal. "I can't believe you did this without telling me."

"I'm sorry." He stepped forward and tugged her close. She clutched onto him like she was holding on for dear life while he stroked her back, trying to bring her comfort. "I didn't mean to upset you, really I didn't. Just forget about it, okay."

She looked up at him. "Promise me . . . promise me you're not going to do anything stupid, that you won't go anywhere near Daniel."

"I promise." He held her close, feeling the tremors shaking her body. He was so mad at himself, he had to bite back the curse on his lips. "I'm sorry. I didn't mean to screw up the last few minutes we had together."

She pushed away, wiping tears from her eyes, looking anywhere but at him. "Yeah, well, if you don't leave now, you'll be late, and Rob will go ballistic."

"You're shaking, Charlie."

"Of course I am!" she shouted. "I'm freaking out that your P.I. is going to do something stupid—become a blip on Daniel's radar—and somehow lead him back to you."

"That's not going to happen. Jerry is exceptional at what he does."

"You can't underestimate Daniel!" She started pacing again, talking faster and faster. "He has lots of enemies, which makes him extremely paranoid, and he's always watching his back. If he thinks he's being pinched, he'll go after your P.I. to find out who he's working for. You have to call him off, get him away from Daniel. Make sure he knows who he's dealing with."

"I will. I'll tell Chet as soon as we're in the air."

"Good." She crossed her arms, putting a barrier between them. He reached out for one of her hands. She resisted at first but allowed him to twine his fingers with hers. "Am I forgiven?" he asked.

She was quiet.

Would not even look at him.

Give her space. She's just processing.

I hope.

He waited patiently, stroking the back of her hand with his thumb. When she finally looked up, it was clear she was still furious.

"I forgive you, but that doesn't mean I'm not angry with you." Her words were measured and cold.

"But I can't leave if you're angry with me."

"You don't have a choice."

"Are you going to answer the phone when I call you tonight?"

She just looked at him.

"Hunter?"

They both turned to see Chet standing at the edge of the patio. "We need to leave if you're going to make it back in time."

"I know. Just give me a minute." Once Chet disappeared around the side of the house, Hunter tugged on Charlie's hand. "I'll call tonight."

She didn't acknowledge him. She just turned and walked back into the house.

Hunter slammed his hand against the dash as soon as he got into the side-by-side.

"What happened?" Chet asked.

"I screwed up big time."

Charlie walked into the house, shoving the sliding glass door closed behind her. She let out a scream, her fists clenched at her sides. She couldn't believe Hunter would do something so stupid, so careless.

Did he not listen to anything I said?

Doesn't he understand how dangerous Daniel is?

Scenario after horrible scenario raced through her mind as her blood pulsed through her veins. Her head began to spin, and the room started to tilt. She was going to be sick.

It was happening again.

Chapter Sixty-Eight

Needing time to settle her stomach and process what Hunter had done, Charlie called Diana and postponed their lunch until tomorrow.

Curled up on the couch, she wrapped her arms around her legs and perched her chin on top of her knees. She watched as diamonds of light danced across the surface of the pool, reflecting the late-afternoon sun. But she felt none of the sun's warmth. She was chilled.

Chilled to the bone.

What have I done?

Squeezing her eyes shut, she tried to prevent her tears from falling. She'd been on the ranch less than twenty-four hours, and everything had already gone terribly wrong.

Her stomach ached from another round of retching and her pulse throbbed in her chest, her ears, and her neck. Tremors shook her body no matter how tightly she tried to hold herself together. "How could he?" she whispered to herself.

How could Hunter have gone behind my back and talked with someone about Daniel? Was this his plan all along? Get me on the ranch, then go after Daniel?

Why would he do that?

Why would he take such a chance?

But maybe . . . just maybe Hunter knew someone he could trust. Not everyone in law enforcement was corrupt. And they were in Texas, not Florida. Surely Daniel's reach didn't extend this far.

Jumping up from the couch, she decided she couldn't sit still any longer. Even though she wasn't in the mood for company, she had to do something, go somewhere. Anything but sitting around, allowing thoughts of Daniel to fester in her mind.

Hurrying to her room, she quickly drew her hair back into a ponytail, pulled on her boots, and headed for the stables.

Winded by the time she got there, she stood quietly inside the entryway, catching her breath, and listening to see if anyone else was around. Convinced she was alone, she found the tack room and gathered Goliath's equipment.

"Hey boy," she whispered as she threw his saddle over the rail of the stall, then quickly stepped inside. Goliath danced around and tossed his head, making it harder for her to get him saddled. "Stand still, boy, or we'll never get out of here."

"Need a hand?"

Charlie whirled around to see Evan standing in the aisle.

"Evan. Hi. I didn't see you there." She smiled nervously as she continued to work on Goliath's tack.

"Want some company?"

"Huh?"

"On your ride. Would you like some company?"

"No thanks," she turned back to Goliath, cinching the saddle tight. "I'll be fine."

"But the terrain can be pretty tricky."

"I can handle it." She was polite but firm.

"Yes, ma'am, I didn't mean to suggest you couldn't. It's just that the ranch is unfamiliar to you and you could get turned around."

"Wait a minute," she looked at the young man over the top of Goliath's back. "Did Hunter put you up to this?" The kid looked away. "He did, didn't he?"

"Only for your protection, ma'am, until you get use to your surroundings."

She smiled, appreciating the gesture. "Thanks, but I'm not going far. I just wanted to spend a little time with Goliath."

"Okay, well, if you're sure. But let me show you something

before you leave."

After Goliath was saddled and ready to go, Evan walked with them out of the stables.

"See that bluff over there?" he pointed to a rise in the distance.

She nodded.

"If you get turned around, just ride up the bluff. You can see everything from there, and you'll be able to get your bearings."

"Thanks. I'll keep that in mind."

She had been riding for almost half an hour when the homestead came into view. Immediately, a peace she could not explain washed over her.

Was it a sign?

She wrapped Goliath's reins around a low-slung branch, then pulled the hoof pick from the tie strap on her saddle. Once inside the musty cabin, she walked over to her stack of boxes and carried the one labeled *WINTER CLOTHES* to the bed. With her hands clenched in her lap, she just sat there—staring at the box—for how long she didn't know.

Finally, she wiped her sweaty palms on her jeans, then used the hoof pick to slice open the box. Reaching inside, she pulled out the ski boots and sat them on the bed. She had never worn them. She didn't even ski. The only reason she bought the secondhand boots was to have an obscure hiding place for the one and only bargaining chip she had against Daniel.

With a shaky hand, she pulled out the flash drive that was hidden in the toe of the left boot, never thinking she would have the courage to use it against Daniel.

But now she had someone on her side.

Someone she could trust.

Closing her eyes, she remembered the night she had acted on instinct. When she found Daniel passed out, a flash drive lying on his desk, she just reacted.

Taking the drive, she downloaded the information onto

her laptop, then quickly put the device back on Daniel's desk. Terrified he would somehow know she'd been tampering with his computer and come looking for the information on hers, she created a false file of recipes and buried the information deep within it. When Daniel went to work the next day, she copied the information to an old thumb drive and erased everything from her computer. But, knowing information could still be retrieved, even after being erased, she staged a poolside accident, her laptop ending up at the bottom of the deep end.

Daniel taunted her for days, calling her stupid and irresponsible, but she didn't care. Her ruse had worked. He never once suspected her of anything more than being clumsy.

Now, staring at the flash drive in her hand, she wondered if the information on it was enough to put Daniel away. She'd only opened the files once, months after she left. But when she realized the information was in some sort of code, she was crushed. Without knowing what was on the drive, she could not take the risk of letting it fall into the wrong hands. Daniel had friends in high places and powerful people in his hip pocket—corrupt people. Not knowing who to trust, she held onto the drive, hoping one day to use it as a bargaining chip to buy her freedom.

She lay back on the old wood-framed bed and stared up at the rough-hewn beams that crisscrossed the ceiling.

Maybe it's time.

Chapter Sixty-Nine

The next morning after breakfast, Charlie decided to give Diana a call, to see what time she should expect them for lunch.

"Jennings' residence."

Courtney's little voice sounded so sweet, she couldn't help but smile. "Hi, sweetie. This is Charlie. Is your mommy there?"

"Hi, Miss Charlie," Courtney nearly shouted with excitement. "I made you a surprise for lunch. Well, Mommy said we would have to wait until after lunch or it will ruin your apple tight."

"My what?"

"You know, your apple tight. It's in your belly."

She suppressed a laugh not wanting to hurt Courtney's feelings. "Oh . . . my appetite."

"Yeah, your apple tight. That's why you're not supposed to eat cookies in the mid—"

Charlie heard Diana's voice in the background, interrupting Courtney's explanation.

"Here's mommy, Miss Charlie."

"Hi. Sorry about that. I thought I heard the phone ring, but I didn't know Courtney had picked it up. She's learning how to use the phone but is supposed to ask *before* answering it."

"It's okay. She and I had a fun conversation. But the reason I called was to see what time you want to have lunch and if I need to make anything."

"No. I have a new recipe for chicken salad I want to try. Actually, it's more fruit than chicken. It has coconut, avocado, pineapple, chutney, peanuts, and raisins in it."

"It sounds amazing, but I hate for you to go to all that trouble. I would be fine with a green salad."

"Are you kidding, I finally have someone to try out new recipes with. Jake is a meat and potatoes kind of guy. The kids would eat peanut butter and jelly or macaroni and cheese every day of the week if I let them. And Irene is pretty traditional, and not one to experiment. Oh, but what about your stomach? Do certain foods aggravate it more than others?"

"No. There's no rhyme or reason to my stomach issues. That's why I still think it has to be related to stress somehow."

"About that," Diana said hesitantly. "I'm really sorry for saying what I did yesterday. It was none of my business."

"But you were just checking off boxes, the same any medical professional would've done if I was a new patient."

"Well, I'm sorry it came off so—"

"No more apologies, okay? Let's just forget it happened and move on. Besides, if we don't, I won't get my surprise."

Diana laughed. "You've got yourself a deal. I still have to make lunch for the guys, so Courtney and I will be over sometime after one o'clock."

"I'm looking forward to it." Charlie hung up the phone, thankful the day was off to a good start.

After talking with Diana, she found herself wandering around the house, studying the pictures on the walls, admiring the personal touches, and all but memorizing the movie selection in the media room.

I need to find myself a hobby.

Looking at her watch, she sighed. It was only ten o'clock. "Well, if this is what it's going to be like, I need to start some kind of routine," she said out loud as she walked to her room. "I can't just sit around and do nothing all day." Pulling on her boots and her old tattered hat, she headed toward the stables.

"Good morning, ma'am," Evan said as she walked toward

Goliath's stall.

"How about if you call me Charlie? Then I won't feel so old."

"Yes, ma'am . . . I mean, Charlie." Evan blushed at his slip-up, cleared his throat, then asked, "Were you going to take Goliath out this morning?"

"Actually, I came to see you about a job."

"A job?" he repeated, clearly confused.

"I want to help around the ranch. Earn my keep. I figured you could use a hand with the horses. I put myself through college working at a racetrack, so I have plenty of experience."

"But no one said anything to me about you working."

"I know. But I can't just sit around the house all day. I'm used to being outdoors with Goliath, mucking his stall, doing small fixit jobs. And I know how it works on a ranch. Low man oversees the crappy jobs . . . literally," she chuckled. "I figured if you had some help, you would have more time to do other things."

"Well, yeah, but . . ."

"Then it's settled. What can I do to help?"

Charlie spent the next hour and a half shadowing Evan. He explained the chart of chores hanging in the tack room and showed her where the different pieces of equipment were kept. Then they walked from stall to stall as Evan told her a little about each horse: their temperament, background, and customized eating regimen. It reminded her of the days she spent at the track.

"So, that's about it," Evan said as they ended up back in the tack room looking at the chart. "I'm usually out here around five-thirty, but you don't have to be here that early."

"Why would she be here at all?"

She turned to see Jake standing in the doorway, looking sweaty and agitated.

"Hey, Jake," Evan said with a hesitant smile. "Charlie asked me to show her around so she can help out in the mornings."

Though Jake's eyes stayed trained on her—barely visible underneath the brim of his well-worn hat—he spoke to Evan. "Lunch is ready at the house. Tell Diana I'll be there in a minute."

"Umm, yeah. Sure." Evan glanced at her before slipping past Jake and out the doorway.

She could tell from Jake's hard exterior this wasn't going to be a pleasant conversation.

"So, tell me again why you're out here?"

"I just want to contribute." She tried to sound upbeat. "I don't do bored well, and I have a lot of experience with horses. I worked at a race—"

"So, you decided all on your own to insert yourself with *my* crew, without asking me?"

"I'm sorry. I was under the impression that this was Hunter's ranch." The minute the words were out of her mouth, she regretted them. Belittling Jake would not get her anywhere. "I'm sorry. I didn't mean that the way it sounded."

"Yes you did. You wanted to put me in my place, remind me I'm nothing more than a glorified hired hand who just happens to share Hunter's last name."

"No, really," she said, trying to sound as genuine as possible, "I didn't mean to insult you. I just want to help. I want to feel like I belong here."

"But that's just it, maybe you don't."

She clenched her jaw, the dull pain reminding her of their previous confrontation. "Why won't you give me a chance? Am I really that big a threat to you?"

"Because you're hiding something. And even though Hunter told me all about your sordid past and your abusive husband—if that's even true—there is something more going on here. And when I find out what it is, I'm going to prove to Hunter you're a liar and a manipulat—"

"I'm sick!" she yelled, tears rolling down her cheeks, hands fisted at her sides. "I'm sick and I don't know what's wrong with me. There! Are you satisfied?" She leaned against the wall behind her, her legs barely holding her up.

"And you haven't told Hunter?" His words were sharp but not as callous.

She stared at the toes of her boots and watched as her falling teardrops darkened the leather. "No."

"Why not?"

Using the sleeve of her shirt, she wiped her face. "Because I thought it would go away," she whispered, finally acknowledging to herself that she'd been in denial all these months.

Knowing she had nothing to lose, she took a deep breath and continued. "At first, I thought it was just a bug, or maybe it was from the stress of looking over my shoulder twenty-four seven. I figured either my immunities were shot, or my body was pushing back because of all the turmoil I've internalized over the years. But it hasn't gone away. I've lied to myself, not wanting to acknowledge it could be something more, but I can't lie anymore. It's happening more and more often."

Jake pushed his hat back off his brow. "Like when you got sick playing with Courtney."

She nodded as she toed the scattered hay. When he didn't say anything, she looked up, unable to read the expression on his face.

"So, where does Hunter fit into all this?"

"What?"

"Hunter? Why did you attach your wagon to his? Because of his deep pockets?"

Her mouth dropped open, astonished he still thought her interest in Hunter was only about money. "You're unreal, you know that?" Realizing it was no use talking to him, she walked to the door and tried to move past him but didn't get far.

He grabbed her arm and turned her around. "So now what? Are you going to tell Hunter?"

"Tell him what?" she snapped as she yanked her arm away. "I don't know anything yet."

"Yet?"

"I'm waiting to hear back on some test results."

"And then you're going to tell him?"

"Regardless what I find out, I'm not going to say anything to Hunter until he's done with the tour."

"So why are you out here?" His tone softened slightly as he referred to the stables. "If you're sick, shouldn't you be conserving your energy?"

She just shrugged. "Like I said, I don't do bored well. If I sit in the house and do nothing, it will give me too much time to think. I'll go crazy."

Their conversation stalled. She watched as Jake walked across the aisle and leaned his elbows on a top rail. He pulled off his hat, scratched his head, then pushed it back on.

Hooking her fingers in the loops of her jeans, she waited for him to say something. Finally, she asked, "Are you going to tell Hunter?"

He rubbed his jaw, contemplatively. "He's going to be pissed when he finds out I knew something he didn't."

"So . . . you're not going to tell him?"

He finally turned to her, and for the first time she didn't see hatred in his stare. "Not yet. But I'm not making any promises."

"Thank you." She walked away mumbling a quick prayer. *Please, God, don't let Jake screw this up for me.*

Chapter Seventy

Charlie relived her conversation with Jake while she waited for Diana and Courtney to come over.

I can't believe I told him. What if he tells Hunter? No secrets. No lies. That's all Hunter has asked of me.

But that was exactly what she was doing: keeping secrets.

What would Hunter do if Jake told him? Would he feel betrayed? Would he understand she was just trying to protect him, that she didn't want him to worry needlessly? Or would Jake twist her words to make Hunter believe she was looking for someone with "deep pockets" like he accused her of doing?

Let it go. There's nothing you can do about it now.

On the patio, she watched the dancing waters of the pool from where she sat under the pergola. The breeze brushed against the surface of the water, causing it to ripple and glisten. Its tranquility was therapeutic. Hypnotizing. She could feel herself being lulled to sleep.

Glancing at her watch, she realized she didn't have time for a nap, because Diana and Courtney would be there any minute. But a quick dip in the water sounded nice.

Walking to the shallow end, she yanked off her socks, rolled up her jeans as high as they would go, and stepped into the crystal-clear water. She tensed, the water colder than she expected, but it still felt good.

Sitting on the pool's edge, she stretched out her legs in front of her, leaned back, and turned her face toward the sun.

Peace. This is what it feels like.

A few minutes later, that peace was interrupted by the sound of the sliding glass door. She looked over her shoulder to see Diana. "Hi."

Diana smiled as she slid the door shut behind her and walked across the patio. "Don't you look relaxed."

"I am." She stepped out of the water and walked over to the table. "I really need to get a swimsuit, so I can enjoy the pool the right way." Glancing past Diana, she looked into the house. "Where's Courtney?"

"Umm . . . she's at home with Cody and Evan. All of a sudden, the three of them were immersed in a game of Chutes and Ladders," Diana said as she stared at the pool. "I snuck out. I thought we could talk without little ears being around."

She realized Diana wasn't making eye contact with her. In fact, she was looking anywhere *but* at her. "You heard from the doctor, didn't you?"

She nodded but didn't say anything.

Taking a deep breath, Charlie pulled out a chair and sat down. Diana took the seat beside her. "It's not a virus, is it?"

"I'm afraid not," Diana whispered.

If her instincts were right, she could tell by looking at Diana that she needed to prepare herself for the worst. "Then what?"

"We won't know without further tests."

"But you have your suspicions."

"Charlie, it's not healthy to speculate. The important thing is to get you in for more—"

"Come on, Diana, the tests were in your name. Your doctor wouldn't fool around with you." She leaned forward, clasping her hands in front of her. "He told you something, his suspicions. Just tell me." She waited for Diana to say something, then finally asked what she feared most. "Could it be cancer?"

Diana reached for her hand and held on tight. "It could be a number of things. Fissures. An ulcer. These home tests can be really finicky. If you don't do them just right, they can give false readings. So we shouldn't automatically assume the worst."

"But cancer is a possibility."

Diana nodded. "A possibility, yes, but we won't know until you take the next step."

"Which is?"

"A colonoscopy. It will give the doctor more to go on."

She was silent. What was there to say?

"Charlie . . ." Diana squeezed her hand. "Come on, talk to me. What are you thinking?"

It took a minute for her to feel composed enough to speak. "How soon do I need to do something?"

"As soon as possible."

She walked over to the sliding glass door and pushed it aside. In the kitchen, she saw the salad Diana had brought and a small tray of cookies. After tucking the salad inside the refrigerator, she leaned against the counter and stared out the kitchen window, processing.

When she heard the sliding glass door close, she sensed Diana standing behind her.

"Charlie, you can go to Dr. Kinsey. I'll explain everything to him. He'll work it out. I know he will. Let me call him and get it set up."

"I don't want to do anything until Hunter is home," she said as she continued to stare out the kitchen window.

"But Charlie, you shouldn't wait. You've been ill for too long already."

"No." She turned around. "I'm not going to do anything to upset Hunter."

"And you don't think he'll be upset when he finds out you waited this long to get medical attention?"

No secrets. No lies. Hunter's words continued to haunt her.

"Charlie, I—"

"Diana, please," she quickly cut her off, "I know you're just trying to help, but I need some time to think. Okay?"

"Sure. Of course." She reached across the granite countertop and placed her hand on top of hers. "Just call if you have any questions or if you want me to set up an appointment."

Charlie waited until she heard the front door shut, then sank to the floor, overwhelmed with emotion.

Chapter Seventy-One

Charlie spent the rest of the afternoon in a fog. Psychologically, she was exhausted. Her entire life had been one emotional roller coaster after another.

Her mother's abandonment.

Aunt Bev's death.

Her volatile life with Daniel.

And now, just when she thought she had a chance at real happiness with Hunter, her body betrays her.

She needed to tell him—she knew that—but how could she without having him overreact?

Curling up on the couch, she stared outside at the pool, craving the tranquility she had felt earlier. In the distance, the sun was just beginning to set, causing brilliant rays of orange and goldenrod to streak across the Texas sky. But even with all its warmth and beauty, it left her cold.

She just couldn't wrap her mind around what she was dealing with. Which was exactly why she needed to wait until after she had more information before telling Hunter. But to keep him in the dark, especially now that Jake knew, would be continuing with the secrets and lies.

Exactly what he asked me not to do.

Reaching for her phone, she scrolled her contacts and dialed.

"Hey, Charlie," Diana said in a somber tone. "Have you decided what you're going to do?"

"Actually, I was hoping to talk to Jake."

"Oh . . . well . . . ahh . . ."

She could tell it caught Diana off guard.

"He hasn't come in yet. He and the guys are working some cattle on the far side of the creek, but he should be home any minute. Do you want him to give you a call when he gets in?"

"If it's not too much trouble."

"Sure. I'll let him know."

She didn't have to wait long for Jake to call. She had closed her eyes for only a minute or two when her phone vibrated in her hand. Gathering her thoughts, she hesitated slightly.

Here goes nothing.

"Hello?"

"Hi, Charlie."

She was surprised to hear Irene's slight southern drawl.

"I hope you don't mind that Hunter gave me your phone number."

"No. Not at all."

"Well, I don't want to seem like a meddling mom and suffocate you, but I did want to check in . . . make sure you're doing okay?"

"I'm doing fine, Irene. Hunter's place is very relaxing."

"That's good, sweetheart. I'm glad to hear it. But don't feel like you have to stay all buttoned up in that big house of his. You're more than welcome to hang out here with me. I'm usually up and dressed by seven in the morning and I don't go to bed until after ten at night. I'd love to have some company in the evenings. We could watch a movie together, even share meals. At least until Hunter gets home."

"Thank you, Irene. I would love that too. But can I take a rain check for a few days while I get settled in?"

"Absolutely. Just give me a jingle."

She smiled at the warmth in Irene's words. "I'll do that."

No sooner had she put her phone down, there was a knock at the front door. Wondering if it was another one of Hunter's surprises, she rushed to the entryway and pulled it open. "Jake! What are you doing here?"

"Diana told me you called. I didn't want her or the kids overhearing our conversation and asking a lot of questions."

He walked through the doorway, removing his hat as he took long strides into the living room.

She closed the door and followed him.

He planted his feet wide and crossed his arms. "Well?"

Abrupt. But then, what did she expect? "I need your advice."

"You're kidding?" he cocked his head like it was a joke.

"No. I'm not. You know Hunter better than anyone. So, I need to know how he will react."

"To what?"

"The test I took. It came back."

"And?"

"I have to take more tests. And since I really don't have any answers, I see no reason to worry him while he's away." She sank to the edge of the couch. "But how will he react if I don't tell him about the tests until after I have an answer?"

"He'll be ticked."

It was the answer she expected, but she still didn't know what to do.

"How long has this been going on?" he asked.

"For a while."

"And you haven't told him you suspected it was something more than an upset stomach?"

"I didn't suspect anything until Diana questioned me about it."

"Diana knows about this?" he snapped.

"Yes, but please don't be upset with her for not telling you. I asked her not to say anything, and being a nurse, she had to keep it confidential."

He stewed, clearly upset, then asked, "So what do you want from me?"

"You're help. I know I need to talk to Hunter, but I'm afraid he will overreact and do something stupid like cancel a show or something. But if I wait until he's done with the tour, I can tell him—"

"No. You can't wait."

"But if I call him, he will—"

"You can't call him either. You need to tell him in person. Make him understand there's nothing he can do."

"How?"

He looked at her with a raised brow and a smirk. "I guess you're going to your first Hunter Jennings' concert."

She quickly stood, shocked at what he was suggesting. "I can't do that. Someone will see me. People will ask questions."

"No they won't." He started toward the front door.

"You don't know that!" she snapped as she followed behind him.

He stopped and turned around abruptly, a smile on his face. "We snuck girls into our hotel rooms and tour busses all the time without anyone knowing. Chet can fly you there and get you to Hunter without anyone noticing. I'll set it all up."

He reached for the door, but she grabbed his arm, turning him to face her. "I won't do it. I'm not going to risk being photographed with Hunter."

"Look," he shoved his hat on his head. "You asked for my help, so I'm giving it."

Stunned, Jake was almost out the door before she asked, "When?"

"I'll ask Chet about Hunter's schedule and get back to you."

Chapter Seventy-Two

Her phone rang twice . . . three times before Charlie reached for it. Preparing herself, she picked it up from the bedside table.

You can do this.

Be casual.

Calm.

Assure him there's nothing to worry about.

Against Jake's advice to visit Hunter—which absolutely terrified her—she decided she would tell him an abbreviated version of her health issues over the phone. She wouldn't say anything about the test she had already taken. She would just explain that Diana thought it would be wise to get checked out by a doctor, so she could get antibiotics or whatever was necessary to kick the lingering bug she was dealing with.

She had rehearsed all evening, what she would say to justify her willingness to see a doctor. Spending time with Cody and Courtney was the perfect excuse. She would tell Hunter, she just wanted to make sure whatever she had wasn't contagious. And since Diana assured her Dr. Kinsey would keep everything confidential, there was no reason to worry.

She would quickly change the subject, chatter on about what she'd been doing since arriving at the ranch, confident that if she sandwiched her health news between other bits of information, Hunter would see it as a normal precaution.

All these thoughts raced through her head as she

answered the phone. "Hey there, cowboy," she said in the most casual tone she could muster.

"Hey yourself," he chuckled. "You sound wide awake."

"I got caught up in a movie and didn't realize how late it had gotten."

"Really. What movie was that?"

"Ahh . . ." Charlie closed her eyes, visualizing the spines of the DVD covers she had all but memorized. "Air Force One. It's one of my favorites. Well, any Harrison Ford movie really."

"Oh. So you have a thing for Harrison Ford?"

"What can I say? I find older men attractive."

"So now you're calling me old."

"Not old. *Older*," she teased, realizing they had never really discussed their age difference. Mainly because, to her, it didn't matter. "Hey, if you can have a thing for Sandra, I can have a thing for Harrison."

He laughed.

Perfect. This is exactly what I need. Easy banter. Playful conversation.

"So how did it go tonight?" she asked, trying to keep the conversation normal.

"Without a hitch. But I'm telling you, cramming nine concerts, twelve personal appearances, drop-ins on late-night television, and an award show performance all in one month is ridiculous. If I had not decided already to hang it up, this last stint would have made the decision for me. If I'm not performing, I'm sleeping. And don't even ask me what city I'm in. But . . . something cool did happen."

She heard a change in his tone. "What?"

"You'll never guess who showed up tonight."

"Who?"

"Rider Daniels."

"Wow! I've heard he's a major up and comer."

"You heard right. He has amassed quite the following in the short amount of time he's been on the charts."

"Did you know he was coming?"

"I knew it was a possibility. He was in town for some charity event and had contacted Rob. Turns out he's a big fan. When I took my break in the middle of the set, he was watching from backstage, so I asked if he wanted to do a song together."

"The crowd must have loved that."

"It was crazy. The minute he took the stage, the crowd went wild. We ended up singing a couple of songs together, and had a great time doing it. He hung around backstage until I was done, and we talked a little before he left."

"Sounds like you had a great time." She was beginning to lose her nerve. He was in such an upbeat mood; she didn't want to bring him down by talking about her health situation. Especially since she didn't know what that was.

"Actually, that isn't the only interesting conversation I had today."

"Really."

"Yeah. Rob wants to extend the tour."

"Extend the tour?" She was shocked. Not so much that Rob wanted to milk Hunter for everything he was worth, but the tone in his voice made it sound like he was actually thinking about it. "But you're not going to, are you?"

"Well . . ."

She sunk to the side of the bed, shocked he was even considering it.

"I'm thinking about it. But only because it gives me bargaining power toward buying out my contract."

"I don't understand." She flopped back on the bed, completely defeated.

"I told Rob I'd consider extending the tour by six weeks, eight weeks tops, so we could record it. Then I could release a live album at the end of the tour as part of my contractual obligations."

Another two months. Hunter would be on tour for another two months.

With boyish enthusiasm, he continued to lay out his plan while her thoughts spiraled.

"I'm tellin' you, Charlie, before tonight, I wouldn't have even considered it. But after singing with Rider, it got me thinking. I could do a duet album. Invite other artists like Blake, Carrie, and Luke to sing with me. If we used previously released hits, it would cut production time in half. No finding new material. No messing with arrangements. In fact, scheduling wouldn't even be an issue. Everyone could lay down tracks in their own studios, then it would be up to the engineers to work their magic. After that release, I'd only have a greatest hit album left to do."

She could tell he had already given it a lot of thought, and the excitement she heard in his voice told her this was something he needed to do.

"So, you see, I would be meeting my contractual obligations without having to do another tour. And the PR would only consist of a round on the late-night talk show circuit and a few morning shows. I laid this all out for Rob twenty minutes ago. And though he wasn't willing to give his stamp of approval just yet, I could see it in his eyes. It's a good plan. A solid plan. And he'd be a fool to pass it up."

She continued to listen, but all she could think about was his extended timetable and how that would botch up her carefully thought out plan. All day, she'd been preparing herself to tell him about her condition. She had convinced herself she'd be able to relay the information in a way that downplayed it, that it was something they could address at the end of his tour. However, if she told him now, he would put his plan on hold. A plan he had just laid out with genuine enthusiasm.

"Charlie?"

"Sorry." She pretended to yawn, realizing she had checked out while he was talking. "I'm listening, but the late hour is catching up with me."

"So, what do you think? I know it means more time apart now but in the long run, it would be worth it."

"I think you should do it." She tried to sound supportive, as supportive as she could with tears streaming down her face.

"You don't sound too convinced. Be honest. If you think it's a bad idea, just say the word. I'll nix the whole thing."

"No. Don't be silly. You're right," she said as she dried her eyes on the hem of the pillowcase. "What's another few weeks if it will take years off your contract? I think you should go for it."

"Really? You're sure you can handle another month or so apart? Because if you can't, I—"

"Are you kidding? Your fans are going to love it."

He was so excited, he didn't even pick up on the fact that she had side-stepped his question. Which only confirmed she was right in *not* telling him about her condition.

She listened for another twenty minutes as he explained in detail what songs he wanted to sing with which guest artist and why.

When they finally said their goodbyes, she dropped her phone on the bed, sunk back against the pillows, and closed her eyes.

I guess I'll have to go with Jake's plan, after all.

It would be the only way to ensure Hunter didn't have a knee-jerk reaction. If she told him in person, she could answer every question, appease all his concerns, and most of all, make sure he didn't alter his plans.

I can do this. I can convince Hunter it's not a big deal.

At least, I hope I can.

Chapter Seventy-Three

The next morning, Charlie was mucking stalls, her thoughts ping-ponging around in her head. She continued to practice what she would say to Hunter, emphasizing words like: standard, common, routine, and simple.

Who am I kidding? I'm coming out of hiding. It will be a dead giveaway that I'm not going in for a simple check-up.

"I talked to Chet."

She whirled around, startled to see Jake standing behind her. With her hand to her chest, she took a deep breath. "You scared me half to death."

"Sorry about that." He leaned against the stable rail and continued. "Hunter's schedule is pretty tight right now. Chet is flying him back and forth between venues and publicity junkets because Rob has booked every second of this last leg of the tour."

"I know. I talked to Hunter last night. He told me Rob has him on an impossible schedule."

"True. But he's going to be playing two shows at the Peoria Civic Center this weekend. That's only a twelve-hour drive from here."

"*Drive?*"

"Yeah, drive. Like I said, Chet is too busy chauffeuring Hunter from one event to another. He doesn't have time to fly here and back. So, if we leave around nine in the morning, we'll get to the venue during Hunter's set and wait for him in his bus. But I don't want him to know we're coming. It will throw off his performance, and he'll ask too many questions."

"We?"

"Yeah, we."

"If you think I need to tell Hunter in person, fine, but I don't need a babysitter. Just let Rob know I'm coming."

"Are you kidding? I can't tell Rob. He would just screw things up. And without me, you won't get anywhere near the buses. You can't just bat your pretty little eyes to get your way. At least not without bringing attention to yourself, which I'm assuming you don't want to do."

"Why would you do this for me?"

"Because I don't want to see Hunter get hurt. Believe it or not, I love my brother. And even if I think this whole situation is jacked-up, I don't want him to be blindsided. You, showing up out of nowhere, dropping a bombshell on him, is going to knock him back on his heels. And the only way I can make sure he doesn't do something stupid—like cancel the rest of his tour dates—is to assure him Diana and I are helping out with whatever you need. We'll downplay it as much as possible. I'll explain that Diana is taking care of everything with Dr. Kinsey, and that he might run further tests as a precaution."

"But that's just it. Won't Hunter think it's strange we went to all this effort to tell him in person if there's nothing to worry about?"

"Tell him you missed him, or you wanted to surprise him. Tell him whatever you need to. Just make him believe it's no big deal."

"You want me to lie to him?"

"Isn't that what you're doing right now?"

The truth hurt like a sucker punch to the gut.

"When do we leave?"

"Friday," he said over his shoulder as he walked away.

Chapter Seventy-Four

Today was the day.

And she was completely exhausted.

She had stared at the nightstand clock for the last two hours, seeing every minute that ticked by. Hunter had called later than usual because of a midnight meet and greet Rob had arranged. She knew he was dreading the late-night event, so she was a little surprised when he called in such an upbeat mood. But, when he started talking about the duet project, she understood why. She couldn't help but smile at the excitement she heard in his voice.

He had secured two more artists for the album and explained in detail how he had strong-armed his favorite engineer into committing to the project. Then he spent the rest of their conversation going over his entire song catalog, narrowing the list to his top fifteen. By the time they hung up, it was after four in the morning.

Since then, she'd done nothing but toss and turn, fixated on the clock, sleep eluding her completely. Rolling over, she closed her eyes.

God, I don't want to do this. I don't want to lie to Hunter again. Because when he finds out—which he will—he's going to be so hurt.

He had asked only two things of her. "No secrets. No lies." What would he do when he found out she'd been keeping her condition a secret since the beginning of their relationship? And, to add insult to injury, she had involved Jake and Diana. Hunter's relationship with his brother wasn't the best, and this would strain it even more. She was sure of it.

Glancing at the clock one more time, she knew she needed to get up and get ready. Today was bad enough knowing what lay ahead of her. But, having to spend the next twelve hours with Jake would be the proverbial salt in the wound. She certainly didn't want to make it worse by being late.

Finally, she dragged herself out of bed, showered, and got dressed. When she reached for her hairbrush in the bottom of her overnight bag, she saw the flash drive she had tucked away inside. Picking it up, she had an idea.

"That's it! I'll give Hunter the flash drive. I'll explain what it is—or at least what I think it is—and tell him I'm ready to ask for help."

But it won't explain why I dragged Jake all the way to his concert.

She paced, moving puzzle pieces around in her head.

The tour extension. I'll tell him I was going to give it to him when the tour was over, but with talks of an extension, I didn't want to wait any longer.

She stood in front of the mirror, brushing her hair, gathering her thoughts, talking to herself.

"I'll just explain that I would feel safer moving forward if Daniel was in prison."

Then, before we leave, I'll casually mention that Diana convinced me to see her doctor, thinking a round of antibiotics might help with the bug I've been dealing with. I'll mention it almost as an afterthought. Like it's no big deal. Hopefully, he'll be so fixated on the flash drive, he won't give a mundane doctor's appointment much thought.

She continued to drag the brush through her hair, reciting what she would say, formulating a script in her head. When she was done, she pulled on her boots, slipped the drive into her purse, and prayed the trip with Jake would go smoothly.

Chapter Seventy-Five

Jake had been driving for hours. Though they had exchanged a few sentences here and there, most of the drive had passed in silence, which was fine with her. It gave her more time to rehearse her imaginary script. Over and over, she silently practiced what she was going to say to Hunter, praying she would be able to pull it off without sounding suspicious.

"Okay," Jake huffed while reaching for the dash. "I can't take the silence any longer." He pressed the knob on the radio, and the truck immediately filled with a country ballad by Thomas Rhett.

"Why didn't you say something sooner?" she snapped, irritated he was blaming her for the quiet.

He shrugged. "Every time I looked over, you were so deep in thought I didn't want to bother you."

"And every time I tried to engage you in conversation, I got one-word answers, so I figured you preferred the silence."

"Well, sorry I'm not a better conversationalist. Small talk isn't my thing."

Not having the energy to spar with him, she bit back the retort on the tip of her tongue and turned toward the passenger window. As she watched the countryside rush by, she prepared herself for the questions Hunter might ask, and came up with nonchalant answers she hoped would diffuse his concerns.

The next few hours seemed to go by faster, the radio adding the right amount of distraction. She had listened to Jake quietly sing along with familiar country tunes, his smooth baritone recognizable from the harmonies he'd sung with Hunter on his earlier hits. When she realized the truck was slowing down, she glanced at him as he turned off the highway.

"I'm stopping for gas and something to eat," he said as he pulled into a station that shared a parking lot with a drive-thru burger joint.

She sat up straighter and combed her fingers through her hair. "Then I'm going to use the restroom while you're filling-up," she said as she got out and stretched.

"Okay, but remember, we're on a schedule."

She rolled her eyes as she walked away, irritated he thought he had to remind her. *Good thing you said something. I might have confused this for a leisurely Sunday drive.*

After waiting her turn in the small two-stall bathroom, she quickly ran a brush through her hair and blotted her face with a wet paper towel. Walking back around the corner of the little convenience store, she saw that Jake was already in the truck ready to go.

Climbing into the cab, she fastened her seatbelt as Jake pulled forward. Merging into the sparse traffic, he passed two more fast-food restaurants and a generic roadside diner before turning back onto the highway.

"I thought you said we were going to get something to eat."

"I did." He pulled out a stick of beef jerky and a bag of chips from the side pocket on his door.

That's when she noticed the mega soda nestled in the center console.

"Sorry. I just figured you would've gotten something for yourself when you went inside."

"But I didn't go inside. The bathroom was outside and around the back."

"Well then, here," he extended the bag of chips across the console. "You can have mine."

She stared at the bag of Xxtra Flamin' Hot Cheetos,

355

knowing they would rip up her stomach, even on a good day. "No thanks. I'm really not that hungry anyway."

"Are you sure? I mean, I would turn around, but the next off—"

"No. Really. I probably shouldn't eat anyway. The less on my stomach the better."

"You're sure?"

She couldn't tell if he looked remorseful or annoyed. Either way, she just nodded, then focused again on the countryside whizzing by.

With the radio playing softly, she closed her eyes and began to drift, but when she heard the D.J. say Hunter's name, she quickly reached for the dial, Jake beating her to it.

"You heard it right, folks, it was just announced. Hunter Jennings is extending his sold-out tour with twelve more dates. So, if you missed him the first time around, this is your chance to see him."

Jake looked at her. "Did you know about this?"

She nodded. "Hunter told me last night, but I didn't think they'd be able to pull it off this quick."

He shook his head. "Knowing Rob, he probably had this up his sleeve all along."

"Actually, it was Hunter's idea."

"What?" He glanced her way, then back to the road in front of him. "Why would he agree to extend the tour? All he's been crying about lately is giving it all up . . . so he could be home with you."

"He told Rob he would be willing to extend the tour, but only if the performances were recorded for a live album. That way, he could fulfill one more contractual obligation without another full-blown tour."

She watched as Jake mulled it over, then smiled. "What do you know? He still has a brain in that thick skull of his after all."

"He's also going to record a duet album."

"A what?"

"An album with other artists. He figures the promotion for

NO SECRETS NO LIES

it would be minimal. Interviews on late-night TV and performances on a couple of the morning shows. Again, no major touring. He's already secured a few artists, with several more showing interest."

"And you're all right with Hunter extending the tour?"

"Yes. I want whatever's best for him."

"Right, as long as he gives up his career and everything he's worked for, just so he can be home with you."

She sighed at the barely veiled belligerence in his tone. "I never asked him to do that."

"Uh-huh, just like you didn't know he would have to choose between his celebrity status and a life hiding away with you."

"Again, I didn't ask him to do that. He pursued me, remember? I told him to leave me alone. I told him it would never work out between us, but he wouldn't take no for an answer."

"Oh, you poor thing. Being pursued by a multimillionaire superstar must be so taxing on you. Pining away in a five-thousand square foot house, knowing all you have to do is ask, and Hunter will give you anything you want . . . and give up everything."

"Dang it, Jake!" She slammed her right hand against the dashboard, gasped, then immediately pulled it to her chest, pain shooting through her wrist. "Why do you have to be so ugly? Am I really that big of a threat to you? Is that it? Because I don't deserve to be treated this way. Believe me, if I was the conniving person you think I am, and was after Hunter for his money or what he could give me, I certainly would not be living on a ranch with his mother and brother. And just so you know, I am as dumbfounded as you are that Hunter loves me. Even so, just because I don't understand it, and you don't like it, doesn't mean I don't deserve to be loved."

She felt tears coming but didn't care.

"You have no idea the life I've led or how hard I've fought to keep my head above water when it would've been easier just to go under. I never dreamed I could love again, or that I would find someone who could love me in spite of my screwed-up life. And just when I allow myself to think things could be different—convince myself Hunter and I really do have a shot—my body betrays me. I'm going to lose everything. I know I am. I don't get miracles. I don't get reprieves."

She turned toward the window and cried silently to herself, her hurting wrist pressed against her chest.

"You're scared, aren't you?" he asked, a hint of compassion in his tone.

She leaned her head against the window and closed her eyes.

"Terrified."

Chapter Seventy-Six

Charlie drifted in and out of sleep, the pain in her wrist keeping her from any true rest. When she could take it no longer, she reached for her purse on the floorboard and plopped it in her lap.

"There's a place coming up in about five minutes. I'll stop there so you can get something to eat," Jake said, as he rolled his neck.

"I'm not hungry," she said as she rummaged around in her purse, "but I could use something to drink." As she searched the bottom of her bag for the bottle of ibuprofen, her fingers brushed against the flash drive.

Could she do it? Could she really give it to Hunter?

She debated for the hundredth time but didn't see that she had an option. She needed to downplay her health issues as best she could. If Hunter thought—even for a second—that she was sicker than she had led him to believe, he would overreact and do something stupid like cancel a concert or axe the extra tour dates. She couldn't let that happen. At least, not until she knew something for sure. And, the only way to divert his attention from her health was to give him something just as important to fixate on.

When Jake pulled into the truck stop, she went inside the mini mart. After using the restroom, she roamed the aisles looking for something to eat, but nothing looked good. After buying some water, she got back into the truck.

"I went ahead and bought a few snacks," Jake said,

referring to the sack on the center console. "Just in case you change your mind."

She looked at him, wondering why he was suddenly treating her like a real human being, but didn't bother to ask, figuring it wouldn't last long. Twisting her wrist to open the water bottle, she gasped, dropped the bottle, and cradled her wrist.

"What's wrong?"

"My wrist," she said, gritting her teeth and holding her forearm.

"Ah, yes, your little temper tantrum," he smirked.

Ignoring him, she reached for the bottle on the floorboard, then gently laid her arm in her lap.

"Let me see it."

"What?"

He twisted sideways in his seat. "Let me see your wrist."

"It's fine."

"I didn't ask if it was fine. I want to take a look at it."

She stared straight ahead, ignoring him.

"We're not going anywhere until I look at your wrist."

She sighed, throwing her head back against the seat. "Really? What, now you're a doctor?"

"I've seen my share of sprains and breaks."

"It's not sprained *or* broken. I tweaked it is all."

"Fine. Have it your way." He rested his head back against his seat, pulled down his cowboy hat low over his eyes and began to whistle a tune.

"Are you kidding me? What is it with you Jennings' men? Do you always have to get your way?"

"Usually."

"Fine." She lifted her arm and gently laid it on the center console.

He sat up straighter. "Well, it's definitely swollen."

"Ya think?"

He carefully slid his hand under her wrist and slowly rotated it from side to side. "Does that hurt?"

Clenching her jaw, she nodded.

With two fingers, he gently felt around her wrist, pressing as he went.

"Ouch!"

"Sorry."

She had to bite her bottom lip to keep from cursing, as he continued to poke and prod.

When he finally laid her arm on the console, he pushed his hat back off his forehead and looked at her. "Well, I don't think it's broken, but we should probably wrap it, to give it some support."

"It's all right," she said, moving her forearm back to her lap. "I'll be—" But before she could finish, Jake was out of the truck and walking towards the minimart.

She groaned. *Why is he making such a big deal about this?*

When he returned a minute later, he hopped back into the truck, holding an ace bandage.

"Do you really think that's necessary? It's just going to be one more thing I have to explain to Hunter."

"That shouldn't be hard," he chuckled. "It's not like he hasn't seen your temper before. Now, bring your arm over here so I can wrap it."

She winced and moaned as he wrapped her wrist.

"There, that should help. At least you won't have to ride the rest of the way cradling it the way you were."

She hated to admit it, but it did feel better. "Thank you."

"No problem. Now I won't have to listen to you whine for the next six hours."

One minute he's nice. The next he's a jerk.

She turned to say something and was met with a devilish smile. "Why do you do that?" she snapped, frustrated he had the ability to get her so riled up. "One minute you actually act like a decent human being, and then you ruin it with a smart-aleck comment."

He smiled even broader. "Oh, come on. If I'm too nice to you, you might actually start liking me. Where's the fun in that?"

Chapter Seventy-Seven

They had driven another hour when Jake turned down the radio and asked, "So, have you thought about what you're going to tell Hunter?"

"Yeah."

"Because the minute we show up, he's going to know something is wrong. I'll do my best to convince him Diana's got it covered, but you will need to downplay it, or else he'll go into control-freak mode."

"You mean, like you just did over a tweaked wrist?"

"Don't get cute." He turned serious. "I'm warning you, if you don't downplay it . . . if you say the wrong—"

"I'm not *just* going to downplay it," she interrupted. "I'm going to mention it as an afterthought."

"An afterthought to what?" He glanced at her, then back to the highway. "What would be more important than your health?"

She carefully dug around in her purse and pulled out the flash drive. "This."

"What's that?"

She took a deep breath. "Hopefully information that can put Daniel behind bars."

He shook his head. "I don't get it. If you've had it all this time, why haven't you used it before now?"

"One time . . . when Daniel had—"

She stopped, choking on emotion that sprang up out of nowhere.

Taking a sip of water, she cleared her throat, then

continued. "Once, when I was in pretty bad shape . . . I told Daniel I'd had enough. I threatened him . . . told him the next time he laid a hand on me, I would go to the police. That's when I found out he owned not only the police chief, but county and government officials all the way to the governor's office. He warned me if I ever tried to ruin his name or his reputation, he would find out, and I would pay with my life."

She shuddered, remembering that night like it was yesterday. Daniel had pinned her against the wall, a knife to her throat, smiling as he pricked her skin. She remembered the chill she felt as her own blood trickled down her neck, and Daniel glared at her like a possessed man.

That glare.

That laugh.

They still haunted her.

With her heart racing out of control and sweat running down her spine, she tried to breathe, but it didn't feel like there was enough air in the truck.

What if Daniel's power stretches beyond the state? What if I endanger Hunter and his family by turning over the flash drive? What if . . .

"Charlie?"

She jumped, jarring her from her panic. She looked at Jake but quickly turned away. "Sorry," she whispered, brushing tears from her cheeks.

"Don't be."

It took a moment to gather her composure and force down the terror Daniel always imbued in her. Taking another swig of water, she explained. "One night, I copied information from Daniel's computer—information he always kept locked in his safe." She held up the flash drive. "I'm pretty sure this has the names of the officials he's either paid-off or blackmailed. I'm hoping Hunter can give this to Chet's brother-in-law . . . and that the information is valuable enough to put Daniel away for a very long time."

"How do you know about Jerry?"

"Hunter had him locate Daniel."

"Why in the—" Jake shook his head. "No. Forget it. I don't even want to know."

They drove in silence as Jake worked his way through an interchange. Once he was back in the steady flow of traffic, he asked, "So, how are you going to bring up your tests?"

"After I give Hunter the flash drive and explain what's on it, I'll wait until we are ready to leave. Then I'll casually mention that Diana arranged for me to see her doctor. I'll explain that it is no big deal; I just want to make sure I don't have something contagious that I could pass on to the kids. I'll let him know it's merely a precaution."

Jake arched a brow skeptically.

"What? It's true. Well, most of it. I *don't* know what I have. I *don't* want the kids to get whatever it is. And if it ends up being nothing, I'll have done it as a precaution."

Jake chuckled. "Wow . . . you're really quite skilled at massaging the truth."

She closed her eyes, feeling the slap of his indictment.

"I . . . I didn't mean it like that."

"Sure you did." She bent forward and turned up the radio.

Jake quickly readjusted the volume. "No, I didn't. Really."

The look of regret in his eyes was genuine.

"For what it's worth, I'm sorry for the pain you've suffered. No one deserves to be treated like a doormat. And, I know I haven't made it easy on you . . . you or Hunter. I just don't want to see him get hurt."

She sighed. "Neither do I."

Chapter Seventy-Eight

They were getting closer.

Hours had passed since the last time they stopped. Jake had been pretty quiet, so she had tried to rest as much as possible, a few times even drifting off. But when she saw a sign for Highway 155, she realized they only had about an hour to go.

Sitting up straighter, she stretched her neck and glanced over at Jake. She could see the fatigue in his shoulders, and the way his eyes strained against the oncoming headlights.

"Are you doing okay?" she asked.

"Yeah."

"You look tired."

He shrugged. "Not too bad. But it does bring back memories."

"Memories?"

"Yeah. When it was just Hunter and I traveling from one honky-tonk to another. We would drive for hours, play a set for tips, then drive to another roadside bar and do it all over again." He smiled. "Those were hard times, but they were good."

"You sound like you miss being on the road."

"Sometimes."

A sobering look transformed his expression. She watched as he stared out the windshield, headlights from the other direction reflecting off the hood of the truck, lighting memories in his eyes. Happy memories if she read his expression right.

"Don't get me wrong," he continued. "I wouldn't trade what I have with Diana and the kids for anything, but those first few years . . . Hunter and I . . . we were so hungry for fame, so determined to see our dreams come true. We busted our butts for eight long years. And then it happened. Hunter Jennings was an *overnight* success."

She waited for his expression to change from happy to bitter, but it didn't. "Was that difficult for you? Working just as hard as Hunter but not getting the recognition?"

He shook his head. "Not really. I always knew Hunter was the real talent. I was just happy to be along for the ride. It allowed me to keep an eye on him, make sure he didn't get in over his head."

Jake's humility surprised her.

"Don't look so shocked," he grinned. "Like I told you before, I love Hunter. He's my brother and my best friend. I just don't want to see him throw away everything he's worked so hard for. Living with regret can be a bitter pill to swallow."

Not wanting Jake to see her tears, she turned away, pulled her feet up underneath her, and wrapped her arms around her raised knees.

"I didn't mean that the way it sounded. I just don't want him to regret giving up his career."

"I know."

She wanted to reassure him that she had no intentions of hurting Hunter but realized *telling* him wasn't going to do it. She had to *show* him her feelings were real, *prove* to Jake that she wasn't after Hunter for his money or what he could provide for her.

But it would take time.

Time she would hopefully get.

Closing her eyes, she took a deep breath. They would be there soon, and she needed to get her thoughts together and keep herself from freaking out.

"What do you think you're doing?" Jake shouted. "Move over! Move over!"

Startled, Charlie snapped, "What are you talking about?"

She turned around, just in time to see the eighteen-wheeler headed straight for them.

Chapter Seventy-Nine

Hunter was ready to take the stage for his second encore when someone grabbed his arm from behind. When he turned around, Rob stood there, looking ill. "What's with you?" he shouted over the roar of the crowd.

"You're done for the night, Hunter. We need to go."

"Done? I'm not done. I have two more songs."

"Hunter . . . listen to me." Rob stared at him, a look in his eyes he had never seen before. "There's been an accident. A helicopter is waiting for us outside. We need to go."

He tried to process what Rob was saying. "What do you mean, an accident? On the ranch? Is someone hurt?"

"Not on the ranch," Rob said calmly. "I'll explain on the way." He turned and hurried toward a set of double doors a stagehand was holding open.

Hunter picked up his pace to keep up with Rob, panic fueling his steps. They both rushed through the doors and were met with the deafening sound of rotor blades. After climbing into the helicopter, the door was slammed shut behind them, and they were quickly lifted into the air. Hunter grabbed the headset in front of him and motioned for Rob to do the same.

"Who got hurt? What happened?" Hunter shouted.

"It's Jake. He was driving with—"

"Jake!" *God, no.* "What about Diana? The kids? Are they okay?"

"Diana and the kids are fine. Chet is headed to the ranch to get Diana and your mother. They'll meet us at the hospital. But Hunter—"

"Where was he? What happened?"

"He was on Highway 155 when an eighteen-wheeler crossed the center line. From what the police can tell, Jake veered out of the way, but in doing so, the truck flipped . . . several times. He was thrown clear of the wreckage, but—"

"Highway 155? That's just outside of here. What was he doing there?"

"He was on his way to see you. He and—"

"Why was he coming to see me? I don't get it. Why wouldn't he just—"

"Hunter! Stop interrupting!" Rob shouted. "You need to listen!"

Flinching at Rob's outburst, Hunter sat back in his chair. "Fine! I'm listening!"

"Hunter . . ." Rob took a deep breath, blew it out, then looked him in the eyes. "Jake is going to be okay. His injuries are not life-threatening."

"Thank God." He closed his eyes, relieved.

"But Hunter . . . there's more."

"More?"

Again, he watched as Rob took another deep breath, his expression twisted with sadness . . . grief even.

"Hunter . . . Charlie was with him."

Immediately, it felt like the helicopter was spiraling out of control. He felt dizzy, like he was going to pass out or puke. Or both. In the space of a nanosecond, a thousand questions rushed through his mind.

Why were Jake and Charlie together? Why were they coming to see me? Was it Daniel? Had he found her? Was he responsible for the accident?

Choking back emotion, Hunter stared at his hands. "But she's going to be okay, right?" When Rob was silent, he turned to him. "Tell me she's going to be okay?"

"The doctors aren't sure, Hunter. She's in critical condition. I'm so sorry."

Chapter Eighty

It felt like an eternity before they landed at the hospital and were met by a liaison.

"Mr. Jennings, I'm Heather Moore." The woman holding a tablet pressed to her chest extended her hand. "It's an honor to meet you. I'm so sorry it's under these circumstances."

He shook her hand out of reflex, then followed her as she hurried them inside and down a brightly lit corridor.

"Just tell me she's alive."

She looked back over her shoulder and offered a timid smile. "She's alive."

"Where is she? Can I see her? Is she conscious?"

"Mr. Jennings, I'll tell you everything I know. But let's go somewhere we can talk and not be interrupted."

Each step felt like he was walking through mud. It took forever to zigzag through hallways and corridors before entering a smartly furnished room—obviously for VIPs.

"Have a seat, Mr. Jennings." She pointed to a leather wingback chair.

"I don't want to sit down. I want to see Charlie."

"Please, Mr. Jennings. I have a lot of information to dispense. It would be better if you were sitting down."

"Come on, Hunter."

Rob put a hand on his shoulder, led him to the couch, and took a seat next to him.

"How is my brother?" Hunter asked as Ms. Moore crossed the room and pulled two bottles of water from a small refrigerator.

After placing the bottles on the coffee table in front of them, she sat down on the edge of the side chair. "Your brother is going to be fine. Though he sustained a concussion, some bone fractures, bruised ribs, and some facial lacerations, he's stable and extremely fortunate. He will be sore for a few weeks but should make a full recovery. He's still in the ER being attended to but will be moved to a room soon. You can see him once he's settled."

"What about Diana and my mother?"

"They were contacted immediately and are on their way. Your brother has been in communication with his wife."

Hunter took a deep breath, afraid to ask about Charlie. Terrified that the reason the woman had escorted him to this isolated room was so he could fall apart in private. If he didn't ask, she couldn't tell him. He wouldn't have to hear her say how very sorry she was.

Please, God. Please let Charlie be okay. I don't want to live life without her.

Slowly, he blew out the breath he was holding. "And Charlie?"

"Mr. Jennings, she's in critical condition. We won't have any real answers until after surgery, but I promise, as soon as I know—"

"Just tell me she's going to be okay. That's all I care about. Injuries . . . recovery time . . . those are all things we can deal with later. Right now, I just need to know she's going to be okay."

"Mr. Jennings," she whispered, "It's not that simple. Miss Foster has sustained life-threatening injuries. Our doctors are doing everything they can to assess and treat those injuries, but each one comes with its own complications."

"You're not telling me anything," he said coldly, pinning the woman with his stare. "Just tell me . . . is she going to die?"

She hesitated, her eyes filling with tears. "I don't know."

Hunter felt like he was going to suffocate from the lack

of oxygen in the room. "Okay," he took a breath, trying to stay in control of his emotions, "then tell me what you *do* know."

"She's in surgery with one of the best teams of doctors possible. Dr. Thomas, a thoracic surgeon, Dr. Jones, a cardiac surgeon, and Dr. Carter, a neurosurgeon. These men are the very best in their field."

More information without telling me a freakin' thing.

He clenched his fists together, doing everything he could to maintain his composure. "What exactly are her injuries?"

"The extent wasn't known prior to surgery."

"Stop it!" Hunter darted to his feet and paced across the room. "Stop talking in circles! What are we dealing with?" he shouted. "Broken bones? A spinal injury? Missing limbs?"

"Come on, Hunter," Rob tried to calm him.

"No!" He spun around and pointed an angry finger at his manager. "Do *not* tell me how to act right now!"

"Mr. Jennings, like I said, we won't know more until after surgery. I think it would be best for you to wait until the doctors can thoroughly explain Miss Foster's injuries, along with what they were able to do for her."

"No." He shook his head and paced. "Tell me now. I need to know what we're up against before the doctors hit me with all kinds of unintelligible medical jargon."

Clearly, the woman did not want to divulge any information, but when her eyes met his, he could tell she was beginning to cave. "Please, Miss Moore," he pleaded, tears blurring his vision.

"Mr. Jennings . . . I was led to believe Miss Foster was one of your staff members . . . but she's more than that, isn't she?"

"Yes," he gasped, no longer caring about secrecy.

She sat up straighter, took a deep breath, and looked at the tablet in her lap. "Miss Foster wasn't breathing when the EMTs arrived on the scene. She was intubated and suffered cardiac arrest while being transported. But . . . they were able to stabilize her before surgery. She suffered broken ribs, which accounts for a punctured lung and some of the internal bleeding. A ruptured spleen was also evident, but her bleeding was extensive, leading the doctors to believe she had other internal injuries. She also sustained a skull fracture."

Not breathing? Cardiac arrest? Skull fracture?

He needed to sit down before his legs went out from under him. He lowered himself to the edge of the couch, hands clutched in front of him.

"Mr. Jennings, I know this is a difficult time, but please know Miss Foster is in very capable hands. Though her injuries are extensive, you need to stay positive."

Did you hear that, God? I'm supposed to stay positive, even though the woman I love—more than anything in this world—is broken and bleeding . . . maybe dying.

The last few months flashed through his mind.

Meeting Charlie.

Spar with her.

Wooing her.

Breaking down her walls.

Finding out about Daniel.

Falling in love.

It can't be over now, God. It can't be. Please. I'll do anything. Anything!

Just don't let her die.

Chapter Eighty-One

When Jake was finally assigned a room, Hunter pulled himself together and quietly walked inside. Immediately, his brother turned to him, tears rolling down his cheeks.

"I'm so sorry, Hunter. This is all my fault."

He rushed to his brother's side and clenched his good hand, never having seen him so emotional. "Don't talk like that, Jake. I met with the police while I was waiting for you to be moved to a room. They said your quick thinking is what saved your lives. It's a miracle either one of you survived. But I still don't understand. Why were you coming to see me?"

He closed his eyes, a pained expression creasing his face. "Charlie needed to talk to you about—"

"Jake!"

Hunter turned and saw Diana rush into the room, followed by their mother. He stepped out of the way and watched as his sister-in-law collapsed against his brother's chest, causing him to wince in pain.

"Sorry," she stood up quickly, scanning his face, the bed sheets, the sling around his arm. She gently touched his bandaged forehead, tears streaming down her face. "I don't know what I would've done if I lost you."

Jake reached for her hand, brought it to his lips and kissed it. "I'm going to be fine."

Glancing at his mom, she looked ready to collapse. Hunter could only remember one other time when she had looked so fragile and weak.

The night they found out about Amy.

He quickly pulled a chair over to Jake's bedside, and helped her sit down. Resting his hand on her shoulder, she clutched it, as if she was holding on for dear life. No one said anything for several minutes, everyone fighting to keep their emotions under control. Finally, Diana asked, "Hunter, how's Charlie?"

"Still in surgery," he answered softly.

She let go of Jake's hand and wrapped her arms around him. Holding him tight, she looked up. "Charlie's tough. She won't go down without a fight. You have to know that."

Hunter held onto Diana, needing her strength, needing to believe what she was saying, but his hope was waning. Though he prayed every second of every minute that Charlie was going to come through this okay—that she was going to be whole again—he was afraid this was God's answer to her difficult dilemma. Yes, God was finally releasing Charlie from a life of fear and hiding. He just wasn't doing it the way Hunter wanted or ever would have imagined.

Still trying to piece things together, Hunter waited until everyone had their emotions intact, then asked for a second time, "Why were you and Charlie on your way to see me?"

He watched as Diana and Jake exchanged glances.

"Okay, I can tell from those looks it wasn't Charlie being impulsive and deciding she wanted to see me perform." Something he had clung to these last few hours, even though he knew it was a stretch. But it was better than the other reasons spinning around in his head.

"Is it her husband? Did he contact her or find out where she was hiding?"

"Husband?" his mother gasped. "What are you talking about?"

Hunter hung his head. *I can't do this right now.* He didn't have the emotional stamina to back up and try to explain everything to his mother.

"Irene," Diana jumped in, "I can explain that to you

later. What matters right now is Charlie."

"And if someone doesn't tell me in the next two seconds why she was in the middle of nowhere on her way to see me, I'm going to snap!"

Diana looked at Jake, then back at him. "Charlie is sick. Not just flu sick, but something more. We thought it was best for her to tell you in person, because we were afraid you would overreact if she told you over the phone."

"I don't understand. How does she know it's not the flu?"

"Last month, when she told me how sick she'd been, I explained to her that it was extremely rare to get the flu so many times in one year. I finally convinced her to do a test to see what was up. She put my name on it and sent it to Dr. Kinsey."

"The doctor you use to work for," Hunter clarified.

"Yes," she nodded. "Well . . . he called to tell me there were some abnormalities, and he wanted to run further tests. When I told him the test results weren't mine, he just about had a heart attack, dictating to me what constituted malpractice, and how I had put his medical license in jeopardy. I begged him to trust me, explaining a little about Charlie's situation. After a lot of pleading and groveling, he agreed to see Charlie—off the record—using my name for any lab work he needed to run."

"Is that what Charlie was coming to tell me, that she's really sick?"

"No. She was coming to tell you she was going through with the additional tests."

"Do the doctors here know there might be something wrong with her, other than the accident?"

"Yes. When the hospital called to tell me Jake and Charlie had been in an accident, I told them she was being seen by a doctor for a preexisting condition, and that they should contact Dr. Kinsey."

Hunter didn't know how much more *unknown* he could take. Looking at the clock on the wall, his heart plummeted. It had been hours since Charlie was taken into surgery, and still no word.

"I can't do this anymore," he said as he stalked toward the door, bumping into Rob, who was on his way in. He looked at his manager, seeing it in his eyes. "What?"

"The media found out. It's on the news and reporters are outside."

Jake hurried and pushed the buttons on his bedside rail, the TV bursting to life. He quickly clicked through the channels until a reporter, standing outside the hospital, filled the screen.

"Though we don't have all the details, the police did say there was an unidentified female in the vehicle at the time of the accident. She sustained critical injuries and was transported from the scene by life flight. Jake Jennings, brother of superstar Hunter Jennings, is said to be in fair condition. The driver of the semi-truck failed a sobriety test at the scene of the accident and has been arrested. He sustained no injuries. Hunter Jennings arrived by helicopter some time ago, cutting his concert at the Peoria Civic Center short. Though fans were initially upset when the superstar didn't retake the stage, their anger quickly turned to support when the reason for Jennings' departure was explained. As you might remember, Jake Jennings was an integral part of Jennings' career when he first emerged on the country music scene. Not only was he a band member, but he was also Jennings' personal manager. Jake retired when he married, turning in his guitar for a lasso. He now manages Hunter Jennings' thirty thousand-acre Texas ranch. That's what we know for now. We will update you as information becomes available."

"Mary, any word on who the unidentified female might be?" the in-studio anchor asked the reporter.

"Yes. Though we still don't have a name, Diana Jennings, wife of Jake Jennings, identified her as a family friend, squashing the immediate rumors that Jake Jennings' was having an affair. Of course, that only leans to more speculation regarding the woman's identity, and if it's possible Hunter Jennings was secretly involved with this woman. That's what we know for now. Back to you in the studio."

Everyone turned to Hunter, waiting for his reaction. He glanced at the clock, then headed for the door. "It's time I get some answers."

Chapter Eighty-Two

Needing some answers, Hunter stormed from Jake's room. However, when he saw a team of doctors walking his way—their expressions fatigued and somber—he wasn't sure he was ready to know.

"Mr. Jennings, I'm Dr. Thomas," one of the men spoke as he extended his hand. "This is Dr. Carter and Dr. Jones."

Hunter shook their hands as his heart raced out of control.

"Why don't we go in here so we can talk privately." The man in the blue scrubs pointed to a door that read "Authorized Personnel Only."

"Just tell me if she's alive," Hunter said, bracing himself for the answer.

Dr. Thomas stared at him with exhausted eyes. "She made it through surgery, but . . . she has a long way to go."

Hunter bent over, his hands on his knees, tears splashing his boots. *Thank you, God. Thank you.*

"Come on," one of the doctors put a hand on his back. "You need to sit down."

Hunter stood back up, releasing the breath he'd been holding for the last several hours. "Can we go in here?" he pointed to Jake's room. "My family is in there, and I don't know if I'll have the strength to repeat what you're going to tell me."

"Not a problem."

When Hunter walked back into Jake's room—flanked by the three doctors—his brother immediately silenced the television and struggled to sit up. Diana quickly moved to the far side of Jake's bed and stood with a reassuring hand on their mother's shoulder. Rob slipped out, saying something about taking care of the media.

After introductions were made all around, Dr. Carter lowered the bedrail and motioned for Hunter to take a seat. "You look a little shaky."

He felt a whole lot shaky, so he took the doctor's advice.

"I'm going to give a brief overview of what we know and what is being done for Miss Foster at this time. I'm not going to get overly technical. Just the basics."

Hunter nodded, or at least he thought he did.

"Miss Foster—"

"Charlie!" Hunter snapped but quickly apologized. "I'm sorry. I didn't mean to be rude, it's just that *Miss Foster* sounds like a stranger. Can you please call her Charlie?"

"Sure," Dr. Carter smiled, then turned serious. "*Charlie* sustained multiple internal injuries. A ruptured spleen, lacerated liver, collapsed lung, pericardial effusion, fractured ribs—"

"Wait," Hunter interrupted. "What is pericardia . . . whatever you said?"

"Pericardial effusion," the doctor repeated. "It's when there is too much fluid around the heart, causing excess pressure."

"Okay." Hunter nodded for him to continue.

"We removed her spleen, drained the fluid from around her heart, put in a chest tube, and repaired her other injuries. Everything went as well as could be expected under the circumstances."

Hunter felt a *but* coming.

Dr. Carter looked around the room, then back to him. "But Charlie also sustained a skull fracture and a subdural hematoma."

"Bleeding on the brain," he mumbled to himself, then dropped his head and closed his eyes, praying it didn't get any worse.

"Yes. And the bleeding along with swelling is causing

intracranial pressure. In order to release the pressure on her brain, we've inserted a drain and . . ."

Hunter looked up when the doctor paused. "And?"

Dr. Carter sighed. "We've placed Charlie in a medically induced coma."

A coma. Hunter closed his eyes again. *I've lost her. I've truly lost her.*

"Mr. Jennings." The doctor waited until he had his attention again. "I know that sounds devastating, but it will actually help Charlie. We need to curtail her body's natural triage mechanism, which shuts off blood flow to injured areas. However, that blood flow is necessary to support the healing process. Also, the body instinctively goes into fight-mode after trauma, causing it to work overtime. By inducing the coma, we're allowing Charlie's brain not to work as hard, relieving stress and allowing it time to rest."

It took a minute to find his voice. After he swallowed back the bile in his throat Hunter asked, "What is Charlie's prognosis?"

"Until we see some reduction in the brain swelling, I'm sorry to say it's hour to hour. We are watching her closely for any signs of increased swelling. If we're able to manage that, her odds increase significantly."

"I know this is a lot for you to take in," Dr. Jones added, looking extremely fatigued. "But just know we are doing everything we can. We have an exceptional staff, and Charlie is getting the best care possible. You know, it's a miracle she didn't have more extensive injuries to her limbs. She has contusions and several small lacerations from glass, but usually, with such a catastrophic collision, legs are crushed, severed, or at the very least pinned into the wreckage causing massive tissue and muscle damage."

"She was sitting cross legged on the seat."

Everyone turned to Jake.

"We were talking. The subject matter got a little heavy. Just seconds before the crash, she pulled her feet up on the seat and turned toward the window. I don't even think she saw the truck coming at us."

"Well, whatever the reason, it probably saved her life. Her body would not have been able to tolerate just one more traumatic injury."

"When can I see her?" Hunter asked, knowing he wasn't going to take no for an answer.

"Shortly. Once she's settled in a room."

When the doctors excused themselves, everyone once again went through the formality of shaking hands, but before the doctors could leave, Diana spoke up. "Dr. Carter, I know right now your focus is on Charlie's injuries, but I was wondering if anyone contacted Dr. Kinsey? When I was called about the accident, I explained that Charlie was already seeing a doctor for some preexisting issues."

"Yes," Dr. Thomas spoke up. "It appears Charlie has been suffering from atrophic gastritis caused by a H. pylori infection. She most likely contracted the infection as a child, but it only started presenting recently."

"Praise God," Diana said, tears falling from her eyes.

Hunter looked at her, angered by her reaction. "What do you mean, 'Praise God?' That's just one more thing she has to battle."

"Hunter, it's actually a good thing," Diana calmly explained. "My fear was Charlie had stomach cancer. Gastritis is easily treatable."

He looked at the doctor for confirmation.

"She's right. A couple rounds of antibiotics will take care of the gastritis. It's minor in the grand scheme of things. Also, her right wrist was already wrapped when she got here. We x-rayed it to be sure nothing was broken."

Hunter turned to Jake.

"We had a disagreement," he said sheepishly. "She got mad and slammed her hand against the dashboard."

Hunter fumed. "And now she's lying in a hospital bed, fighting for her life. Are you—"

"Like I said," Dr. Thomas interrupted, "it's minor. And getting angry isn't going to change anything. What matters now is staying positive and focusing your energy on Charlie. She needs all the prayers and emotional support you can offer her."

Hunter nodded and waited for the doctors to exit. When they did, he got up from where he sat on the bed and walked to Jake's private bathroom. After throwing up, he sank to the floor and sobbed quietly to himself, feeling as if his very heart was being crushed inside his chest.

Chapter Eighty-Three

It had been over an hour since the doctors had spoken with them. Hunter had cleaned up after purging his stomach and waited impatiently for someone to come and get him. His mother slept in the chair that converted into a bed, while Diana rested, her head laying on Jake's bed, their hands folded together. And Rob was still out dealing with the media circus.

While Hunter paced, he watched his brother try to get comfortable. It was obvious he was in a fair amount of pain, but Jake didn't say a word. Even so, Hunter watched him push the button on his medication pump more than once.

"How are you feeling?" he whispered, not wanting to disturb Diana.

"Okay."

"You're pretty banged up."

"Worse than any bar fight I've ever been in."

Hunter plopped down in the chair next to his brother's bed and leaned forward. "So . . . tell me again what you two were doing?"

"I told you. She was sick and needed to talk to you in person."

"Sure. I get why Charlie was coming to see me. What I want to know is why *you* were with her?"

Jake played with the monitor wires clipped to his finger. "Because she was scared. Not just because she was sick, but because she was afraid to go out in public. Besides, I knew I would be able to get her into your bus without being hassled. If I remember correctly, the first time she went to see you, she almost got arrested. I figured I could run interference for her."

Hunter grinned. "So . . . you were *helping* Charlie?"

"More like keeping her out of trouble."

He watched as his brother tried to mask a grin. "You couldn't ignore a damsel in distress, could you?" he teased.

"Whatever." Jake closed his eyes while Hunter stared at his watch.

"I heard about your extended tour on the radio," Jake said, keeping the conversation going. Charlie explained your reasoning behind it. It's a good idea. The duet album is too. They're smart ways to fulfill your contract without having to commit to another full-blown tour."

"That's the idea."

"Selling off the back acreage is a good idea too. I was just ticked because you didn't include me in the decision-making process."

"You had every right to be mad. It's *our* property—always has been. I just didn't want to hear a lecture. You reacted exactly the way I thought you would, blaming it on Charlie. I should've said something sooner, but I knew you wouldn't understand what I was trying to do. Charlie deserves so much more than what she has had to deal with. Stability. A home. No more running or looking over her shoulder. That's what I wanted to give her. But now . . ." Hunter stopped, having to swallow back his emotions. "Now, she's in intensive care fighting for her life . . . all because of me."

"Come on, Hunter, you can't think that way. This isn't your fault. Every decision Charlie made was because of the dirt-bag husband she left behind. Wait a minute," Jake leaned back, his hand to his forehead, "The drive. I forgot about the drive." His sharp tone caused Diana to stir.

"What's wrong?" She sat up, but still looked half asleep.

"Nothing, honey. We were just talking. Go back to sleep."

"Hunter, have you been able to see Charlie, yet?" she

asked, fighting back a yawn.

"No. Not yet."

She nodded, laid her head back down on Jake's bed, and closed her eyes.

"What are you talking about?" Hunter whispered. "What about the drive?"

Jake inched up on the mattress, grimacing in pain. "Not *the* drive. *A* drive. Charlie had a flash drive in her purse."

"Okay . . ."

"It has information on it she stole from her husband's computer. Charlie's convinced whatever is on it can be used against him. She figured you could give it to Jerry, and Jerry could make sure it anonymously ended up in the right hands. And, if it did prove her husband bought off government officials, it could be enough to put him behind bars."

Hunter moved to the edge of his chair. "Where is the drive now?"

"I don't know. I don't know where any of our stuff is. But someone must've collected everything at the scene. Hopefully, it's still inside her purse."

"I need to find out who has it."

Hunter got up from his chair and headed to the door, just as a nurse entered.

"Mr. Jennings, I can take you to see Miss Foster now."

Chapter Eighty-Four

Hunter stood at the foot of Charlie's bed, doing his best not to break down. Tubes and wires snaked around her body, in her side, her head, and in her mouth. Her right arm was in a sling, her head bandaged, her face swollen and bruised.

But he could still see her.

He could still see the woman he loved.

"You can hold her hand, if you'd like," the nurse whispered.

Hunter positioned himself on the left side of the bed and laid his hand over Charlie's.

The nurse quickly pulled a chair around so he could sit down.

"Thank you."

"You can talk to her too, but only positive things. Don't reference the accident. Talk to her like you would over breakfast."

"What's wrong with her arm? The doctor said she had a sprained wrist but didn't say anything about her arm."

"It's just a dislocated shoulder. Minor. That's probably why he didn't say anything. It will be fine in a few weeks."

Silently, he stroked Charlie's hand, afraid he would say the wrong thing. He studied the machines around her, familiarizing himself with the beeps and squiggly lines. He stared at her closed eyes, willing them to open, then realized, even if she wanted to wake up, she couldn't. She was supposed to stay asleep. The doctors needed her body and mind to rest. He brushed back a strand of hair from her face, lightly touching her swollen cheek.

Not knowing what to say, he began to hum her favorite songs, jumping from one to another.

"You know," he finally spoke after humming and stroking her hand for almost an hour, "I could write another verse to "Memories in the Making" . . . just for us," he whispered.

> *Recollections make me smile,*
> *when I think how we began.*
> *You a firecracker,*
> *me an angry man.*
> *Missed cues and apologies,*
> *instead of dinner dates with wine.*
> *But I wouldn't change a minute,*
> *those days that made you mine.*

He continued to hum and improvise lyrics, all the while praying God would use this time to mend Charlie's broken body. When he felt a tap on his shoulder, he knew what it meant.

"Okay, sweetheart, I'm supposed to let you rest now, but I'll be back to finish our song."

He pushed to his feet and tried to let go of her hand but couldn't. He was too afraid if he did, she would slip away forever.

"Mr. Jennings, I understand this is hard for you. But trust me. She's in good hands."

He turned to the nurse behind him and saw compassion in her eyes, and something more. When he glanced at her badge, it almost knocked him to his knees. It took him a second to find his voice. When he did, he smiled and gave the nurse a hug. "Thank you, *Amy*. I feel better knowing you're watching over her."

And as he walked away, he thanked the One who was truly in control.

Message received, God. I know she's in Your hands.

Chapter Eighty-Five

At the twenty-six-hour mark, Charlie experienced a non-convulsive seizure which sent everyone into a tailspin. Thankfully, Dr. Carter was present when it happened. Even so, seeing the concern on his face when he exited Charlie's room nearly caused Hunter's knees to buckle. Dr. Carter led him to a chair, explained what had happened and the course of action they were taking, but clearly, he was still worried.

Now they were at the four-day mark, and Charlie had not experienced any further setbacks or complications. Pacing the hall right outside her room, Hunter waited for the doctor to finish his exam, praying his prognosis would continue to be positive.

Smiling as he swung the door open, Dr. Carter pulled off his gloves, tossed them in the trash, and pumped the hand sanitizer dispenser on the wall. "She's a fighter, Mr. Jennings, clear and simple." The doctor patted him on the back as they walked toward the nurses' station. Setting down the computer tablet with Charlie's chart on it, he shook his head. "Ninety-six hours ago, she was in the fight of her life. Today everything is clicking. She's healing nicely, and we are continuing to see a reduction in swelling."

"When will you be able to wake her?"

"It's too soon to tell, but I'm very optimistic."

Hunter sighed. He had no words.

"Listen, I heard your brother is being released today. Why don't you go see him off, grab a shower, maybe even

389

close your eyes for twenty minutes or so?"

Hunter looked over the doctor's shoulder at Charlie's room.

"She's stable, Mr. Jennings, why don't—"

"Come on, doc, I keep asking you to call me Hunter. It doesn't sound so . . . bleak."

He smiled. "Okay . . . Hunter, why don't you move around, go outside? You haven't left this floor in four days. You need to get some fresh air."

"Easy for you to say. I haven't left because the staff on this floor knows what I'm going through and have been respectful of my privacy. Here I'm just a man concerned for his woman. I'm not sure that will be the case elsewhere."

"True. I get it. But, if you need some fresh air, talk to Heather Moore. She can get authorization for you to be on the roof. You can have the place all to yourself, as long as we don't have an incoming patient. I would suggest the staff terrace, but I'm afraid you're right. I've heard the nurses talking, or should I say panting," he laughed. "You wouldn't get the solitude you're looking for there either."

Hunter thought about the last few days. In some respects, they had melted together into one long, grueling stretch of time. In other ways, it was like he had closed his eyes for only a second and his world had changed completely. He tuned out everything but Charlie. As far as he was concerned, nothing existed outside these walls. When he wasn't holding her hand and humming tunes, he was grabbing a quick shower in the doctor's locker room, or a bite to eat in the VIP room he had been escorted to that first night. Though Rob had offered to sit with him, Hunter didn't want him around. He didn't want to talk business, or concerts, or media footage. He just wanted to focus on Charlie.

The only distractions he had allowed himself was Jake's recovery and the flash drive he'd spoken about that first night. Hunter thought about the drive when he paced the halls or closed his eyes to rest, wondering if it was possible it held the answers they were looking for.

It's time I find out.

"I think you're right, Dr. Carter. I'll go see my brother before he leaves. But I won't be gone long."

Hunter smiled when he walked into Jake's room and saw him dressed and standing by the window. "Raring to go, huh?"

"Are you kidding? One more day in that bed and I was going to lose it. But now that I have my walking papers, I'd like to stay with you. I don't feel right leaving you here alone."

"No, bro, Cody and Courtney need to see you, and not just on Facetime. They need to be able to touch you, hug you, and see for themselves that their daddy is okay."

"I know. But you need someone too. The last few days have been rough."

Hunter rubbed his bristled jaw, doing everything he could to maintain his emotions. "Go see the kids and spend some time with Diana. When she gets tired of you," he teased, "come back and hang out with me for a few days; bring a couple of guitars when you do."

"Deal."

Walking to the far side of the room, Hunter looked out the window at the media circus taking up residence in the parking lot. "I can't believe they're still here. I made it perfectly clear I would not be making a statement."

"Doesn't matter. Now that they know Charlie is your significant other—someone they knew nothing about—you couldn't pay them to go away." Jake said, glancing out the window.

Hunter tensed, thinking about the janitor he had wrestled to the ground, grabbing his phone, seeing the picture he had clicked of Charlie. The man was pressing charges for assault, but Hunter didn't care. Bloodying the man's face had given him just a hint of satisfaction.

When Diana walked into the room, they both turned around.

"You got it!" Hunter rushed to her side.

"Yes. I was told everything collected at the scene is in

here," she said, handing him the plastic bag.

He took it and pulled Charlie's purse from it, but there wasn't much in it. A brush. Some gum. A package of tissues. He searched every pocket before turning the large leather bag inside out. "There has to be more."

Dumping the evidence bag onto the bed, he rifled through the stuff that must have been in Jake's truck. Stuff now covered in dirt and grime. Loose CDs. Broken CD cases. A phone charger. Crumpled registration and insurance papers. Charlie's wallet and broken phone. "These must've fallen out of her purse. What if the drive did too, and it's still out there somewhere?" Hunter cursed under his breath.

This can't be happening.

It has to be here.

When he picked up Charlie's phone, he saw it lying there. The drive. Exposed. Without a cap. Minuscule grains of dirt embedded inside the connector.

"What is that?" Diana asked.

Hunter held it up. "Hopefully, it's what Charlie thinks it is. Evidence to put her husband away."

"You're kidding. How did you know she had it?"

"She was taking it to Hunter," Jake said. "It was her other reason to go see him."

"And you didn't tell me?" Diana looked confused.

"I didn't know. Not until we were almost there."

Hunter stared at the filthy drive, praying the information could still be retrieved, then handed it to Jake. "Give it to Chet; make sure he gives it to Jerry ASAP."

"Will do."

Hunter pulled his brother into a hug, careful not to hurt his injured arm. "I love you, man. I don't know what I would've done if I had lost you."

"I love you too, bro. And I ain't goin' nowhere. I plan on being a colossal pain in the butt for the next fifty years."

"I'm gonna hold you to it."

Both men brushed away tears before the three of them walked to the elevator. "I'm going up," Hunter said, "but I'll ride down with you guys."

"No need," Jake pushed four. "We're going up too. Chet chartered a helicopter and got permission from the hospital administrator to land on the roof. The chopper is waiting to take us back to the airport. Chet will fly us home from there."

When the elevator opened, Hunter stepped out and pressed his hand against the door, preventing it from shutting. "Come with me to see Charlie."

Jake shook his head, stepping back against the elevator wall. "I can't. It's my fault she's here. I don't want to do anything to interfere with her recovery. If I hadn't been such a jerk—if I hadn't forced her to go talk to you—none of this would've happened."

Hunter looked him straight in the eyes. "And . . . if I hadn't fallen in love with a woman with a crazy past, none of us would be here. But I did. And I'm not sorry. And Charlie is going to be fine. So, you can either get out of the elevator and come say hi, or I can deck you just like I did the janitor. What's it going to be?"

"Knock it off, both of you!" Diana snapped as she pulled his brother out of the elevator, then turned to him. "But Jake has a valid point. He's part of the accident. Hearing his voice could spark something in Charlie, something negative." She turned to her husband. "I'm not saying you're responsible for Charlie's condition. I'm just saying it could be painful for her if she connects your voice with the accident. I, on the other hand, would love to see her." She reached for Hunter's hand, gave it a squeeze, then smiled. "Take me to your lady."

"Yes, ma'am."

Hunter stood back and watched Diana interact with Charlie. She was a natural comforter. Her tone, the way she held Charlie's hand between her own. It was obvious why she had become a nurse. She was a caretaker at heart.

He listened as Diana talked about Courtney, and how she was making plans for when Charlie got home. "She has tea parties and dress-up days already scribbled on her Paw Patrol calendar, Diana said. "She can't wait to spend time with you. Unfortunately, Cody isn't quite as excited as Courtney. He isn't sure how he feels about having to share his Uncle Hunter's time with a girl, but he'll get over it."

Diana peered over her shoulder at him and smiled, before turning back to Charlie. "Well, I have to be going, but I know we'll talk again real soon." She stood, leaned over the bed, and kissed her bruised cheek. "Don't be afraid, Charlie," Diana whispered. "Everything is going to be fine."

Chapter Eighty-Six

Three weeks.

Charlie had been asleep for three weeks.

But now it was time for her to wake up.

The swelling was gone, the chest tube and drain in her skull removed, and her condition had been downgraded from critical, to serious, to guarded.

The weaning-off process had started earlier that morning, and now Dr. Carter was checking Charlie's progress while Hunter stood at the foot of the bed.

Watching.

Waiting.

Praying.

"Well, Hunter . . . so far, she's doing great. Charlie is actually breathing on her own, which is the first hurdle. If she can go twenty-four hours without assistance, we'll be able to remove the ventilator completely."

"And then she'll wake up?"

"Like I said before, there is no exact timetable to the waking up process. Think of it as a light switch with a dimmer. The light doesn't go from off to on with the flip of a switch, it's gradual. And since Charlie has been under for a few weeks, it could take a little longer. Each patient is unique and has a different set of circumstances.

"But remember, when Charlie does wake up, she could be disorientated, agitated, even combative. Her body is trying to wake up but doesn't understand why it's so difficult. She might not even remember the accident, so her first reaction to her surroundings could be confusion. The ventilator can also be an issue. If she wakes before we can remove it, she could panic because she can't talk or communicate. A patient's first instinct is to pull out the tube. We have to make sure that doesn't happen. It could cause damage if not removed properly."

"So, what do I do?"

"What you have been doing. Talk to her. Sing to her. But now you can also encourage her to wake up. Tell her it's okay. Reassure her everything is all right. Remind her who you are. Where she is. Her mind will try to protect her from reliving the fear and terror of the accident, or it could confuse it with past traumatic events. That's why it's important to keep reassuring her everything is going to be okay. That she's safe. That nobody is going to hurt her."

Their eyes met, an unspoken understanding passing between them, reminding Hunter of the confidential conversation he had with Dr. Carter the day Charlie suffered the seizure. When the doctor explained there were several reasons for the seizure, one being a physical manifestation of past psychological events, Hunter broke down and explained—without giving names or particulars—that Charlie had been in an abusive relationship. That she had already experienced one life-threatening accident, and her life had been threatened more than once.

Dr. Carter handled the information like the professional he was, never asking for more details than necessary. However, it did help him understand why the administration staff insisted Charlie didn't exist on paper. Other than her driver's license, they could find no record of her. Dr. Carter immediately ran interference, alluding to the fact that Charlie's *case* involved the government, and the admin staff was to delve no further.

"I'll be back to check on you two in just a little while. If Charlie wakes up, keep her calm, and call for one of the nurses." The doctor patted Hunter on the shoulder before stepping away.

Sitting down next to Charlie's bed, Hunter held her hand,

and watched her eyes.

"Did you hear that, sweetheart? It's time for you to wake up. It's time we make plans for the future. Solid plans. There's nothing holding us back now. I promise."

He wanted to tell her everything but was afraid the mention of Daniel's name could have a negative effect. He just needed to be patient, knowing God would allow her to wake up when the time was right.

He began to hum while stroking her hand, juggling words and lyrics in his head. When he felt he had a decent first verse, he scooted closer to Charlie's bed and sang softly next to her ear.

> *You can dream,*
> *as long as you're dreamin' with me.*
> *You can rest,*
> *as long as you're restin' in my arms.*
> *It's time we plan.*
> *I'm holdin' your hand,*
> *every minute for the rest of your life.*
> *Wake up, Charlie, and be my wife.*

"Wow, sounds like a hit."

He turned to see Jake and Diana standing behind him. He quickly got to his feet and gave his brother a hug. "I see you got your cast off," he said while embracing him.

"Yep. Just now. But I still need to wear the sling, at least for another week."

"And you came all the way back here to get it off?"

He shrugged. "What can I say, they treated me well here. Besides, we wanted to check on you. It has been almost a week since I last came."

"Hey, Diana," he hugged her close.

"So, today is the big day, huh?"

"Yep," Hunter exhaled. "And she is already knockin' it out of the park. Dr. Carter said she's breathing on her own. If she can keep it up for twenty-four hours, they'll be able to take out the tube."

"That's great." Diana moved to the other side of Charlie's bed. "She looks so much better than the last time I saw her."

"I know. The bruising and swelling are pretty much gone. And she doesn't have tubes sticking out of her everywhere." He sat back down and reached for her hand. "Now all she has to do is wake up."

"So . . . the song you were singing when we came in . . . it sounded pretty good," Jake said.

"Yeah . . . well . . . it's only for Charlie. No one else needs to hear it."

"So . . . speaking of Rob . . ."

Hunter groaned. "What now?"

"He called me the other day, said you haven't talked to him for almost two weeks. He sounded pretty desperate."

"That's because he didn't like what I had to say the last time we talked."

"So, it's true? You're quitting?"

"I'm not *quitting*. Even though I'm not going to reschedule the extended tour, I assured Rob I would make good on the dates I had to cancel. I also told him I'd go through with the duet album once life settles down, but after that, I'm through. Hunter Jennings will be officially retired."

"But why? It's not like you have to choose between your career and Charlie anymore. Now you can have both."

"You're right. And maybe someday down the road I'll pick it back up again. But I don't want to think about that right now. I don't want to worry about schedules or deadlines or meetings about what direction to take my career next. I just want to go back to the ranch with Charlie, make her my wife, and do all the simple things honeymooners do. Like curl up in front of the TV and watch a Longmire marathon. Go for a ride at sunset. Lounge by the pool. Stay in bed all day, just because we can."

"Okay . . . Okay . . . that's enough," Diana chimed in. "We get the picture."

"Yeah, shut up before I have to poke out my mind's eye."

Jake gave him a brotherly shove.

When Hunter turned to say something, he felt a tremor under his hand. He whipped his head back around and moved his hand, so he could see Charlie's.

"Did you see that?"

"See what?" Diana asked.

"Charlie's hand . . . it just moved."

"What?" Jake hurried around the bed and stood next to Diana.

"I felt it. Under my hand. Charlie moved her hand." Hunter stared at her face, hoping to see even the slightest movement. "Come on, babe, do it again. Let me know you're there."

He darted his attention back and forth between her face and her hand. And then he saw it.

Diana gasped.

"You saw it too, right?"

"Yes," Diana burst into tears. "I saw it. Her fingers twitched."

Hunter fist pumped his right hand into the air and let out a holler. Within seconds, Amy and an older nurse named Connie rushed into the room.

"What's wrong?" Connie asked as she positioned herself in front of the monitors.

"Her fingers moved. Charlie's fingers moved."

The nurse studied the screens, while Amy laid a hand on Hunter's shoulder. "See, I told you she'd be okay."

Hunter kept his attention on Charlie's hand. "Do it again, sweetheart. I know you can hear me. Do it again."

Everyone stared at Charlie's hand. No one breathed. No one blinked.

And then it happened again.

"I'm going to page Dr. Carter," Connie said as she hurried to the door. "Remember, keep her calm if she wakes up."

"Wake up, Charlie. I know you can do it. I'm right here."

Hunter continued to stroke her hand as he encouraged her to wake up, desperate to see a flinch or a tremor. It wasn't long before the doctor showed up, but it felt like an eternity.

"I heard we had some movement," Dr. Carter said as he pulled on some gloves and approached the bed. Jake and Diana quickly stepped back.

"Yes. Her fingers twitched three different times."

"That's great," Dr. Carter said while he studied the monitors.

"Come on, sweetheart. Show the doctor what you're made of," Hunter said while holding her hand in his.

He continued to talk to Charlie while the doctor did his thing, but the longer it dragged on without a response, the more disappointment seeped into his voice.

"It's okay, Hunter. Don't get discouraged. Remember . . . a dimmer, not a switch."

"I know. But she was right there. I could feel her."

"And she still is. But even a few reflexes can exhaust her. She has been immobile for weeks. Just keep your tone positive. Let her know you're here, and that she can take her time. Reassure her. Don't pressure her."

He nodded, swallowing back his emotion as he stroked her hand. "You go ahead and rest, Charlie. I'll be right here when you're ready."

Chapter Eighty-Seven

It was midnight.

Another day had gone by and all was quiet.

Dr. Carter broke the rules once again, allowing Hunter twenty-four-hour access to Charlie's room. Just like he had altered the protocol that would've had Charlie change rooms as her condition improved.

After seeing relentless fans and media invade the hospital, the doctor did not want to take the chance of Hunter being approached or someone slipping by the staff to gain access to Charlie's room. She had been on the fourth floor for three weeks. That's where she would remain for the duration of her stay.

Same room.

Same staff.

Same everything.

Hunter agreed one hundred percent. He felt a special bond with the fourth-floor staff, like he too was a patient and they were seeing to his needs as much as they were Charlie's.

Especially Amy.

She was always there with a comforting hand on his shoulder or a reassuring word the moment fear or discouragement crept in. Every time Amy entered Charlie's room or checked on him in the VIP room, Hunter thought about his sister. However, instead of feeling sadness, he was comforted. Maybe that was why his trust in the young nurse ran so deep. She had so many qualities that reminded him of his sister. She genuinely seemed to care about him, not as a fan, but as a person who understood the worry and anxiousness he felt. When she prayed with him, tears streamed down her face. When she made her rounds, she always had time to sit down and talk with him. She lifted his spirits the moment he felt discouraged and was always there when he needed someone the most. He was so thankful for the care and concern she, along with the rest of the fourth-floor staff, had given him.

As he reflected on the last few days, Amy walked into the room.

"How is my favorite patient doing?" she asked, glancing at the monitors, then at Charlie, before smiling at him.

"Resting, I guess."

"Come on, Hunter, don't get discouraged," she whispered, pulling up a chair at the foot of the bed. "She's off the ventilator, breathing on her own. All good steps. After everything you've told me about her, she's not going to give up now. She has too much pluck for that." Amy sat back in the chair, like she was settling in for a long evening. "Tell me again about the time you startled her in the barn and almost got yourself impaled."

Hunter chuckled, remembering the fire he saw in Charlie's eyes that day—fire that immediately ignited something inside him.

"Or how she pummeled you with the toe of her boot when you laid down your motorcycle."

He didn't remember telling Amy about the motorcycle incident, but he laughed as he recalled the memory. "You know . . . I have told you more about my relationship with Charlie than anyone else." He looked her in the eye. "You remind me of my sister. She was always such a good listener and encourager. Her name was Amy too."

"I know," she smiled back. "You told me."

"Then you can understand how betrayed I would feel if these private conversations ended up in a rag magazine."

"Don't worry. I consider it a privilege to be here with you.

Believe me, your secrets are safe with me."

She sat with him for a while—like she had all the time in the world—even though he knew she must have other patients to attend. When silence stretched between them, he sighed. "I feel guilty keeping you away from your other patients."

"No need. I'm an extra body tonight, another scheduling error."

"Again? That's three nights this week."

"Yes, but don't tell anyone. The extra money is good, so don't jinx it for me."

"Not me. Admins' screw-up is my gain. Seriously, if not for our conversations, I think I would've gone off the rails more than once already. Nights are the worst. Everything is so quiet." He looked at her and smiled. "You've been such a tremendous help, Amy. I can't thank you enough."

She stood and curtsied. "You are more than welcome." Sliding the chair back where it belonged, she smiled. "I guess I should see if I'm needed elsewhere, you know . . . show impartiality. But I'll be back to check on you in a little while. In the meantime, get some rest. You need to look your best when your girl wakes up." She patted his shoulder. "It shouldn't be long now."

He smiled at the hopefulness Amy always instilled in him.

With Charlie's hand still cocooned in his, he slid the somewhat reclining chair into a more comfortable position and closed his eyes.

Chapter Eighty-Eight

Something woke him.

He opened one eye just enough to look at the clock on the wall. *Three in the morning.* He had actually slept for a few hours.

Stretching, he sat up in his chair.

That's when he saw the most amazing pair of brown eyes staring back at him.

"I thought you would never wake up," Charlie whispered with a sigh.

He gasped. Tears immediately filled his eyes as he watched hers close. "Charlie?" He swallowed back sobs, not believing his eyes or his ears.

Am I dreaming?

Did Charlie really just speak to me?

Her eyes were open. I saw them.

Leaning forward in his chair, his shaking hand stroking her cheek, he whispered, "Talk to me, sweetheart. Say anything. Open your eyes. Let me know I wasn't imagining it."

He waited for a tremor, a flinch, a nudge. Anything. He was afraid to blink, not wanting to miss even the smallest sign.

Then her eyes opened again.

"God have mercy . . . you're really awake."

She didn't say anything, but she smiled before closing her eyes again.

He knew he needed to alert the nurses, but he didn't want to leave, or let go of her hand, or do anything to interfere with this moment. *She doesn't seem confused or agitated like Dr.*

Carter warned. He looked at her. Stared at her. *She seemed like . . . well, like Charlie.*

Standing, he picked up the empty plastic Coke bottle from the nightstand and threw it at the glass wall separating them from the nurses' station. Immediately, the two nurses sitting there looked up. He didn't have to do or say anything, obviously the look on his face said it all. They both jumped into action. One picked up the phone, the other rushed toward the room.

Hunter sat back down, his eyes concentrated on Charlie. "She woke up," he said when he heard the door open. "She talked and everything."

The nurse hurried to the bedside, looked at the monitors, at Charlie, and back again. "Dr. Carter is in the ER with an emergency. I'll page him to come up as soon as he can."

"Charlie . . . open your eyes. Let me see those amazing brown eyes of yours."

Her eyelids fluttered.

"Squeeze my hand. Open your eyes. Say something."

"You sure are bossy," she whispered and grinned before opening her eyes.

He choked, emotion stealing his words.

Don't cry, she mouthed as she squeezed his hand.

He brought their laced fingers up to his lips, kissed hers, then pressed them to his cheek. "Sorry, but I can't hold back." When she closed her eyes, Hunter lurched forward. "Don't go, babe. Stay with me."

"Don't worry," she spoke, sounding a little stronger even though her eyes remained closed. "I'm not going anywhere."

Over the next hour, Charlie opened her eyes half a dozen times, smiled, but went back to sleep. She never spoke, worrying Hunter. He talked with her, encouraged her to answer, but she just sighed and closed her eyes.

He looked at the nurse. "Should I ask her some questions? See if she knows where she is or why she's here?"

"No. Asking questions she might not be able to answer could confuse her, make her anxious. We don't want to do anything to upset her before the doctor gets here."

When Dr. Carter walked into the room a few minutes later, Hunter could not contain his emotion. Tears once again ran down his face.

"Catch me up." The doctor smiled at him while he looked at the tablet the nurse handed him.

"She woke up at three o'clock and scolded me for being asleep."

Dr. Carter laughed.

"She has opened her eyes several times since then and was able to focus on me. She spoke a few times and knows who I am. She wasn't agitated or upset. Not even confused. She's moaned a few times. Winced. But she hasn't spoken for a while."

"That's okay. These are all good signs." He handed back the tablet to the nurse. "Was her speech slurred at all? Did she mumble?"

"No. It was perfect. Quiet but perfect."

The doctor leaned on the bed rail. "Charlie . . . can you hear me?"

They all waited for confirmation.

Her eyes slowly fluttered opened.

"Hi, Charlie. Do you know where you are?"

She glanced at Hunter and smiled, then looked around the room. With her brows knit together, and fear coloring her eyes, it was as if she was noticing her surroundings for the first time. "Hunter, why am I here? What's happened to me?" She squeezed his hand. "Hunter, I'm scared."

Her heart rate soared, setting off an alarm.

"Charlie, listen to me." He leaned in close to her face. "Look at me."

She turned to him, but her eyes quickly darted around the room again. "Only at me, Charlie. Look only at me." She looked at him, studied his face, focused on his eyes. "You're safe. Do you hear me? You're safe. Everything is fine, but you need to calm down."

Hunter glanced at the number that continued to climb. 135 . . . 141. "Charlie, take a deep breath with me." Hunter inhaled and waited for her to follow. When she did, he let his breath out and watched her to the same. "Again. Deep breath . . . let it out." Her numbers began to drop. 115 . . . 108 . . . 103. "You're doing good." She continued to mirror Hunter until the alarm finally silenced itself. Charlie closed her eyes, looking exhausted. He looked at the doctor.

"She'll only be able to handle small doses," Dr. Carter smiled. "One step at a time, Hunter. One step at a time."

Chapter Eighty-Nine

Charlie's mind was a scrambled mess.

Moments in her life danced before her eyes, but they were strangely distorted. Fragmented. Like the frames in a kaleidoscope fractured into something completely different.

A picture of her mom morphed into a picture of her aunt.

The stables at the racetrack morphed into the stables at Daniel's home.

A picture of Daniel on their wedding day morphed into the night he held a knife to her throat and threatened to kill her.

She felt her body shake and her heart race. She squeezed her eyes tighter, not wanting to see anymore. But then everything changed. Darkness turned to light. Her body calmed, and her heart slowed. The pictures no longer fractured and changed. They were constant. Solid. Memories that warmed her heart.

Hunter standing on her porch with a saddle in his hands.

Down on one knee begging forgiveness in her barn.

Riding with her side by side.

Exploring the homestead.

Lying on the couch together.

Planning their forever.

But why am I here?

She knew she was in a hospital. The smell. The machines. A man in a starched white coat.

Why?

She realized she'd have to wake up if she wanted answers to her questions.

Opening her eyes, she tried to focus.

Immediately, she saw movement out of the corner of her eye. It was Hunter, sitting beside her. Looking at him, her heart fluttered.

"Hey, babe, you're back." He stood up and pressed a kiss to her forehead.

She nodded, then groaned. Her body felt stiff, like it had been crammed inside a box for way too long. She tried to stretch, but her legs and arms felt like lead.

Am I paralyzed?

She panicked for a second, wondering.

Would I be able to feel anything if I was paralyzed?

She looked at her left arm, at her hand nestled between Hunters. She willed her fingers to clench and unclench.

"Why is it so hard to move?" she asked.

Hunter smiled as his hand brushed against her cheek. "You've been asleep for a while, and your body is very weak. But don't worry, it's normal."

The man in the white coat stood to her right. "I'm so glad you decided to join us, Miss Foster. I'm Dr. Carter."

She smiled, not sure what to say. But she did know what she wanted to ask.

"Why am I here? I don't understand."

The doctor glanced at Hunter and back to her. "But you do remember this man."

She stared into Hunter's eyes, and every memory she had of him filled her heart. "Yes." She started to cry.

"Don't cry, sweetheart. Everything is going to be okay." Hunter brought her hand up to his face. "What do you remember?"

What do I remember?

Good question.

She closed her eyes. Really concentrated.

"Driving." She opened her eyes. "I was in a truck, driving somewhere. No . . . Jake was driving." She closed her eyes again, feeling confused. "That can't be right. Why would I be with Jake?"

Hunter squeezed her hand. "But you *are* right."

She turned to him.

"You were with Jake. Do you remember why?"

She remembered talking with him. *But why was I with him in the first place?*

"What are you thinking?" Hunter asked.

"I remember being with Jake, I just can't remember why." She watched as Hunter glanced at the doctor, and the doctor nodded back. *What did that mean?*

"Do you remember Diana?" Hunter asked.

Charlie thought for a moment. "Yes. Diana is Jake's wife. She's a nurse."

It was like solving a sliding puzzle game. Tiles shifting, falling into place. She looked at Hunter, panicked. "I'm sick. That's why I was with Jake. We were on our way to see you. Is that why I'm here? I'm so sick Jake had to bring me to a hospital instead?"

Hunter shook his head. "No. You're not here because you're sick. You were coming to see me. Do you remember anything else?"

She closed her eyes to concentrate but felt so tired. It was like her mind was a muscle she hadn't used in years. It actually ached from trying to remember.

"Let her rest, Hunter. There's no reason to rush this. Her speech is good. Her comprehension is good. We need to be satisfied with that for now. She just needs time."

Charlie heard the doctor's summation of her condition, and it angered her. She could barely lift her arm—let alone move her legs—and her thoughts and memories were a jumbled mess. *She* was not satisfied with that.

"I don't want to rest," she said, even though she didn't open her eyes. "Please . . . just tell me why I'm here." When no one spoke, she looked at Hunter. "Please."

He squeezed her hand a little tighter and looked at her with tear-filled eyes. "You were in an accident. You and Jake."

She thought for a moment, but nothing came to mind.

"You don't remember?" Dr. Carter asked.

"No." She tried again. "I remember driving with Jake but then my mind goes blank." She blinked a few times and took a deep breath. "I don't remember anything else, other than waking up and seeing Hunter asleep beside me." She looked at the doctor. "That's bad, isn't it?"

"No. Actually it's not uncommon. There's a good chance you may never recall the accident, and that's okay," he said, offering her a sympathetic smile. "The mind has the ability to block out circumstances too traumatic or too painful to remember. What's important now is your physical recovery."

"Wait a minute," she turned to Hunter. "What about Jake? Is he okay? Was he hurt?"

"He's doing fine. A broken arm and a concussion. He was released after only a few days."

"A few days?" That freaked her out. "I've been asleep for a few days?"

Hunter scooted closer. Bringing her hand up to his lips, he kissed her fingers, then smiled, not wanting her to be scared. "Babe, you've been asleep for three . . . weeks."

"Weeks?" she whispered. "How can that be?"

"Your body sustained massive trauma, Miss Foster."

She looked at the doctor, then at her feet, forcing herself to wiggle both big toes. She looked at her arm in the sling. It ached, so she knew she could still feel it, and her other hand was wrapped in Hunter's, and she could feel the warmth of his kisses. *Thank you, God. I still have my arms and legs.*

"What kind of trauma?" she asked, turning from Hunter to the doctor.

"Internal injuries. But you also sustained head trauma."

"Head trauma," she repeated.

"Yes. And because of that, we placed you in a medically induced coma so your body could rest and heal."

Coma. I've been in a coma. She began to panic. *What if I'm still in a coma? What if I'm hallucinating or having an out of body experience? What if—*

411

An alarm sounded, shattering her thoughts.

"You're okay, Miss Foster. You just need to calm down," the doctor encouraged.

Hunter squeezed her hand. "Look at me."

She turned to him.

"Breathe, Charlie. Slow breaths. In and out."

Like before, she studied Hunter's face and followed his breathing pattern. Her racing heart began to slow, but she still had a question to ask. It was the only thing that really mattered. "Hunter, tell me the truth. Don't lie to me."

"Tell you what?"

"Am I going to die?"

He teared up, causing her to cry.

No . . . No. Please, God, I want more time.

"Don't cry, sweetheart" He wiped the tears from her cheeks. "Eventually . . . one day . . . you will die, but not before I make you my wife and we grow old together, surrounded by our kids and grandkids."

She fell asleep, holding onto the dream of what life would look like with Hunter, forever by her side.

Chapter Ninety

Finally, alone with Hunter. Charlie sighed with euphoric exhaustion.

The day had been filled with tests, assessments, questions, doctors, nurses, and a physical therapist. Though Hunter had been by her side through it all, this was the first time they were actually alone together since she had woken up.

Truly woken up.

She smiled at him, realizing he looked as tired as she felt. "You're exhausted."

"Well . . . let's just say I haven't been sleeping much these last few weeks."

"Then get some sleep, in a real bed, not that stupid chair."

He sat forward, elbows resting on his knees, a glint in his eyes. "Is that an invitation?"

His grin was devilish, and sexy, and wonderful. She laughed. "Do you think we would get in trouble?"

"One way to find out." He stood.

She watched as Hunter closed the blinds on the picture window, blocking the view of the nurses' station. Moaning and groaning, she slowly inched toward the side rail while making sure she didn't disturb the wires and monitors still attached to her.

After toeing off his boots, Hunter dropped the other rail and slipped in alongside her. He nestled his head against hers, his hand resting carefully on her hip. "Are you comfortable? I'm not hurting you, am I?"

Giggling, she whispered, "I'm fine. More than fine. But why do I feel like a schoolgirl, afraid of getting caught with a boy? My hands are sweaty, and my heart is racing."

He nuzzled her ear. "I don't know, but if you don't calm down, you're going to set off an alarm, and we'll get caught red-handed."

She looked at the monitor and watched as her heartrate escalated. Hunter laughed beside her as she forced herself to take slow, even breaths.

"How am I doing?"

He leaned up to look at the monitor. "Umm . . . a little better. You've gone from *sneaking a boy into your room so you can have your way with him,* to *I have a crush on you, do you want to make out?*"

She laughed but quickly covered her mouth.

"Here," he propped himself up on one elbow, "let me do that."

His kiss was slow . . . tender . . . gentle.

"Come on," she looked into his eyes and teased. "I deserve better than that. After all I've been through. I mean . . . I *was* practically dead."

"You!" he huffed. "You slept through the whole thing. I'm the one who died a thousand deaths waiting for you to wake up."

She shrugged, then moaned. "I guess you're right."

"You bet I am." He rested back against the pillows. "You know . . . they prepared me for the worst. Paralysis. Amnesia. Loss of motor skills. But you blew them all away today. You're talking *and* walking. It's nothing short of a miracle."

"Well, I certainly didn't do it gracefully. I would've fallen flat on my face if you hadn't grabbed me."

He laughed. "That's what you get for being so stubborn. The doctor warned you, but nooo, you wanted to do it on your own."

"But I didn't think walking to the bathroom was that grand of a gesture."

"Well, now you know. Until you gain back some strength, no unsupervised strolls."

"Whatever." She closed her eyes for a second. "Hey, what about my other symptoms? The reason Diana had me do that test? No one has said anything about that."

"You have what's called atrophic gastritis."

"What?"

He shrugged. "I don't remember all the specifics. Your other injuries kind of took precedence. But I do remember it had something to do with an infection. One you have probably had since you were a kid. You've been given antibiotics and something to control the acid in your stomach. Other than that, you're going to be fine."

They lay together. Quiet. Not needing words. Charlie tried to enjoy the simplicity of the moment, but her mind wouldn't stop spinning. She kept thinking about everything she'd been told. Her list of injuries. Having major surgery. Losing three weeks of her life. Then it struck her.

If Hunter has been here with me, what must the media be saying? What kind of publicity was this for him? He would've had to cancel shows. Disappoint fans. But he hasn't said a word.

"You're awfully quiet," Hunter whispered.

"Just thinking."

He nudged her ear with his nose. "About what?"

"You haven't said anything about the media. What are they saying about all this? Do they know about us? About me?"

"Yes and no. One of the rag magazines paid off a janitor. He sneaked into your room and took a picture while you—"

"What?" She tried to sit up.

"Relax. He never made it down the hall. When I realized what happened, I decked him and had him arrested. He screamed and hollered all the way to the cop car, telling the press you weren't just a *family friend*, that we were involved romantically. But he wasn't able to leak the picture of you."

"So, people know we're an item?"

"Yep."

"And they aren't going to rest until they know who I am?"

"Probably not."

"What are we going to do?"

"We're not going to worry about it. Not anymore."

Slowly, she rolled over to face him. "How can you say that? The accident changes nothing. No, I take that back. The accident changes everything, because now people know you are seeing someone."

"You're right, everything has changed."

She watched as he rolled off the side of the bed and squatted down next to a duffel bag lying against the wall. He rooted around inside, grabbed some newspapers, and crawled back into bed.

"What are those? Reports of the accident?"

She reached for the papers, but he held them at arm's length. "This isn't what you think. They're not about the accident."

"What are they about?"

With a sobering look, he handed them to her. "They're about Daniel."

Chapter Ninety-One

"He's dead? Daniel is dead?"

She couldn't believe the headlines, even though they were right in front of her.

"I don't understand. How is that possible?" She shifted, trying to sit up. "I can't breathe."

Immediately, Hunter stood, adjusted the bed to a sitting position, and propped a pillow behind her head.

"Is that better?"

"Yes . . . I guess so." But her head continued to swim, and she felt nauseous.

Hunter glanced at her monitor, causing her to look too. Her heart rate was climbing . . . fast. If she didn't calm down, the alarm would go off and the nursing staff would come in, asking a hundred questions.

"Come on, Charlie, deep breaths, just like before."

She closed her eyes and concentrated on the rhythm of Hunter stroking her hand.

"That's it, babe. Slow, even breaths."

After a few minutes, she chanced opening her eyes. The room had stopped spinning, and she no longer felt like she was going to be sick.

"Are you with me?" Hunter asked, still stroking her hand.

She nodded, then looked at the papers laying in her lap. She picked up the top one, read the headline again, but her eyes would not focus on the small type, the words a jumbled mass of black and white specks. She looked up at

Hunter, needing answers. "What happened?"

He hitched his hip up on the bed and sat alongside her. He looked like he wanted to say something but was hesitant.

"What's wrong?"

"I don't want you to freak out."

"I'm already freaking out. Tell me what happened."

Hunter continued to stroke her hand. Finally, she grasped his and forced him to look at her. "What . . . is . . . wrong?"

"Charlie, you need to rest," he said as he brushed a strand of hair back from her face. "This has been a big day for you, and you're not supposed to overdo it. I shouldn't have shown you the papers. I just wanted you to know it's over. The running . . . the hiding . . . you're free. Daniel can't hurt you anymore."

She shook her head and massaged her brow, feeling overwhelmed. "How do we know for sure?"

"That he's dead?" Hunter looked perplexed. "It's right there in black and white. He was shot in police custody."

"They could have been paid off. Daniel could've set the whole thing up. Maybe he wanted to disappear. He wouldn't be the first person to orchestrate his own death."

"But that isn't what happened."

"How do you know?"

"Come on, Charlie, we can talk about this tomorrow . . . when you're stronger."

She glanced at the clock on the wall. "I don't think a few more hours are going to make me that much stronger. *But,* spending that time wondering what you're *not* telling me, will most definitely push me over the edge."

Hunter pulled at the back of his neck, then rubbed at the scruff on his face. But he wouldn't look at her.

A chill raced down her spine. *No . . . he couldn't have.* She looked at Hunter. Studied him. There was no way Hunter was capable of . . . that. *But why won't he look at me?*

"Hunter, please tell me you had nothing to do with Daniel's death?"

He finally looked up. "I could, but that would be a lie."

When the alarm went off, Charlie could do nothing to control it. Her whole body tingled, and she felt like she was going to pass out. Her heartrate jumped to one-ninety and continued to climb.

"Talk to us, Miss Foster," Connie said as she rushed to her bedside. Two younger nurses hurried in with her. One stood across from the older nurse, watching everything she did, while the other stood at the foot of the bed next to Hunter.

"I'm . . . all right," she said, gasping for air.

"Well, the monitors are telling us differently." Connie reached for the oxygen mask draped to the side of the bed and secured it over her nose and mouth. "I need you to take slow, even breaths, Miss Foster."

Charlie tried, really she did, but all she had to do was look at Hunter and the distraught expression on his face, and her sense of control went right out the window.

"Page Dr. Carter," Connie instructed the young nurse across from her.

The woman hurried out of the room while Connie continued to give Charlie instructions. But she couldn't focus on what she was saying. All she could think about was that Hunter was somehow responsible for Daniel's death.

Charlie watched as Connie inserted a syringe into her IV port. After only a few seconds, she felt her heart begin to slow. She took a deep breath, pulling oxygen in through her nose.

"That's better, Miss Foster, slow and even."

"This is my fault," Hunter said from where he stood at the foot of her bed. "I gave Charlie some upsetting news."

Connie glanced at him, "You should've known better, Mr. Jennings. Though Miss Foster exhibited remarkable progress today, her condition is still considered guarded. Dr. Carter warned you she could experience a setback if faced with information that was disturbing, or if she was pressed to recall something she couldn't remember."

Charlie pulled the mask away from her mouth. "No. It's not Hunter's fault. I asked him to tell me."

"Please, Miss Foster, leave the mask in place and concentrate on breathing."

"But Hunter and I need to—"

"Miss Foster, I'm going to have to ask Mr. Jennings to leave if you can't calm down sufficiently."

Charlie could not bear the thought of Hunter not being at her side. Closing her eyes, she tried her best to take control of her body.

------- • -------

"This is my fault," Hunter whispered to Amy standing beside him. "I should've known she wasn't ready."

"You didn't purposely try to upset her. You just wanted her to know she's safe."

Hunter was too choked up to say anything. He just acknowledged Amy with a nod while he watched the numbers on Charlie's monitor fluctuate.

"Here," Amy said. "I have something for you." She handed him an old patch in the shape of a tire. It looked worn and frayed, like it had been used before. Hunter read it. *Jesus Take the Wheel.* He couldn't believe it. *One more thing she has in common with Amy.* "That was one of my sister's favorite songs."

She smiled. "I really wanted to get you a new one. I thought for sure I'd find it on Amazon or eBay, but I didn't, so I pulled this one off my old backpack. Whenever I was going through a rough time, it reminded me who was in control. Nothing happens outside of God's plan, Hunter. Even the hard stuff. You just need to have faith."

"Thanks, Amy." He tucked the patch inside his back pocket, knowing she was only trying to distract him. But his attention stayed riveted on Charlie and her monitors. Feeling powerless, he closed his eyes and prayed. *Please, God. Don't take her from me now. This can't be—*

When he felt a rush of air he turned and saw Amy leave as Dr. Carter walked in.

"Okay, Miss Foster," the doctor said while working sanitizer into his hands. "You promised you'd be a model patient if I allowed Hunter to stay after hours. So, what's this all about?" he asked, a concerned smile on his face.

"It's my fault," Hunter spoke up, glancing at the newspapers on Charlie's lap.

Dr. Carter nodded his understanding. "Okay, Connie, Miss Foster's numbers are looking much better now. Why don't you give us a few minutes?"

"Sure thing, Doctor."

Hunter waited until the nurse was gone, and the door was closed before talking to Dr. Carter. "I'm sorry. I thought if I showed Charlie that she was safe, it would help."

"Hunter . . ." Both he and Dr. Carter turned to see Charlie with the masked pulled down to her chin. "We can talk about this later."

He moved to her bedside. "It's okay. Dr. Carter knows."

"Knows what?" she said, panic in her eyes.

"He knows about Daniel and that Charlie Foster isn't your real name. He knows everything."

"And before you get upset with Hunter for telling me," the doctor said as he turned to the monitors, "he did the right thing. And let me assure you, I've told absolutely no one. My only concern is for your well-being and your full recovery."

Hunter could tell Charlie wasn't sure how to respond.

"Babe, he needed to know. I needed his help to run interference with the administration staff when they started asking all kinds of questions about who you were, if you had insurance, did I know your social security number, and why none of that information was in your wallet."

"You're a brave woman, Miss Foster. Many women never find the courage to leave their abuser."

Hunter could tell Charlie was having a hard time with

the thought that just one more person knew her secret. But it no longer mattered.

That's what he was trying to tell her.

Pulling the chair closer, he sat alongside the bed, and reached for her hand. "I did not have Daniel killed, if that's what has you freaking out. But I'm not innocent either."

"That's not helping, Hunter." She looked at him, tears in her eyes. "What did you do?"

"The *other* reason you were coming to see me. Do you remember what that was?"

She sighed, clearly frustrated. "There was no other reason. I was coming to let you know I was sick and had to have more tests done."

"I know, sweetheart," he spoke calmly, hoping she would follow suit. "But there was more. You had a flash drive you wanted to give me."

———— • ————

The flash drive.

More tiles slid into place.

"I remember. I was going to give it to you, to give to Chet's brother-in-law."

"And that's what I did."

She started putting two and two together. "You said Daniel was shot in police custody. What was he doing there?"

Hunter sat back in his chair. "The flash drive. It had valuable information on it. When Jerry saw what he had, he turned it over to someone he trusted in the Organized Crime Division of the FBI. I don't know all the details, but the FBI was going to cut a deal with Daniel. They wanted his help to expose the federal employees who were on the take, in exchange for a lighter sentence in a luxury prison somewhere. The plan was to have Daniel arrested on trumped-up charges, with the intentions of putting him into protective custody. From what Jerry gathered, Daniel was considered a small fish in a big pond, and the FBI wanted to use him to get to the real sharks. Daniel never made it. Obviously, someone wanted him silenced before he could talk."

"But isn't the FBI curious where the information came from?"

"Nope. To them, it was an anonymous tip. Jerry doesn't even know where it came from."

"But what if—"

"Charlie . . ." Hunter scooted forward in the chair and smiled. "There are no 'what ifs.' It's over. It's time for us to start making plans."

Chapter Ninety-Two

Finally, it was time for Charlie to go home.

Dr. Carter was pleased with her recovery, and even though she still needed physical therapy to strengthen her body, he was willing to release her to further recuperate at home.

"Congratulations. Today is the big day," Amy said as she walked into her room.

Charlie had just gotten dressed and sat down in the chair, feeling winded. "I know. I can hardly believe it."

"You realize you're a walking miracle, right?"

"That's what they tell me," she said, breathing heavily.

"Well, I never doubted you for a second." Amy walked around the bed, tidying the nightstand and straightening the room. "What you and Hunter have is truly special. I see it in his eyes. He absolutely gushes when he talks about you. There was no way God was going to end your love story prematurely. I talked to Him at length about it."

"I know. Hunter said your talks gave him a lot of hope when he was discouraged."

"Not Hunter. I talked to God. He and I are pretty tight."

"Oh?" Charlie wasn't sure what to say.

"I just explained to Him that a love like you and Hunter have only comes around once in a lifetime, and you both deserve to be happy."

"Well . . . ahh . . . thanks for putting in a good word for us."

Amy smiled. "Actually, I've been a fan of Hunter's for as long as I can remember. I never told him that, because I didn't want him to think I was a stalker or anything. But seeing him so broken up was hard to watch. He's a good man who has had his share of struggles. He deserves to be happy. So do you."

Charlie didn't know what to say. Previous to this, Amy was more like a cheerleader, encouraging her to wake up. Reminding her what was waiting for her—*who* was waiting for her. In fact, other than hearing Amy's voice while she was trying to wake from her coma, Charlie hadn't talked to the nurse. Though Hunter had told her about Amy, and how he felt a connection with her because of his sister, Charlie was beginning to wonder if the young woman might have played on Hunter's emotions and was a stalker after all.

"I'm sorry," Amy said standing across from Charlie. "I didn't mean to make you feel uncomfortable." She knelt in front of her, so she was eye level. "I promise, I only want good things for you and Hunter. I didn't mean to creep you out by saying all that stuff. Believe me, no one knows about the conversations I've had with Hunter, and no one will. Just remember, I'll be praying for you both." She stood and walked toward the door, but before she left, Amy turned and smiled. "Take good care of him."

Charlie was still rehashing her conversation with Amy when Hunter, Jake, and Diana walked in, a lively conversation going on between them.

"I'm telling you, Hunter, I would hit it head on," Diana was saying. "Give them what they want so they'll leave you alone. Otherwise, they will continue to print speculations and lies."

"No," Jake shook his head. "It won't do any good. You could have a sit-down conversation with Diane Sawyer, and the rag magazines are still going to print what they want."

"But what about my fans? They've been so supportive, even though the media has printed some pretty outrageous things."

"Hey, hey, hey," Charlie jumped in. "What are we talking about?"

"Hi, sweetheart." Hunter smiled and bent down to give her a kiss. "You look great!"

"Ha!" Charlie huffed. "I'm sweating like I just ran a 10k, and all I've done is slip a dress over my head, run a comb through my hair, and brush my teeth. I don't even have the energy to bend down and pull on my sandals."

Hunter squatted in front of her, his brows knit together with concern. "Do you think we're rushing this? Maybe you should stay here for a couple more days?"

She slapped his arm. "Bite your tongue! I'll go stir crazy if I have to stay even one more hour."

He pretended to be wounded, rubbing his arm. "I guess if you have enough energy to assault me, you're well enough to go home."

"Very funny."

Hunter laughed, then kissed her on the nose. "So, are you ready to go?"

Taking a deep breath, she smiled. "Absolutely."

The next few hours felt like an eternity, zapping Charlie of what little energy she had. After Hunter made a brief statement to the press—mostly thanking his fans for all their support—everyone loaded into the chartered helicopter that was waiting for them on the hospital roof. After transferring to Hunter's private plane, Chet flew them home, but had to take a longer route to stay out of the path of an incoming storm. When they finally touched down at Hunter's ranch, Evan was waiting for them by the Polaris.

Charlie said goodbye to Diana and Jake at the airstrip, but only after promising Diana she would call her with any questions or concerns. Hunter assured his sister-in-law that she was on speed dial before carefully helping Charlie into the passenger side of the vehicle.

The short trip from the airstrip to the house seemed to take forever. She watched as Hunter maneuvered around every rut in the road and slowed for even the smallest bumps. But once the house came into view, Charlie felt her whole body sigh.

As soon as Hunter killed the engine, she swung her legs outside the vehicle.

"Wait for me," he said as he hurried around the bumper, pulled his duffel bag from the back, and looped it over his head.

"I'm fine."

But when she stood, her legs were like noodles, and she felt a little lightheaded.

Immediately, Hunter reached for her.

"Wow. I guess I'm a little weaker than I thought."

"Um-hum." Hunter swept her up into his arms, carried her through the doorway, and straight to her bed. Sinking into the down comforter, she couldn't help but cry with relief.

Finally.

She was home.

Chapter Ninety-Three

Hunter lay next to Charlie while she slept.

Flipping through channels, he tried to avoid the news, tired of seeing replays of the statement he gave outside the hospital. Even though he did what he set out to do—thank his fans—the entertainment shows continued to speculate regarding his and Charlie's relationship.

But it no longer mattered to him. They could say what they wanted because nothing was going to change the truth. Charlie was home. She was no longer in danger, and they could finally move forward.

Together.

As a couple.

"You're going to wear out the remote if you keep flipping through channels," Charlie mumbled as she stretched beside him.

"I just don't get it. What good is it to have hundreds of channels if every one of them is going to play the same thing?"

Charlie rolled over closer to him and snuggled underneath his arm. "Didn't you have your fill of TV in the hospital?"

"Yeah, but I have to watch something."

"Hunter," she leaned back and scowled at him, "you don't have to stay with me 24/7. I'm fine. I can get around by myself. I'm sure you have more important things to do than laying here watching me sleep. What about the duet album? Where are you with that?"

Hunter scooted up against the headboard and silenced the

TV. "It's coming along. In fact, there has been so much interest, we're thinking about making it a double album."

"That's exciting."

"I've also decided I'm going to donate the proceeds."

Charlie smiled. "That's great. Do you have an idea where?"

"Yeah," Hunter nodded. "The Amy Jennings Foundation."

Immediately, Charlie's eyes welled up. "That sounds awesome."

Hunter had to swallow a few times to hold in his emotion. "I want it to be a place where women can go to get away from abuse. Where they can get legal help, daycare and schooling for their kids, even learn a trade if they haven't had the opportunity to go to college. And if need be, new identities if their current relationship is considered life-threatening. I know there are thousands of women out there just like Amy. If I can help even a handful, I've got to try."

"Wow. You've given this a lot of thought."

"Well, I've had a lot of time to think lately."

"I'm proud of you, Hunter. Amy would be too."

"I just wish I could've done more for her. I guess talking with Amy in the hospital made me think."

Charlie paused, looking like she had something more to say.

"What?"

"Huh?"

"You looked like you wanted to say something."

"Umm . . . yeah . . . I didn't say anything sooner because the day was pretty hectic, but I had kind of a weird conversation at the hospital before I left."

"With who?"

"Amy. Right before you, Jake, and Diana came into my room. We were talking, and the conversation just got a little weird."

"Weird? Like how?"

"She talked like she had known you for years. I guess it was just the way she said things."

"Like what?"

"Like, you've had your share of struggles, and you deserve to be happy. Then, right before she left, she told me to take good care of you. She even apologized for sounding creepy. I don't know . . . it just felt weird."

He cocked his head and smirked.

"Don't give me that look. I'm not jealous. Really, that's not what this is about."

"But you had other conversations with her, right? Did those feel weird too?"

"No. That's just it. I never really had a conversation with her. In fact, I remember *hearing* her more than talking with her. It was like she was the voice in my head when I was in a fog. When I was trying to wake up, she encouraged me to keep fighting. To hang in there. To wake up because you were waiting for me. Things like that."

"Hold on . . . you mean you never really talked with her?"

Charlie thought a moment. "Not until today. I mean, I saw her in my room on occasion, and she always had something encouraging to say when she was making her rounds. And of course, you told me what an encouragement she was to you. But I can't remember ever really carrying on a conversation with her before today. Oh, and another thing she said . . . that she had 'talked to God' about us."

"But that's not weird. She told me numerous times that she was praying for us."

"No. She said she 'talked to God.' That she and God were pretty tight, so she explained to Him that a love like ours only came around once in a lifetime. I mean, those weren't her exact words, but that's still kind of weird, don't you think? She never used the word *pray*. She said she 'talked to God,' like He was sitting on a park bench next to her."

Hunter thought a minute but refused to think badly of the nurse who had pulled him through his most desperate hours. "You know what . . . it doesn't matter. Maybe she was a kook, and I just didn't see it. All that matters now is that you're home lying next to me."

She smiled at him. "You're right. She was just trying to be encouraging. I'm sure she had nothing but good intentions." Charlie leaned forward and kissed him, right before he scooted off the side of the bed. "How about I fix you some dinner? What sounds good?"

She thought a moment, then smiled. "A grilled cheese sandwich."

"One grilled cheese sandwich, coming right up."

Hunter waited until he was in the kitchen, then pulled out his phone. "Yes. Connie, I'm so glad you're still there. It's Hunter." He listened to the head nurse chatter on. "Yes, thank you. We're home, and she's doing fine. Tired but fine. Hey, Connie, the reason I'm calling is that when it came time to leave, there was a lot going on, and I never got the chance to say goodbye to Amy."

He cleared his throat.

"Amy. She usually worked the night shift."

This isn't happening.

"Then maybe that's her nickname? No. I'm very sure. I even told her Amy was my sister's name."

Hunter was losing his patience. Or better yet, maybe he was losing his mind. "You were in the room with her that night when Charlie got so upset. No . . . I know who Cindy is. She was working with you, but Amy was standing beside me at the foot of Charlie's bed."

Hunter broke out in a cold sweat as he raced up the stairs. "No . . . I'm sorry. It was a stressful time. I probably just got my names confused. Yes. Thanks again for everything you and the staff did. Have a good evening."

He disconnected the call, hurried to his bedroom, and pulled his jeans from the duffel he'd had at the hospital. Checking the back pocket, then rummaging through all of them, he came up empty.

No patch.

Sitting on his bed, breathing heavy from running up the

stairs, he closed his eyes and started to cry. He had never been a mystical person. Yes, he believed in God, and he liked the idea of Amy being his guardian angel, but he had never given any *real* thought about angels, and if they really existed or not.

"It was you, wasn't it?" He spoke to his sister like it was the most natural thing to do. "You were there with me. Encouraging me. Encouraging Charlie. You never let us give up."

He waited for his tears to dry, then went to the stairwell and looked at the picture of his sister hanging on the wall.

"Thank, Amy. I love you too."

Chapter Ninety-Four

"I'm fine. Really."

Charlie had been home for almost a month, and though her lack of strength was vastly disappointing, she was tired of her every step being watched when she moved from one room to another or Hunter scolding her for being on her feet too long.

"I still don't think riding is such a great idea," Hunter said as he drove the side-by-side toward the stables. "You could easily lose your balance or not have the strength to keep yourself in the saddle."

"And I won't know until I try." She crossed her arms in defiance.

"You have to be the most stubborn woman I know."

"I'm not being stubborn . . . just confident." Smiling, she rested her hand on top of his as he shifted gears. "Dr. Carter cleared me to go riding. And you'll be right beside me. I know you won't let me fall."

He pulled up in front of the stables, cut the engine, then leaned in real close. "Do you know how much I love you?"

Smiling wider, she tapped her chin in contemplation. "I'm gonna guess somewhere between your love for this land and your guitar collection."

"Oh, I don't know . . ." he said as he stepped out of the vehicle and walked around to her side. "This land is *pretty* darn special, and it has taken me years to gather my guitar collection."

She elbowed him in the ribs as she got out.

He grunted at the blow and laughed. "Okay, you edge out my guitar collection, but only slightly. Just keep in mind, my guitars don't jab me. So, if you want to hold on to your ranking, you have to be nicer to me."

"How nice?"

He stepped in close, pressing her against the vehicle. "This nice." His kiss was slow. Indulgent. When he pulled back, the smolder on his face nearly made her knees buckle. "Think you can handle that?"

"Oh . . . I can handle anything you can dish out, cowboy."

He looped his arm around her shoulders and walked toward the stables. "I'm counting on it."

Evan met them in the breezeway, Goliath and Superman already saddled. After giving her a generous leg up, Hunter mounted Superman. "How do you feel?" he asked.

She held onto the horn and shifted her seat, before looking at each foot. "I think I'd feel better if the stirrups were a little shorter. I usually like them loose, but I think I'm going to need the extra support."

Hunter stood up in the saddle to dismount, but Evan cut him off. "I've got it." He hurried to Goliath's side and made the adjustments. "There," he said, taking a step back. "How does that feel?"

She stood in the stirrups and sat again. "Better. More secure."

"You're sure you are ready for this?" Hunter asked again, as Superman sidestepped, anxious to get going.

"Come on, I can handle a leisurely ride."

"But does Goliath know it is just supposed to be a leisurely ride? It has been almost two months since you've ridden him. He might act out."

"He'll do fine, won't you boy?" she leaned over and stroked his withers. "He'll follow my lead."

"Okay . . ." Hunter said, not sounding convinced as he walked Superman past the rink and to the trail.

Goliath and she brought up the rear until they were side by side. "How about we head to the homestead? We can take it slow and rest there for a little while before heading back."

He grinned. "Sounds perfect."

She wasn't sure why Hunter's agreeability bothered her, but she let it pass. She was outside. In the saddle. Exactly where she wanted to be. Riding was just the therapy she needed. It made her feel almost normal again.

They carried on short conversations between bouts of silence. They were satisfied just being together, not needing constant chatter to feel connected. *God, I can't believe this is what it's going to be like.*

The tranquility.

The calm.

The exact opposite of how she'd been living her life.

Though she and Hunter had not opened themselves up to public scrutiny yet, she knew they would be able to handle it, because they'd always come back to this place to do life.

"What are you thinking?" Hunter asked as they slowly loped toward the homestead in the distance.

"That I'm so thankful to God for blessing me the way He has."

"Even after everything you've been through?"

She nodded and inhaled deeply to prevent herself from crying. "I know it's such a cliché, but I never would've met you if it wasn't for the fact that I was hiding out in Connor. It's hard to process that everything in my life led me to this moment. My mom leaving me. My aunt dying. Meeting Daniel. Even the abuse that forced me into hiding. If it wasn't for all those circumstances, our paths never would've crossed. It is almost more than I can comprehend. But God knew it all along."

Having to work past the emotion, she cleared her throat and continued. "There were so many times in my life when I felt alone and abandoned. Now I realize God was there all along. The verse in the Bible that keeps running through my head is the one in Genesis that reminds us what men intend for evil, God can use for good." She wiped at the tear that got away and looked at Hunter, seeing emotion in his eyes too. "I've never been happier in my life than I am at this very moment."

He reached out his hand to her. And, if she didn't know better, she would think Goliath and Superman understood what a special moment it was. The two normally feisty males moved closer to each other, allowing Hunter to lean over and give her a kiss. Righting himself, he grinned. "I hope that helps make the moment even happier."

She smiled. "It does. But you know what would make it even better? Beating you to the homestead."

Before Hunter could react, she and Goliath took off like a shot.

It felt so good.

So free.

No limits. No boundaries.

She held on tight, laughing as she gave Goliath free rein. And even though Hunter would probably read her the riot act for being so careless, she knew Goliath wouldn't let her down.

With the homestead just around the bend, she glanced over her shoulder, surprised Hunter wasn't even chasing her. She pulled on the reins slightly, slowing Goliath. Still looking behind her, she worried that Hunter was angrier than she anticipated. Turning around, she rehearsed her apology as she waited for him to catch up.

He slowed Superman to a walk as he approached, never breaking eye contact with her. When the horses were almost nose to nose, he stopped.

"I'm sorry. I know that was foolish, and careless, and you're probably angry at me. But it felt so good."

"I'm not angry," he said calmly, his grin mischievous.

"You're not?"

"Nope."

"Then why didn't you try to keep up?"

He shrugged, in his oh-so-sexy way. "Because I have a surprise of my own."

"What do you mean? What surprise?"

"Give me your reins." He put out his hand.

"But Hunter, I—"

"Ah-ah-ah. Just give me your reins and close your eyes." While she allowed Hunter to lead her and Goliath, she was pretty sure she had guessed his surprise. A picnic at the homestead. Just like before.

It warmed her heart. Not only because of the romantic sentimentality, but because it meant he knew all along she was strong enough to ride this far. His hemming and hawing at the house was just an act.

"Okay. You can open your eyes now."

Ready to do her best to fake a surprised smile, she opened her eyes and gasped.

Chapter Ninety-Five

She was shocked. No . . . stunned.

She sat astride unable to move or say anything.

When she felt Hunter's hand on her thigh, she turned to him, and let him help her down. When her feet were firmly planted on the ground, she finally found her voice.

"I don't know what to say."

She looked at the homestead and saw that it was decked out with flowers—an exorbitant amount of flowers—in every color imaginable. The beams of the porch were wrapped in beautiful sprays and huge bouquets lined the pathway leading to the steps. Irene, Diana, and Courtney stood on the porch in beautiful dresses. Jake and Chet, even Cody stood opposite them, decked out in black jeans and starched white shirts.

"What is all this?" she mumbled, trying to take it all in.

Hunter dropped to one knee. "Hopefully, it's the shortest engagement on record." He held her hands, and she was so thankful he did, because she feared she might crumble.

"Charlie, I love you, plain and simple. I love you more than I can express in words."

"But you did," she whispered. "In the hospital. You sang to me."

"You heard that?"

"Yes. But it wasn't until last night that I remembered it. You were humming the same tune after dinner, and again this morning when you were making breakfast."

"Why didn't you say something?"

"I don't know." She shrugged nervously. "I think I was a

little scared."

"Scared?"

She nodded. "Since I woke up, you haven't talked about getting married. I thought maybe you needed more time."

"No way," he laughed. "I would've married you in the hospital, but I didn't want to overwhelm you. Dr. Carter urged me to be patient, allowing you enough time to adapt and adjust. But I've run out of patience. So . . . will you dream with me, plan with me, and let me hold your hand for the rest of your life? Because, Charlie . . . I want to make you my wife."

She watched as he pulled the most beautiful wedding band from his pocket. "This is just a token of my love. I didn't want to ruin the surprise by talking about ring styles, so if you want something different . . ."

"No. It's beautiful. It's gorgeous."

"But if you want a solitaire or something more traditional."

"No. I want the ring you chose for me. It's absolutely breathtaking."

"Well, I did put some thought into it. The band has twenty-one diamonds. One for every day I prayed that God would give you back to me."

He placed it at the tip of her ring finger. "Charlie will you be my wife?"

"Yes." She nodded until she felt dizzy. "Yes. I want nothing more than to be your wife."

He slid the ring onto her finger, stood, and swallowed her up in a hug, lifting her off her feet.

"Hey," Jake yelled from the porch. "Are we going to do this thing or not?"

Charlie pulled back and looked at Hunter. "Now? We're getting married now?"

"That's the plan."

"But look at us. We're in jeans and dirty old boots. We can't get married like this."

"That's why my best suit and a dress Diana picked out

just for you are waiting for us inside. If you want a big fancy wedding later, we can do that too. But please, don't make me wait another day to call you Mrs. Aaron Hunter Jennings II."

She almost pinched herself, just to make sure it was real.

"Well?" Hunter looked at her, smiling his sexy smile.

"Okay. Let's do this."

They walked hand in hand to the porch, where they were greeted with hugs, tears, and congratulations.

"Come on," Irene said, tugging on Charlie's arm. "We have to get you ready."

When they walked inside, a sheet had been strung on the diagonal. "Hunter, your stuff is over there," his mom said. "Charlie, we have got everything you need right over here."

When she saw the dress hanging from a hook on the wall, she teared up.

"Do you like it?" Diana asked as she slipped in behind her. "I took you for someone who would like simplistic with just a hint of . . . daring."

Charlie stepped forward and fingered the beautiful lace dress. Its sleek silhouette would be figure hugging, and the neckline was a little *daring*, but it was absolutely gorgeous. "I love it. It's incredible."

"And I get to help with the kajillion buttons on the back," Courtney said proudly.

"Who hung the sheet? I barely have enough room over here to turn around," Hunter grumbled.

"You don't need room," his mom scolded. "You got dressed in cramped quarters the whole first part of your career, but Charlie is going to need some help."

"That's for sure," she said when she turned and looked at the sheer-back dress and the *kajillion* buttons running from neckline to waistline.

"I know newer dresses have a zipper beneath the buttons," Diana said, "but this dress is vintage. It requires a little extra work, but I think it's worth it."

"You're absolutely right." Charlie smiled. "It's stunning."

"Then let's get started," Irene said, looking like she was

going to burst from excitement.

Half an hour later, Charlie was standing in front of the full-length mirror, looking at her reflection. "I don't know how you did it, Diana, but it fits perfectly, even the shoes." She glanced down at the old-fashion white lace boots. "And Courtney, you did such a good job helping with all the buttons. I couldn't have gotten dressed without you."

The little girl beamed in her cute white sundress and wreath of flowers in her hair. "You look like a princess, Miss Charlie."

She looked again in the mirror, admiring the crystal encrusted headband tucked behind her ears. "I feel like a princess."

"And last but not least." Irene held out a pale blue handkerchief. "This belonged to my great-great-grandmother. You and Diana are the sixth generation of women to hold it during their wedding vows. Welcome to the family, Charlie. You're the best thing to happen to Hunter." Irene squeezed her hands. "Pray for him. Stand beside him. And love him with a love only God can give."

"Come on, Mom," Diana quickly pulled tissues from the box and passed them around. "You can't start crying now, or you won't stop."

Everyone laughed while wiping the moisture from their eyes.

"Ready?" Diana asked.

"Absolutely."

When Irene opened the door for Charlie, Hunter was already standing on the porch waiting.

"Wow!" His eyes instantly glossed over with emotion. "You look . . . Wow!"

Feeling nervous, she teased. "Two wows. That must be good."

"Are you kidding? It doesn't even begin to describe how gorgeous you look."

"Well, you don't look so bad yourself, cowboy." Charlie

stared at him in his black suit, crisp white shirt with a Nehru collar and black buttons. Topped off with his black Stetson.

"Okay, okay," Jake grumbled. "You look good. He looks good. Can we just get this thing started?"

"Jake!" Diana scolded. "Be patient. Charlie still has to walk down the aisle."

"Really? Isn't that a little unnecessary since there aren't any guests?"

"No," Diana scolded while nodding toward Courtney. "If Charlie doesn't walk down the aisle, your daughter can't spread her flowers."

"Yeah, Daddy, I have to make sure Miss Charlie has flowers to walk on. It's tree-dishen."

Jake looked at his daughter and visibly melted. "You mean *tra-dition,* sweetheart. And you're right. Miss Charlie *has* to walk on flowers to make if official."

"You are such a pushover," Hunter teased.

"Oh yeah, wait until you have a little girl who looks at you with puppy-dog eyes. You'll be putty in her hands too."

"Well then, let's get started, so I can see for myself one day real soon."

Charlie blushed just thinking about what the night held in store for them.

"Okay, everyone, let's take our places," Chet said, holding a Bible in his hand.

Hunter walked Charlie to the end of the flower-lined path, handed her a single purple rose and gave her a kiss.

"Purple . . . that's different," she said, seeing a twinkle in his eye.

"I know red signifies love, but what we have is so much more than that. So, I did a little research." He grinned. "A purple rose means love at first sight."

"Does it?" She smiled. "I never knew that."

"It also means adoration, fascination, magical, and . . . infinite possibilities. I think that describes what we have perfectly."

She threw her arms around his neck—tears sliding down

her cheeks—and kissed him. "I love you so much."

"I love you too." He kissed away her tears then took a step back. "Don't keep me waiting," he said with a sexy wink, then sauntered toward the porch.

She waited for Hunter to take his place next to his brother. Feeling a slight tug on her dress, she looked down at Courtney standing beside her, a flower basket in her hands.

"Can I spread my flowers now, Miss Charlie?"

"Yes, sweetheart, it's time."

She watched as the little girl carefully sprinkled purple rose petals on the ground in front of her.

When Charlie took her first step, Jake began strumming his guitar. She smiled when she recognized the tune. The same song Hunter had whispered to her when she was fast asleep. But now he sung a second verse.

She stared into his eyes, transfixed.

Dreams,
they do come true.
Trust,
our faith renewed.
It was in God's plan.
Now I'm holdin' your hand,
For today and the rest of our life.
Thank you, Charlie, for being my wife.

When she stepped onto the porch next to Hunter, she whispered, tears running down her face again. "That was beautiful."

He brushed away her tears with the tip of his thumb. "I wasn't sure if I was going to be able to get through it."

"I'm glad you did. I will cherish this moment always."

"Are you two ready to begin?" Chet asked.

They both nodded.

Charlie turned to Diana standing next to her and handed her the single purple rose, knowing she would need to hold on to Hunter with both hands.

Chet read from Scripture and recited a simple ceremony. She didn't hear it all because she kept finding herself lost in Hunter's eyes. However, when Cody stepped forward with his white satin pillow, he broke the spell.

Hunter bent slightly, straightened, then reached for her hand. She was stunned when he slipped two more rings on her finger, the same as the one already there. "These three rings will represent what we have in Christ. A marriage built on a sure foundation. We are far from perfect. I know I'll fail you, and you will fail me, but Christ will not fail us."

Charlie looked at her hand, diamonds shimmering in the sunlight, then looked at Hunter. "I don't have a ring for you."

"Yes, you do," Irene said through tears.

Charlie looked down at the pillow Cody was holding and saw a simple gold band. She picked it up, her hands shaking.

"It was my grandfather's," Hunter said, choking back emotion. "He was an amazing man of God. Every day, when I look at it, I'll be reminded of the shoes I have to fill."

She slipped the ring on his finger and looked into his eyes. "I love you."

"I love you too."

"Then let's finish up," Chet said with a smile.

"Charlotte Elizabeth Fuller, do you take Aaron Hunter Jennings II to be your lawfully wedded husband?"

She leaned forward and whispered, "How did you know my middle name?"

"I did a little investigating. Since I knew Charlie Foster wasn't your legal name, I wanted to make sure there weren't any loopholes for you to wiggle out of."

"There will be no wiggling. You're stuck with me."

"Not until you answer my question," Chet said, rolling his eyes while everyone else laughed.

"I do. I do. I promise, I do."

Hunter squeezed her fingers and smiled.

"Aaron Hunter Jennings II, do you take Charlotte Elizabeth Fuller to be your lawfully wedded wife?"

"Yes sir, I do."

Chet smiled, a glint in his eyes, maybe even a tear. "By the powers vested in me by the state of Texas, I now pronounce you husband and wife. Hunter . . . she's all yours."

The adults clapped and the kids threw Courtney's flower petals, while Hunter dipped Charlie backwards and indulged in a long, *long* kiss.

"Okay, Hunter, let the girl come up for air." Jake said with a pat on his shoulder.

He righted her footing and made sure she was steady before turning around to embrace his brother, then Chet. Hunter's mom and Diana each gave her a hug, then she watched as Irene gave Hunter a tearful peck on the cheek.

When Charlie turned around, she was face to face with Jake. He gave her a lopsided grin and asked, "Can I give my new sister-in-law a hug?"

She smiled. "Of course."

His embrace was firm, and his show of affection surprised her. "Welcome to the family, Charlie," he said next to her ear, then took a step back. "You're good for Hunter."

"Thanks, Jake, that means a lot to me."

"Well, I'm glad I didn't scare you off, because I've never seen him happier."

She welled up, his acceptance meaning the world to her.

"Miss Charlie, Miss Charlie, do you know what this means," Courtney said as she excitedly tugged on her hand.

Carefully, she knelt down next to her. "What?"

"You're no longer Miss Charlie. Now you're *Aunt* Charlie. For reals."

Courtney's simple declaration was almost her undoing.

"Okay, if I can have my bride back," Hunter said, helping Charlie to her feet, "I have one more surprise."

"You do?" She was beginning to feel a little light-headed from all the excitement and emotions. She only hoped Hunter's next surprised wasn't a whirlwind

445

honeymoon. If so, she would have to finally admit she was weaker than she pretended to be.

Hunter let loose an ear-piercing whistle. And out from behind the homestead pranced two white horses complete with a Cinderella-style carriage, Evan at the helm.

Hunter turned to her and bowed. "Mrs. Jennings, your carriage awaits."

She took his hand and walked with him the short distance to the carriage. "Oh my gosh," she gasped. "I forgot about Goliath." She looked around realizing the stallion could be anywhere.

"Don't worry. Goliath and Superman were taken back to the stables the minute you stepped inside to get ready."

Relieved, she turned and watched as Evan placed a small box on the ground, so they could step up into the carriage. The only problem . . . there was no way her fitted dress was going to allow her that much leeway. "I don't think I'm going to be able to make it." She looked again at the distance between the carriage and the box.

"Never fear," Hunter said swinging her up into his arms.

She laughed as he hoisted her up just far enough for her feet to clear the carriage frame. She settled on the seat, and Hunter hopped into the carriage and sat down beside her. "Not as elegant as I planned, but I still think it added to the overall effect. Go ahead, Evan, we're ready."

As the carriage lurched forward, Charlie heard the celebratory whoops and hollers from Hunter's family. Threading her arm through his, she rested her head on his shoulder. "Today was perfect. You gave me something I've always wanted."

"What's that?"

"An amazing family. Something I always knew was missing from my life. Now I have a sister, a niece and nephew, even a bossy brother. And a mom—a godly woman I can turn to when I need advice."

Hunter pulled back and shrugged. "Wow, so I guess I'm just chopped liver?"

"No," she nudged his arm. "You are an amazingly attractive, incredibly sexy, stud of a man who can send chills up my spine by merely holding my hand."

"That's better."

She cuddled closer to him. "So, any more surprises?"

"No. The rest of the day will be somewhat low key. After we have a bite to eat, we only have a few things left to do."

"And what would that be?"

"One . . . we need to get you out of that dress."

"Hunter!" she quickly lowered her voice. "What if Evan heard you?"

"He's a fairly intelligent young man. I think he knows what's going to happen next."

She felt her face flush at the implications.

"Two . . . we're going to silence our phones and bar the doors and windows."

She laughed. "Did you just say, 'we're going to bar the doors and windows?'"

"Yep."

"I don't understand?"

"Because I don't want any interruptions while we work on a family of our own."

ABOUT THE AUTHOR

Tamara Tilley writes from her home at Hume Lake Christian Camps, located in the beautiful Sequoia National Forest. She and her husband, Walter, have been on full-time staff at Hume for more than twenty-five years. Tamara is a retail manager who loves to read, spend time with her grandkids, and craft greeting cards. Visit her website at www.tamaratilley.com to read excerpts from her other books.

www.ingramcontent.com/pod-product-compliance
Lightning Source LLC
Chambersburg PA
CBHW070858260626
47162CB00007B/2501